Their Splendid Love

Kathleen walked hesitantly toward the bed. "Can I, please, Martin—can I sit on the edge of your bed?"

He took her hand, and she sat gingerly on the bed's frame. She was shivering. "Please, Martin," she said. "Please hold me."

He pushed his blanket aside and eagerly sat up straighter and took her in his arms. He held her close. "Kathleen," he whispered hoarsely, pressing his cheek against hers. "Kathleen, dearest one," he said softly. Then he lay back gently on the bed, taking her down with him.

She raised both hands to his cheeks and kissed his mouth, timidly, lightly. He held her close and kissed her hungrily again and again. He felt himself harden against her inner thigh. She groaned and dug her fingers into his back, then suddenly released him, and struggled to move away from him.

"Kathleen, marry me. I love you. Please marry me."

In the moonlight, Martin could see the tears in her eyes. "I can't, Martin. I . . . I wouldn't make you a proper wife. Forgive me . . . I can't . . . I can't just lose another child."

Other Bantam Books by Joseph Csida
Ask your book store for the titles you have missed

REMEMBER THIS HOUSE

THIS PLACE TO HONOR

Joseph Csida

An Arthur Pine Associates Book

BANTAM BOOKS
TORONTO • NEW YORK • LONDON • SYDNEY • AUCKLAND

THIS PLACE TO HONOR

A Bantam Book / December 1985

ISBN 0-553-25287-9

Published simultaneously in the United States and Canada

Bantam Books are published by Bantam Books, Inc. Its trademark, consisting of the words "Bantam Books" and the portrayal of a rooster, is Registered in U.S. Patent and Trademark Office and in other countries. Marca Registrada. Bantam Books, Inc., 666 Fifth Avenue, New York, New York 10103.

PRINTED IN THE UNITED STATES OF AMERICA

H 0 9 8 7 6 5 4 3 2 1

To DeDe
Supermatriarch
with love

PART ONE

Ned Van Gelder, Maureen Morrissey, and
Martin Morrissey, Jr.

John, Anne, and Mary Deasy

Billy (the Butcher) Brannigan
and Five Points

"It's ridiculous! A man could walk from Albany to Schenectady and get there ahead of one of Clinton's scows!"

—Daniel D. Tompkins (ex-governor of New York State and Vice-President of the United States), commenting on Governor De Witt Clinton's stubborn campaign to continue work on the Erie Canal in 1820

"The aquatic display celebrating the arrival of the Clinton party in New York harbor transcended all anticipations . . . and steamboats, barges, ships, pilot boats, canal boats and the boats of the Whitehall firemen . . . appeared to move as by magic."

—Cadwallader C. Colden, report on the opening of the three-day festivities honoring the completion of the Erie Canal, in New York City, November 4, 1825

"Tolls collected on the Erie Canal in the past fiscal year amounted to $495,000 . . . 13,110 boats and rafts passed to and fro on the junction canal between Watervliet and Albany. . . . More than 40,000 people passed Utica on freight and packet boats during the season, an average of forty-two boats, arks and cribs per day."

—Canal Commission, report on the canal's first year of operation, 1825–1826

1

"I can hardly write," the old man scrawled in his unsteady hand, "word will come soon, this very day . . ."

Magically the rolling boom of a distant cannon fulfilled his prophecy. Ned Van Gelder listened to the lingering sound of the explosion. He put down his pen, pulled a large cotton handkerchief from his back trouser pocket, wiped his misty eyes, and blew his nose. With astonishing dexterity, considering he had only one arm, he rolled his chair away from the writing table to the window. It was a clear, unusually mild day. Out on Rivington Street, fifteen yards from the window, a small knot of people, four men and two women, had congregated beneath a sturdy elm, and were chattering and gesticulating animatedly.

The small group was obviously in a great state of excitement. A tall, robust man in a stovepipe hat seemed to be dominating the exchanges. Beside him stood an attractive, expensively attired young lady.

Van Gelder frowned as he recognized John Deasy and his daughter, Mary. He realized that everyone in the city would be excited today. His own stomach and head churned. But he uttered a grunt of displeasure as Deasy put his arm around the narrow shoulders of a small bearded man in the group, and headed with him and Mary toward the entrance of 106 Rivington Street, the Van Gelder and Morrissey Restaurant and Tavern. Ned rolled his chair to the door of his room and turned the lock. He did not wish to be disturbed on this day. By anyone. And certainly not by John Deasy, whom he disliked. He hoped—realized that probably—Deasy and his daughter had come to talk with young Martin Morrissey. His nephew-in-law, Martin junior and Martin's mother, Maureen, were minority partners with Ned Van Gelder in the tavern just beyond the northeastern boundary of Five Points.

Back at his writing table Van Gelder stared at the last words he had written. What would he say now? Was he jubilant? Strangely, yes. To a degree. How could he not be? For almost half a century he had dreamed of, and played a part in, the incredible adventure, the successful culmination of which was being celebrated today. But unhappy memories flooded in on him as well. He was a prisoner in this wheelchair because of an accident that had befallen him in the course of the work on the project. His brother-in-law and best friend, Martin Morrissey senior, had died in that same accident. Another friend, Vincent Boyle, the first husband of Van Gelder's beloved late wife, Bridget Morrissey, had also died during the earlier phases of the construction.

How many men had died since 1793 when the first ditches were dug, the first trees felled, the first rock obstructions blasted? He did not know. Hundreds? Thousands? He doubted whether anyone knew. Yes, he was sad. And though he struggled not to be, he was bitter! For now that the cannon blast had heralded the beginning of the festivities, he felt a keen disappointment that he would have no active part in the glorious celebration.

He had all but memorized the report in the *New York Evening Post* explaining how news of the celebration would reach the city. This morning, as he awoke, he could see each element of today's activities in his mind's eye. Standing on the deck, or perhaps the cabin roof of the *Seneca Chief*, the flagship of the flotilla of canal boats near the western terminal, Governor De Witt Clinton would make his brief speech:

"On this day, October 26, 1825, the Grand Erie Canal is declared open for navigation for its entire course from Buffalo to Albany. May it serve the noble purpose for which the citizens of this State have built it."

The newspaper report had estimated that it would take approximately an hour and a half between the time the first cannon was fired to celebrate the official opening at Buffalo and the final shot, which Ned Van Gelder had just heard. Cannons at strategic intervals, running roughly east from Buffalo, eight to ten miles apart, were to fire successive shots. As each easterly location heard the thunder of the gun to the immediate west, it would fire its own gun, until the last shot was heard in New York.

In each village, beginning with Buffalo (which already had a population of more than five hundred), parades would march the dusty streets; bands would play; at nightfall fireworks would splash the autumn skies. As he pondered what he should write next, Van Gelder thought of his twenty-eight-year-old son, Christopher, and his wife and three small children, who lived in Buffalo, marching in the parade there. He smiled as he imagined his precocious nine-year-old granddaughter, Laura, strutting at the head of the church group, no doubt flanked by her seven-year-old twin brothers, Ned and Fred.

In a little more than a week, on November 4, the governor's *Seneca Chief* would arrive at Sandy Hook and New York City would hold its own full-fledged celebration. And Ned Van Gelder would have no more part in it than any of the other citizens of the city, or the thirty thousand out-of-city visitors who were expected to come in to witness the festivities. A spectator! That was all he would be. But he supposed he should be grateful he was still alive to see the celebration of the completion of the great work to which he *had* made a substantial contribution.

He began to write, slowly, the arthritis stiffening his fingers with a mild pain, which he grimly ignored.

". . . The sound of the cannon reverberates in my ears. I think of the day in 1791 when James Rivington burst into our house, this very house on Rivington Street, then Van Gelder Road, to announce that the State Legislature had granted charters for the first two companies authorized to build canals. De Witt Clinton's uncle George was Governor then."

There was a knock at his door.

"Yes?"

Maureen Morrissey's husky voice said, "Mr. Deasy is here, Ned. With a man from the *Evening Post* . . ."

"I'm busy, Maureen," grumbled Ned loudly.

"The man from the paper wants to talk to you about the early canals. Martin and me, we thought maybe . . ."

Van Gelder wheeled to the door and unlocked it.

"Of course, Maureen. Of course. Bring them back, and maybe a bottle of good whiskey."

Stupid, thought Van Gelder. His dislike of Deasy had almost caused him to turn away an opportunity to talk with a journalist about his and Martin's part in the building of the canal. Maybe he would be part of the celebration yet.

Everything about the *Post* reporter was small. Five three. Small head on a narrow body. Brief Vandyke beard. Short, thin nose and close-together, shrewd dark eyes. His name was Elias Scribner.

"Eli is the finest reporter and editor in the city, Mr. Van Gelder," said Deasy in his deep, resonant voice. "He found out a bit about your work on the early canals, but he didn't know where to locate you, and he knows John Deasy is the man to come to if you're needin' information about anybody in New York town. Am I correct, Eli?"

The journalist smiled tolerantly at Deasy and said to Van Gelder, "I'm most gratified to meet you, sir."

"Tell Eli about the malaria epidemic, Mr. Van Gelder," said Deasy.

John Deasy was forty, ruddy, square-jawed, graying prematurely, oozing power. He called most people by their first names, but he always addressed sixty-nine-year-old Ned Van Gelder by his surname. Most people did. Ned Van Gelder simply did not seem the type of man you would call Ned. There was a lopsided strength and dignity about him. After he lost his left arm at age twenty-five, in 1781, just before the War of the American Revolution ended, the muscles in his right arm, right shoulder, and the right side of his neck developed to an extraordinary degree. And just four years ago, in 1821, when he had become paralyzed from the waist down, the right arm and entire upper right side of his body gradually became even more pronouncedly muscular.

Young Martin had built him the special wheelchair, which he steered by maneuvering a sturdy oak bar attached to its single small front wheel. And once having set his direction, he placed the upper part of the bar firmly in his right armpit, and with his powerful, gnarled hand spun the right one of the two rear wheels of the chair to move forward or backward. In addition to this constant use of the right arm, he also exercised regularly each morning, by pulling himself up and lowering himself twenty-five or more times on a trapezelike bar Martin had suspended from the ceiling over his bed.

"I know about the malaria epidemics, John," said Scribner now. "There were several."

Deasy launched into a long tale about how he had had his own doctor tend more than a dozen malaria victims who had made their way back to the city.

"Near death they were, those poor bog-trotters," he declaimed, "but old Doc Warner pulled 'em through. And old JD paid all the bills, o' course."

Ned Van Gelder frowned at Deasy. He was unfailingly irritated by the man's relentless take-charge manner, his boasting, and the respectable front he affected. For the past five years Deasy had been one of the major subcontractors on the Erie Canal project, doing a thriving business in paying for the transportation from Ireland of hundreds of desperate, starving Irish farmers and their families. He enrolled many of the men as laborers on the canal. Most of the women he placed as cooks, housekeepers, maids, or seamstresses with the city's more affluent families. All turned half their meager earnings over to him until they had repaid the cost of their voyages, plus a handsome profit for Deasy.

A goodly number of the rougher, ignorant, and immoral younger men he steered toward the Five Points gangs. They had always proved helpful to him at election time, and now that the state legislature was about to pass a bill permitting foreigners to vote, they would become even more useful. He took no responsibility for some of the more attractive girls, some as young as ten or twelve, who turned to prostitution. His connection with the city's bawdy-house operators and pimps was as difficult to prove as his relationships with the Five Points gangs. He owned six prosperous saloons, three race horses, and promoted various sporting events. He was also a behind-the-scenes power in the new Tammany political organization.

Upon their very first encounter, Ned Van Gelder had learned that Deasy had influence with at least one gang. Four thugs had come to the tavern threatening young Martin Morrissey with misfortune if he didn't pay five dollars per week to the Brannigan Protective Association. Ned Van Gelder, in the wheelchair, bellowed curses in helpless fury as one of the brutes swept a dozen glasses off the bar with one swing of a thick forearm.

"See, Morrissey!" said the hoodlum. "Like that . . . accidents like that an' worse kin happen all the time."

Martin grinned at the heavy-jowled man, reached below the bar, and came up with a small club, which he banged against the head of the glass-breaker before the foursome knew what was happening.

"Or like that!" he shouted.

Nimble as an acrobat, he leaped over the bar, and though one gangster stabbed him in the shoulder and another eventually wrested the club from his grip, he knocked two more into the same state of unconsciousness as the man he had clubbed. The fourth roughneck raced from the barroom.

The representatives of the Brannigan Protective Association did not return. The next day John Deasy came into the bar at dinnertime. He introduced himself to Maureen, Martin, and Ned, and after a huge meal he told Maureen, in her early fifties but still handsome, that her skills as a cook were surpassed only by her sparkling Irish beauty. He drank several brandies and when the dinner rush had passed, he had a long and serious talk with Martin and Ned. He had heard what Martin had done to the hoodlums and he offered Martin five dollars if he would fight a boxer named Jem McCool on the following Saturday afternoon in the big yard behind his saloon on Water Street near the East River. He said he thought he could assure Martin and Ned that the Brannigan representatives would not bother them again if Martin would agree to become one of his boxers. Bare-knuckle boxing was illegal, but somehow the police never interfered with Deasy's bouts.

Over his mother's tearful objections and his uncle's warning that he could be seriously hurt, Martin accepted Deasy's offer. It did not take a mental giant to figure out that John Deasy had some influence with Bill Brannigan and his Protective Association.

In the two years that had passed since Martin began his career as a boxer, and he continued to work eighteen hours most days at the restaurant and tavern, Ned Van Gelder had become not one whit fonder of John Deasy. He glared at Deasy now as the ruddy Irishman continued to interrupt Scribner's interview.

"If you don't mind, JD," said the journalist finally, "I did come here to interview Mr. Van Gelder."

"O' course, my friend. Old JD was just tryin' to be helpful."

Elias Scribner had briefed himself on much of the history of the state's efforts to build canals. He resumed his discussion with Van Gelder in his nasal, high-pitched voice.

"I understand, Mr. Van Gelder, that you were paralyzed in the unfortunate incident in the Schoharie Valley, when that innocent-appearing creek went on a rampage in twenty-one."

"Yes, six of us were swept off the deck of a Durham. My best friend, my wife's brother, Martin Morrissey, drowned. I was lucky to come out alive. Martin was the most daring and expert blower ever to work on the canals. In the early days, with the old black powder, he could set a charge that would be almost as effective as what we did later with the new DuPont blasting powder. He was absolutely fearless, but he was smart too—"

"Excuse me, please, Mr. Van Gelder. I don't mean to interrupt, but I've got many stories of the blowers," said

Scribner. He looked at the empty sleeve tucked into Van Gelder's trouser belt.

"If you don't mind my asking, sir—the newspaper accounts said nothing of your having lost an arm in the Schoharie incident. . . ."

"No, no," said Van Gelder. "That was long ago. In my youth. I was in the French navy. A cannon backfired during a battle in Chesapeake Bay near Yorktown, off the coast of Virginia."

Deasy poured himself another drink.

"Mr. Van Gelder's son was in our own navy during the War of 1812," he interrupted again. "Wasn't he, Mr. Van Gelder?"

Van Gelder nodded.

"He was wounded too. In the battle of Lake Erie. He was on Perry's flagship, the *Lawrence*."

"Was he also incapacitated?" asked Scribner politely, although scarcely able to conceal his eagerness to get back to canal matters.

"No," said Van Gelder, "his wounds were not serious. It turned out most fortunately for him. In the hospital in Buffalo he met a young nurse. He married her and they have three children."

"Fine family, the Van Gelders," said Deasy heartily. "One of the oldest families in the city. They and the Morrisseys, both fine families."

"I don't mean to stir up depressing memories, Mr. Van Gelder," said Scribner, "but I've been through the records of the early canal companies, Western Inland Lock Navigation and Northern Inland, and I understand you lost a considerable amount of money in those pioneer companies."

Van Gelder smiled a twisted smile.

"I never did understand business too well. I lost everything, except my house here. But that was back in 1810 when the companies went bankrupt. Martin and me, we continued to work on the canal—young Martin, too, from the time he was thirteen. We got along well enough."

He shrugged.

"But a year or so after Schoharie we were almost penniless. Young Martin and Maureen, Mrs. Morrissey and me, we made the house into a restaurant and saloon."

Scribner took a yellowed pamphlet from his coat pocket.

"I came upon this in Albany, Mr. Van Gelder. It's a treatise you wrote in 1791 proposing the route a canal from Buffalo to Albany might take. A remarkable document."

Van Gelder beamed proudly.

"I made journeys over almost every inch of the territory. Would you like to see some of my early maps and specifications?"

"I would indeed, sir!"

Deasy followed Van Gelder as he wheeled himself to a broad shelf beside the writing table, and reached for a large metal strongbox.

"Here, here. Let me help, Mr. Van Gelder."

"Never mind. I can do it."

He managed to lift the box and set it on a bench between himself and Scribner. He stacked the neatly leather-bound Van Gelder ancestral memoirs on his writing table. Then for the next three hours the journalist and Van Gelder pored over scores of his own ancient papers, with Ned animatedly explaining each map and page of notes, and relating anecdotes pertaining to them. Scribner expressed amazement that Van Gelder had not been discouraged by what seemed to be the hopelessness of getting support for the canal project in the early years.

"Good people believed in me and my dreams of the inland waterways," said Van Gelder. "My aunt Elizabeth supported me every step of the way. When she died she left me a good deal of money, which enabled me to carry on the work. James Rivington, who was like an uncle to me, helped me in many ways. My dear wife, Bridget—God rest her soul—would not let me become discouraged. And Kilaen Borsum, he helped me greatly."

"Borsum was a member of the assembly, wasn't he? And of course I know that James Rivington was one of our pioneer newspaper editors and printers."

"Without them I would never have been able to do this work."

"I believe you should be an honored guest during the festivities at Sandy Hook when the governor's party arrives there on the fourth," said Scribner. "Perhaps the account I shall write of your work will help."

"I can talk to some important people in Tammany," said Deasy. "Mr. Van Gelder's contributions should surely be recognized as well as my own."

"I'm meeting Governor Clinton's party at the Lockport Fives," said Scribner, "and will come the rest of the way with them. I will talk to the governor then. I wrote some articles which helped him occasionally through the years of his own long struggle to make the great canal a reality. I believe he owes me a small favor."

Van Gelder's bright brown eyes filled with tears. He even felt kindly toward John Deasy.

"I thank you, Mr. Scribner, with all my heart. And you, John, I thank you. It would give me great joy to participate in the festivities at Sandy Hook."

"John Deasy's always proud to be of service to a distinguished citizen, Mr. Van Gelder," said Deasy unctuously.

2

Two years earlier, when Mary Deasy was eighteen, Martin Morrissey fought Jem McCool in a grueling sixty-three-round bout lasting two hours and forty minutes. Women were not permitted to attend the contests, but Mary, curious, willful, and venturesome as always, had found a place in a storeroom in the rear of the second floor of her father's saloon on Water Street, near the East River. She had an excellent view of the action in the yard. It was the most thrilling spectacle she had ever seen. Close to a hundred rowdy men, most of them more than half-drunk, crowded around a twenty-five-foot square of dirt in the center of the yard. Heavy oak poles were buried deep in the four corners of the square and thick ropes extended from pole to pole. One strand of ropes came almost to the shoulder blades of a grown man, and the lower strand to a height just above the knees.

Jem McCool and Martin Morrissey, neither of whom were known to Mary Deasy, were clad in a fashion which excited her. Both wore tight-fitting breeches, McCool's black, and Morrissey's yellow, from their waists to just below their knees. Perhaps underwear, rather than breeches. Mary had never seen men in their underwear. Whatever the apparel, it was so form-fitting that the contours of the men's genitals and their muscular thighs and buttocks showed plainly. They wore white cotton stockings and high-topped shoes. From the waist up they were naked. She watched her father going among the crowd, collecting money and making notations in a small pad he carried.

McCool was some six inches shorter than Morrissey, but twenty pounds heavier, with a bulletlike head and a flattened nose on his broad face, the dominant feature of which was a pair of thick black eyebrows.

Martin, at twenty-five, was eleven years younger than McCool. He seemed nervous, and kept staring down at the dirt at his feet as one of the two men at his side rubbed his slender but muscular back and neck vigorously. The second man with Martin was a silver-haired gentleman with one arm. He was in a wheelchair. The chair rolled agitatedly inches forward and back and skidded occasionally from side to side as the old man made various punching motions, looking up at Martin, and speaking earnestly all the while.

Mary Deasy always told herself that she had fallen in love with Martin Morrissey even before she knew his name, that day of his first bout. Although he was almost a head taller than McCool, he seemed frail compared to the squat monster across the ring. Mary Deasy had no way of knowing how agile Martin was; how much strength there was in that gangly, lithe body; how much punishment he could absorb; nor how much power there was in those long, tautly muscular arms and bony fists. She saw only a youth who seemed not much older than herself. The youthful impression was created by the shock of raven hair with the cowlick standing up over his forehead, just above his left eyebrow. And most of all by the extraordinarily large ears, which stood out from the sides of his head.

Mary Deasy was soaked in perspiration by the time the savage contest ended. She was emotionally drained, but she had never been so thrilled by any experience in her life. Not even the time a year earlier when she had permitted herself to be seduced by her more or less steady escort, Timothy O'Leary. Timothy was one of the fastest-rising politicians in the city, and a wealthy businessman. He was a partner of her father's in several enterprises.

Mary found him cold and pompous and an uninspired, mechanical lover. She had continued to share his bed occasionally only because she had no wish to become promiscuous, but still sought the thrills of lovemaking, scant as they were with O'Leary. He had asked her to marry him, but she told him she was not ready for marriage. Now, watching the furious bout, it passed through her mind that the fearless young boxer would undoubtedly make a much more satisfactory lover than Timothy O'Leary.

Often during the bloody battle she shouted triumphantly when Martin landed a telling blow, or screamed and cried when McCool grasped Martin in a bearlike hug, and it seemed he would crush the younger man to death.

However, Martin lost the bout when his second, his uncle Ned, refused to let him take any more punishment and declared him beaten. But McCool could barely walk out of the ring when it ended. Back in the tavern, Martin's mother treated his wounds, alternately commiserating and scolding all the while. Battered as he was, Martin told her and his uncle, through swollen lips, that he had enjoyed the fight and would fight again. Maureen told him he had lost his senses, but Ned Van Gelder understood.

Van Gelder knew from the bright gleam in Martin's eyes, the grim set of his jaw, that he had enjoyed the encounter, even at the moments when he was taking severe punishment. Indeed, during some of those moments, he grinned at McCool. It seemed strange that so fundamentally gentle a young man should get such pleasure out of this brutal, illegal sport.

For days after the McCool fight, Mary Deasy could not get Martin Morrissey out of her mind. She lay awake most of several nights trying to figure out how she could ask her father who he was and somehow arrange to meet him, without revealing that she had sneaked into the saloon through a side door and witnessed the fight. She was almost prepared to confess bluntly that she had seen the bout and wanted to meet the gangly young man with the cowlick and the big ears. She knew that her father would admire and be amused by her interest in boxing, rather than be shocked and disapproving. He was aware of her often nonconformist, sometimes unfeminine, attitudes and interests. She was more than an adequate substitute for the son he had never had. He spoiled her thoroughly.

Her mother, Anne, on the other hand, fretted and worried over her, to no avail. Mary paid as little attention to the woman who had borne her as did her husband. Anne Deasy lived in fear of John, who was not averse to cuffing her about now and then. However, it turned out to be unnecessary for

Mary to confess her surreptitious witnessing of the fight. On the second Sunday after it took place, John Deasy had Martin Morrissey, his mother and uncle as guests for supper.

The Deasys lived in one of the new row of houses north of Rivington Street, and about a half mile south of St. Mark's-in-the-Bouwerie Church where Peter Stuyvesant was buried. The developed section of the city was just beginning to reach as far north as Fourteenth Street. The Deasy house was an attractive two-story edifice with dormer windows, high front steps, and an ornately carved doorway. A plump and hearty Irishwoman named Fanny cooked and served a plain meal of roast pork, mounds of thickly buttered mashed potatoes, and cabbage. The Deasys had no black slaves, since they held Negroes in even greater contempt that most New Yorkers held Irish immigrants. Indeed, John Deasy predicted there would be great trouble with the niggers in a couple of years. Ten years earlier a state law had been passed stipulating that on July 4, 1827, all slaves born after July 4, 1799, were to be freed.

Tonight, like the shrewd politician he was, Deasy spent the first part of the evening asking endless questions about the Van Gelders and the Morrisseys. Old Ned was reluctant to say much, but Maureen Morrissey boasted that the Van Gelders had settled in New York when it was New Amsterdam under the Dutch. She told about the memoirs that Ned's forebears, his great-great-grandfather Willem; his great-grandfather Harman; and his aunt Elizabeth had written. Elizabeth Van Gelder had practically raised orphaned Maureen, and had permitted her to read all the family histories.

"The city was beautiful and spacious years ago," Maureen said, "but there were some terrible times too."

"And would you be writing your memoirs, too, Mr. Van Gelder?" asked Deasy.

"No. I'm just beginning to write the story of my work on the early canals. Since Schoharie, it is all I can really do."

That launched Deasy on an account of his own activities in bringing impoverished Irish families to America.

"It costs me a pretty penny," he boasted, "but as my holy friend Father Boland says, a man must do his share of good works."

By that time he had consumed enough wine so that he

could no longer control his strong desire to boast of his many properties and activities. It was then that Ned Van Gelder began to develop an active dislike for the bragging Irishman.

"I've got great plans for you, young man," Deasy finally said to Martin. "I believe you can become a truly fine box-fighter. Someday soon the sport'll be legalized, and champions'll be heroes here just like they are in England."

"Thanks, Mr. Deasy," said Martin. "I don't mind the fighting at all."

Deasy laughed heartily.

"I could see that plain enough, and I'll wager old Jem would testify to it. The day's comin' fast when a young man with your skills and strength can make a fortune."

"How so?" asked Van Gelder.

"You know, I'm sure, that with more and more immigrants comin' into the city—Irish by the thousands, and now Germans too—there's a resentment developin' on the part of people who were born here. They think the city belongs to native Americans."

"That's ridiculous," said Van Gelder. "The Indians are the only natives."

"Jesus, Mary, 'n' Joseph, Mr. Van Gelder! You couldn't be righter. But you're a rare exception. I know some powerful politicians who are tryin' to organize a party of native-born Americans to oppose the entry of immigrants, voting rights for them, schools . . . any benefits. And one of these politicians has arrangements with some excellent boxers of the same persuasion—or perhaps no persuasion at all, except to make money."

He finished yet another glass of wine and refilled his glass and Martin's. Van Gelder's glass was still full.

"Someday in the not-too-distant future a bout between a boxer representin' the position of the natives and an Irish champion could be held in a locale where hundreds, maybe even thousands, of people would pay to see the contest. And the wagerin' would be staggerin'."

"I must say, Mr. Deasy," said Maureen, "I would much prefer it if Martin didn't fight at all."

Martin grinned at her.

"It's like I told you, Mom. It's a fine sport. The bruises heal soon enough."

"I believe you could be the Irish champion, young man," said Deasy. "Under my guidance and with Billy Brannigan's help you could become famous in sportin' circles, and rich in the bargain."

"Brannigan!" exclaimed Van Gelder. "Isn't that the gangster who sent those hoodlums to our place?"

Deasy chuckled again and nodded.

"Billy does have a tendency to operate some of his enterprises with a bit of unnecessary force, but he's not really a bad lad. He keeps that bunch called the Dead Rabbits from doin' a lot more mischief than they would if he wasn't the boss."

"He's a pig!" said Mary Deasy vehemently.

"Oh, now, Mary dear," protested Mrs. Deasy feebly. They were the first words she had spoken in more than an hour. Deasy chuckled again.

"Billy is very fond of pretty young girls, but is not too gentle in his handlin' of them. He approached our little Mary a bit too aggressively at a Tammany ball last month. She slapped him, and he came to me, furious he was. 'J.D.,' says he, 'if that wench wasn't your daughter I'd bust her head.' "

"I'd just like to see him try," said Mary defiantly. After supper Mary persuaded Martin to accompany her on a walk. They strolled slowly in the cool night to the Bowery, and walked north along the busy street, which had become the entertainment center of the city.

"I saw you fight McCool," Mary told Martin.

He looked surprised.

"How could you? There were no ladies . . ."

In the light of one of the new gas lamps on the street, he saw the twinkle in her deep green eyes.

"I saw it," she insisted. "I do many things ladies don't do. You were wonderful."

He smiled at her uneasily. Her aggressive manner made him uncomfortable. They heard the oompah music of the German bands as they passed several of the new beer gardens, and came to a darker place, where thick elms lined the street, blocking both the light of the moon and the nearest gas lamp. Mary took his hand and pulled him toward the trunk of a tree in the darkest part of the street.

"Wha—wha—what are you—" he began to say.

She put her arms around his neck and held her face close to his. He could feel her breath against his chin. It smelled a bit of the pork gravy.

"Kiss me, Martin," she said.

When he made no effort to do so, she put a hand behind his neck, and pulled his head forward till his mouth was on hers. In his twenty-five years Martin had, of course, often thought about eventually establishing an alliance with a young woman. He had frequently dreamed of how exciting it would be to make love to a woman, although he feared he would be awkward and clumsy. He had occasional erotic dreams. And four times he had escorted girls of his acquaintance to dances, or taken them on boat rides, or gone for walks with them. But none of them had really interested him, and it never occurred to any of them or to him to do such a daring thing as kiss. Green-eyed, flame-haired Mary Deasy was an attractive young lady, with a fetching hourglass figure, but she not only did not interest Martin, she terrified him.

When she moved her lips away from his tightly compressed mouth, she said angrily, "Jesus, Mary, and Joseph, Martin Morrissey! What *is* the matter with you? Don't you like me?"

"Y—y—yes, of course, I do, Mary. It's just—it's just—well, we just met!"

"I can see it's going to take me a long time to teach you to make love, Martin."

Now two years had passed and she had not yet been able to teach Martin how to make love. Reluctantly, when she persisted with such frequency that to refuse her again would be unforgivably insulting, he agreed to take her to an occasional ball or assembly, to the theater, or on boating and fishing trips. He even learned to return her energetic and passionate kisses with a certain cooperative politeness. But never ardently. Once she boldly took his hand and placed it on her breast as they were kissing. He withdrew the hand as if the cloth over the firm bosom were on fire. He was hopeless for two reasons. He did not love Mary. And her aggressiveness made it totally impossible for him to learn to love her. But she was her father's daughter and knew no other way.

In those same two years, Martin had also become increasingly disenchanted with boxing. John Deasy had persuaded him to sign an agreement providing that Deasy and Bill Brannigan would get fifty percent of whatever Martin was paid for bouts promoted by others than Deasy himself. As his skills improved he won bout after bout, and there were an ever-increasing number of contests staged by entrepreneurs in secluded places in Long Island, upstate New York, New

Jersey, Boston, Philadelphia, and even Virginia. He was paid as much as twenty-five dollars for some of these fights, and on Deasy's advice he often wagered his share of the purse and won.

However, the people with whom he had to deal as a boxer were for the most part unsavory and unscrupulous. Brannigan himself was the worst of all. The gangster had been through more than a hundred savage street fights and more formal boxing matches from the time he was twelve years old until his present age of forty-one. Four years earlier, in 1821, he had killed Dandy Jack Duggan, the leader of the Dead Rabbits gang, in the kind of bloody knife battle that had earned him the nickname of the Butcher. Thus he had become the new, undisputed leader of the gang.

As the king, he considered it beneath him to do any of the actual brawling any longer. He assembled seven of the strongest, most cold-blooded and obedient brutes in Five Points around him, and gave each of them the exclusive rights to a share in the profits of one or another of the criminal areas in which the Dead Rabbits operated. One-Eye Mulchahy got ten percent of all collections of the protective association; Terrible Tommy Malone received ten percent of all the proceeds from thefts from ships on the waterfront; and so on. Three of this unholy seven were defectors from other Five Points gangs, and all were killers of the first order. They were King Billy's courtiers, and his bodyguards at the same time. They became known in Five Points as the Butcher's slaughterers.

Within the limitations of dilapidated Five Points, King Billy made every effort to set himself up in style. The area derived its name from the fact that it was bounded by five streets, whose corners touched upon each other. They were Anthony, Orange, Cross, Little Water, and Mulberry. The section was less than a ten-minute walk north of the City Hall, and not too far southwest of Rivington Street. Ned Van Gelder often remarked that Five Points was the most depressingly dramatic evidence of the city's decline. His great-great-grandfather (as a very young man) had slept on the banks of a pond one night after he left the then tiny village of New Amsterdam to seek his fortune. Willem Van Gelder described it as the Collect, a freshwater pond surrounded by woods and meadow; serene and beautiful beyond his poorly educated power to describe.

Ned remembered going ice-skating and boating on the

Collect Pond as a boy, although by that time the practice of washing laundry in the pond, the filth from the tanneries, and the dumping of garbage had already begun to pollute it. By 1811 it had become so malodorous as to be considered a public-health hazard and the city had filled the pond with tons upon tons of garbage and dirt. The fill had proved inadequate, and over the next fourteen years the underground waters began to ooze to the surface in many places and the area was constantly damp and swampy. Soon anyone who could afford to moved out of the filled-in Collect and it became Five Points. The houses and buildings were neglected and rapidly decayed. When the enormous influx of Irish immigrants began, the penniless sons and daughters of Erin moved into the deserted, rat-infested houses, and, where there was room, built wooden and canvas shacks of their own.

The *Evening Post* and the other city newspapers made frequent references to the festering slum.

"Five Points strikes even the practiced eye and hardened olfactories of a veteran New Yorker as particularly foul and loathsome."

"Five Points is the most dangerous place in our City. All manner of outrages are committed there daily."

"Five Points is the great center ulcer of wretchedness, the very rotting skeleton of civilization."

The oldest and still one of the sturdiest buildings in Five Points had been constructed on the south shore of the Collect in 1792. Ned Van Gelder was in his midthirties then, and he remembered it well. It was Coulder's Brewery, and they made one of the finest beers in the city, a brew so good it became popular in most of the eastern states. But now, in 1825, like most other buildings in the Points, it had become a dank, dark, evil-smelling ruin. Still called the Old Brewery, it was a five-story building, and the lower four of its floors had been compartmentalized into small rooms, most of them windowless, with a maze of dim, foul-smelling hallways and corridors running through them. These rooms were occupied by more than a thousand prostitutes, sexual deviates, thieves, and murderers, ranging in age from sickly five- and six-year-old children to scurvy forty- and fifty-year-old cripples and hags, though not many reached such advanced years. They were practically all Irish.

The top floor of the brewery had also been converted, most recently after Brannigan's ascension. He had directed the reconstruction himself. This upper story was no longer a hive of small rooms. More than a quarter of the south end of the floor was King Billy's court.

Deasy had brought Martin to the Old Brewery near midnight three days after his second bout. Martin had knocked out a burly opponent in three and a half minutes, and Deasy said Brannigan was anxious to meet him. They rode the short distance from Rivington Street in a carriage, accompanied by Francis Xavier Mulchahy, better known as One-Eye, and Thomas Ernest Malone, the cutthroat Terrible Tommy. The two Dead Rabbits kicked and shoved a dozen or more filthy men, women, and children out of the way as they climbed the stinking, creaking stairs leading to the fifth floor. When Brannigan opened the door to their coded knock, Martin saw three giggling, nude young girls scamper through a large doorway beside the rear of the bar. A thin brunette closed the door quickly behind them.

Brannigan greeted them effusively. He was the largest man Martin had ever seen. Martin himself was almost six feet, but Brannigan stood at least eight inches taller. He was not only tall, he was heavy. Like many men who are extraordinarily active and underfed in their younger years, and then become sedentary and gluttonous, Brannigan had gone to fat. But hard fat. His head was round as a cannonball, topped by short-cropped black hair over less than two inches of forehead.

"Ya come a bit sooner'n I expected ya, Johnno," he said to Deasy in a deep, hoarse voice as he led the group to the bar. He shoved stocky Mulchahy roughly, and ordered, "Pour us some whiskey, ya one-eyed donkey!"

Mulchahy sullenly went behind the bar and filled thick glass tumblers. Martin stood at the bar beside Deasy.

"Thanks, Mr. Brannigan," he said, as Brannigan lifted his glass, readying a toast, "I don't drink."

"Holy crise!" said Brannigan. "An Irishman, an' a barkeep ta boot, who don't drink! Here's to ya, anyway, young Morrissey, yer one helluva box-fighter!"

There was a wooden platter with an ample supply of dark bread, cheese, and sausages on the bar, and beside it a large glass jar, filled with a cloudy pinkish liquid, and what Martin assumed to be pickled pigs' knuckles. Many saloons served that delicacy. Brannigan, Deasy, Mulchahy, and Malone drank. Brannigan grabbed a sausage and waved it at Martin.

"Have some grub, son," he invited. Then he noticed that Martin was staring at the glass jar. He laughed.

"No, me bucko. Those ain't pigs' knuckles. Just a few fingers, ears, and noses of some unfriendly fellas, mostly Bowery B'hoys."

He led the way to the table, chewing an overstuffed mouthful of sausage, and waved them to seats.

"We're gonna make a lotta money, son," he said, talking as he chewed. "Johnno, tell the lad how we work."

It was at this meeting that the financial arrangements had been made. Since then, in the twenty-three months that had passed, Martin had had twenty-one bouts and had won them all. Only the third, fifth, and ninth of the matches had been difficult. He had come within a punch or two of losing twice. But from the tenth contest on, although his opponents were reputed to be experienced, respected fighters in sporting circles, he had knocked each of them out in less than twenty-two minutes, after no more than fourteen or fifteen rounds. Many of them stayed down on one knee and refused to continue after Martin knocked them down for the first time.

Martin was pleased with his success, but had an uneasy feeling about it. He had become a huge favorite with virtually all of the characters who were involved in, or followed, the outlawed sport. Brannigan himself, and his seven slaughterers, particularly admired him. Their fellowship pleased him not at all, and when they started to frequent the restaurant he discouraged them. Which was difficult without insulting them. Financially, of course, his boxing career proved more lucrative than he had ever expected. It enabled him to have considerable renovations made on both the exterior and the interior of the old house at 106 Rivington Street. Indeed he spent so much that his uncle Ned insisted on assigning half of the property to him. The money also enabled him to provide the cost of transportation from Ireland for his cousin Stephen Boyle and Stephen's wife and two small children. His mother and uncle were particularly eager to bring the Boyles to America and help them. Their arrival date was uncertain, but Martin had sent the money.

In spite of his spectacular success, he felt uncomfortable and discontented with boxing for a number of reasons. He knew he had quick hands, and power in both his left and right. He also could absorb punishment. But somehow his last eleven bouts had seemed to him too pat, too mechanical;

almost like those melodramas he had seen with Mary Deasy at the Park or the Bowery theaters. And there were other aspects of the illegal sporting scene that had brought him to the point where he was seriously considering quitting in spite of the fact that a championship fight had been arranged.

Now, just three days after Elias Scribner, the *Post* reporter, had visited the restaurant, the very day his praiseful story about Uncle Ned appeared in the paper, Martin, once again, sat at the round oak table in Brannigan's vast room in the Old Brewery. He had committed himself to the upcoming fight, obviously the most important of his career, and one about which Brannigan and Deasy were more excited than he had ever seen them. It was midday and a bright October sun filtered feebly through the dirty windows. On this occasion Brannigan was not in his underwear and no naked ladies scampered from the room. He was dressed in black-and-white-checkered trousers and a red silk shirt, which seemed to have been painted upon his bulky torso and arms. Under the broad collar of the shirt, hanging down between his bulging breasts and resting on his hard paunch, was a broad emerald-green cravat. This was fastened to the taut shirt with a diamond pin. He was clean-shaven.

Brannigan poured himself and Deasy generous drinks of whiskey. Deasy immediately gulped down his drink. To Martin he seemed uncharacteristically edgy.

"Well, now, Martin, me lad," said Brannigan. "In less'n a week ya'll be fightin' the English champion. How're ya feelin'?"

Martin shrugged.

"Fine enough."

"Ya think ya kin beat Cribb?"

"I don't know. I've never seen him fight."

"But ya know all about 'im. . . ."

"Only what you and John've told me. That he's been the champion in Europe for seven years. He must be good."

"He's big," said Brannigan, "big as I am."

"I know. You told me they call him the Lancashire Giant."

"I also told ya that the Frenchman I saw 'im fight last year almost knocked 'im out. If he'd been able t' land one more solid blow . . ."

"I'll do my best, Billy. You know that."

"That's what I'm afraid of," said Brannigan.

Martin wasn't sure he had heard right. There was a sly look in Brannigan's squinted ice-gray eyes and a grin on his thick lips. He stuck the spittle-soaked end of his unlit cigar in the corner of his mouth, but kept grinning at Martin.

"Afraid?" said Martin. "You're afraid I'll do my best?"

"At yer best I think ya kin beat the goddam Englishman," said Brannigan. He put the cigar down in a dish and drank his whiskey. He belched and said, "We don't want ya to beat him, Martin."

"You don't want me to? You don't want me to beat him?"

"Explain it to him, Johnno," Brannigan ordered.

Deasy coughed, finished his whiskey, and poured himself another.

"It's a business, son. You know that. We had to guarantee Cribb and his people five thousand dollars to come over here to fight you. The big barn on Long Island, buildin' the benches, payin' people to spread the word o' the bout all this week of the canal celebrations all adds up. We've built you up so big all the gamblers here are bettin' on you even though Cribb's the champion. There's no money around except what Cribb and his own people are willin' to bet . . . and they're bein' careful. The only way we can make any money on this fight is to bet on Cribb—and make sure Cribb wins."

He paused and stared intently at Martin. He licked his lips nervously and gulped his fresh drink.

"You understand, lad?"

"You want me to lose . . . deliberately?"

"Yeah, fight 'im hard fer as long as ye want to, but don't knock 'im out," said Brannigan. "When ya git a bit tired stay down."

Martin shook his head.

"I don't think I can do it. It's not right."

"You're still gonna be the champion, bucko," said Brannigan. "Tell 'im the rest, Johnno."

"You give Cribb a hard fight, the hardest fight of his life, Martin. He and his people take word back to jolly ol' England. They've already got a racecourse at Worcester booked for next July. July fourth to be exact. They're goin' to build grandstands that'll hold close to thirty thousand people. You can beat Cribb then . . . July fourth . . . right in front of his own people. No special arrangements then. Just fight him with all you've got. . . . We'll all make a fortune, lad. And you'll be champion o' the world!"

Martin stared at him and turned to stare at Brannigan, who was again chewing on his cigar. He removed it once more and said, "An' when ya come back the champion o' the whole fuckin' world, me boy, those native Americans'll have built up Henry Wilson, a youngster they're groomin', and we'll stage a bout between him and the pride o' the Irish, Martin Morrissey. Only thing I don't know is where we'll find a place big enough t' hold the goddam match."

Martin, hands clasped between his knees, looked down at the floor, and shook his head.

"I don't care about being champion, one way or the other. But I can't lose the fight on purpose. I wouldn't feel right—"

"Horseshit, me bucko. We do it all the time. How in holy crise's name d'ya think ya beat some o' them good fighters so easy!"

Martin's eyes widened as he stared at Brannigan.

"You mean they—they deliberately lost? I didn't really beat them?"

"It's just business, Martin," said Deasy nervously. "The way we build up a boxer. There's nothin' wrong with makin' an honest dollar. . . . You'll be able to open another saloon soon, or—"

Brannigan finished his drink and stood up.

"I got a man from City Hall comin' in in a coupl'a minutes. That's the way it's gonna be done, young Morrissey."

He grinned down at Martin.

"I've taken a great likin' to ya, lad," he said, "and so have me slaughterers. Matter of fact they'll be bettin' heavy on ya to beat the Englishman, 'long with everybody else."

He laughed heartily.

"Won't hurt the bastards ta lose a little o' their ill-gotten gains."

He clutched Martin's shoulder in a beefy hand and squeezed.

"We've all become more than passin' fond of ya . . . but if ya don't lose ta Cribb a little piece of ya'll wind up in that jar over there."

"Jesus, Mary, 'n' Joseph!" burst out Deasy. "That's not necessary, Billy."

Brannigan chuckled and gave Martin's shoulder another affectionate squeeze.

"Good! Good! I'm glad it's not gonna be necessary. See ya both out on Long Island the night of the fifth."

He slapped Martin's cheek playfully, but hard enough so it

stung. He belched and strode to the door beside the bar, and walked into the bedchamber.

3

Martin's mother and his uncle had been puzzled over his troubled demeanor for the past week. Though Ned had long since joined Maureen in her desire to see Martin get out of the dangerous, corrupt, and illegal world of boxing, neither of them could understand why he was not more excited about the championship match. And Martin could not tell them. In the meantime the jubilant atmosphere in the city over the impending November 4 New York celebration of the completion of the Grand Canal was nearing a hysterical crescendo. From midmorning until late at night every restaurant, tavern, and saloon in the city was crowded. The Van Gelder and Morrissey establishment on Rivington Street had built a fine reputation and got more than its share of both local and out-of-the-city celebrants.

Walking home from his meeting with Deasy and Brannigan, Martin thought how much he would like to discuss his dilemma with his uncle. Yet he had seen how elated Ned had been with the story in the *Post* that morning, and he felt it would be a shame to dampen Ned's joy by involving him in this problem. And he never even considered telling his mother about Brannigan's ultimatum. She would simply demand that he lose the fight, and get out of the boxing business once and for all! He suspected that his Uncle Ned might well urge him to fight to win. *That's what your father would have done, lad!* he imagined Ned saying. *Brannigan and Deasy be damned!* Yes, he thought, he would talk to his Uncle Ned.

Van Gelder was at a rear corner table surrounded by more than a dozen friends, local merchants, some men from the shipyards, and two tanners. They were still talking about the story in the *Post*, asking Ned endless questions on matters the report had not covered. Martin had not seen his uncle so exhilarated in years. When he joined his mother behind the bar, she smiled at him broadly.

"Oh, I'm so happy for him, Martin," she exclaimed. "The publisher of the *Post* came by just after you left, and brought him an invitation to be aboard the journalists' vessel during the ceremonies at Sandy Hook next Friday."

She drew a beer from a keg for a stout man in the mob at the bar, and turned back to Martin.

"And that's not all. He'll also be a guest at the banquet Governor Clinton is giving for all the most important men who worked on the canal."

Martin smiled warmly in the direction of his flushed and excited uncle.

"That's wonderful!" he said, as he donned his bartender's apron. He made up his mind he was not going to cloud his uncle's hard-won days of glory with his own ridiculous predicament.

It was three hours after the tavern had closed. Outside there were still occasional shouts and laughter as some drunken passersby continued their celebration. Martin, his mother, and his uncle sat in the large kitchen of the restaurant, steaming cups of tea before them. Although they had been awake for almost twenty-four hours they were not sleepy.

"I only wish old Martin could be here," said Ned Van Gelder, moisture forming in his brown eyes.

Maureen reached across the table and put her hand on Ned's.

"I do, too, Ned, but I'm sure he's looking down from heaven and enjoying all this as much as we are."

"Having you recognized this way, Uncle Ned, is just like having Pop recognized," said Martin.

Suddenly Ned's hand darted to his chest. An expression of pain twisted his lined face. Martin leaped to his side. Ned shook his head and waved him away. He gasped, taking short breaths until, finally, he was able to hold and exhale one long, relieved whoosh of air. Then he breathed more evenly again.

"Damned chest pains!" he muttered. He slumped in his chair, closed his eyes, then opened them again, and smiled a strained smile at Martin.

"With all this talk about me and the canal ceremonies," he said, breathing with some effort, "I haven't even thought to ask you about the fight. Did Deasy and Brannigan have anything new to say today?"

Martin shook his head.

"No, the bout's still scheduled for Sunday, the night after the official canal celebrations. Deasy's got a regular fleet of flatboats ready to take people over to Port Jefferson. He's charging a dollar each way."

"I won't rest easy till you come home again," said Maureen. "I'm always worried something terrible's going to happen to you in these cursed fights."

Martin smiled at her.

"I'll be all right, Mom. And maybe this'll be my last fight."

"I've sensed you're getting tired of the boxing business, son . . . and I don't blame you," said Ned. He spoke with some difficulty, but he forced a smile. "So you're planning on retiring as champion of the world!"

Martin shrugged. His uncle patted his shoulder.

"Good! Good!" he said. "That's the time to quit!"

"Will you, Martin?" asked Maureen eagerly. "Will this *really* be your last fight?"

"We'll see," said Martin. He looked at Ned, and said solicitously, "Uncle Ned, you're looking kind of weary, and by the time the celebrations are over you'll be needing a long rest. I think it might be a good idea if you didn't come to the fight. It might just be too much."

Catching his breath between sentences, Ned nevertheless protested vehemently.

"What's the matter with you, Martin! Have you taken leave of your senses? You're fighting the champion of the world and you want me not to be there! I haven't missed a single one of your bouts since the time you fought McCool. I—I surely have no intention of missing this one!"

Martin grinned at him and rose.

"In that case you'd better start keeping more sensible hours," he said. "Ready for bed?"

Maureen came around the table and kissed her brother-in-law's cheek.

"Happy dreams, Ned," she said.

Martin wheeled him into his bedchamber.

Van Gelder lay beneath his trapeze in the darkness and dreamed. During brief stretches of sleep, and longer spans of wakefulness, and hours when he was not certain whether he was awake or asleep, he dreamed. The visions came in disconnected fragments. He recalled the shock he felt the day his beloved wife, Bridget, sister of his dear friend Martin Morrissey, told him she was with child. Normally he would have been overjoyed at the prospect of fatherhood, but

Bridget was then thirty-eight years old. She had almost died giving birth to her son, Vincent, by her first marriage to Vincent Boyle. She had only been seventeen at that time, and she had been told she could bear no more children. Ned pretended to be overwhelmingly pleased at the news and not at all worried. He assured Bridget that everything would be fine. But at the first opportunity he had confessed to his aunt Elizabeth Van Gelder how deeply concerned he was.

"I don't know what I'll do if I lose Bridget, Aunt Liz," he had said. And Aunt Liz, who was then already sixty-eight and ravaged by a degenerating heart, somehow convinced him that Bridget would have a healthy child and survive the birth. Aunt Elizabeth had always been Ned's greatest source of strength. She had been a mother, rather than an aunt, to him.

"Look at Maureen," she had said. "They told her she could never bear a child after young Vinnie raped her so brutally."

Ned remembered the traumatic days when he and Martin had returned from Herkimer after another season of working on the canal. Pretty teenage Maureen Kerrigan told Martin she could not marry him in spite of the fact that she had agreed they would be married this winter. She gave Martin no reason, but she had told Elizabeth and Bridget that Bridget's eighteen-year-old son, Vinnie junior, had raped her. She considered herself damaged goods, and unworthy of a fine man like Martin. Bridget had driven her incorrigible son from the house and he had left the city despite feeble protests from his father. The following winter, urged to do so by Aunt Elizabeth and Bridget, Maureen had told Martin what had happened, and he insisted on marrying her despite her violent deflowering.

Just three months after the wedding, Martin had come to Ned in a panic.

"Jesus Christ, Ned! She's pregnant!"

"Congratulations, lad," said Ned. "I hope it's twins."

"The doctor told us Maureen's life would be in danger if she got pregnant, Ned. Don't you remember? That filthy rapparee nephe· · o' mine hurt her—"

"Doctors are wrong more often than they're right, Martin," Ned recalled saying, although he was as worried as Martin. But Maureen had borne Martin junior, a healthy six-pound four-ounce boy with a promise of oversize ears like his father, and within two weeks after the birth Maureen was back working in Walker's cake shop. A year later, Bridget bore a son, too, almost a pound heaver than Martin. They named him Christopher, after a long-time idol of Ned's, Christopher Wren. But Bridget had almost died in the course of giving birth, and regained her health painfully slowly in the months that followed.

Lying in bed now, Ned remembered how she had insisted on attending the joyous christening. Weak as she was, he had never seen her so happy. They were all happy. Aunt Liz had said, "I feel as though you and Bridget have given me a grandson, Ned."

Now Ned's reverie was interrupted by a sudden knock at the door. It was light, but repeated insistently, and Maureen's voice called, "Ned! Ned! Are you all right?"

"Yes, Maureen, of course, I'm fine."

"Sorry to disturb you! I thought I heard a groan."

It was possible, thought Ned. The pain in his chest was coming and going, but he was ignoring it. He might have dropped off to sleep and made some sound.

"Probably someone outside," he said loudly.

"Yes, probably. Good night, Ned."

What a wonderful woman, what a friend Maureen had always been. After Christopher's birth, Ned felt it might be better if he did not return to the canal project. It would keep him and Martin away all through the spring, summer, and fall. But Bridget insisted he go, and Maureen gave up her job at the cake shop and took care of Bridget and Elizabeth, as well as the two babies. When Ned and Martin returned to the house on Rivington Street the following winter, an episode occurred in which Maureen once again demonstrated her sweet and noble nature.

Bridget had gone to the door to accept a letter from the postboy. She began to read it on the way back to the kitchen where Ned, Elizabeth, Martin, Maureen, and the two babies sat at the long oak table, halfway through dinner.

"Holy Mary!" exclaimed Bridget. "It's—it's from Vinnie—from a Father Neely for Vinnie." She took her seat and continued to read. Tears began to roll down her gaunt cheeks, and finally she handed the letter to Ned at her side. The priest, acting as Vincent Boyle junior's amanuensis, wrote in a clear, bold hand, but was not a very good speller. Nevertheless the message was clear. After he left New York City, Vinnie had worked in the West Indies for a time, but had eventually made his way to Ireland. In Templemore County in Tipperary he had met a fourteen-year-old girl, named Annie Riordan, and married her. Annie had just given birth to a boy, whom they had named Stephen, after Annie's father. The birth of his son had had a profound spiritual effect on young Vinnie, who had lived a dissolute and wicked life until his marriage.

He begged Bridget's and his father's forgiveness for all the troubles and sorrows he had caused them. (He did not know that his father had died during a malaria epidemic while working on the canal.) Now he was working on a farm leased from a wealthy English landholder by Annie's father, and he swore he would work hard, and hoped someday to save enough money to come back to America so that his parents could see their grandson. He also pleaded with Bridget to show the letter to Maureen Kerrigan, and tell Maureen that he prayed every night that the terrible thing he did to her had not blighted her life, and that she, too, might find it in her heart to forgive him.

Ned's eyes were moist as he finished reading. He took Bridget's hand, and passed the letter across the table to Maureen.

"Is he all right, Ned? What has happened?" asked Elizabeth Van Gelder in alarm. Ned nodded and stuttered a reply. "He's—he's—had a son too."

Maureen began to read the letter aloud so that Martin, at her side, and Elizabeth would be aware of its contents. Her voice cracked as she came to the part referring to herself. When she finished reading, she came around the table and put her arms around Bridget.

"We do forgive him, Bridget, don't we?" she said. "He has found the Lord. One day we'll see him again."

Bridget nodded happily, sniffling and wiping her eyes with a kerchief.

Ned had often pondered the strange ways of fate. Vinnie's letter was testimony to one of its oddest turns. Ned and Bridget now had a young son and a grandson who were almost the same ages. And to compound the felicitous picture, they also had a nephew just a year older than their son, Christopher. Ned drifted off to sleep remembering Christopher's and Martin's infanthood. Happy days they were. He and

Bridget, and Martin and Maureen, and Aunt Elizabeth and the babies lived busy, fulfilling lives in the house on Rivington Street.

But then one night in the winter of 1798, when Christopher was two and Martin, three, Elizabeth Van Gelder died quietly in her sleep. She was in her seventieth year. And Bridget had died a much more painful death two years later, stoic to the end, fighting back the agony of the cancerous growth in her abdomen. The day before she died, a letter from Father Neely, again writing for Vinnie Boyle, arrived. Vinnie's second child, a one-year-old baby daughter, named Bridget, had died the week before the letter was written. Young Stephen was healthy enough, although times were hard in Tipperary and many people were starving. Annie Boyle was pregnant with yet a third child.

Ned's dream turned macabre. Aunt Liz, in a flowing white robe, led a small procession down a street he had never seen. The street was flanked by trees that seemed to be made of translucent glass with leaves like large tear drops. Aunt Liz was holding a sleeping infant in her arms. Ned did not recognize the baby. At Aunt Liz's side was a tall, broad-shouldered man in the scarlet-coated uniform of a British officer. Aunt Liz's husband, Richardson Thorpe, had died before Ned was born, but in his dream, Ned knew that the handsome soldier was his deceased uncle.

Ned was aware, even as he slept, that his heart was pounding irregularly. He saw himself standing beneath one of the glass trees, staring wide-eyed at the people in the procession as they walked solemnly by. Behind Aunt Liz and her husband were three people: his mother, Gloriana; his father, Preston; and James Rivington. Gloriana walked regally between the two men. She was dressed in a low-cut gown as scarlet as Richardson Thorpe's coat. Rivington was carrying an American flag. Behind his mother, father, and Rivington came another threesome. Bridget, at age sixteen, fresh and lovely as the day Ned had first met her, walked on one side of her first husband, young Vincent Boyle. Francine Bressuire, the blind French girl who was Ned's first wife, walked on the other. Bridget stared straight ahead with the same unseeing cast in her green eyes as in sightless Francine's. While they were students at Oxford, Ned and Vincent Boyle had been best friends. Ned, in love with Bridget, had introduced her to Vincent, and, to his dismay, they had married.

A sudden sharp pain stabbed Ned's chest, but he did not awaken. In the dream a brilliant flash of golden orange light streaked through the unfamiliar street, and the trees melted into a placid stream, which rose higher and higher until all the people in the procession sank slowly out of sight. The water, initially a milky aqua, turned an ugly blackish green and became choppy, and Ned found himself in the raging stream, swimming desperately toward two distant figures. They were both drowning. As he drew closer, gasping for breath, he saw that one was his son, Christopher. Christopher was bleeding from a gash over his right eye. The other was his brother-in-law, Martin Morrissey. He got an arm around Christopher and managed to swim to shore with him. Christopher was dressed in the uniform of the American navy. Ned could hardly breathe as he swam back through the raging sea toward the place he had seen Martin, but his best friend was gone.

Now young Martin Morrissey was shaking him. The gray light of dawn filled the bedchamber. Ned was soaking wet with perspiration. He was gasping for breath. Martin sat on the edge of the bed and clutched his shoulder, taking his trembling hand.

"Are you all right, Uncle Ned? You were making some terrible sounds."

Ned stared at his nephew. He had heard that a man's life often passed before his eyes in the moments before he died. He was having so much difficulty breathing that he thought he might well be dying. He struggled to a sitting position, and Martin sat with his arm around his shoulder.

"I—I—I was just having a—a dream," he managed to say. Later, reflecting upon the nightmare, he thought how amazing some of the symbolism seemed. Bridget, it had turned out, had surely been blind in marrying Vincent Boyle rather than him. He and Bridget had always been meant for each other. And he shook his head over the significance of James Rivington carrying the flag in the procession. His adoptive uncle James had died on July 4 in 1802. The scarlet gown his mother wore spoke eloquently of her wanton life.

On Friday, four days later, the dream no longer occupied his thoughts. Elias Scribner stood behind his wheelchair at the rail of the steamboat, rocking gently in the waters off Sandy Hook. He hardly knew where to look first. The sights and sounds surrounding him were the most festively spectacular he had ever heard or seen. To the north and east, the south and west there were boats, barges, and ships of every description. He counted thirty steamboats, more than a dozen barges, three boats of the Whitehall firemen. Every vessel was crowded with privileged New Yorkers. And every vessel was garlanded with flowers and boughs, and flying pennants and flags, and draped with bunting. Whistles tooted, bells clanged, cannon boomed their prearranged signals for the succession of magical formations into which the colorful mixed flotilla moved. A blast sent the vessels into straight lines; two booms, and they rocked into squadrons; three shots, and they slowly curved themselves into a circle surrounding the canal boats, which were at the heart of the remarkable aquatic celebration.

These freshly painted, elaborately garlanded flat boats, the *Seneca Chief*, the *Lion of the West*, the *Commodore Perry*, the *Buffalo*, and the *Superior*, had made the long joyous journey on the new waterway, greeted by cheering throngs everywhere from Buffalo to Albany. The waterfront streets of the city, the roofs of the buildings in the interior streets were crowded with thousands of excited, cheering spectators as the canal boats and their steamboat escorts cruised southward through the upper bay. In the crowd at the Battery were Martin Morrissey, with Mary Deasy clutching his arm possessively, and Maureen Morrissey with John and Anne Deasy. They did not know which steamboat bore the journalists and proud Ned, so they waved indiscriminately at all the ships that moved by.

Then the flotilla made its way through the Narrows into the lower bay and anchored ten miles farther south off Sandy Hook, where the bay joined the Atlantic. The journalists' vessel was not twenty yards from where the *Seneca Chief* danced in place in the sea. Ned could see Governor De Witt Clinton standing on the foredeck of the *Chief*, in the center of a small group of distinguished gentlemen and their ladies.

Wide-eyed as a small boy at a circus, Ned stared across the water as two smartly dressed deckhands emerged from the governor's quarters on the *Seneca Chief*. They were carrying undersized, exquisitely made cedar kegs.

"Those are the ceremonial kegs," said Scribner. "They're filled with water from Lake Erie."

The deckhands stood the kegs before the governor, and he

addressed the group on the deck of the *Chief*. Scribner and Ned could not hear the ceremonial words, but Ned felt a prideful thrill as the governor finally lifted one keg and poured its water into the ocean, then proceeded to do the same with the other.

"The wedding of the waters," said Scribner. He directed Ned's attention to a young artist at the rail near them, busily sketching the scene. Another man in top hat and greatcoat, much younger than the governor, now stepped forward to the rail.

"That's Dr. Samuel Mitchell," Scribner told Ned. "He's only in his early thirties, but he's probably the most famous geographer in the nation."

Ned watched with some puzzlement as the young man took a vial from the box and poured its contents into the sea. He repeated this with another vial, and then another, and a third.

"He's pouring water from all the world's great rivers into the ocean," explained Scribner, as Mitchell, with flourishing gestures, emptied nine more vials.

The following day was the most jubilant Ned could ever recall in the city, and he and Maureen became completely wrapped up in the final day's celebration. Vendors pushed through the crowds, hawking pottery and dishes, silk handkerchiefs and neckties, and other assorted items decorated with paintings of the *Seneca Chief*, the Lockport Fives, and other canal scenes.

More than two hundred ornately and garishly decorated floats, pulled by teams of horses, rolled by. The bands of some twenty-nine societies and civic organizations marched by, drumming, fifing, and blaring triumphant music. Affiliated groups and military units followed their bands, strutting and carrying flags and banners and signs extolling Clinton and the canal. By the time the last of the parade approached the spot in the street where Ned and Maureen stood it was late afternoon.

"Ned," Maureen said, "I think it would be a good idea if you rested for a couple of hours when we get home. I'm afraid the day may be too much for you."

His chest did feel tight, but he smiled up at her.

"Nonsense, Maureen. I'm fine. I can hardly wait for the banquet tonight!"

The banquet surpassed Ned's wildest expectations. After

Martin had wheeled him to his place at the right-hand side of the dais in the brilliantly gas-lighted, bunting-bedecked room he met and exchanged canal stories with two eminent men flanking him. One was Judge Benjamin Wright and the other Nathan Roberts. At the center of the dais was Governor Clinton. At the governor's right sat the President of the United States, John Quincy Adams, and at his left the Marquis de Lafayette, now in his sixty-eighth year, and on his last visit to the country he had helped so immeasurably during the revolution against Britain. Beside President John Quincy Adams sat his father, John Adams, who had been the nation's second President. The elder Adams was in his ninetieth year. At his right was the nation's third President, Thomas Jefferson, who, at eighty-two, still sat erect and keen-eyed. Mystically enough, both these distinguished servants of their country were to die nine months later on the same day, July 4, 1826. The fourth and fifth Presidents of the country, James Madison and James Monroe, sat alongside the French marquis.

Ned did not touch any of the sumptuous dishes set before him. He sipped nervously at the succession of glasses of fine red and white wines which were filled and refilled. He listened, enraptured, to the speeches, glancing occasionally out at the tables before the dais. At one of these, almost directly below him, sat Martin and Maureen, all three Deasys, Elias Scribner, a Tammany officer, and their wives.

Souvenir medals were presented to President Adams, his father, and the other former Presidents. Governor Clinton was given a medal and a wood-mounted bronze plaque.

"Oh, yes," said Governor Clinton, in the speech preceding the presentation of their medals, ". . . the Judge and the honorable Mr. Roberts, who as you know was an attorney, knew how to squint through a theodolite, but we had no reason to suspect that they would become two of the nation's foremost hydraulic engineers."

When the governor completed a brief speech about the canal pioneers, he identified Ned Van Gelder as one of them, and strode down the rear of the dais, directly to Ned's chair, and presented his medal to him. Ned felt his heart would stop as the audience burst into loud applause. Tears formed in his eyes as he thanked the governor, and nodded his appreciation to the crowd in the banquet hall.

Back at the restaurant throngs of his friends insisted on seeing the gold medallion and congratulating him. It was past two o'clock in the morning when Martin wheeled him into his bedchamber. Martin had again considered discussing Brannigan's order that he lose the fight, but when he saw the lines of strain etched in Ned's sallow face, the look of pain in his eyes, he decided he could not.

"Rest well, Uncle Ned," he said as he settled Ned in the bed. "We're very proud of you."

Martin could not fall asleep that night. He relived the joyous moments of his uncle's recognition. He thought pensively about his father.

"You know this medallion belongs to your father as much as it does to me, lad," Ned had told him. Inevitably his mind drifted to his upcoming bout, which was scheduled for seven o'clock that evening, less than sixteen hours away. He had not slept very much for the past several days, but he did not feel tired. He seemed to be operating on an inexhaustible supply of nervous energy. He did not know what he would do in the fight with the Englishman. There was no question in his mind that Brannigan's threat was not an idle one. He had no wish to die, yet he did not know if he was capable of deliberately permitting an opponent to defeat him.

At eight o'clock, still sleepless, he arose and went into the kitchen, where his mother was already preparing his breakfast. At ten, he asked, "Shall we let Uncle Ned sleep, or do you think I should wake him?"

"Oh, let the poor dear sleep for at least another hour, Martin. This past week has truly worn him out."

A few minutes past eleven Martin knocked at the door of his uncle's bedchamber. When he received no response after knocking a half dozen times, he went in. Ned Van Gelder was dead. Like his aunt Elizabeth's, his heart had ceased beating in his sleep. On his strong, lined face was a smile, only slightly twisted by what must have been the last stabbing pain in his chest, the last instinctive struggle for breath.

PART TWO

Stephen, Kathleen, and Jimmy Boyle

Mr. and Mrs. Timothy O'Leary

Honey Bee Volunteer Fire Company Number 5

"That no champion be deemed beaten, unless he fails coming up to the line in the limited time, or that his own second declares him beaten. No second is to be allowed to ask his man's adversary any questions or advise him to give out."

—*Broughton's Rules of Boxing,* Rule IV, loosely adopted by outlaw promoters of illegal boxing matches in New York City in the first quarter of the nineteenth century

4

Martin was bleeding from the nose and his right eye was swollen shut. He had never had as much difficulty hitting an opponent solidly as he was having with the Lancashire Giant. Not only was Simon Cribb tall and strong, with a four-inch reach advantage and a thirty-five-pound weight advantage, but he had mastered the skills of stopping and blocking, hitting and retreating. Without exception, Martin's previous opponents had basically fought the toe-to-toe style, paying little heed to defense. The speed of Martin's hooks, jabs, uppercuts, and combinations had always kept his adversaries from landing too many blows effectively, and prevented them from wrestling him into exhaustion.

Now he was battling out of nothing more than raw courage, sheer instinct for survival, and a mindless pride. He had completely forgotten how close he had come to heeding his mother's pleas not to dishonor the memory of his uncle by fighting on the day he died. Somehow he had convinced himself that his uncle Ned would have wanted him to go ahead with the match. He did not realize that at least part of the reason for his decision was that he knew the fight would take his mind off the overwhelming grief he felt at the loss of his uncle. The question of whether or not he should lose the fight deliberately had also been battered from his consciousness.

Seated in the first row of benches beneath the ring, which had been set up on a stage in the middle of the huge barn in Port Jefferson, Billy Brannigan was in a purple-faced rage. Martin had been knocked down fourteen times in the past hour and nine minutes. The match was being fought under the Broughton Rules of Boxing, which had been followed in England since 1743, when they had been introduced by Jack Broughton. All it would take for Martin to be declared the loser would be for him to fail to rise after a knockdown and return to his side of the ring before the half-minute time limit expired. No matter how vicious or powerful the blows which knocked him to the boards, Martin had struggled to his feet and to his position at the ropes each time before the thirty seconds elapsed. And he had either blindly staggered or rushed forward at the champion on the opposite side of the ring for the fresh set-to immediately upon the signal from the two umpires.

Brannigan cursed bitterly as Kevin Muldoon, one of Martin's seconds, helped him to his feet and half-carried him to his position when he was battered to the floor for the fifteenth time.

"The stupid sonovabitch!" screamed Brannigan. He was referring to Muldoon. Brannigan would not concede, even to himself, that it was his fault that Martin's seconds did nothing to keep him down beyond the half minute, or prevent him from going back into the fray at the umpires' command. Brannigan had felt he was being clever in bringing the fewest possible number of people into his scheme to have Martin deliberately lose the fight. He believed that the promise of riches to come, buttressed by the death threat, was more than sufficient to guarantee Martin's cooperation.

"He's got to stay down sooner or later, Billy," said John Deasy with as much conviction as he could muster.

Hardly had he spoken when the umpires once more signaled the fighters to resume. The Lancashire Giant was beginning to breathe heavily and his arms were becoming weary, both from battering his opponent and blocking Martin's blows. He failed to raise his brawny right arm against a sweeping left hook and Martin's hard-knuckled fist caught him squarely on the side of his head. He toppled to the boards, rolled over on his back, then onto his stomach. He got up on his hands and knees, and both his seconds grabbed him, one by each arm, and staggered with him to his position at the ropes. He made it by one second. The umpires waved Martin to the opposite side of the ring.

"Morrissey, ya dumb bastard!" bellowed Brannigan, leaping to his feet. But his hoarse curse was lost in the monstrous roar of the frenzied crowd. Almost to a man they had wagered on Martin, and this was the first time in the bloody evening he had knocked down the champion. The sound shook the walls of the huge barn, sent swirling the thick clouds of tobacco smoke lying flat near the ceiling, caused the wagon-wheel chandeliers holding the oil lamps to sway. The pandemonium even seemed to stir up the ancient odors of cow dung and hay and the present smell of nervous sweat, cigar smoke, and alcohol.

"Morrrr... isssseeee... Morrrr... isssseeee!" they screamed.

The Lancashire Giant stumbled toward the center of the

ring and threw his arms around Martin. Martin twisted his own arms to break Cribb's grasp and tried to uppercut the champion with both fists. Grunting, Cribb slid down Martin's sweat-slick upper body and clutched him around the buttocks.

"Rule seven! Rule seven!" yelled Kevin Muldoon. Broughton's rule seven stipulated that "no person is to hit his adversary when he is down, or seize him by the ham, the breeches, or any part below the waist."

Muldoon was a conscientious second. He had studied the British rules carefully. He also had bet more money than he could afford on Martin. Fortunately for him, Brannigan could not hear his admonition to the umpires over the continuing waves of eardrum-splitting noise. Cribb slid from Martin's thighs and fell to one knee. Again his seconds rushed in to get him to his feet and back to his side of the ring before the half minute expired. Martin became overconfident when they met each other in the next, the seventeenth set-to or round. As Cribb back-pedaled away from him, skillfully blocking one punch after another, Martin lowered his head and charged, bull-like, at the champion. Cribb sidestepped his rush, and at the same time swung a brutal, chopping blow downward. It caught Martin at the base of his skull, just above the neck. He felt as if everything inside his head was exploding. At the same time the most excruciating pain he had ever experienced coursed through his entire body, spreading out into both arms and legs. It seemed an eternity of agony, although it was actually less than a second before he pitched forward to the rough boards. He lay on his right cheek, blood oozing from both his nose and mouth. His arms were outstretched and they and his legs twitched spasmodically.

It was a full three days before Martin was sure of what he was doing and what was going on around him, even part of the time. He did not regain consciousness until the ferry carrying him back to Manhattan was halfway across the bay. When he did come to, there was a steady buzz and a severe ache in his head. His mouth was dry. The blood had caked on his smashed lips. He felt completely disoriented. The world seemed to be rocking. He did not realize he was lying on a cot in the sheltered stern of the boat crossing the choppy waters. He blinked out of his good eye up at the group of people standing over him. His vision was blurred. A man with a handlebar mustache, whom he had never seen before, was putting a strange instrument in a black bag.

"It'll be some time," he heard the man say, "but I think he'll be all right." Through the persistent buzzing in his head the man's voice sounded far away.

Beside the mustachioed man stood John Deasy and, towering over them all, Billy Brannigan. Brannigan, the soggy cigar stuck in the corner of his mouth, grinned down at him.

"Yer one goddam crazy stubborn mick, young Morrissey. Fer a minute there, we thought ya was gonna win."

Martin wondered what he was talking about. He only vaguely remembered the fight. Mary Deasy pushed Brannigan aside and reached down and touched Martin's shoulder.

"Oh, you're a brave one, Martin. So brave . . ."

It was Mary who made him feel as though he were either dreaming or losing his mind. She was dressed as a man, in a fine wool suit, with a stiff white-collared shirt and a red cravat. Her hair was tucked beneath a derby hat and she even had a mustache. He wasn't really sure it was Mary until she spoke. It was hours later, back at the house on Rivington Street, that they were able to explain to him that Mary had disguised herself because no women were permitted to attend the fight. She had made Timmy O'Leary take her, but dressed as a male companion. On the ferry her father had been too concerned about Martin to chastise her or do anything about her costume.

As the days and nights passed, the buzzing in his head continued and the pain was as severe as ever, but it stopped occasionally for brief periods. Now he became increasingly aware of aches in other parts of his body, his ribs, his abdomen. He began to remember portions of the fight vividly, particularly the moment when he knocked Cribb down. He also began to recall fragmentary episodes of his uncle Ned's wake and funeral. He was disturbed that his mother was so worried about him. He kept assuring her that he would be fine and he swore he would never box again.

Somehow he had not been aware that Ned Van Gelder's son, Christopher, his wife, Jennie, and the twin boys and little Laura had come east from Buffalo for the funeral, although he had talked with them at some length, and even played with the children. Maureen had decided to close the restaurant for a fortnight to honor Ned's memory, and Christopher and his family were staying at the house for an extended visit so Christopher could be present when his father's will was probated. It was a full week before Martin seemed to become aware that they were there.

At supper on a Sunday night, he said cheerily to Christopher, "I'm glad you all could come for dinner tonight, Chris. I'm sorry you missed your father's funeral."

Christopher, Jennie, and Maureen looked at each other with puzzled concern. The twin boys giggled, and Laura looked mystified.

"You're going to stay a while, I hope," said Martin.

"Oh, yes, Martin," said Christopher, "I hope you and I will be able to take the boys fishing or boating this week."

"I want to go too," said Laura.

There was a knocking at the door, and Martin went out to answer it. A gaunt young man in a wool cap, a young woman with a partially unraveled wool shawl around her shoulders, and a thin child stood there, shivering in the chill November night. The man clutched a bulky object wrapped in rags under his left arm. The woman held a dirty, stuffed sack over one shoulder. In the wan moonlight Martin could see that they were dressed in tattered, soiled clothes. The skinny boy clutched the young woman's shabby homespun skirt and looked up at Martin with round, frightened eyes. All three stared in awe at Martin's discolored, swollen face. The man held out a thin, bony hand.

"Oi—Oi'm—Stephen," he said hoarsely. There was a pleading, nervous note in his voice.

Martin looked at him quizzically. He did not take his extended hand.

In a weary voice, speaking very slowly, the young woman said, "It's the Boyles we are, sir. Stephen 'n' Kathleen." She tapped the boy's capped head. "An' this one is our Jimmy."

The memory mechanism of Martin's mind was still malfunctioning. He did not recall knowing anyone named Boyle.

As a matter of fact it had been many years since Father Neely had written his last letter for Vinnie Boyle, Bridget Van Gelder's son, and Stephen's father. It was to inform Bridget, Ned, Martin, and Maureen of Vinnie's death. They had heard nothing further until some five years ago, when they received a totally unexpected letter from Stephen Boyle, who was then twenty-two. He wrote a poor hand, but was able to make himself understood. It was a sad letter. His mother had died four years after his father. Of Vincent and Annie Boyle's five children, Stephen was the only surviving child.

Stephen had married a fifteen-year-old girl, Kathleen Hennessy, who had borne four children in the five years they had been married. Jimmy was the eldest, and seemed in passing fair health. Francis, the next eldest, and the two youngest, Bessie and Fanny, were sickly a good part of the time. Stephen was a potato farmer, like his father. Times had been extremely hard. The death rate from malnutrition and diseases like cholera and tuberculosis, especially among infants and young children, was climbing steadily.

Stephen had come across a packet of letters his father had received from Bridget Van Gelder, Stephen's grandmother, and another kind lady, named Maureen Morrissey. He was desperate, and, though he said he was ashamed to do so, he felt he must plead with his grandmother to send him some money. Otherwise they would be dispossessed from the farm, and then he did not know what would become of them. Maureen wrote Stephen Boyle that his grandmother had passed away, but that she was happy to send him twenty-five dollars, from herself, Martin, and Stephen's step-grandfather, Ned Van Gelder. She wrote that they would all pray that God would make things better for the Boyles and all the poor farmers in Ireland.

Maureen received a maudlin letter of thanks for the money, but no further word until ten months ago when another communication, even more desperate than the earlier one, arrived. There had been another blight on the potato crop, a tragedy which occurred at irregular intervals in many parts of Ireland. A shocking number of farm families in their area were literally starving to death. Bessie and Fanny had died within weeks of each other. Francis and Jimmy had developed the bloated belly of extreme malnutrition. They had little to eat. Stephen begged Maureen to ask his grandfather and her son to send enough money for them to come to America.

"Ile work day an nite evry day incloodin Sunday ef the Good Lord will forgive me to repay the money," he wrote. "And Kathleen an me, we'll pray to God to bless you an all the family evry day of yer lifes. Fer the sake uv our two boys, plaize, plaize, send the money."

Martin, flush with funds from his burgeoning but miserable boxing career, had sent the money immediately.

Maureen came running from the kitchen now. She had

been expecting the Boyles, and as she greeted them warmly, she saw that there were only three. With a shock she realized that one of the boys must have been left behind in Ireland...or must have died, since they had last heard from Stephen.

Maureen put her arm around Kathleen and said, "Oh, we're so glad you got here. Come in! Come in!"

With that greeting the relationship between Maureen, more than thirty years older than the younger woman, and Kathleen was established. It was as though they were mother and daughter. Maureen set platters before the Boyles and they ate ravenously, with Kathleen apologizing all the while for their manners. Kathleen said nothing about her absent son until much later that night, when the rest had retired and she and Maureen sat alone in the kitchen, drinking tea.

"Oi prayed and prayed," she told Maureen then, "but the little angel was in a bad way when we boarded the ship. Three days out he come down with a fever, and on the fourth day the good Lord took 'im from us. Buried at sea, 'e was. Oi wanted to throw myself into the sea after 'im, but there was still Jimmy. 'E needs me, an' for that matter so does 'is father."

By the following morning Martin had recalled the correspondence with the Boyles, and he and Christopher Van Gelder took Stephen and Jimmy along with Ned and Fred and Laura on a fishing excursion. Jimmy was a shy, introspective little boy, small for six and emaciated looking, but the Van Gelder children's easy acceptance of him and their exuberance soon put him at his ease. When they returned from the East River bank where they had spent the morning, Kathleen Boyle rushed to her son, knelt before him, and took him in her arms.

"Are ye all right, Jimmy boy?" she asked anxiously, and when he nodded eagerly, and she noted the sparkle in his eyes, she kissed him, and got to her feet, smiling. Martin was moved by the obvious, if extreme, concern she showed for the child. It was no wonder, he thought, since they had lost their three younger children. At breakfast he had observed the Boyles with great curiosity. Stephen was that rarity in an Irishman. He had long, almost straw-colored blond hair. Somewhere in either the Boyle or the Riordan ancestral lines a Scandinavian must have become involved. He had a long, square jaw and high cheekbones and blue eyes. As a trencherman and a drinker Stephen proved a more orthodox son of Erin. He not only ate copious quantities of food, but after drinking three mugs of beer with his breakfast, he asked if he might have a nip of whiskey. He drank four cups of whiskey before they set out on the fishing trip. He seemed to have a great capacity, for he was not drunk at all when they left.

Martin paid considerably more attention to Kathleen Boyle at breakfast than he did to Stephen. She fascinated him as had no other young woman he had ever met. She had a small oval-shaped face with large, round eyes of an indescribable color, a mix of hyacinth and violet. But it was not the striking color which intrigued Martin. It was the expression. Exaggerated no doubt by their unusually large size, their roundness, the thick dark lashes, and possibly most of all, the inverted purplish black arches beneath them, the eyes spoke of a vulnerability, of a heart often wounded. Yet a spark of indomitableness shone behind the sorrowful surface. Martin thought he must be getting this impression from the manner in which she held her hollow-cheeked head, small chin high. Her brown hair was dry and lusterless, but she kept it neatly brushed. She was a slight girl, almost androgynous of figure, but again her carriage and general posture gave a contradictory impression of hidden strength.

Soon after the Boyles' arrival, Ned Van Gelder's will was probated. Christopher was bequeathed his father's interest in the property and restaurant-tavern at 106 Rivington Street and, of course, all the family memoirs. The medallion commemorating his pioneering efforts on the canals Ned left to Martin. He must have had a premonition of death, for he had scribbled a note bequeathing the medal to Martin on the night he died. Christopher had no interest in remaining in New York City and operating the restaurant, so he sold his interest to Martin for a modest amount, payable in easy installments. He and Jennie and Ned and Fred and Laura returned to their farm in Buffalo.

The Boyles and the Morrisseys became a single family in the Rivington Street establishment. The Boyles blossomed in their new environment. The miracle of eating three meals a day, especially fare other than potatoes, seemed God-sent. Kathleen could not do enough to earn her keep. She actually embarrassed Maureen with her eagerness to be of service. Maureen and Martin were surprised to discover that Kathleen was quite a literate young lady. In Ireland her father and the local Catholic priest had been close friends, and the priest had taught her to read and write both English and Gaelic. She, in turn, had taught Stephen what little he knew, and from the time the boy was three, she had been teaching young Jimmy. Now, whenever she was not working at her chores around the tavern, in the kitchen, the rooms upstairs, or tending bar or waiting tables, she sat with Jimmy, reading to him, or teaching him to write. Maureen and Martin had never seen a mother lavish such affection, nor show such unrelenting concern over a child.

Stephen also worked around the tavern, but with a seeming reluctance, which Martin could not quite identify. He continued to devour extraordinary quantities of food, as though he were trying to make up for the many meals he had missed. And he drank great quantities of beer and whiskey. Yet his metabolism was such that he gained little weight, and never seemed to be drunk. His greatest contribution to the thriving business the restaurant and tavern enjoyed eventually came, remarkably enough, from his talents as an entertainer. He had carried his small Irish harp all the way from Mallow. Stephen often said that his grandfather's and his mother's playing and singing had been most responsible for enabling the Riordans and the Boyles to survive their darkest days. And Kathleen shyly said Stephen's troubadouring had been a most persuasive part of his courting her in Mallow.

On the second night after their arrival at Rivington Street, after Stephen had had several drinks, he asked if they would permit him to play a few tunes. He unwrapped the harp and sat cross-legged on the floor in the kitchen. He felt most comfortable in that posture. He closed his eyes and fingered the strings of the harp expertly and delicately, playing a melancholy introduction. Stephen's hands were the hands of a potato farmer, thick-veined and calloused, but the fingers were long and supple. Martin and Maureen marveled at the way they plucked, then thrummed, then plucked again at the harp strings. Stephen sang, softly at first, in a rich, tenor voice.

The minstrel boy to the war is gone,
In the ranks of death you'll find him;
The hero's sword he has girded on,
And his wild harp slung behind him.

The vibrato in the tenor voice increased, as he sang with greater emotional intensity.

"Land of song!" said the warrior bard,
"Tho all the world betrays you,
One sword, at least, your rights shall guard,
One faithful harp shall praise you!"

Now he rocked from side to side as he sang.

The minstrel fell, but the foeman's chain
Could not bring the proud soul under;
The harp he loved ne'er spoke again,
For he tore its chords asunder.

He thrummed a dark, staccato, minor chord and sang on.

. . . and said, "No chains shall sully you,
Your soul of love and brav'ry!
Your songs were made for the pure and free,
They shall never sound in slavery."

Martin applauded. Maureen fought back tears.

"That's beautiful, Stephen," she said.

"When we open the restaurant again, Stephen, perhaps you could sing for the patrons," asked Martin.

"Oh, Oi'd be proud to, Coosin Martin!" said Stephen.

"But do you sing only sad songs of war?" chided Maureen.

"Aaagh! No, indeed!"

He strode to Maureen, and standing before her, a twinkle in his blue eyes, began to play and sing brightly and up-tempo.

It was on a fine summer's morning,
The birds sweetly sang on each bough,
And as I walked out for my pleasure
I saw a maid milking her cow.
Her voice so enchanting, melodious,
Left me quite unable to go,
My heart it was loaded with such love
For the pretty maid milking her cow . . .
For Maureen dhas cruthen namoe.

Moore's original song used the name "Coleen," so Maureen's name sang very well. Stephen dropped to one knee, and stared worshipfully up into Maureen's eyes and played on.

Then to her I made my advances;
"Good morrow, most beautiful maid
Your beauty my heart so entrances—"

He paused and plucked a tinkling arpeggio, then sang again, raising his voice an octave higher.

"Pray sir, do not banter," she said.
"I'm not such a rare precious jewel,
That I should enamor you so.
I am but a poor little milkmaid,"
Says Maureen dhas cruthen namoe.

He dropped his voice to the lower pitch once more, and sang.

The wide world affords no such jewels,
So bright and so beautifully clear.
Please be not unkind and so cruel,
Consent but to love me, my dear.
If I had the lamp of Aladdin
Or the wealth of the African shore,
I would rather be poor in a cottage
With Maureen dhas cruthen namoe.

Maureen giggled and blushed and slapped Stephen's shoulder playfully. Martin grinned foolishly. Kathleen rose and said in her brogue, "I think I heard Jimmy stirring. If ye'll excuse me, I'll say a good night to ye all."

Stephen asked if he might have another drink and Martin joined him.

Four hours later Martin was awakened by sounds from Stephen and Kathleen's bedchamber, which adjoined his on the second floor of the house. He could only occasionally make out isolated phrases and words, but the tone was unmistakable.

Stephen (cajoling): "Sure an' it can't hurt ye, sweet Kathleen . . . just a wee bit . . . wanna suck those li'l bitty titties—"

Kathleen (angrily): "No . . . get away, Stephen . . . no—no—I can't."

Then silence, but not for long.

Stephen again (angrily, but slurring his words slightly): ". . . hus'ban . . . some goddam rights, woman—"

Scuffling sounds, bed webbing straining, and footsteps across the floor. And Kathleen (desperately): ". . . no more . . . dying . . . can't stand dying . . . no more . . . never . . . never." And sobbing.

Stephen was sullen the following day, but Kathleen went about her chores quietly, and spent the entire evening reading to Jimmy.

Two days later, Mary Deasy came to visit. Martin introduced her to the Boyles. Stephen was all obsequious charm at meeting this voluptuous, elegantly dressed young lady. After a pleasant supper Mary persuaded Martin to come for a stroll with her. They walked to the Bowling Green and sat on a bench there. Mary chatted idly for a time, commenting on how nicely Martin's bruises were healing, telling him what a handsome cousin he had, and how much she liked Stephen's strangely quiet wife. Finally she said, "Martin, do you realize I'm twenty years old?"

Martin looked at her in surprise.

"Well—yes—I suppose—"

"When are you going to marry me?" she demanded.

"I—I—I don't want to get married, Mary."

"Timothy O'Leary has just been appointed to the City Council to replace old Mr. Collins, who just died. Did you know that?"

Martin shook his head.

"Do you know that Timothy O'Leary owns more real estate in Manhattan than my father?"

"No, I didn't—" said Martin.

"I love you, you oaf!" she said.

"I—I—I wish you wouldn't say that, Mary. A smart, beautiful girl like you . . . you can do much better—"

"I know I can, Martin Morrissey. Last night Timothy O'Leary asked me to marry him—again!"

Martin grinned and nodded enthusiastically.

"Oh, good! Congratulations, Mary. I mean—that O'Leary! What a lucky man!"

"I hate you, Martin Morrissey," she said bitterly. Tears were beginning to form in her eyes. "My father wants me to marry Timmy. He says he likes you better, too, but you'll never be as rich or powerful as Timmy."

"Please don't cry, Mary. Please. He's right. Your father's right. I'll never—"

"My father says I can learn to love Timmy."

"Of course. I'm sure you can. Timmy is a smart man and—and—very nice—and—and I know he loves you."

"And you don't!" she said accusingly, but with a touch of sadness.

"I do! I do, Mary! Like a friend. Like a real good friend!"

"Are you in love with your cousin's wife?"

Martin was shocked. He had certainly become intrigued with Kathleen Boyle, he admired her, but he had never considered the possibility that he could be in love with her. How could he? She was his own cousin's wife!

"With Kathleen? How can you say that? I—I—"

"I saw the way you keep looking at her. Women can tell about such things."

"She's Stephen's wife, Mary. How could I—"

"You're not very smart, Martin. About love you're an absolute blockhead."

She took a kerchief from her fur muff and dabbed at her eyes. "You're sure you won't marry me?" she asked.

He lowered his head and watched a small army of ants parade out from under the foot of the left side of the bench.

"I know you and Timmy will be very happy," he said, not looking at her.

5

John Deasy's new saloon was one of the largest, and by all odds the gaudiest and most popular of the new places on the Bowery. On Friday and Saturday nights, particularly, the four-leaf-clover-ornamented, orange velvet and gilt room was packed with revelers. On the last Friday of September in 1827, the five-man Irish band played the final lively number of their midnight set. The jig and reel dancers, sweating and panting, staggered and stumbled to their tables, and Deasy himself introduced the entertainer they had all been waiting to hear.

"And now, me good friends, John Deasy's Shamrock Palace brings you once again that handsome singin' rogue, Stevie Boyle!"

Stephen, cradling his harp, walked jauntily in from the stage right wing of the small raised platform. He bowed over and over again to the boisterous, whistling, applauding crowd. He grinned broadly and stopped at center stage.

"I love ye all, each an' ev'ry one o' ye; bless yer hearts!" he said, speaking so softly, they had to hush to hear him.

John Deasy joined his daughter, Mary, at a small table directly beneath the stage. Occasionally, on a Friday or Saturday night she missed the earlier two of Stephen's shows, but she always attended the final midnight show. She took a drink of the dark amber liquid in her glass as her father sat down opposite her. He noticed the slightly glazed look, with which he was familiar, come into her eyes as she smiled at him.

"Mary, I wish you wouldn't drink so much," he said. "It's not good for you."

Mary took another sip and smiled at him again. She supposed he had admonished her thus two or three hundred times since her wedding night a little more than a year ago. It was automatic. He knew she had no intention of discontinuing drinking. She had been half-drunk—it was the first time in her life she had drunk whiskey at all—when she and Tim O'Leary went to their nuptial bed on the night they were wed. It did not seem to make much difference to her groom. His love-making was as passionless and mechanical as on any previous occasion.

She had always been aware that O'Leary had courted her, tolerated her obvious infatuation with Martin Morrissey, and finally married her because of his political and business connections with her father. In recent months she had often heard them discussing a new joint venture in a cotton brokerage operation, which was apparently turning out to be phenomenally successful. It also necessitated occasional trips by O'Leary to Virginia, Maryland, and Georgia for meetings with plantation owners. Indeed he was absent on such a journey at this very time.

Mary never accompanied him on these trips. She hated traveling and had never adjusted completely to being around Negroes. After their wedding she and her new husband moved into a high-stooped, three-story brick mansion in fashionable Washington Square, and O'Leary brought in Negro slaves, who had been made free by law on July 4, this year, 1827. O'Leary paid them a paltry monthly wage since they were no longer slaves. They shared housekeeping duties. One, an older woman named Mandy, additionally served as cook; the other, a buxom young mulatto named Tilda, as Mary's personal maid.

Mary stared in rapt attention now at the handsome blond young man on the stage. She had heard him do this opening song, his entire repertoire for that matter, scores of times, but she never tired of his performance. The song Stephen was singing was also a favorite of the crowd.

Quick, we have but a second,
Fill round the cup while you may,
For time, the churl has beckoned
And we must away, away . . .

He strutted to the stage right wing and back across to the left, smiling and winking at the ladies at the tables directly below the raised platform. He had that natural-born romantic entertainer's knack of convincing each of the women, in turn, that he was singing especially to her. He blew a kiss to Mary, as he stood before her table. He fixed his blue eyes upon her, as he resumed playing and singing.

See the glass how it flushes
Like my own anxious lips,
And half meets yours and blushes
That you should delay to sip . . .

For forty-five minutes Stephen strolled cockily back and forth across the stage, plucked his harp, and sang and stole the hearts of the predominantly Irish audience, men and women alike. The males responded with loud cheers to his songs of derring-do, of brave men dying in a hopeless cause: *The Minstrel Boy to the War Is Gone, Drink to the Swords of Former Time, Let Erin Remember.* He titillated the men and their consorts and mistresses with novelty and romantic ditties, *The Pretty Maid Milking Her Cow, To Ladies' Eyes,* and the tongue-in-cheek tragic tale of *Eveleen*.

And then, with a boldness that shocked many in his audience (for there was gossip about this) he leaped from the stage and knelt on one knee before Mary. As though they were alone in the smoky, now hushed and crowded room, he stared fixedly into her eyes. There was an expression of utter sincerity on his face. In sweet tenor tones, he sang,

Believe me if all those
Endearing young charms

Which I gaze on so fondly today—
Were to change by tomorrow
And flee from my arms
Like precious gifts fading away,
You would still be adored,
As this moment you are,
Let your loveliness fade as it will.
And around you, my dear
Each wish of my heart
Would entwine itself verdantly still.

The song had the same hypnotic effect on Mary as it had had the first time she heard it at the reception on the evening of her wedding. On that night Stephen had introduced it by saying, "The words of this song are in Mr. O'Leary's heart this joyous day. Oi sing them for him to his loverly bride."

The song worked such magic on her that night that for a few fleeting hours, she thought she might actually be in love with Timothy O'Leary. The groom himself disenchanted her when he climbed into bed beside her, and began to fumble at her in his silent, businesslike way. Since then Stephen had sung the tender ballad to her many times. Indeed, ever since his first performance at the Shamrock Palace. It had always moved her. Now it excited her. For now, only months after her first wedding anniversary, Stevie Boyle had become her lover, and had demonstrated his deep and passionate desire for her in the most uninhibited physical ways she had ever dared fantasize. Over and over and over again.

She was still not sure she was really in love with Stevie Boyle. Nor was she certain what had motivated her in becoming his mistress. After Martin Morrissey had finally and flatly rejected her, a spasmodic bitterness frequently possessed her. Whenever she saw Martin in the presence of Kathleen Boyle, and became convinced anew that it was for Kathleen he secretly yearned—whether he would admit it or not—she resented the slender, quiet girl. She did not know how much that bitterness toward Martin, that resentment toward Kathleen, had to do with her taking Stephen Boyle as her lover. She did know, sinful and shameful as it might be, that after each ecstatic night she could hardly wait for the next assignation.

She had been enchanted with his singing on her wedding night, but her heart and mind were filled with the struggle between trying to assure herself she could learn to love O'Leary, and the determination to forget Martin. She knew it would not be easy because she still felt a sharp pang of jealousy each time he danced with Kathleen Boyle. Up until the day of her wedding, Stephen had performed only at Morrissey's restaurant and tavern, where he had built a loyal if small following. The day after her wedding her father had persuaded Stephen to sing in his newly opened saloon. Deasy handled the arrangements in his usual smooth, politician's fashion.

"The lad's so good," he told Martin, "it's a cryin' shame t' hide 'im here in your little establishment. I can pay him ten times what you could afford."

Martin felt under some obligation to Deasy because Deasy had talked Billy Brannigan out of doing physical harm to Martin when Martin refused to continue his boxing career. Deasy stalled Brannigan for months, and then they found Brannigan's body one morning behind a warehouse on Water Street. The head was missing, but there was no question it was Brannigan. Official opinion was divided as to who had done the deed. Some police believed the rival Bowery B'hoys had beheaded him; others were certain One-Eye Mulchahy or Terrible Tommy Malone had killed him (they were presently engaged in a power struggle among themselves for the leadership of the Dead Rabbits); still a third faction felt he had been killed by some of the more oppressed but aggressive Negroes who had moved into Five Points when they were legally freed. Deasy was of the latter belief. To him it was just one sign of the troubles he had long predicted would come when the Negroes were set free by the New York legislature. In any event Martin felt obligated to Deasy, but he said, "It's really up to Stephen, John. He's a grown man."

Martin was not too surprised when Stephen told him he had decided to accept Deasy's offer.

"It's not that Oi don't appreciate everythin' ye've done fer me an' Kathleen an' Jimmy, Coosin Martin," he said, "but Oi know ye'd want me t' take advantage o' this opportunity yerself, now wouldn't ye?"

"It's up to you, Stephen, purely up to you."

By this time Martin had developed very mixed feelings about his cousin. He had found Stephen to be selfish, greedy, conceited, and cunningly opportunistic.

One of the regular patrons of the Morrissey tavern was

Blasius "Blaze" Ditchett. Ditchett was a lean, sturdy, forty-year-old type founder and foreman of Honey Bee Protection Engine Company Number 5. This was one of the oldest of the many volunteer fire companies, which dotted the residential and business areas of the city. Ditchett had followed Martin's boxing career and he admired Maureen. He developed an avuncular affection for quiet Kathleen and little Jimmy. He came to Morrissey's almost every day for dinner, and rarely missed one of Stephen's performances on a Saturday night.

Stephen made a concerted effort, exerting all his charm, to win Ditchett's friendship. The volunteer fire companies were a political force in the city and were influential in many ways, and Stephen believed that if he could join a distinguished company, it might lead to fame and fortune. Soon Ditchett had him accepted as a member of the Honey Bee Company.

The company's firehouse, coyly called the Hive, was at 105 Fulton Street in the backyard of the Old North Dutch Reformed Church. It housed the company's gooseneck engine, the hose reel, the firemen's boots, hats, and other equipment, including Ditchett's brass trumpet with its engraved beehive. The company was the first in the city to wear red flannel shirts, and even had a life-size, colorful glass and brass honeybee pin as its emblem. Stephen took to wearing both shirt and pin most of the time, and became impatient and nasty when Kathleen permitted several days to pass before she laundered the shirt when it became too soiled or gamey to wear.

Stephen also took his turn, along with every other member of the company, patroling the streets all through his assigned night, watching for fires. While Martin resented Stephen's taking so much time away from his work at the tavern, he had to admit that Stephen's membership in the Honey Bee Company was bringing quite a few influential politicians, merchants, and craftsmen into the tavern. They were all members of the company. Stephen also proved to be an eager and able firefighter. He responded to every alarm, no matter what time of day or night, and contributed to upholding the Honey Bee Company's reputation as the fastest and most efficient company in the city. It had been the custom for years to award a thirty-dollar prize to whichever fire company arrived first at a major fire. The Honey Bee Company had won the prize twenty times in five years, twice as often as any other group.

But Martin felt that even if Stephen did not spend as much time at the tavern as he should, he certainly owed it to Kathleen and Jimmy to spend more time with them. He not only ignored both his wife and little boy most of the time, but on several occasions had even become abusive.

Three weeks before Mary's wedding, Martin, Maureen, and Jimmy had all been awakened in the middle of the night by a sudden outburst of shouting, screaming, and crying from Stephen and Kathleen's bedchamber. As Martin quickly stepped into a pair of breeches and rushed from his room, Kathleen crashed into him. In the darkness in the hall he could not see her features. She threw her arms around him, shrieking, "Stop him, plaize! Plaize stop him!"

And directly after her came Stephen. Martin sensed rather than saw the blow Stephen struck against the side of Kathleen's head. She screamed again and groaned as Martin turned her away from her raging husband. Stephen, still punching, struck the back of Martin's neck. Martin released Kathleen, whirled and swung a sharp right hook against Stephen's jaw. It was as savage a blow as he had ever delivered in his boxing days. Stephen dropped to the floor and lay on his back, unconscious. Maureen and Jimmy had come out of their rooms. The seven-year-old lad, weeping hysterically, ran to his mother. Maureen put one arm around Kathleen's shoulder, the other around Jimmy's, and led them down to the kitchen. Soon the terrified child was soothed and put back to bed. Kathleen sat with him, and crooned him to sleep. Stephen was revived. He made abject apologies to all, and especially to his wife.

"Oi'm sorry, Kathleen," he cried. "The divil possessed me. Oi'll niver touch ye agin. Oi swear it on me sainted mither's grave."

And the next day Stephen tried to explain the situation to Martin, man to man.

"It's drivin' me out o' me mind, Coosin Martin," he whined. "Ever since little Francis died on the way over, she hasn't let me touch 'er. She's afraid we'll have another wee one. She lives ev'ry blessed day fearin' fer Jimmy's life. It's enough t' drive any man crazy! Ya understand, Coosin Martin? Do ye?"

Martin was not sure he did understand. Ashamed of it as he was, he admitted to himself that in the past several months he had felt great desire for Kathleen Boyle. He had made no effort to woo or possess her, no matter how great the temptation. But then he was not her husband. Perhaps husbands had certain rights. At the time he simply said to Stephen, in a voice full of quiet menace, "Don't ever do that again, Stephen. Ever. I know she's your wife, but don't ever hit her again."

For a moment it looked as though Stephen would challenge Martin, but when he saw the cold look in Martin's eyes he remained quiet.

Two weeks after Stephen went to work as an entertainer in Deasy's Shamrock Palace, he had found himself, after a midnight performance on a Saturday, in the large, canopied bed of the O'Learys. Timothy was in Georgia. Mary was in Stephen's arms. And Stephen made love to her as only a virile, highly sexed, and egocentric young man, starved for the feel and taste of a beautiful young woman's body, could make love. His hands, his mouth, all of him explored her, literally from head to toe. He caressed her and kissed her and licked her and bit her and entered her. Burning and rigid. He exploded inside her almost immediately, but within minutes was erect again, and fondling and hugging and devouring her till she thought she would be unable to breathe. Yet she responded with a passion to match his own. It went on all night, and when he left at dawn, Mary O'Leary, pleasurably sore and bruised, sank into the most blissful sleep of her life.

In these two households in New York City, then, the O'Learys on Washington Square and the Morrisseys and Boyles at 106 Rivington Street, a sustained, awkward roundelay of deception began. Stephen Boyle was not certain he was successfully deceiving his wife or anyone else in his torrid affair with Mary O'Leary. Mary was equally uncertain whether she was successfully concealing her mad affair from her husband, her father, her mother, or any of her friends. In spite of the fact that Stephen had taken to staying away all night two or three Fridays and Saturdays successively every two or three months—he said he was taking an extra shift on the fire patrol, or playing cards with his Honey Bee colleagues—neither Kathleen, Maureen, nor Martin questioned him. Even after they became aware that Martin's all-night absences coincided with Timothy O'Leary's trips to the Southern plantations, they said nothing to each other or to Stephen.

O'Leary became conscious of the fact that his wife seemed happier and more energetic after his trips to the South than during his periods at home in between, but he said nothing either. Even after the maid Tilda told him his wife had a handsome young blond lover. He had taken to bedding Tilda now and then when Mary was off visiting her parents. On his Southern visits he had discovered that, for reasons he neither understood nor attempted to analyze, he derived far greater pleasure from copulating with Negro women than with his wife.

With Stephen and Mary the affair quickly became an unholy obsession. When O'Leary's business prevented him from leaving the city for unusually extended periods of time, they became desperate with their carnal desire for each other. Once they even took a room at the Shakespeare Hotel, but the fear that they would be discovered destroyed the exquisite pleasure they normally found in their erotic couplings. Occasionally they talked of divorcing their spouses, but both were Catholic and realized they could not do that. One night Mary suggested Stephen devise some foolproof means of killing Timothy and Kathleen.

"Maybe we can get them together in some place and set it afire," said Stephen.

"Don't be such a fool, Stevie," said Mary angrily. "How would you ever get them together?"

But this murderous plotting came toward the end of a time when they hadn't been able to spend a night together for almost three months. And O'Leary left for Georgia the following week, so they dropped the dark schemes. O'Leary was gone for nine weeks, and Stephen and Mary rendezvoused and reveled to the point of erotic exhaustion.

Another movement in the roundelay was performed daily at 106 Rivington Street. Martin pretended he was interested in Kathleen only as a good friend. She blossomed in her new environment. Gone were the sick, purplish circles beneath her hyacinth-violet eyes. They glittered now with good health. Her brown hair had a sheen that to Martin often appeared halolike. There was a glow in her cheeks, which were no longer sunken. Even her boyish figure had filled out. And as the months passed Martin fell more hopelessly and desperately in love with her.

If she was in love with him, she gave no indication of it. One means Martin used to be close to her and participate in activities with her was to spend considerable time with her and Jimmy. Jimmy was in school now, and Martin often walked with Kathleen and the boy as they left for school each morning. He took Jimmy fishing and told him stories about his days on the canal and in the ring. He became more of a father to the boy than Stephen. Stephen did not seem to mind at all. He was drinking more than usual and he spent little time around the tavern. His earnings from his performances at the Shamrock Palace were more than sufficient for the Boyles' needs, and he found his pleasure in the company of his Honey Bee colleagues. Since the night Martin had threatened him, they seemed to have become increasingly distant, although not overtly unfriendly. At one point Stephen had suggested to Kathleen that they find a place of their own, but she had refused. She wished to stay with the Morrisseys. She and Maureen had become closer than the closest mother and daughter. And most important of all, young Jimmy was happy and thriving. He loved Martin and Maureen. Kathleen continued to work happily in the tavern. There was no indication that any romantic feelings for Martin might have played a part in Kathleen's decision. As far as anyone could see, Kathleen Boyle and Martin Morrissey were simply good friends.

Maureen, of course, had long since realized that her son was in love with Stephen's wife—and she suspected Kathleen might be in love with Martin, but she said nothing about it. She merely suffered silently as she watched Martin concealing his true feelings day after week after month after year. It made for an unnatural, strained atmosphere around the house, which the surface show of industrious contentment only partially camouflaged. But it had a beneficial effect on the business. All of them worked so hard every waking moment that the Morrissey establishment became the most popular in that section of the city.

By September of 1831 the O'Leary-Deasy cotton brokerage business had stabilized to such an extent and political matters in New York demanded so much of O'Leary's attention that he did not leave the city for almost nine months. Mary O'Leary became an alcoholic shrew; Stephen Boyle began to lose a great deal of his boyish appeal as an entertainer. He was beginning to look extraordinarily dissolute and he had developed a bit of a paunch and a sullen manner. John Deasy would have terminated his services except for Mary's fanatic insistence that he keep the young man on.

Mary and Stephen once again began to discuss ways and

means of murdering Timothy and Kathleen. They were becoming desperate. And then, late in June of 1832, a newly arrived Irish immigrant woman named Mrs. Fitzgerald and her two small children were found dead in their shabby apartment at 75 Cherry Street. Cherry Street had once been a fashionable lane in the city, but it was now part of the decaying Irish ghetto. The authorities were shocked when the city's leading doctors informed them that the deaths had been caused by Asiatic cholera. The poor Fitzgeralds had brought to the city a disease that threatened to wipe out all of its two hundred thousand inhabitants.

New cases were discovered daily. By mid-July the plague had claimed hundreds. On Saturday the fourteenth of July alone, one hundred and fifteen new cases and sixty-six deaths were reported; Sunday brought a hundred and thirty-three new cases and seventy-four deaths; Monday, a hundred and sixty-three cases and ninety-four deaths. The wealthy made frantic preparations to leave the city. Timothy O'Leary suddenly decided that he had urgent business in Virginia. He told Mary he expected he would be delayed there a long time, perhaps for months. She chose not to accompany him. Her father and mother made plans to flee to Connecticut, and as hundreds more died each week and the plague spread throughout the city, Mary decided she must join them. But she insisted they take the Morrisseys and the Boyles along with them.

Martin refused to leave the business. Maureen refused to leave Martin in the city alone.

"We'll be all right," she said confidently. "We're both strong and in good health." But she turned to Kathleen.

"You go, Kathleen. Take Jimmy and go."

Stephen said, "You're out o' yer mind, Coosin Martin. We should all go. This cursed plague'll kill all who stay."

"Plaize come, Maureen," pleaded Kathleen.

But Maureen was adamant. She would not leave unless Martin would too. And Martin flatfootedly refused.

Finally Kathleen said, "Stephen, you take Jimmy and go. I must stay with Maureen."

Even though he was thirteen years old, and tried hard not to, Jimmy cried, but that was how it was done. The Deasys and Mary O'Leary with Mandy, the older Negro servant and cook, and Stephen Boyle and Jimmy boarded a brig bound for Connecticut. When it landed at Short Beach, a small village south of New Haven, a threatening, grumbling crowd of local citizens met them. They feared that the New Yorkers would bring the terrible disease to their village. The newspapers had reported the incredible spread of the plague and the unbelievably large numbers who were dying daily.

In New York, Kathleen and Martin went to Father Boland's storefront Catholic church and prayed every day. In Short Beach, Mary and Stephen resumed their passionate affair. They turned the care of Jimmy over to Mandy.

In New York City the doctors battled to bring the plague under control. They treated patients with a dozen nostrums, with brandy, with dry friction, with dry heat, with opium—all to no avail. They prayed that the advent of winter's cold would check it. The frigid weather did so, but only temporarily. People kept dying all around them.

Kathleen missed Jimmy terribly. Immediately after his departure she felt she had made a terrible mistake in letting him go. But as the epidemic continued and worsened, she was glad she had insisted he go. In the middle of one of the most tragic weeks of the siege—a week when more than a hundred died—she was surprised to receive a letter from Stephen. The plague had severely disrupted the city's postal service. Stephen wrote that Jimmy was thriving as never before. They were living in a small cottage on the beach, he said, and Jimmy had become a proficient swimmer. Although the boy missed her, said Stephen, he had never been healthier or happier.

"Ta be sure, me love," the letter concluded, "Jimmy and me both miss ye and pray fer ye every nite and wish ye would come join us. We send all our love."

She was tempted for a moment, as she read the letter, with her eyes misty, to attempt to make her way to Connecticut, but then she saw Maureen, haggard and pale, standing over the stove. She was stirring a kettle of broth to take to Mrs. O'Keefe, who had just come down with the cholera, and who had already lost three children to the killer disease. She settled for writing Stephen and Jimmy loving letters, assuring them she was strong and well. She prayed the communication would reach them. By midspring the cholera bug was more virulent than ever. In early June Kathleen came down with it. Maureen nursed her day and night. A week after Kathleen contracted the disease Maureen experienced the same early symptoms: sudden, violent vomiting; diarrhea and an inability to control the sphincter; colicky pains in the abdomen. Martin tended them both under the guidance of a harassed Dr. Mills, who had been the Morrisseys' physician for many years.

By summer's end New York was in total panic. In the last three weeks in August more than a hundred thousand people, nearly half the city's total population, fled. Day after day every road out of the city was clogged with carriages, wagons, and carts, crowded with men, women, and children, piled high with their belongings. Some sat horses, two and three to a mount, while others, having no means of transportation, trudged doggedly along the dusty roads with sacks flung over their shoulders, or wheeling barrows loaded with their possessions before them. Every floatable craft from leaky rowboats to schooners was pressed into service as the city's desperate people tried to escape. Cornelius Vanderbilt's new fleet of steamboats, operating on Long Island Sound, did a thriving, virtual day-and-night business. At many Connecticut ports furious, hysterical locals met the refugees with pistols, pitchforks, axes, and clubs and refused to permit them to land. The craft rowed or sailed or steamed on until they found a deserted beach where the passengers could come ashore.

Kathleen recovered in late July, and slowly regained her strength, but then Martin was stricken. Maureen was fighting a seesaw battle against the disease. She would appear to be better for a few days, then would suffer a relapse and become more severely ill than before. By the time Martin contracted the cholera, Maureen was almost skeletal. Before he recovered, she died. Her sixty-one-year-old body could not stand the ravages of the disease. Martin was so ill himself, he could not attend his mother's funeral. Kathleen handled all the grim details, and she and Father Boland alone saw Maureen buried.

In the early spring of 1834 the epidemic miraculously seemed to come under control. It was seven o'clock in the morning of a cool day in late April, four months after Maureen's death, when Stephen came home. Martin and Kathleen were in the main room of the tavern. A dozen times or more, in their grief and desperation, they had almost fallen into each other's arms. Martin, particularly, felt an overwhelming compulsion to hold her, and tell her how deeply he loved her and needed her. On several occasions their hands touched accidentally, and each time Kathleen moved quickly away. In the evenings, when the last customer had gone, and the cleanup completed, Martin had often asked her to sit and join him for a late cup of tea. But she refused, pleading weariness, and went up to her bedchamber.

Now, as Stephen came into the tavern, she was scrubbing down the tables, and Martin was boiling cups, glasses, and mugs in a tub behind the bar. Neither of them recognized Stephen when he entered. He had obviously been drinking. He staggered toward them. His blond hair had turned a dry, dusty gray at the temples, and was long and unkempt. He had a scraggly brownish-blond beard and mustache. His cheeks were sunken and there was a haunted look in his watery blue eyes. His chest seemed to have caved in, his shoulders were rounded, and his paunch was more pronounced. He stumbled toward Kathleen and fell to his knees before her. He stared up at her with bloodshot eyes. His speech was slurred, his brogue thick as he spoke.

"Oi'm—sorr—Oi'm so sorr—sorry, Kathleen. Our Jimmy is gone. In—in Conn—in Connec—he got the chol'ra. 'E died last week."

He clutched for her full skirt with both hands and threw his arms around her legs. He moaned pitifully and wept into the coarse homespun so uncontrollably that his shoulders shook. Kathleen stared across the room at Martin, her round eyes filled with horror. A scream tore from her throat. Her face contorted into a mask of agony, and tears began to stream down her cheeks.

6

Martin stood just inside the wide oak doors of the Chatham Street Chapel on a hot, humid evening in July, three months after Stephen's return to the city. He was just saying a small prayer of thanks that no white mob had come along to break up the Negro meeting, when he saw a dozen or more Caucasian men, respectably dressed but all carrying heavy-knobbed canes, round the corner and head toward the chapel. He recognized a short, stocky man in a slouch hat at the head of the group. It was One-Eye Mulchahy. Martin gripped the locustwood club in his hand tighter and said to the policeman beside him, "Here they come, Charlie. It looks like we're not going to have a quiet evening after all."

Charlie Walsh, a hefty, red-faced Irishman and veteran of the police force, raised his whistle to his lips and blew a call for help.

The epidemic had taken its toll not only in lives but also in its effects on the economy of the city. Morrissey's tavern was now deep in debt, so Martin had taken a part-time job as a policeman in a force badly undermanned and overworked. Crime had increased during the plague, particularly in the Sixth Ward, which embraced the Five Points area. One-third of all the people who had died during the epidemic perished in the unspeakable Irish ghetto. The behavior of the desperate survivors had become increasingly ugly and vicious. No strong leader had emerged to replace Billy Brannigan, and the gangs were fighting among themselves and running wild in every section of the city. One of the profitable new services they had developed was hiring themselves out to white men and groups who were intent on keeping the newly freed Negroes in their places.

Following the emancipation of the city's slaves by state fiat in 1827, an abolitionist movement had sprung up, the American Antislavery Society. The society was founded in 1833 by Arthur and Lewis Tappan, wealthy dry-goods importers. However, the attitude of most was expressed by Anthony Peck, the stout cigar maker, whose shop was two doors from 106 on Rivington Street. One night in the tavern he had told Martin, "We know slavery is wrong, but this country is founded on it. Here in New York City alone, we do millions of dollars worth of business with the South. We can't let the abolitionists overthrow slavery. It's not a matter or principle, just plain business. We'll wipe out the abolitionists one way or another, mark my words, Martin."

Martin had no strong feelings about the issue. He himself would not care to own a slave, but he had no argument with those who did, especially if they treated their Negroes like human beings. But he did believe in obeying the law, and now, as a policeman, he was sworn to do his best to see that it was obeyed by others.

The small mob approached the church. No assistance had yet arrived. Walsh put the whistle to his lips again, but did not blow it. Mulchahy immediately recognized Martin.

"Well, it if ain't the ol' champ hisself," he said. "I didn't know ye'd turned copper." He sneered at the copper badge pinned to Martin's shirt. The police had not yet adopted uniforms and the badge identified them as law-enforcement officers.

"Hello, Mulchahy," said Martin. "There's a peaceable meeting going on inside."

A tall, bearded man beside Mulchahy said, "Officer, we are all members of the New York Sacred Music Society, and we rented the chapel for this evening. Those niggers are trespassing—"

"Is that why you're all carrying those knobby canes—for a brief song rehearsal?" asked Martin, grinning, but tapping his club in his palm.

Charlie Walsh took the whistle from his lips and asked, "Do you have anythin' to show you rented the place for tonight?"

"Yeah, this!" shouted Mulchahy, and swung his cane at Walsh's head. "Le's go, men," he bellowed and the mob roared after him as he charged into the chapel. Martin blocked one or two of them, and clubbed one to the ground, but soon he was overwhelmed by numbers. A leaded cane head caught him just under the ear, and he fell to his knees. Walsh was blowing the whistle frantically. Inside the chapel there was screaming and shouting and crying as the white mob beat the assembled Negro men, women, and children with their canes. Within fifteen minutes, four policemen arrived to help break up the battle.

As in the days when he had begun boxing, Martin actually derived relief and pleasure from these occasional violent physical encounters. He needed to get away from the tavern, to be distracted by something which absorbed him totally. He needed to put behind him the loss of his mother and Jimmy; the whole terrible experience of the two-year cholera onslaught. Around the tavern it was difficult to do. Kathleen had raced, like a screaming madwoman, to her room when she learned that her son had died. She had not come out for two days, despite Martin's pleading. When she did she was dry-eyed, but tense and silent. She had said little, but was polite and efficient and worked harder than ever.

John Deasy, for reasons unknown to Martin, had chosen not to rehire Stephen to entertain at the Shamrock Palace, so there was no place for him to work but at Morrissey's. He drank from morning to night, and fluctuated when tending bar between an almost hysterical forced jocularity and sudden periods of belligerence, during which he got into loud arguments with patrons. Martin permitted him to work only when he himself was on police duty. And he had been considering forbidding Stephen to work in the tavern at all.

Stephen became more fanatic than ever about fire fighting. He insisted on patrol duty three or four nights each week. He seemed to require incredibly little sleep. When he slept at home he now used Jimmy's room, because Kathleen refused to sleep with him. And anytime he heard the clanging of the fire alarm, he leaped from bed and rushed to the hive. He was always the first member of the company there, and could not wait to get to the fire, large or small. When he returned to the bar after fighting a blaze he would talk about it, wild-eyed and semihysterical, to whoever would listen, for days on end.

Martin wondered what was happening to him. He wondered whether he was actually spending those long nights on fire patrol, or whether he might still be seeing Mary O'Leary. Martin, of course, as had many others, had suspected the affair long before the beginning of the cholera epidemic.

John Deasy came into the tavern a week after the small riot at the Chatham Square chapel. Martin hadn't seen him since the day after his return home from Connecticut. On this night in early August Deasy seemed more troubled than Martin had ever seen him. He and Martin sat alone at a table in a rear corner of the barroom.

"I'm desperate, Martin," said Deasy, after Kathleen had quietly set a tumbler of brandy before him and walked back behind the bar. "I don't know if you can help, but I don't know who else I can come to."

"I will if I can, John, you know that."

"Did you hear that a mob broke into Lewis Tappan's house last night and destroyed everything in it? I knew that idiot and his brother would get in trouble sooner or later, trying to stir up the goddam niggers."

"They were talking about it at the precinct this morning."

"Mary was with the mob," said Deasy, shaking his head. "Maybe led it for all I know. I don't know what's come over the girl. She's drivin' poor Timmy out o' his mind. She fired the old nigger cook, Mandy, while she was still in Connecticut, and when she got back she fired Tilda. She told Timmy she wouldn't stand for havin' any more niggers in the house."

"Well . . . you and Mrs. Deasy never had any nigger help, did you?"

"No, but Jesus, Mary, an' Joseph, we never interfered with them who wanted to keep nigger slaves. Timmy wanted to keep Tilda, but Mary accused him of bedding the wench."

"Was he?"

"I'm sure I don't know, Martin. But if he was, I think maybe it was because he was pretty sure Mary was carryin' on with Stevie."

"Are they still seeing each other?"

"Gad, no! Stevie hasn't been near the house, nor the Palace. An' Mary's so drunk so much o' the time, she hardly ever leaves the house unless it's to go out and beat up some goddam abolitionists or niggers."

"Can't you or Timmy stop her drinking?"

"Aaagh! The more we try, the more she drinks. And last night she told me she's pregnant."

"That's good," said Martin. "Maybe having a baby will bring her to her senses. Maybe it'll bring her and Timmy closer together."

"She'll probably lose the baby if she keeps carryin' on the way she is. . . ."

"Well what do you think I can do, John?"

"Jesus, Mary, an' Joseph, Martin, I don't truly know. But she always respected and admired you. . . ."

Martin shifted uncomfortably in his chair.

"Matter of fact, lad, I wish now I'd asked you to marry her. I think it would have worked out much better than her marryin' Timmy."

Martin said, "Timmy's an important man, John. They'll probably be able to work things out."

Deasy shook his head.

"Talk to her, Martin. At least talk to her. Maybe you can get her to quit drinkin' so goddam much. When she was seein' you, she didn't drink at all. Maybe you can convince her she's got to keep out o' these goddam nigger fights."

"I haven't seen her in a long time, John. Why would she listen to me?"

"She talks about you all the time . . . whenever she gets sloppy, sentimental drunk, especially. She still thinks you're the greatest Irishman ever lived."

Martin winced, but said reluctantly, "I'll talk to her, John. I doubt it'll do any good, but I'll talk to her." He paused. "Is there any chance you can take Stephen back at the Palace?"

"I'd like to, lad. I'd like to, but you know it wouldn't work.

To begin with, he's quit playin' the harp. He told me he'll never play again. An' he's drinkin' as hard as Mary. Sometimes I think he's crazy. He personally wants to put out every goddam fire in the city."

He leaned toward Martin and lowered his voice to a whisper. "When young Jimmy died in Short Beach, he and Mary both seemed to go berserk."

Martin stole a worried, compassionate glance at Kathleen, quietly wiping glasses behind the bar. He nodded.

"I'll pay Mary a visit tomorrow, John," he said.

A short, middle-aged Dutchman, who looked uncomfortable in his livery, opened the door to Martin's knock at the house in Washington Square. Mary was in the ornately furnished living room. She sat in a chair near a large, handsomely draped window on the east side of the room, reading a newspaper. On the small rosewood table beside the chair was a cut-glass whiskey decanter, and a half-filled glass. She put the paper aside, and said, "Well, this is a surprise! To what do I owe the pleasure of this visit, Martin Morrissey, you son of a bitch!"

She looked haggard. Her flame-colored hair was unkempt, hanging carelessly down over her shoulders. Her cheeks were mottled. She wore a green brocade dressing gown. She lifted her glass and drank. Martin stood before her.

"Huh—huhlo, Mary," he stammered. "Huh—huh—how are you?"

"Jesus, Mary, and Joseph! Sit down!" she ordered. "You're just as big a bumbler as ever."

He sat down in a damask-covered chair near hers.

"You want a drink?" she asked.

"No, thanks, Mary, I—"

"You *still* don't drink! Never-changing, *noble* Martin Morrissey!" she said sarcastically.

"Mary, you know—"

"I was sorry to hear your mother died," she said, abruptly serious.

"Thanks, Mary. You know—"

"But then a lot of people died, didn't they?" The bitterness sounded again in her voice. And the sarcasm, as she added, "Your cousin's wife didn't die, did she?"

"Mary, you know I'm your friend."

"That's what you said some time ago."

"I am, Mary, I am. Your father's worried about you."

"Oh, that's why you're here. Old JD asked you to come."

"I would've come anyway if I knew you were in trouble."

"Who says I'm in trouble?"

Martin leaned forward in his chair, reached for her hand.

"Mary, Mary. It's plain you're drinking too much. It's not good for you. It's not good for the baby."

She looked down at her stomach.

"Does it show that much already? Oh, no. Old JD told you, didn't he?"

Martin nodded.

"Maybe having a baby is just what you and Timmy need. You'll make a fine mother, Mary. But you've got to stop drinking. And getting involved in these dumb riots. It's dangerous."

She picked up the paper and waved it at Martin.

"Did you see where they had one at the Bowery Theatre? Ran that nigger-loving, anti-American English actor George Percy Warren right off the stage."

"I know," said Martin.

Mary's expression suddenly softened.

"Do you remember when we used to go to the theater, Martin?"

Martin smiled.

"Yes," he said.

"Do you know the Bowery Theatre now has gaslights?"

"Yes, I know."

"We should go again, Martin. It would be nice."

"You're a married woman, Mary. . . ."

She laughed and finished the whiskey in her glass.

"Come here and kiss me, Martin," she said coquettishly.

Martin grinned at her, but sat still.

"Come on! Come on! It's not goin' to kill you to give an old friend a kiss."

Martin walked to her chair, and leaned over and kissed her cheek. She flailed at him with her left arm.

"Jesus, Mary, and Joseph!" she shouted. "Get the hell out of here, Martin Morrissey. And stay out!"

"Mary, please. Please listen to me."

She pushed herself up out of the chair and shoved him aside roughly with both hands. As she stalked out of the room, she screamed, "Mind your own fucking business, Martin Morrissey! I don't need friends like you!"

* * *

In mid-November of the following year, Stephen moved out of 106 Rivington Street and took a room with an Irish family named Kahan on Fulton Street, only five doors away from the Honey Bee Company hive. He had gotten a job at one of the newly reopened shipyards in late 1834, and from that time on, Kathleen and Martin had seen little of him. And when they infrequently saw him, they had no arguments, nor even serious discussions, about anything. Stephen simply talked to his wife and Martin only when it was absolutely necessary.

In the meantime, Kathleen had gradually worked her way out of her extreme melancholia, and while she was by no means the merry barmaid, she was consistently friendly and pleasant with the patrons and with Martin. Now, when they were alone at the end of a long day, she occasionally did join Martin for a late-night cup of tea. Martin was more desperately in love with her than ever.

After a busy Thanksgiving day, at one o'clock in the morning, Martin sat at the oak table in the kitchen, watching Kathleen at the stove waiting for the kettle to whistle. He had a tremendous urge to take her in his arms. But he sat still, watching her with a warm smile on his face, as she returned to the table and poured the steaming tea. She returned the kettle to the stove and finally sat down, opposite him. She sighed, wearily, but with an air of contentment. Martin reached across the table and took her hand.

"You work too hard, Kathleen," he said tenderly.

She blushed at the touch of Martin's hand, and shook her head. Her brogue had almost vanished over the years.

"I can never work hard enough to repay you and Maureen for all you've done for me," she said.

Martin squeezed her hand, just the slightest bit, and rose in his chair to come to her. Quickly, she withdrew her hand. Her face reddened. An expression of fear, touched with regret, came into her hyacinth-violet eyes. Martin stopped, and stood near her for a moment. Then he went back to his chair.

"I'm sorry, Martin," said Kathleen.

"I—I—I do—" Martin was on the edge of saying, "love you," but altered it.

"I—do understand, Kathleen," he said.

"I—I've been worried, Martin," she said shyly, "about us

living here together with Stephen gone. I don't know if it is right."

Martin seemed surprised. Since he had resisted making any advances to Kathleen until moments ago, and had always respected her position as the wife of his cousin, it had never occurred to him that anyone could see anything wicked in the situation.

"Why . . . ? Why, Kathleen . . . ? What do you mean? What could be wrong about it?"

"I thought people might be talkin'. Last Sunday I asked Father Boland about it after Mass."

"What did he say?" asked Martin anxiously.

Kathleen lowered her eyes.

"He asked me whether there was anything of a romantic, or—or a—a carnal nature between us."

Martin waited. Eyes still lowered, Kathleen said, "I told him there wasn't, there'd never been, none at all, at all!"

Martin attempted to hide his disappointment over her emphasis on this fact, with only moderate success. He frowned involuntarily, and Kathleen continued, "Father said, 'Well, then, what are ye worried about? Let evil-minded people think what they will. If you and Martin are pure in yer hearts, that's all that matters.' "

Martin beamed, relieved. But he understood why Kathleen had withdrawn her hand. He smiled and sipped his tea. They talked for a while about how nice it was that business was improving so steadily. When they finished their tea, Kathleen washed out the cups and kettle, and shyly bid Martin good night.

On Monday, December 15, a fire broke out on Burling Slip on the East River. Before the Kahans could stir themselves awake, their boarder, Stephen Boyle, was out of the house and climbing into his gear at the Honey Bee hive. He did not get back until two o'clock in the morning, but despite the severe cold the fire had been brought under control before it could do too much damage. Blaze Ditchett told Stephen that he was going to recommend that the City Council award Stephen some kind of medal for heroic and effective fire fighting above and beyond the call of duty. Sniffing and coughing all through the night, Stephen was nevertheless pleased.

The following morning the temperature dropped to below zero. It was one of the coldest, most bitter days in several years. At six in the evening it began to snow, and a vicious northwest wind slashed across the city. Stephen insisted on walking watch that night. About nine o'clock as he passed the corner of Merchant and Pearl Streets, he raised his head out of the collar of his greatcoat and sniffed the frigid air. With his stuffed and running nose, and the snow driving against his face, it was hard to tell, but he was almost certain he smelled smoke. He was in the heart of the business district. Now in the third decade of the nineteenth century it was a maze of narrow, crooked streets, lined on both sides with four-, five-, even six-story buildings, recently built by the more successful dry-goods, hardware, and other merchants. Stephen stood before a five-story warehouse at 25 Merchant Street, right on the corner of Pearl. In the cold moonlight he could make out a painted sign at the side of huge double doors: Comstock & Andrews, Fancy Dry Goods Jobbers.

In the seam where the doors met, thick smoke poured forth, increasingly heavy. It spread into small gray-black clouds, only to be whipped away by the savage wind as fast as it emerged. Stephen raced to the next corner and clanged the fire bell. Then he ran through the icy streets, almost slipping and crashing onto his back three times before he reached the Honey Bee hive. Again he was the first member of the company to arrive. He donned his gear and was impatiently testing the pump on the gooseneck engine when Blaze Ditchett arrived. Ditchett grunted a hello, and began to pull his boots on. He said to Stephen, "Crise-awmighty, lad, the divil himself'd have to git outta the way, if you were down there."

"It's over in the business district, Blaze. Those buildings are full of all kinds of flammable stuff."

This Tuesday night marked the beginning of a sixteen-hour holocaust such as the city had never seen in all the thousands of fires which had plagued it down through the years. The volunteer companies had lost many men during the cholera epidemic. Most of those who responded to the Merchant Street alarm had fought the Burling Slip conflagration the previous night and were exhausted. The weather had turned so frigid that the water in most of the wells, hydrants, and cisterns in the city was frozen.

When Stephen and two of his Honey Bee colleagues aimed the gooseneck-engine hose at the now flaming warehouse on Merchant Street and two others pumped furiously, no water came out. The firemen cursed and pumped with all their strength, but the water was congealed in the hose. Stephen climbed on the engine and began to beat on the hose with the flat of an ax.

"We've got to break the ice in the hose," he yelled at his colleagues. Three firemen joined him in pounding the hose several feet apart from each other. After what seemed hours, but was less than fifteen minutes, water began to spray from the hose. As soon as it hit the air, wind-whipped to fifty below zero, it turned into hail. With the northwester driving the flame from one building to another, with the all but impossible water situation, with the shortage of weary, frozen volunteers and malfunctioning equipment, the fire was soon out of control.

By midnight the roaring inferno lighted the entire city. The glow in the night sky could be seen as far northwest as New Haven, and as far southwest as Philadelphia. Martin and Kathleen joined the throngs that clustered on the edges of the spreading holocaust. At Duane Street they saw a fireman who looked like Stephen race up to the front of a burning building and hack away at a scorched pillar with an ax. He and several other firemen were trying to hasten the wooden structure's collapse to keep it from spreading to the next building. They could not be sure it was Stephen, but the Honey Bee gooseneck engine was spraying water on another part of the building nearby.

He's going to get scorched to death, thought Martin as he watched the heroic firefighter. He felt some guilt at being unable to help in any way. But no one, including the city's proud fire companies, every single one of which responded this night, could do much against the spectacular gale-driven hell. The last small fires and sparks were not extinguished until December 19, three days after Stephen had detected the smoke at 25 Merchant Street. Eighteen blocks of lower Manhattan, on more than fifty acres, were an awesome landscape of ashes, charred remnants of wood, brick, and stone. Six hundred and ninety-five buildings, most of them shops and warehouses, had been destroyed. The entire area between Broadway, Wall Street, and Coenties Slip was leveled. All landmarks of the old Dutch town vanished, as the few surviving seventeenth-century houses were burned to the ground.

Molly Kahan came to 106 Rivington Street just after dawn on Friday, the nineteenth. She was a stout, gray-haired woman, and there were tears in her eyes as she said to Kathleen, "Oh, Oi think ye'd best come, Mrs. Boyle! My Frank's gone to fetch Father Boland, but it's you Mr. Boyle's wantin' t' see. . . . He keeps callin' yer name."

Stephen had collapsed in utter exhaustion with a raging fever on Monday afternoon. He had continued to fight the spreading fire, without surcease, from late Friday night, despite the pleas, then the orders, of Blaze Ditchett to quit. He worked like a man possessed. Now he lay in his small room at the Kahans', his lungs ravaged by heat and smoke and congested by the severe pneumonia he had developed. Father Boland stood at his side when Kathleen and Martin came in. The priest was reciting the last rites in somber, quiet tones. He turned to them, when they entered, but then turned back to Stephen and continued praying.

Kathleen rushed to him and knelt at Stephen's side. He stared at her out of his mad blue eyes. His eyebrows and half his hair were singed. His lips were dry and cracked. The left side of his face was badly scorched, but Kathleen could feel the heat of the fever from his entire body. Insane, desperate as he seemed, it was plain he recognized his wife.

"Oi just confessed to the father, Kathleen," he croaked in a rasping, almost soundless voice. "But Oi must confess t' you, too, and beg ye t' fergive me. . . ." He paused, struggling for breath, then continued.

"Jimmy—Jimmy drowned. . . . The nigger woman would've called me t' git 'im . . . but she was afraid t'—t' come into the bedroom. . . . Oi was fookin' Mary O'Leary when Jimmy drowned. . . . Oi know Oi'll burn in the fires o' hell, Kathleen, but—but—"

His back arched suddenly. His body stiffened for a moment, then collapsed. His head twisted to the side and his lashless dead eyes stared at the top of Kathleen's head, resting on her folded hands at the edge of his bed. Father Boland kept praying. Martin lifted Kathleen gently to her feet. She sobbed quietly as he led her out of the room.

On Christmas Day Mary O'Leary's baby was born. It was a boy, eight pounds and six ounces. Martin stood in the small group at St. Peter's, Father Boland's new Catholic church, as the priest flicked holy water upon the infant and spoke the Latin prayers of baptism. Martin heard an older Irish woman whom he did not know whisper to another.

"I think the li'l darlin's got blue eyes, Tessie, an' such light hair."

Martin hoped Timmy, standing at the baptismal font with Mary and the priest, did not hear. They named the baby Michael John O'Leary.

PART THREE

Edward and Patrick Morrissey
and Michael John O'Leary

A Wedding at the Elegant
Astor House Hotel

Max Kessler and His Brewery

The Black-hearted Reverend Whiteheart

Stampede on Fifth Avenue

"The Astor House Hotel represents a bold stride in advance of its time . . . its appearance far surpasses expectations; for size and solidity no building in the United States can compare with it. . . . It is lighted by this gas which everybody is discussing."

—Newspaper commentary on the opening of the new hotel, 1836

"Not only must the cattle drives be banned, but the carting of live animals through the city streets must be prohibited. . . . Such expeditions as we have seen of calves and sheep, with legs tied and heads hanging over end boards, rattled away through Broadway, are enough to provoke the indignation of any person who has a spark of sensibility left. . . . We have seen a wagon seat tossed upon the bodies of these animals and two great boys sitting upon the board as cooly as if lolling upon a sofa, while their weight was fairly crushing the poor creatures beneath."

—*The New York Tribune*, editorial, July 18, 1850

7

Amazingly enough Martin was not surprised when the timid tapping sounded on his bedroom door in the middle of a cold night in January in 1838. He knew it was Kathleen. Somehow he knew she would come to him this night.

It had been a strange year. Martin's comforting and understanding presence brought Kathleen through the traumatic period following Stephen's death. The tavern thrived for a few months, but then the combined effects of the cholera epidemic, the disastrous fire in the business district, and a number of unrelated factors began to take their toll. The city's fire-insurance companies, unable to pay off many of their policyholders, were ruined. Banks were closed and merchants and manufacturers were unable to raise funds to rebuild their shops and factories.

The state had piled up enormous debts building the canals and the new railroads. There had been fanatic speculation in real estate, and President Andrew Jackson decreed that all purchases of public land must be paid for in gold or silver. This further hampered banking operations. In the city the shipyards closed down; building and construction screeched to a near halt. Immigration continued, with the majority of destitute foreigners settling in New York. Unemployment reached new peaks. Poverty-stricken Irish fought freed Negroes for the few remaining lowest-paying jobs. New York and the nation were launched into the greatest depression in history. It was to last a full seventy-seven months.

Martin considered himself lucky. He was working a steadily increasing number of hours on the police watch. As is usual when hard times intensify, crime soared. It was taxing to put in six or eight hours on watch, then work for another ten or twelve in the tavern. It was difficult not only for him but also for Kathleen, who had to carry the entire burden of the restaurant and bar when he did his police work. They could not afford extra help. Neither of them complained.

On this frozen day in January, Martin had gone on duty at eight in the morning, after a hot breakfast with Kathleen. He had returned a little after eight at night, and taken over behind the bar. Kathleen had worked with him until midnight when they closed, after the last of the handful of patrons departed. From their first words at breakfast until their good nights in the kitchen shortly after midnight, Martin had sensed an extraordinary reaching out to him on Kathleen's part. Several times during breakfast, she had touched his hand, or patted his shoulder as she set a plate or filled his cup. It seemed to him there was a special, indefinable tenderness in her voice as she spoke to him; a look, needy, pleading perhaps, in her eyes. And it was not just this day. Martin sensed there had been a deeply affectionate telepathic communication between them for several months.

All day long, that frosty January Friday, he had been thinking about Kathleen. Frozen-faced, he was smiling inanely to himself toward evening, when a stout gentleman with a fur-collared coat and fur hat asked how to get to the Astor House. The city's newest, largest, and most elegant hotel had opened a little less than two years earlier, on an entire block of Broadway between Vesey and Barclay Streets.

Martin, hardly aware that the man had spoken, grinned at him and said, "Hello, sir. A good evening to you."

The man looked annoyed.

"The Astor House! The Astor House!" he repeated irritably. "Where will I find it?"

"Ho!" said Martin. "It's not hard to find, to be certain. Just go two blocks straight ahead to Broadway and then another three blocks to your left."

The stout man trudged off without saying thanks, and Martin went back to thinking about Kathleen. He knew she would come to his bedroom this very night. How he knew he did not know. He just knew it.

Responding to the tapping at his door now, at three o'clock on this bright, moonlit night, he called, "Come in, Kathleen, please come in."

The door opened slowly and she walked hesitantly toward the bed. He sat up, leaning on one elbow. Moonglow filled the room. It cast a silvery highlight on one side of her gleaming brown hair and on one lean, pale cheek. She clutched a long blue wool robe just below her chin. She reached the bed, stood over Martin, and said in a trembling voice, "Can I, please, Martin, can I sit on the edge of your bed?"

He took her hand, and she sat gingerly on the bed's frame. She was shivering.

"Please, Martin," she said. "Please hold me."

He pushed his blanket aside and eagerly sat up straighter and took her in his arms. He held her close.

"Kathleen," he whispered hoarsely, pressing his cheek against hers. "Kathleen, dearest Kathleen."

She pulled him tightly against her and she stopped shivering.

"D'you think I'm terrible, Martin?"

He chuckled.

"Not terrible, wonderful," he said softly, and lay back gently on the bed, taking her down with him. They lay side by side, embracing each other, cheeks still touching.

"Thank the good Lord," said Martin, with great feeling.

She raised both her hands to his cheeks and kissed his mouth, timidly, lightly. He held her close and kissed her hungrily again and again. He felt himself harden against her inner thigh. She groaned and dug her fingers into his back, then suddenly released him, and struggled to move away from him.

"Kathleen, marry me. I love you. Please marry me."

She squirmed her way upright, and sat on the edge of the bed again. In the moonlight, Martin could see the tears in her eyes. She shook her head.

"I—I can't, Martin. I—I wouldn't make you a proper wife. . . . Forgive me!"

She sobbed and abruptly stood up and rushed from the room. Martin lay quietly, looking at the ceiling, waiting for his passion to subside. When it did, he still lay there, pondering. Finally he rose and walked down the hall to Kathleen's bedroom, and knocked firmly.

"Martin," came Kathleen's still choked voice. "I can't—I just can't. . . . It frightens me. . . . I can't lose another child."

Martin opened the door and walked slowly to her bed. He leaned over and stroked her hair.

"We don't have to, Kathleen. Not till you're ready. Never, if you can't. . . ."

He sat on the edge of her bed and wiped the tears from her cheeks with the back of his hand.

"I love you, Kathleen. Marry me."

She took his hand from her cheek and kissed the palm, then held it to her breast.

"I love you, too, Martin. I've loved you for a long, long time. But you're a man. You need a woman . . . in every way. I—I don't want to ruin your life."

"You won't, Kathleen. I promise you, you won't."

It was not until spring that she agreed to marry him. And amazingly enough, the day she said yes, Martin again had a premonition that she would. Again they had had a breakfast during which Martin sensed a special warm eagerness on Kathleen's part as she brought his coffee and buttered brown bread to him.

"Have you ever worked in Yorkville before?" she asked.

"No," said Martin. "It should be a quiet day. It's a bit far out in the country, but a couple of the expensive villas have been broken into, and some of the shanty people seem to be getting out of hand."

"Will you walk?"

"No, I believe I'll take the horsecar. It gives me a chance to read the paper."

It was all simple, homey, almost old-married-couple conversation, but a sound of longing and love transformed the plain words into a romantic exchange.

A Clarence Wilson, who had been an admirer of Martin's in his boxing days, was now an official with the New York and Harlem Railroad Company, and he had given Martin a pass to ride the cars at any time. In addition to *The Evening Post*, two other excellent newspapers were now being published in the city. Benjamin Day had started *The Sun* three years ago, and James Gordon Bennett, *The Herald* just last year. The newspapers were increasingly influential in the city's affairs, and since Martin had joined the police force, he had taken a strong interest in New York's politics and its general activity.

"Have a fine day, Martin, and please be careful," said Kathleen, touching his arm solicitously and smiling at the door as he left. It was a warm and sunny day in early May, and Martin leaned back in his seat on the stagecoachlike horsecar and began to read a report about the progress being made on the new Croton water project. Despite the deepening depression, the city officials had authorized the construction of the gigantic new system because they had determined that one of the probable causes for the cholera epidemic had been the city's brackish well water. Before his death, former Vice-President Aaron Burr had formed a water-purifying company called the Manhattan Company, but it could meet the needs of only a small part of the population. And many of the poorer people could afford neither the Manhattan Company's service, nor the water sold by the street vendors. There were hints in the newspaper story that some politicians were profiting from the huge Croton project. Martin thought it likely that John Deasy and Tim O'Leary were involved in some way.

The NY and H horsecars ran along the Bowery from Prince Street to Fourteenth Street. There they continued up Fourth Avenue through the countryside to the termination at the rural section called Yorkville. Martin put his paper aside. The driver, sitting atop the front of the car, slammed his foot on the brake pedal and pulled the reins to halt the car to let a group of pedestrians cross the street. They were just approaching Fourteenth Street. Martin was thinking of Kathleen again. He decided that tonight he would ask her, once more, to marry him.

A sudden explosion jolted him out of his reverie. He turned toward the sound, which came from behind him. Evidently some construction workers, blasting a rock obstruction, had exploded a charge. The sound had frightened a sleek, copper-colored horse pulling an elegant black lacquered carriage. Martin saw the horse rear, then kick back down to the ground again, almost pulling the coachman from his high seat. Eyes wild, nostrils flaring, the horse charged wildly ahead on the cobble-stoned street, which flanked the car tracks.

The harder the red-faced coachman pulled at the reins, the more unmanageable the horse became. It whipped its head from side to side, mane flying. Then it kicked its front legs high in the air, and again stomped back to the cobblestones and charged ahead erratically. Behind it the carriage rocked and bounced precariously. As the runaway horse drew within thirty yards of the streetcar, racing parallel to it, Martin saw the head and shoulders of a pretty young lady sticking out of the carriage window. Her flower-bedecked bonnet was askew on her head. She was screaming in terror.

Martin was in the rear compartment of the three-compartment coach. He climbed over two passengers to reach the side door. He swung the door open and dropped to the dirt road. The charging horse was fifteen yards away. Martin whipped off his jacket. He stood directly in the path of the onrushing beast, waving the jacket frantically up and down. The horse saw it and veered to the right, rearing up on its hind legs again. The coachman was thrown from his seat, and landed in a crumpled heap at the side of the cobblestoned street. The carriage flopped over onto its side, and scraped along the street. Martin dropped the jacket and grabbed desperately for the harness as the horse's front hooves hit the ground and it began to charge forward again. The weight of the dragging carriage, now on its side, slowed the wild animal. Martin felt a sharp pain as the horse's iron-shod hoof kicked his shin. Grimly, holding the harness in one tight fist, Martin grabbed the horse's mane with the other, and hurled himself onto the animal's back. In his youth in Ireland he had always been good with the landowner's horses. In less than twenty-five yards, half by sheer will, half by muttered persuasion, he brought the panicky animal to a halt. The streetcar conductor and several of the passengers came running to the scene. Over the excited hubbub of the gathering crowd, Martin heard the sustained hysterical screaming of the girl in the wrecked carriage.

Kathleen stood over the narrow hospital bed and stared in grave concern at Martin's grotesque right leg. Two narrow boards, one at the front of the leg, the other at the rear, extended from just below the knee to just above the ankle. The boards were wrapped in thick layers of bandage. The leg rested on several overstuffed pillows. A bare, pale foot stuck out, naked, at its end.

"The doctor said it's a compound fracture of the—I think—the tibula, he said, Martin. Is it terribly painful?" fretted Kathleen.

Martin, sitting up in the bed, shook his head.

"Not unless I try to move it. I think it's just a cracked shinbone. I hope I can leave here tomorrow. Sit down, Kathleen."

She took the chair beside the bed and reached for his hand.

"They told me all about it, Martin. You could have been killed."

"Will you marry me, Kathleen?" asked Martin quietly.

"Martin! Martin . . . your leg . . ."

"My leg will be fine. Will you, Kathleen? Say yes, please."

He squeezed her hand, and raised it to his lips and kissed the backs of her fingers. She rose impulsively from the chair, leaned down and put her arms around him and kissed him on the cheek.

"Yes . . . yes . . . yes, Martin," she whispered fervently, "I will. I will. I love you."

The door to the small hospital room opened and a middle-aged male nurse said, "Mr. Vanderwegh is here to see you, Mr. Morrissey. Can he come in?"

Kathleen, blushing, sat back in her chair, and before Martin could say anything a portly, round-faced man with curly blond hair and an impeccably groomed mustache and Vandyke beard strode into the room. He was dressed in a fine wool suit with the trousers neatly pressed. A gold watch chain rested on the gray vest on his paunch.

"You must excuse me for interrupting, please, my dear Mr. Morrissey, but I have not much time," he said, walking confidently to the bed. He extended a pudgy hand toward Martin.

"I am Conrad Vanderwegh. I have come to thank you from the bottom of my heart for saving the life of my daughter, Liesel. You are a very brave man."

They had told Martin that the young woman in the carriage was not seriously hurt. She had suffered some severe bruises and was in a state of hysteria, but they had taken her home. The coachman was injured severely. He had a broken shoulder and a concussion, and he was in another room in the hospital. Vanderwegh continued to shake Martin's hand all the while he made his small speech. Martin reddened, and looked toward Kathleen. Vanderwegh suddenly released his hand and bowed to Kathleen.

"And this is the good wife, *Mevrouw* Morrissey, I presume. Your husband risked his—"

Kathleen blushed again, but took Vanderwegh's extended hand. As he continued to speak and shake her hand vigorously, she said, "N—not yet, sir. Soon. . . . We—we hope."

Martin grinned.

"This is Kathleen Boyle, Mr. Vanderwegh. We are not married yet, but will be soon."

Vanderwegh clapped his hands together.

"Ach, how wonderful! You must have your reception at the Astor House!"

"Oh . . . I don't think we could afford that, sir," said Martin. "We have a small tavern on Rivington Street, but business has not been good—"

"Nonsense!" said Vanderwegh. "I have been considering how I could reward you for saving my dear Liesel. I am the manager and a stockholder in the Astor House and it will give me great pleasure to host your wedding reception in one of our finest rooms. A small enough reward for so heroic a deed!"

Which was how it happened that in mid-August, after a quiet church wedding at St. Peter's with old Father Boland conducting the ceremony, Mr. and Mrs. Martin Morrissey had their reception in an ornately decorated ballroom on the first floor of the imposing five-story Greek revival hotel on Broadway. Martin had just given up using his crutch in early July and he still walked with a pronounced limp. More than twenty members of the police department with their wives and some of their children were among the guests. As were a dozen or more of the regular patrons of the tavern, including Blaze Ditchett. Conrad Vanderwegh, his plump wife, and eighteen-year-old daughter, Liesel, came. And, of course, John and Ann Deasy and Timothy and Mary O'Leary. Martin had wondered if Mary would accept the invitation. He was glad she had, but her presence did cause him some trepidation.

There was a small band and dancing. And fine wines, whiskeys, and beer, and more food than the entire assemblage could eat: fish and fowl and meats and vegetables and fruits and sherbets and cakes and coffee and tea. It was the happiest day of Martin's life, and—as she told him over and over—of Kathleen's. She told him again as they moved out onto the polished floor for the first dance of the evening, but as they swept by the long, white-clothed buffet table, she whispered, "It's almost sinful, I feel guilty having so much in the middle of such bad times."

Martin nodded and kissed her cheek as they circled the dance floor to the applause of their friends.

"This one night, my love, we won't think about the bad times," he said. "Just thank God for all this bounty, and most of all that we have each other."

Over Kathleen's shoulder he saw Mary O'Leary as they glided by the Deasy-O'Leary table. Mary stared at them as they passed, then lifted her glass to her lips, and emptied it in one long drink. Martin smiled at her warmly. He hoped she would do nothing to mar the occasion. At the church she had kissed his cheek coldly, when the bride and groom passed through the line of well-wishers. She had also kissed

Kathleen's cheek without uttering a word. Every time Martin had glanced over at the table near the bandstand, Mary seemed to be either drinking or refilling her glass.

Shortly after ten o'clock John Deasy pulled Martin over to their table and insisted he sit with them for a while. He had had a good deal to drink himself, and he immediately began to talk politics.

"You should get more involved, lad," he told Martin. "Our little Tammany society is getting more powerful all the time. You know we elected the mayor, don't you?"

It was the first time in the city's history that the mayor had been chosen by a vote of the citizens rather than by appointment. Martin was aware that Deasy and the Tammany group, with a little help from some of the Five Points gangsters, had been instrumental in the victory of the Democratic Tammany candidate, Cornelius Van Wyck Lawrence, over the Whig nominee, Gulian Verplanck.

"Yes, I know," said Martin.

"We're doing very nicely with the Croton water project," said O'Leary. "You know there was a group wanted to pipe in the water from the Bronx River. Wouldn't've been nearly as—"

"Oh, shut up, Timmy," interrupted Mary loudly.

Martin reached over and took Mary's hand.

"I'm glad you came, Mary. I wanted all my good friends here. You and Timmy and—"

The band began to play. Mary rose to her feet, holding on to Martin's hand. He was glad to see she was quite steady.

"Dance with me," she ordered, and pulled Martin to the polished wood floor in the center of the room. The band was playing one of the popular new songs of the day, "A Life on the Ocean Wave," in a slow tempo, and Mary leaned her head on Martin's shoulder as they danced. She felt the perspiration in the palm of his hand, holding hers.

"You're nervous, Martin," she said.

"A little," he admitted.

"For a cripple you dance pretty well."

"How have you been, Mary?" he asked.

"Rotten," she said. "I miss Stevie. Isn't that ridiculous!"

"It—it—must have been terrible—what happened in Connecticut," he stammered. He realized what a blunder it was for him to have brought up the subject when she stiffened in his arms. But that was what he thought she was referring t when she said she felt rotten.

She said, with quiet vehemence, "The goddam stupi nigger woman should have called us right away! We coul have—"

Martin tried to change the subject.

"How's little Mike?" he asked.

The strategy, much to his surprise, worked. Her gree eyes seemed to light up.

"A rascal that one is. Wild, three years old and big as a bo of five. Last week he bit the nanny."

Martin chuckled.

"Week before, he ate one of Timmy's cigars. . . . You kno we're building a new house, a big villa up on Thirty-sevent Street, right on the corner of Fifth Avenue."

"That's pretty far out of the city."

She shrugged.

"Makes no difference to me."

As the music stopped, she took both his hands and looke up into his eyes.

"You're a son of a bitch, Martin Morrissey, but I love yo and I wish you well."

She patted his cheek.

"Stop looking so worried. I won't make any trouble."

She led him back to the table.

A half hour later Martin was dancing with Kathleen agai when the gaslights in the crystal chandeliers on the ceilin and in the silver brackets at the side of the room all went out The room was in total darkness. There were nervous an raucous comments, some hysterical laughter from all aroun the room. In a moment a red-faced, perspiring man carryin an oil lantern came in.

"Please, ladies and gentlemen," he shouted nervousl "There is nothing to be concerned about. We make the gas i our own plant, and there are nearly six hundred guests in th hotel at this moment. Occasionally when there is too great drain on the gas supply, it becomes exhausted. The manage ment offers its apologies, and I assure you steps are bein taken to replenish the supply as quickly as possible."

Moments later a dozen liveried waiters came into the dar room carrying large brass candelabra with six lighted candle in each, and placed them around on all the tables. The happ reception resumed. The candlelight created a special roma tic atmosphere. Just before midnight Martin whispered to Kathleen and they quietly made their way out of the ballroom.

"Oh, Martin, I just can't believe it," said Kathleen as they walked, hand in hand, down the long carpeted hallway to their honeymoon room on the fifth floor. The gaslights had come on again.

"I'd be happy enough celebrating our marriage in the tavern, or anywhere—in a stable, even—but all this elegance . . ." She looked around at the rich wainscoting and the flock-papered walls.

"Is it true that there are more than three hundred rooms in the hotel?" she asked.

"Three hundred and nine," said Martin.

"And do they really have baths and toilets on every floor?"

Martin nodded toward a heavy oak door with brass letters, reading, Bathing Facilities.

"There's ours. And just four doors away from our own room."

In bed, clothed in a fresh nightshirt, and with Kathleen in a soft cotton gown, Martin held her in his arms.

"I'm the happiest man in the world, Mrs. Morrissey," he said.

She turned to face him, and put her arms around him. They kissed and almost instantly Martin became rigidly erect. He arched his midsection away from her, but she had already felt it.

"I'm sorry, Kathleen," he whispered.

He heard her sniffling in the darkness, as she released him and got out of bed. She was sobbing as she walked to the window and looked down upon quiet and deserted Broadway.

"I—I'm so ashamed of myself, Martin. I—I know it's ridiculous. But I'm frightened. I—I can't help it."

He went to her and put his arms on her shoulders from behind.

"Don't worry about it, sweet Kathleen. Perhaps some day . . ."

He kissed her neck and led her back to bed. He took her in his arms again, and by sheer will power controlled himself so he would not have a genital reaction to her closeness. They did not make love on their wedding night. But five months later on a cold night in January, in their bed on the second floor of 106 Rivington Street, his will power deserted him, and he grew large and hard as he hugged her. Again, aching with desire, he arched his pelvic area away from her, but she leaned in toward him and reached behind him and clutched his buttocks and pulled him to her. She kissed him, open-mouthed, and with a passion that startled him. Neither of them said a word. Suddenly she gasped as he slid inside her. For a long moment they lay totally quiet, quivering in each other's arms. Then Kathleen moaned as Martin found her lips, and kissed her as he gently moved back and forth, and in seconds, exploded. Kathleen gasped and held him tightly to her.

"Don't . . . don't leave me, Martin. Please."

She dug her fingers into his muscular back, and he stayed inside her, and miraculously, almost immediately he was swollen and burningly rigid again and now they moved together, and it seemed a blissful eternity before he erupted once more.

It was impossible to say with certainty that that was the night on which Edward Morrissey was conceived, for they made love every night for the next three weeks, and a dozen times, early in the morning as well. Martin was a vigorous forty, and Kathleen a love-starved thirty-three, and they seemed determined to make up for all the years of sharing each other they had missed. Whenever the conception occurred, Edward was born on October 11, 1839. He looked like a miniature Martin. Same unusually large ears. Same bright dark eyes. Even, said Kathleen, the same endearing smile.

8

"You see, Ned, lad," said Martin to his three-year-old son, sitting astride his shoulders, "they've made these magical fountains just for your birthday."

Ned clutched his father's large ear with the pudgy fingers of one hand, while Martin steadied the boy with a firm grip on his ankles.

"Nice rain, Papa," the child acknowledged wearily. He was enchanted by the spray of sparkling water, rising fifty feet high and arching like a bouquet of liquid giant feathers, then splashing back into the bubbling pool at its base. But he could hardly keep his eyes open. It was late afternoon on that

Friday, October 14, 1842, and it had been a long, exciting day. Shortly before noon Martin and Kathleen had taken Ned and his two-year-old brother, Patrick, to the Bowling Green, where they had seen the first of the new fountains created to celebrate the activation of the incredible Croton Water System. The Bowling Green fountain had impressed Martin and Kathleen, but to wide-eyed Ned and Pat it was indeed something out of a fairyland. Yet it was dwarfed by this spectacular jet stream they were now watching at the High Bridge.

After the ceremonies at Bowling Green were concluded, they had walked over to the Bowery and stood on the corner at Rivington Street and watched the parade go by. Virtually every one of the volunteer fire companies marched in the long, jubilant procession. A bright fall sun gleamed on their colorful, brass-trimmed gooseneck engines, hose reels, peaked hats, and polished boots. The foremen waved their brass trumpets triumphantly at the crowds lining the Bowery. Bands accompanied the marchers and blared joyous music. The new system would deliver thirty-five million gallons of water into the city every day. The firefighters would be able to do their heroic work more effectively than they had ever dreamed possible.

Kathleen was a changed woman. When Edward was born she, herself, seemed to experience a rebirth. Despite the fact that the depression had worsened, and they were struggling to keep possession of the tavern, she faced each day with a zest that warmed Martin's heart. The little money he earned in his part-time police work went into paying some of the mounting obligations of operating the tavern. Yet, he, too, was happier than he had ever been in his life. Young Edward, whom they called Ned, had had his share of the typical childhood maladies—teething, an occasional cold, an upset stomach, now and then a moderate fever—but Kathleen showed none of the unreasonable panic and near hysteria that had gripped her whenever young Jimmy as much as sneezed. Martin's confident, positive outlook on life, his passionate devotion to her, transformed Kathleen into a vivacious, capable, and contented wife and mother. She seemed to enjoy every moment of each hard day, and found endless pleasure in the husband and children she adored.

Although Patrick's birth, just ten months after Edward's, had been difficult for her, she lost none of her stalwart spirit nor her love of life. Since it proved impossible for her to run the tavern and take care of the babies when Martin was on police duty, on those occasions they hired a thirteen-year-old Irish girl, Flossie Cassidy, daughter of a street sweeper named Harry Samuel Cassidy, whom everyone called H.S. Sad-eyed H.S. was a longtime patron of the tavern. Flossie loved the children and treated them as though they were her own baby brothers.

Kathleen had even resigned herself to the fact that there was a certain amount of risk in Martin's police work. He had been in several nasty encounters with thieves and gangsters from Five Points, but his locustwood club, his boxing skills, and his natural strength stood him in good stead in these incidents. He had never suffered anything worse than a bloodied nose or bruised knuckles. In late 1839, when the first steam locomotives were put into service, Kathleen worried every time Martin was assigned to an area near the new railways' routes. All kinds of accidents were caused by the noisy, smoke-belching engines in their early days.

On this Friday of the celebration of the Croton Water System, Max Kessler had met the Morrisseys back at 106 Rivington Street after the parade, and had driven them in his brewery wagon up to the High Bridge in Harlem, where they were now witnessing the spectacular jet streams spouting gracefully into the air. Patrick was asleep in Kathleen's arms.

"I think we had better go, Martin. Do you mind, Max?" she asked the muscular young man at her side.

Max Kessler said, "Yes, please, Mrs. Morrissey—I mean, no, I do not mind. Yes, we should leave. I was beginning to worry I would not be home by sundown."

"Oh, I didn't know we were keeping you from anything important, Max. Why didn't you say something?" said Kathleen.

Kessler smiled. "It's the Sabbath. At sundown on Friday the Sabbath begins and I must be home."

"Of course," said Kathleen.

Martin did not know what Kessler meant. He knew Kessler was Jewish and that he attended the Shearith Israel Synagogue, but there were very few Jewish people in the city at this time, less than ten thousand, and the two hundred thousand Irish were hardly aware of their existence, let alone their religious practices. They climbed aboard Kessler's brewery wagon. Kessler had arranged a small wooden cot, covered with a straw-filled pallet, wide enough for the two boys, and a wooden bench alongside it in the back of the boxlike wagon. Martin and Kathleen got Ned and Patrick settled on the cot, and Kathleen sat on the bench alongside them. Even on this clear, brisk day the interior of the wagon smelled strongly of beer, but neither the sleeping boys nor Kathleen were bothered by the aroma. She leaned back against the side of the wagon and closed her eyes. There was a contented smile on her face.

Martin sat alongside Kessler on the wide seat high at the front of the wagon.

"Now, Mr. Morrissey," said Kessler, as he tapped his team into motion with a light flick of the reins. "Now you will have the finest beer in all America. Made only with pure Croton water, the finest hops, the . . ."

Martin was embarrassed. Max Kessler had been supplying the Morrissey tavern with beer for almost two years, and Martin had not been able to pay him a single penny.

Max Kessler had first appeared at 106 Rivington Street one November morning in 1839. A heavy snow had been falling since dawn. Ned was on the floor of the small room that had been Uncle Ned Van Gelder's room, playing with a wooden rattle Martin had made for him. Patrick, warmly bundled, was asleep in his wooden crib. Kathleen had just settled them and joined Martin in the barroom, where he was making preparations for opening for the day at noon. There was a worried look on Martin's face as he turned away from the large beer keg behind the bar.

"I would guess we've got about a three-day supply," he told Kathleen. Cornelius Van Kriek, the owner of the Red Lion Brewery, had been in the day before and told them he could no longer extend them credit. They owed Van Kriek more than a hundred dollars. He was not the only supplier to whom they were in debt. As one business after another in the city failed, as more and more men were thrown out of work, fewer and fewer patrons came into the tavern. They owed the farmer who sold them vegetables, the butcher, the coal man, and others. If it had not been for Martin's earnings as a policeman they would have been forced to close some time ago.

"So we'll do without beer if we have to," said the new, positive Kathleen. "We still serve as hearty a dinner or supper as is to be found in the city."

Martin came around from behind the bar and kissed her

cheek. Outside it was snowing harder. There came a knock at the front door. Martin opened it. A stocky man, effortlessly holding a keg on one shoulder, stood there. Out in the street Martin saw a flat open wagon with a weary horse standing before it. On the wagon a dozen or more kegs were stacked upright. Kegs, wagon, horse, and man at the door were dusted with snow. The man wore a cloth cap, a tight-fitting heavy wool sweater, and baggy black trousers.

"Could I please, sir, to come in?" he asked as Martin stared at him. He had a slight Yiddish accent, which was unfamiliar to Martin, but he spoke well. Martin backed away from the door.

"To be sure, to be sure," he said.

With a springy step, as though he were bearing no burden at all, the man strode to the bar and set the keg down upon it. He bowed to Kathleen.

"We were not expecting a beer delivery today," said Martin. "Mr. Van Kriek was in yesterday and he said—"

The man removed his cap and shook the snow from it. He said to Martin, "It is not the Red Lion Brewery I represent, sir—you are Mr. Morrissey?"

"Please sit down," invited Kathleen.

The man did so and Martin and Kathleen joined him at the table. Martin held out his hand.

"I am—I am Martin Morrissey and this is my wife, Kathleen."

The man shook Martin's hand in a firm grip and bowed in a stiff, courtly manner to Kathleen. Martin was impressed by the power of the handshake. The man was strong. He had broad shoulders and a barrel chest, and the musculature of his arms, shoulders, and chest showed beneath the ragged wool sweater, which seemed too small for him. He had a round, olive-complected face with a sparse coal-black mustache and short, curly coal-black hair. The predominant feature of the face was an exceptionally large, slightly hooked nose. It was the face of a very young man, except for the eyes. Deep mahogany, verging on ebony, they were the eyes of an old man. They shone with what seemed to Martin an expression of sorrow, patience, and wisdom.

"I am Max Kessler," the man said, "and I would like to supply your establishment with my beer."

He stood up.

"Allow me," he said, and walked behind the bar and took a

mug and filled it from the keg he had placed on the bar. He brought the mug to the table and held it out to Kathleen.

"Taste, please, Mrs. Morrissey," he requested.

"But we can't afford—" Kathleen started to say. Kessler shook his head.

"Afford! Afford! Afford we will talk about later. Please to taste."

Kathleen did, and handed the mug to Martin, who also drank. He wiped the foam from his lips.

"Oh, a good brew. Good," he said. "But as Mrs. Morrissey says, we can't afford—we still owe Mr. Van Kriek. . . ."

Kessler sat down at the table again.

"I know. Times are hard. Many establishments cannot pay the Red Lion Brewery. Mr. Van Kriek has many employees, a crushing overhead. He must be paid. The Kessler Brewery is small, but one day it will be the largest in the city. Today I have an old frame house in Harlem, one of the largest there. Soon I think it will fall to the ground. But it is three stories. I live there and also have my brewery there. I have only one employee, a fine Dutch brewmaster, who worked one time at Red Lion, when I also worked there. . . . Drink a bit more," he urged Martin.

Martin sipped again.

"I do not get the water from the city wells," said Kessler. "I go twice each week to the Bronx River, and bring back water to my brewery in Harlem. Then Friedrik and me we brew the beer, and I keg it and make the deliveries."

"But Mr. Kessler," said Kathleen, "we cannot pay—"

"This arrangement we will make. You pay Mr. Van Kriek whatever money you can afford each week or each month until you have paid off your debt to him. I will supply you my good Kessler brew and you will owe me for what you use. When you have met your obligation to Red Lion, and you are making a profit, then you can begin to pay me."

Martin said, "Well, we don't know when—"

Kessler waved a large, calloused, thick-veined hand at him.

"Do not worry, please, Mr. Morrissey. This is a fine country, a fine city. I come here when I am only fourteen years, an orphan, with nobody and no money. Now when I am just sixteen I already have a brewery. We will all work hard and work together and soon the bad times will be over. All will prosper once more."

Now as the new boxlike Kessler Brewery wagon rocked

over the hard dirt road of the upper Bowery, headed for Rivington Street, Martin said to his energetic eighteen-year-old Jewish beer supplier, "Max, Mrs. Morrissey and me, we appreciate your patience, but we already owe you two hundred and forty-one dollars and—"

"Ach, it is not so much. Very soon the depression will be over."

He smiled.

"Look at the miracle of this water system. Twelve million dollars they spend. So maybe the politicians steal a little, but forty miles the Croton water is carried through the aqueducts under the ground to the Harlem River. Then more pipes bring it across the High Bridge and farther on to the reservoir at Yorkville and yet farther to the new distributing reservoir at Murray Hill. Have you seen the Murray Hill reservoir?"

Last Sunday, after church, Martin and Kathleen had taken the babies and strolled with scores of others along the wide promenade atop the slanted, pyramidlike, huge stone walls of the new reservoir at Forty-second Street and Fifth Avenue.

"Yes, Max. It's remarkable, but—"

"And do you know," interrupted Kessler, "that already more than five thousand homes of rich people have pipes connected and they turn on the spigot in their own kitchen and get water right from the reservoir!"

"I know. A friend of ours, Tim O'Leary, has had the water piped in. He has a big villa on Thirty-seventh—"

"Him I know, too," said Max. "The councilman." He hurried on with his optimistic recital.

"Just yesterday I went to my bank on Wall Street. Have you not seen what they accomplished there—depression or no depression—since the big fire! The new Merchants' Exchange Building! The Federal Hall! It looks like a Greek temple! And the Customs House—"

A loud wail sounded suddenly from inside the wagon behind them. Max shoved Martin's shoulder.

"Better than talking, talking, talking about how much you owe me, Mr. Morrissey—you should climb back there and see what is the matter with one of my small friends."

Max Kessler was an accurate prophet. By mid-1843 the city was booming once again. Business at 106 Rivington Street picked up, but in the transition period between relative inactivity and the sudden onrush of dinner and suppertime crowds, the boisterous revelers drinking till midnight, the burden on Kathleen became intolerable. Between caring for the boys and running the tavern during Martin's police hours, she was losing weight and was so constantly overtired she could hardly sleep at night. John Deasy remarked on her haggard condition one Monday night, and suggested a solution.

"Why don't you sell the place, Martin, and join the police force full-time. They're desperate for strong, conscientious constables, and with your record I'm sure you could make sergeant in short order."

Martin and Kathleen talked it over that night and decided it was an excellent idea.

"We still owe Max over two hundred dollars," said Kathleen. "Maybe he'd be interested in buying the place."

Thursday of that week Max came in with his beer delivery. Over dinner Martin broached the notion to him. It seemed the Morrisseys' relationship with Max Kessler was destined to be blessed by fateful coincidences. Just as he had appeared at their door, like some muscle-bound Santa Claus with a keg rather than a sack on his shoulder, to solve their beer dilemma, he now proved the immediate key to their new life. He reached across the table and enthusiastically grabbed Martin's right hand in both his.

"Mr. Morrissey! Mr. Morrissey!" he exclaimed. "I have been talking to real estate agents for two weeks trying to find a building right in the downtown section of the city for a new brewery. You have just sold me 106 Rivington Street!"

Oh, how well it all worked out in the beginning. Martin became a full-time member of the police force, assigned to the Broadway Squad in the precinct at 300 Mulberry Street. A builder had just constructed a row of neat but modest frame houses on West Fortieth Street between Sixth Avenue and Broadway. Kathleen saw the advertisement in *The New York Tribune*, which had been founded by Horace Greeley two years earlier, and was now the Morrisseys' favorite newspaper.

The notice said, "To let—Eight entirely new two-story cottages, piazzas and verandah fronts, courtyards thirty-five feet deep, filled with elegant forest trees. Four bedrooms, two parlors and kitchen and hard-finished walls with cornice and center piece. Possession given immediately."

The rent was one hundred thirty dollars per year. They moved into the new house in the spring. The Cassidys moved into the house next door, so Flossie was available to baby-sit occasionally. And before the year was out Martin made sergeant. He did well on the test, but the promotion was as much in recognition of his work in arresting and supplying the evidence to convict one of the slyest and most successful whoremasters in the city, a Reverend Horace Whiteheart.

9

Father Boland, celebrating his eightieth birthday with a corned beef and cabbage dinner cooked by Kathleen, was the unlikely tipster in the Whiteheart case. Still bright-eyed, though completely bald and wrinkled as a raisin, he and Martin sat in the front parlor of the Morrissey house on Fortieth Street. Kathleen was in the kitchen and Ned and Patrick had already gone to bed. Kathleen had cooked the cabbage to a mushlike consistency and had boiled the beef so thoroughly that the old, almost toothless priest had no trouble chewing it. Now the good Father sipped a glass of brandy and lighted his pipe.

"Aagh!" he said again. "That was as fine a meal as I've had in many a moon, lad. That Kathleen o' yours is a jewel, she is; a genuine emerald, ye might say."

"Glad you enjoyed it, Father," said Martin and lifted his glass of Kessler beer. "Once again, a happy birthday to you!"

"Eh? Birthday, did you say?" The priest nodded and brought forth a bulky, folded paper from the inside pocket of his coat. He looked toward the kitchen to be certain Kathleen was not about to come into the parlor.

"We've got a new ally, lad, in our war on whoredom," he said in a loud whisper, handing the paper to Martin. Martin unfolded it. He had never seen it before. The logo across the top of the front page read, The Whiteheart Guardian, and beneath it, in boldface type, was the legend, Dedicated to Rescuing New York City's Fallen Angels. A two-line headline across the four columns of the sheet said, These Are the Young Women Who Are Today Prisoners in the Dens of Iniquity.

Martin had worked on the police force long enough to be familiar with the city's prostitution situation. The most elegant of the bawdy houses were on Church Street in the Park Place section, a block or two from some of the busiest hotels.

The police department estimated that there were probably ten thousand prostitutes in the city, if one included the freelance independents who worked around the hotels and the pitiful child whores of Five Points and other spreading ghetto areas. It was a depressing fact of life to Martin that most of the prosperous brothels were protected by corrupt police officials and patronized by many of the city's leading politicians, merchants, and businessmen. There was a rumor that two of the largest were actually owned by one of the city's councilmen, though Martin was sure it was not Tim O'Leary.

In recent months a number of shopkeepers and small manufacturers and jobbers had moved into the Park Place district and the plush bordellos were moving to Greene Street and Mercer Street to be nearer the newer hotels on Broadway. Greene and Mercer were the first north- and southbound streets west of Broadway.

Martin was surprised to discover that the entire four pages of the *Guardian* contained nothing more than a list and descriptions of prostitutes at selected whorehouses, interspersed with variations of a single message and a plea for funds. Under Number 8 Greene Street the first girl was described:

> GRETA—14 years of age; recently arrived from Bremen; clear complexion; unusually well developed for her age; bust, 34"; hips, 36"; blue eyes; blond hair. Has been trained and forced to perform acts in the French manner.

After every third or fourth entry, ruled off from the descriptions, was one version or another of the same message and appeal:

> YOUR HELP IS NEEDED!
>
> These unfortunate young ladies who have gone astray need your help. The Home for Fallen Angels is the only refuge in the city where repentant prostitutes are housed and cared for without cost until they can become self-supporting through honest labor. Support this good work by donating regularly to the following churches, which are patrons of The Home for Fallen Angels, or send your contributions directly to Reverend Horace Whiteheart at the address noted on page 4.

* * *

Beneath the solicitation were listed six places of worship: two Protestant; two Dutch Reformed; one Anglican and the Catholic, St. Peter's. Martin put the paper aside, and in a disbelieving tone, asked, "Did you say '*Ally*,' Father?"

"No! No! No lie, lad! The gospel truth! The Reverend Whiteheart has saved the soul of many a wayward lass."

Martin realized that Father Boland was not only becoming senile but was suffering increasingly diminished hearing. He indicated the *Guardian* and said in a voice, several decibels louder, "This is nothing more than a directory of whores!"

The old priest shook his head impatiently.

"We don't bring whores to the rectory, lad. The Home for Fallen Angels . . . that's where they go!"

"Is St. Peter's really supporting this—this charlatan?" yelled Martin. His voice was so loud now that even the deaf old Father was aware that Kathleen might hear. He looked toward the kitchen in alarm, then whispered, louder than he realized, "No, Martin! The church doesn't support the harlots! Whiteheart has this home—"

Kathleen came in then, and Father Boland hastily put the paper back in his pocket. He coughed into his hand and said, "Well, Kathleen, ye've made my birthday a truly happy one. Martin and me, we were just discussin' the new Ladies' Missionary Society. I'm told they're plannin' to take over the Old Brewery in Five Points."

"I've read about it," said Kathleen. "Now that the boys are a bit older, I'm thinking of offering my services."

Father Boland waved a shaky hand.

"Nothin' to be nervous about, colleen," he said. "Martin can tell ye, the area's well policed when the ladies are there."

The next day Martin began a quiet investigation and found that two of the clergymen were in league with Whiteheart and were being paid by him. The other three were as advanced in years and as susceptible to deception as the octogenarian Father Boland. Martin and three of his trusted officers, along with a reporter from the *Tribune*, descended on The Home for Fallen Angels on a Saturday night two weeks after Father Boland's birthday. The home on Greene Street was indeed decorated and furnished in the prim and simple style of a refuge for wayward girls. In the reception hall there was even an altar complete with cross and candles, and religious paintings and mottos on the walls. The small rooms of the girls were plain and clean, with comfortable beds. But the young women were hardly repentant. They dispensed their sexual favors with as much diverse technique and enthusiasm as the ladies in the most rococo brothels in the city. Whiteheart, who, of course, was a counterfeit reverend, and the two venal clergymen in league with him were arrested and convicted. Whiteheart was sent to prison for five years, and the clerical accessories to two years each.

Although arrests and convictions of this kind earned Martin a reputation as an able and honest law-enforcement officer, they did nothing to further his career. The powerful politicians and high-placed police officials who were growing wealthy on graft and corruption of every kind feared Martin. The *Tribune* and other newspapers were behind him, so his superiors dared not demote or fire him, but they saw to it that he did not win a precinct captaincy. John Deasy and Tim O'Leary were among those who constantly chided Martin, in a jocular and good-natured way, for his unswerving refusal to take advantage of any opportunity to enrich himself by overlooking what they called minor violations of the law, or occasionally abetting a moderately illegal operation. But Martin was content with his life. And so was Kathleen. The boys were growing, healthy and bright. And while Martin would furiously (and sometimes with physical violence) reject any proffered bribes to turn his back on or participate in illegal activities, he was not reluctant to accept gratis admissions and other small favors from the many friends he developed in his police work.

He was on excellent terms with the owners and/or managers of the city's theaters, museums, and other places of amusement. He and Kathleen had both come to love the theater and often went to the Park or the Bowery or the Purdy National. On special occasions he took her to Niblo's Garden or Castle Garden to see various acts or popular singers or dancers. When these entertainment centers featured an attraction which would appeal to the boys, Martin and Kathleen would take them along. At Niblo's one week the European Ravel Family of Pantomimists were performing. At one point in this astonishing act, what appeared to be a huge grindstone was "accidentally" rolled over Garibaldi Ravel, the father of the family. When the shocked family members lifted Garibaldi from the floor he looked like a great cutout of a cardboard man, flat and thin. They placed the cutout on a lounge and the sturdiest of the sons rushed offstage in pantomimic panic and returned with an enormous bellows. He inserted it into the cutout and pumped and pumped and the cut-out figure swelled, and soon Garibaldi, in his normal size, sprang up from the lounge and bowed to the amazed audience. Ned and Patrick were speechless at this miracle.

The boys also enjoyed the visits to Barnum's American Museum on the corner of Broadway and Ann Street. They stared up in wide-eyed wonder at the giant-sized paintings of fierce beasts and strange creatures, and the colorful flags of all nations, which covered a goodly portion of the front and sides of the building. Inside they were awestruck. Martin introduced them to old P.T. himself, and Barnum told them a few outrageous stories about some of the monstrosities in the display case. He introduced them to General Tom Thumb, the world's smallest man. Both Ned and Patrick were already taller than the Barnum midget, who was a lad named Charles Stratton. Barnum also gave Martin and Kathleen choice seats to the Jenny Lind concerts at Castle Garden.

Another favorite of the Morrisseys was the Original Christy Minstrels, who played continuously at Mechanics' Hall at 472 Broadway. The star of the show was George Christy, who introduced what the minstrel showmen called "wench" characters. His blackface "Lucy Long" and "Cachuca" were hilarious caricatures. George's real name was Harrington, but he had adopted the Christy name at the urging of the owner of the group, E. P. Christy.

Through another friend, Harvey Hutchings, captain of the harbor police, whose headquarters was City Steamboat Number 1, Martin secured season passes for the entire family on the commercial pleasure steamboats, which made regular excursion trips up the Hudson. Of all the family activities, the one Kathleen loved best was to steam up the sparkling green river, sitting quietly with Martin on a bench near the prow, holding hands, luxuriating in the soft summer breeze and talking about how good the Lord had been to them, how happy they were over the life they had made together. Drifting lazily by the lush verdant banks on both sides of the river reminded them both of Ireland. When they disembarked far north of the city proper, Kathleen would spread a sheet and lay out a picnic repast, while Martin played games and roughhoused with the boys.

One of Martin's friends in the municipal government was Alexander Cartwright, who was a city surveyor. Cartwright and several other cricket players and followers developed a game based on a sport originated by an Abner Doubleday in Cooperstown, New York. Cartwright designed the game with four bases, placed to shape a diamond. The bases were approximately sixty feet apart, and there was a path from the home base to the center of the diamond, where a pitcher threw the hard ball to the batter at home base. Cartwright organized a team called the New York Knickerbockers and arranged a contest with another team named the New York Nine.

Martin and Tim O'Leary took Ned, Patrick, and Mike O'Leary to see the game. On the ferry across the Hudson to Hoboken, eleven-year-old Mike and seven-year-old Ned raced all over the boat, getting into one mischief after another, much to the annoyance of some of the passengers. O'Leary ignored his son, and Martin yelled at Ned every now and then to behave, while listening to O'Leary's derogatory comments on the new mayor, James Harper, who was a partner in the book-publishing company of Harper and Brothers. Harper was a reform candidate, and the flow of profitable arrangements in municipal-government operations had been considerably slowed down.

"The man is a nativist as well as a would-be reformer!" said O'Leary. "You remember the 'No Popery' banners they used during his campaign."

Martin nodded, reached out and caught Ned by a shoulder as he raced by with Mike in hot pursuit.

"Sit down there with your brother and rest for a minute, lad," he ordered gruffly, shoving Ned toward the bench where Patrick was engrossed in his first-grade primer. Both the boys were attending the ward school. Ned was only a fair student, but Patrick was exceptional. He seemed to have an almost unnatural hunger for learning. He was not as proficient a one-o'-cat or two-o'-cat ball player as Ned or Mike, but he was as interested in the game they were going to see as they were. They arrived finally at Elysian Fields and cheered and yelled as they watched the New York Nine defeat the Knickerbockers by a score of 23 to 1 in a four-inning game.

The relationship among the Morrisseys, the O'Learys, and the Deasys survived through the years. They visited and occasionally dined at one another's homes or attended various events in a number of combinations. Sometimes the entire families participated; sometimes the Morrisseys visited with either the Deasys or the O'Learys. As the years passed young Mike O'Leary was an increasingly vivid living reminder of Stephen. He not only had Stephen's blond hair and glittering blue eyes but as he matured he displayed more and more of the same neurotic, yet carefree and often reckless, attitude toward life.

The similarity to Stephen Boyle was so striking that no member of any of the three families (excepting, of course, Mike himself and Ned and Patrick) could be unaware of it. As the likeness became ever more evident with each passing year, John and Ann Deasy had discussed it from time to time. Martin had once made a comment on it, but Kathleen had quickly cut off the conversation and Martin had never brought it up again.

Neither Tim O'Leary nor Mary ever mentioned it. O'Leary had been cold and indifferent to Michael from the day of his birth, and Mary had worshipped him and tended him lovingly if spasmodically during his first three years. But as she increased her drinking, carried on occasional casual affairs, and got involved in her personal war against the day's abolitionists, she left his care almost exclusively to his nannies, and treated him with an indifference that all but matched Tim's.

O'Leary was a twenty-four-hour-a-day politician. He and Mary had separate bedrooms in their elegant villa, and had had no intimate relations in years. Mary suspected that Tim had a Negro mistress, but said nothing about it. She was still an avid follower of boxing. The fanatic rivalry between native Americans and the Irish, which her father and Billy Brannigan had predicted years earlier, had developed with a vengeance. Mary delighted in dressing in fine men's clothes, concealing her gray-flecked auburn hair beneath a stovepipe hat, and attending bouts with Tim. At forty, she easily passed as just another of the florid-cheeked, red-nosed prosperous Irishmen in the boisterous fight crowd.

Boxing was the one pastime in which she and Tim had maintained a mutual interest. Indeed, O'Leary derived great amusement out of accompanying his masquerading wife to the matches. He turned a blind eye to the casual affairs she carried on from time to time with some of the Irish boxers.

Tim and Mary traveled to Still Pond Creek near Baltimore on a bitter cold day in February to see the first contest for the heavyweight championship of the United States. It was between Tom Hyer, a powerful young native American, and a vicious fighter named James Ambrose, who was born in Ireland but called himself Yankee Sullivan in the ring.

Tim and a group of fellow politicians had bet five thousand dollars on Sullivan. Hyer's father, Jacob, a Dutchman born in New York City, had been a fighter in his own time, and had defeated a prominent heavyweight named Tom Beasley as early as 1816. He had taught Tom well, and young Hyer battered the tough Irishman into submission after sixteen bloody rounds. Mary had a brief affair with the defeated Sullivan, but he left New York, and she lost track of him.

His departure did not bother her. She soon became involved with a rough scar-faced newcomer to the city, Isaiah Rynders, who had gained considerable political power. He owned seven saloons in the Paradise Square area of the Five Points, and had established a headquarters called the Empire Club, where most of the city's politicians (including Tim O'Leary and John Deasy) came from time to time to make deals. Most important, Rynders had been able to form a coalition of all the Five Points gangs, and he was their unquestioned leader. One-Eye Mulchahy and Terrible Tommy Malone had been liquidated along the way in undisciplined gang wars. Rynders made the gang services available to any individual or group who could pay. Mary often joined him and members of the special riot groups on the occasions when they went out to break up abolitionist meetings.

Mary's relationship with Kathleen was potentially explosive. There was a guarded hostility between them, which surfaced only on the relatively few occasions when Mary would become drunk enough to make some sarcastic remark about Kathleen's good works, the time she spent with the Ladies' Missionary Society or in various charitable activities concerned with St. Peter's. Infrequently, when she was drunker than usual, she would make some derogatory comments about Ned or Patrick and compare then unfavorably to her bold, handsome Mike. Kathleen ignored such remarks, usually pretending she had not heard them or naïvely misinterpreted their meaning. Martin would cut Mary off curtly now and then, but usually he ignored her too.

All in all, however, John and Ann Deasy, Mary and Tim

O'Leary, and Kathleen and Martin Morrissey had come to accept young Mike's existence as an obvious, unchangeable fact. They lived with it without comment, each of them reflecting on the boy's origins and surrounding circumstances only as the tragic, star-crossed episode surfaced occasionally in their consciousness or in their dreams or nightmares. Young Ned Morrissey idolized Mike O'Leary. He was fond enough of his brother, but found him dull compared to Mike. He followed enthusiastically wherever the older boy led. The summer after the first baseball game at Elysian Fields Mike led him into the most traumatic and painful experience in his eight years.

One of the summer adventures Mike and Ned shared was waiting at the ferry landings on the Hudson on mornings when scores of cattle from various New Jersey farms were herded ashore and driven to one of the west side slaughterhouses several blocks inland. There was real excitement in watching the cowherders on their well-trained horses whip and guide the mooing and bleating beasts through the streets. Mike found the slaughtering of the animals in the open pens even more thrilling than the drives. The mournful wailing of the terrified beasts, the sight of the blood spurting from their slashed throats made his heart beat faster, his palms sweat, and his blue eyes glisten madly. Ned enjoyed the cattle drives but hated the slaughtering. Yet he feared to admit it lest Mike think him feminine and cowardly. He had all he could do to keep from vomiting, not only at the gory sight but at the horrible smells coming from the open abattoir. On most occasions he was able to hold back till Mike left him when they reached the O'Leary villa on Thirty-seventh Street, and Ned continued north, heading for Fortieth. Then he would throw up and retch until he thought his stomach would catch in his throat.

The city's population had been growing and more livestock, as well as foodstuffs of every kind, were being brought in daily. The slaughterhouses had originally been exclusively on the West Side close to the ferry landings or railroads on which the beasts were brought in.

In the second week of a hot and humid July, Mike had learned that an unusually large consignment of cattle was going to be driven all the way across town from the ferry landing on the Hudson to the Stanton Street slaughterhouse. He had saved several packages of fireworks from the Fourth of July celebration at the family villa just a week earlier.

"This will really be a lark, Ned," he told the younger boy the day before the Wednesday on which the crosstown cattle drive was to take place.

"You know how busy Fifth Avenue is in the middle of the day. Just when the herd begins to cross Fifth, we'll light a couple of strings of crackers and throw 'em into the pack."

"Don't you think somebody might get hurt?" said Ned.

"Nobody's gonna get hurt. They'll all just scramble like the devil's chasin' 'em. The horses'll run round like crazy and the people in the streets—"

Ned interrupted, a nervous, troubled look on his face. "We could get in a lot of trouble," he said.

"Well, you don't have to do it if you're scared," said Mike contemptuously. "I'll do it myself. I don't know why I bother with you anyway. My mother's right. I ought to run with kids my own age, not babies—"

They did it. They waited in the doorway of a dry-goods store on Fifth Avenue, just south of Twelfth Street. The avenue was extremely busy at this hour of the sunny summer morning. Pedestrians ambled along the street; carriages, wagons, and carts wheeled and rocked at various speeds north and south along the cobblestoned road. Suddenly from the west came the sound of the cattle, like distant thunder. Then as the herd crossed Sixth Avenue and came closer, the yelling of the cowhands and the complaining lowing and bleating of the doomed bovines could be heard, counterpointing the beat of their hooves on the dusty dirt road. It sounded like a thousand muffled Indian drums.

Ned licked his dry lips and crossed one foot over his opposite shin, squeezing to keep from wetting his pants. The large string of firecrackers were becoming moist in his sweating hands. He wondered if he would be able to steady himself enough to light the explosives.

"Get ready, Ned!" said Mike, his voice trembling with excitement. The pedestrian and horse-drawn traffic on the avenue staggered erratically to a halt as the herd from the west came closer. Then the ragged line of cattle, shouting cowboys riding their flanks, came through.

"Wait till half of 'em are almost across the avenue, like I told you," ordered Mike excitedly. He lit his own long string of firecrackers and just as the last twenty or thirty of the herd were entering the avenue behind the like number which had preceded them, he stepped from the doorway and hurled the firecracker. It fell into the herd's midst. Ned's hands were shaking so hard he could not light his own string of explosives. After several fumbling tries, in panic, he threw the unlit string in the same direction Mike had thrown his.

In seconds the busy avenue at Twelfth and just north and south of the intersection erupted into an ear-shattering, chaotic scene out of a dreadful black comedy. Mike's string of potent fireworks crackled like gunshots and spat terrifying sparks into the eyes and snouts of a knot of steers and cows roughly in the center of the herd. Startled and frightened, these beasts snorted and lowered their heads and charged, digging their horns into the cattle blocking their paths leading away from the darting flashes and whiplike sound of the explosives. Crazed animals broke out of the mass and stampeded and hurtled in every direction.

Above the bellowing and bleating, the wailing and the snorting of the bovine pack, rose the furious cursing and shouting of the cowhands, skillfully racing, whirling about on their horses, futilely attempting to whip the panicky beasts back into an orderly group. In the street more wild shouting and screaming came from the drivers of carriages, wagons, and carts and from individuals on horseback.

Two gaunt cows, racing almost in tandem, blindly ran into a farmer's wagon broadside. The wagon was carrying three score of chickens in thin wooden slat crates. The vehicle toppled, crates shattered, and the air around the cursing farmer, who had been driving, was suddenly full of feathers and hens and roosters, furiously beating their wings. The birds fell to the street, cackling indignantly, mincing about in wing-flapping confusion, like sixty Chicken Littles warning of falling skies. A man in fashionable riding apparel tried to rein his horse out of the path of another onrushing steer. He had just succeeded in wheeling the gelding to the left, when the steer charged into the horse's flank, ripping the flesh to the bone. The horse toppled to his side, kicking frantically. The rider managed to stumble clear as he fell.

On the sidewalks men and women raced into doorways for safety. Five yards from Ned a young woman in a long white taffeta dress and broad-brimmed, beflowered bonnet was pushing a baby in a tasseled, hooded carriage. Ned heard the woman scream and saw the desperate look in her wide eyes. He looked in the direction in which she was staring, and saw a snorting steer, plunging toward the carriage. Ned dashed forward and dived to push the front of the carriage hard into the young woman standing behind it. She staggered backward several steps, then fell onto her behind, screaming, but pulling the carriage with her. The carriage rocked from side to side for a moment, but the startled, crying baby did not fall out. The charging bovine, head lowered, slashed his left horn into the fleshy part of Ned's buttock as he roared by. The animal raised his head, snorted again, and galloped back to the herd as one of the cowhands rushed forward on his horse, snapping his long whip and shouting.

The pandemonium continued, but in less than forty minutes, the cowhands, aided by several of the sturdier farmers in the crowd and three policemen, who had rushed to the scene from the Sixteenth Precinct on West Twentieth Street, brought the cattle back under control and the drive continued on to the Stanton Street slaughterhouse without further incident. A walrus-mustached man had seen Ned throw his string of firecrackers and he came forward hysterically to identify him for the policemen. Mike had slipped away when the officers from the Sixteenth came dashing into the street. The young woman whose carriage Ned had pushed out of the path of the steer pleaded with the officers that he should not be punished.

"He saved my baby's life," she testified tearfully.

But the officers took him to the precinct anyway. There a doctor treated the seven-inch-long, half-inch-deep gouge in the meaty part of his right buttock. They assumed he had accomplices in the idiotic adventure, but he insisted he did not. No one had seen Mike throw his fireworks, and Mike did not come forward. Because Ned was the son of the well-respected Sergeant Morrissey, he was released after being questioned for most of the rest of the day. However, Martin had to pay the farmer whose chickens were scattered about, for the damage to his wagon; the man who owned the carriage the steer had punctured; and the price of the gelding, which had been gouged by the steer and later died. The young woman whose baby Ned had saved wrote Martin and Kathleen a letter saying they should be proud of their son, and thanking Ned again for the valiant deed. Martin did not thank him. He rarely spanked the boys, but when Ned insisted he had done the foolish deed alone with fireworks he had taken from the July Fourth celebration at the O'Learys, Martin turned him over his knee. Gouged buttock notwithstanding, Martin paddled him until Ned finally could stand the pain no longer, and cried and wailed in agony. Kathleen cried, too, when Ned limped off to his room, tears streaming down his face.

"Maybe you were right in paddling him, Martin," she said, "but I'm proud of him. . . . And I'm sure Mike O'Leary put him up to it."

"That may be, Kathleen, but if so, he lied to us on top of endangering people's lives. And he's responsible for his own actions, no matter who tries to influence him."

"He just didn't want to be an informer. And he did save Mrs. Vandemeer's child," insisted Kathleen.

Martin nodded and grinned at her.

"I'm proud of him too," he said.

Ned could not sit down for ten days.

The event had something to do with another change in city policy. In 1850 all cattle drives below Thirty-fourth Street were forbidden. But the drives were only one part of the growing city's problems with livestock. Disposal of the inedible and unusable remains of the animals was yet another. A neighbor of the Morrisseys on Fortieth Street, William Reynolds, was part of the solution. He held a contract with the city to pick up and dispose of the remains of any dead animals, offal, and other heavy and unsanitary refuse that collected in the streets. A profitable part of his operation was picking up the horns, hooves, and other large bones from the abattoirs (just as the tanners bought the hides) and selling them to the bone-boiling works in the city. Brush handles were made from a few of the suitable bones, and the rest, along with the horns and hoofs, were ground into bone-meal fertilizer or used to produce glue. The stench emanating from the bone-boiling plants was extremely offensive to neighboring residents.

In response to their protests the Health Department closed down all the bone-boiling works. With the profitability removed, Reynolds, of course, ceased picking up the bones from the abattoirs and they simply wound up in various streets with the other mounting refuse. The city's street sweepers, like Flossie Cassidy's father, H.S., could not handle the carcasses of animals, small and large, which littered so many streets, nor the heavy bones, which were discarded after the butchers and tanners got through with the slaughtered animals. The street sweepers' efforts were limited to sweeping up minor litter and primarily the manure, which the horses drawing the streetcars and other conveyances dropped in persistent profusion. (Thus, incidentally, Harry Samuel Cassidy's initial nickname, H.S. There was always a slight aroma of manure about him.)

Martin, H.S., and Bill Reynolds were discussing the situation one night during a poker game at the Morrisseys.

"The city's got to do something about it," said Reynolds. He showed the men the tally of what he had removed from the streets in the past month: The carcasses of more than 500 horses; 850 dogs; 163 cats; 22 hogs; 6 sheep; 1303 tons of butcher's offal; and 67 tons of refuse bones.

That summer the council leased Reynolds an island in Sheepshead Bay, far from the city, where he could dispose of his collections without offense to Manhattan's residents. But abattoirs and animal carcasses were only two of the problems the city faced. For Martin, Kathleen, and the boys, for the Deasys and the O'Learys, for Max Kessler, for all New Yorkers there were many others. Some pregnant with the potential for destroying the metropolis.

PART FOUR

Sergeant Morrissey

Tessie Kearns and Helen Van Wirtz

William Macready, Edwin Forrest,
Isaiah Rynders, and Ned Buntline

Riot at the Opera House

An Excursion on the Steamboat *Henry Clay*

"Our good city of New York has already arrived at the state of society to be found in the large cities of Europe; overburdened with population, and where the two extremes of costly luxury in living, expensive establishments and improvident waste are presented daily and hourly in contrast with squalid misery and hopeless destitution."

—Philip Hone, ex-mayor and distinguished citizen of New York, diary entry, 1847

"Pack the traffic of the Strand and Cheapside into Oxford Street and still you will not have an idea of the crush in Broadway."

—Isabella Lucy Bird, a London visitor to New York City, 1854

"The other day they were tearing down the Irving House. It is too old; it has been built at least ten years. New York is notoriously the largest and least loved of any of our great cities. Why should it be loved as a city? It is never the same city for a dozen years altogether. A man born in New York forty years ago finds nothing, absolutely nothing of the New York he knew. If he chances to stumble upon a few old houses not yet leveled, he is fortunate. But the landmarks, the objects which marked the city to him as a city, are gone."

—*Harper's Magazine*, June 1856

10

Martin had had a worrisome, sleepless Sunday night. The cause for Martin's insomnia was the uneasy situation that had been developing over the appearance of the well-known English actor William Macready in *Macbeth* at the Astor Place Opera House, the large theater of the elite at Astor Place and Broadway. The nativist groups in the city had become increasingly aggressive and fanatic with the mounting influx of foreigners into the city. They seemed ready to make trouble now by taking advantage of a well-publicized feud between English and upper-class supporters of Macready and working-class American admirers of the more melodramatic native player Edwin Forrest. Forrest was opening in a drama called *The Gladiator* at the Broadway Theatre, just a mile south of the Opera House on this same Monday night, May 10, 1849. Martin had not become aware that there had been any trouble in the Macready situation until the previous Saturday. After finishing his tour of duty that evening he had dropped in to visit his old friend Max Kessler. Kessler, now sturdier than ever and a prosperous twenty-five, had completely renovated the building at 106 Rivington Street. He had given up the restaurant and tavern over a year ago.

"There are today more than five thousand taverns in the city and almost two thousand beer gardens," he had explained to Martin. "There is no reason why I should compete with my own customers."

Max had also added a third story to the two-story edifice, and put a handsome brick facing over the front of the building. Across the entire width of 106, between the first and second floors, was a neat sign in large gold letters against a black background, which read, Kessler Brewery. Max's living quarters were on the newly constructed third floor, and on this Saturday night Martin sat with him in a parlor, furnished in a comfortable masculine mode.

"So how is Mrs. Morrissey and the boys?"

"Good, Max, good. We worry a little about Ned, but they're fine."

Max waved away Martin's concern.

"Ned is a good boy. We have more to worry about than a

little Irisher's mischief. Did you hear what happened last night at the Opera House?"

Martin had not. Although the theater's managers, Bill Niblo and Jim Hackett, were friends and always invited Martin and Kathleen to their openings, they rarely attended. The high-brow Shakespearean plays and operas did not appeal to them.

"I went last night with my friend, Professor Schoenbrun, who has just arrived from Germany. We are both fond of Shakespeare, especially *Macbeth*. But that fine actor Macready was driven from the stage by a large number of roughnecks in the audience."

"Was anyone hurt?"

"No, they threw only tomatoes, rotten eggs, and a few rocks, then Macready ran off. But it ended the evening. These Know-Nothing lowlifes are becoming very difficult!"

After church the following day Martin asked his friend Tom Shea, police captain in the Eighth Ward, whether he had heard any more details about the disorder at the Opera House.

"Yeah, I'm sure Rynders was behind it. And that goddam Buntline was out front before the show, making patriotic speeches."

The police department had been keenly aware of and deeply concerned by the increasing number of nativist secret societies that had sprung into being. There were organizations called the Supreme Order of the Star-Spangled Banner, the Wide Awakes, and at least fifty others. Horace Greeley, in his *Tribune*, lumped all these fanatics under a single name, the Know-Nothings. Shea also told Martin that Macready had decided to cancel the balance of his engagement after the Friday episode, but Niblo and Hackett had quickly organized a committee consisting of some of the city's most distinguished citizens, including Herman Melville and Washington Irving, and they had persuaded the English actor to reopen on Monday. Many of the city's newspapers had carried sensational stories, half-true, about the long-standing hostility between Macready and Forrest and their respective supporters.

"It could be serious," Shea told Martin. "Matter of fact we're meeting with the sheriff and Sanford of the National Guard at Woodhull's office this afternoon. Woodhull's worried."

Caleb Woodhull, a Whig and the city's new mayor, had been in office less than a week and he was in a state of near hysteria over the possibility of a larger and more serious riot at the Opera House.

As soon as Martin arrived in his office at Mulberry Street on the Monday morning following his discussion with Shea, he had been instructed to be prepared to take a force of men to the theater that afternoon at four o'clock. And now, shortly before noon, as he sat at his desk, plotting the positioning of his squad along the Broadway side of the playhouse, the man who looked like Mulchahy's ghost stood before him. At the startled expression on Martin's face, the one-eyed man said, "It's me, Sergeant. Mickey! Mickey Mulchahy!"

In a flash Martin remembered. One-Eye Mulchahy had had three sons, all approximately the same age, each by a different common-law wife in Five Points. During his earliest days as a part-time constable, Martin had arrested all three of them, young boys then, sometimes together with other young thieves, and occasionally each of them in separate petty thefts. He had liked Mickey. He considered him the least corrupted and the most stable of the three. The other two were sly, conniving, and much more vicious than Mickey. Much more like their father.

"Sit down, Mickey." Martin indicated a chair alongside his desk. "I didn't know you were back in the city. I thought you might've stayed in Mexico."

Mickey shook his head and took a soiled and folded heavy paper poster from the pocket of his ragged jacket.

"No," he said in a hoarse nervous voice, "I been back some time. I brung ya this, Sergeant. There's gonna be big trouble tonight."

Martin took the paper, unfolded it and read:

> WORKINGMEN!
>
> Shall Americans or English rule this city? The crew of a British ship recently arrived in our harbor has threatened all Americans who shall dare express their opinion on this night of May 10 at the English Aristocratic Opera House! We advocate no violence, but a FREE EXPRESSION of opinion to all public men!

"Where did you get this?" asked Martin.

Mickey took his cap from his shaggy head and wiped it across his sweating brow, then lifted his eye patch and dabbed at the sweat beginning to roll down his cheek from the eyeless socket.

"They gimme a hundred of 'em. I wuz supposed t' stick 'em all up an' down Stanton, Essex, and Rivington. They got twenny, thirty boys spreadin' 'em all aroun' town. They wanna pay me a dollar t' run my ass off. Rynders says 'e can't git me no decent job. He thinks all I'm good fer is puttin' up 'is fuckin' posters like some dumb schoolboy."

To Martin the poster indicated that Rynders was working toward a more substantial riot this night than the disturbance on Friday. Yet the poster's language did not sound like Rynders. Martin said so to Mickey.

"No. I know. They read it t' me. It's that Buntline wrote it. Fuckin' Rynders can't write no more'n I can."

Ned Buntline, whose real name was Judson, was a political propagandist and agitator, who had won considerable fame and fortune as the author of scores of dime novels of adventure. He also published a rabid nativist weekly, called *Ned Buntline's Own*, and was head of a nativist organization, the American Committee.

"I appreciate your bringing this in, Mickey," said Martin. "What happened to your eye?"

"Lost it in the fuckin' war. Them rifles they give us wasn't worth a damn. First time I fire mine, powder explodes right into my eye."

"Didn't you get out of the army?"

"Didn't wanna git out!" said Mickey. "They wuz glad t' have me. Fight jus' as good with one eye as two."

"Well, at least you came out alive. What happened to Francis Xavier and Xavier Francis?"

Martin knew that all three brothers had enlisted in the army in the second year of the Mexican War. Both Mickey's brothers were a few months older than he, and One-Eye Mulchahy had insisted they be named after him. When Mickey was born, he wanted to name him F. X., but the common-law wife who had borne him resisted.

"They wuz hanged, the dumb bastids," said Mickey. "Fuckin' Santa Anna, the Mex president, gits word t' all us 'Merican so'jers we should come over an' fight for the Mexskins. 'What the hell ya wanna fight fer a country hates Irishmen an' Cat'lics; fight fer a Cat'lic country,' 'e says."

"So your brothers went over?"

"Yeah, but not 'cause they listen t' that kinda bullshit. Santa

Anna says anyone who comes over'll git three hundred twenny acres o' free land. Me dumb brothers like the country an' specially them Mexskin women, so they desert. They wuzn't the on'y ones. More'n three hun'red stupid bogtrotters git together an' form a whole fuckin' battalion fer the Mexes. They even call it the San Patricio Battalion. Would ya believe them crazy fuckers! I wuz in the battle of Churubusco when we win the war. These ig'nerant Irishmen fightin' fer Santa Anna even got green banners with a harp an' a shamrock on 'em, and they come into the battle singin' Irish war songs."

"I never heard anything about that," said Martin.

"No, I guess the gov'ment here wouldn' want that kinda shit t' git around."

Martin shook his head.

"So you were fighting against your own brothers."

Mickey nodded.

"I didn't see 'em durin' the fightin'. But later I was in the hangin' party, when we strung up about fifty of 'em we captured, on a gallows right in front o' the San Jacinto Church. When I saw me brothers, I jes' walked away. I didn' wanna watch 'em hang. The fuckin' colonel got mad and said he wuz gonna shoot me. I told 'im t' go fuck hisself. That's when they threw me outta the army. Goddam war wuz over anyway."

He paused abruptly and looked apologetically at Martin.

"Jeezus Crise, Sergeant, ya got me talkin' about the fuckin' war like it wuz important or somethin'. I come t' tell ya that Rynders and Buntline're plannin' big trouble tonight."

"Thanks, Mickey."

"You wuz always pretty good t' me. An' maybe ya kin help me git a job."

"I'll talk to some people, Mickey."

President James Polk's longtime effort to acquire New Mexico and California was not of great importance to many in New York City. Mickey, his brothers, and hundreds of other New York Irishmen did not join the army out of patriotic fervor. They signed up for the cash bounty and because of the elemental fact that they would be able to eat regularly and be better clothed than they were in the Five Points. Polk had offered Mexico twenty-five million dollars for New Mexico and California, but after the war, the peace treaty signed at Guadalupe Hidalgo stipulated that the United States would acquire these territories for fifteen million. Despite the cost in a substantial number of lives, the war had saved the nation some ten million dollars, and had given valuable training to American career army men, such as Ulysses Grant, William Tecumseh Sherman, George McClellan, Robert E. Lee, Stonewall Jackson, and Jefferson Davis.

The poster Mickey brought in to Martin did indeed appear all over the city that Monday. And the riot it subtly urged did take place. More than ten thousand American workingmen, whipped into a frenzy by the fanatical Buntline and some of Rynders's more eloquent rabble-rousers, gathered around the Opera House and hurled insults, rocks, and paving stones at the combined forces of the police and the National Guard, who attempted to prevent them from breaking into the playhouse.

There were over three hundred police, some stationed inside the theater and others along the four streets that bounded the eighteen-hundred-seat Gothic entertainment palace. There were also eight companies of Guardsmen, who took a tremendous amount of verbal and physical abuse all through the long evening before they were forced finally to fire into the crazed mob.

When it was over, a little before ten o'clock that night, every window in the Opera House was shattered. The doors were battered down, and benches were ripped from their moorings. Macready escaped, but twenty-two people were killed. Five more died of their injuries in the week that followed. More than a hundred and fifty others were injured. Eighty-six rioters were arrested. Rynders got away, but Buntline, still ranting and raving, was taken in. Ten of the eighty-six rioters were convicted. Most got prison sentences of a month to a year. Buntline got the maximum penalty of a year in prison and a two-hundred-fifty-dollar fine. Martin Morrissey got a severe gash over his right eye, a headache that lasted two days, and a heartache that lasted much longer.

He was truly heartsick over what he saw happening in the city. A newspaper editorial the Saturday after the riot summed up his feelings. He read it to Kathleen at breakfast.

" 'There is a bitterness and a rancor remaining behind this tragic riot, which we fear will manifest itself on future occasions. It leaves behind a feeling to which this community has hitherto been a stranger, a feeling that there is now in our country and in New York City what every good patriot has hitherto considered it his duty to deny, a HIGH class and a LOW class.' "

"It's terrible, it is, but I fear it's too true," said Kathleen. She took Martin's platter and cup and saucer to the wooden tub on the counter.

"Holy Mary!" she screamed. "Stop them, Martin! Stop them!"

Martin dashed to her side and stared out the window in the direction she pointed. In the backyard Ned and Patrick were standing toe to toe, battering each other furiously, with hard, tightly clenched fists. Ned was four inches taller than Patrick and far stronger. Yet Patrick held his head down and traded blows with his brother without flinching. Martin raced out of the house into the yard and charged between the two flailing boys. He grabbed ten-year-old Ned by the shoulders and flung him four feet into a sturdy elm. There were tears in Patrick's eyes, the flesh beneath the left one was blackish blue, and blood flowed from his nose. Martin handed him a kerchief and stomped toward Ned.

"Now, what was that all about, you lout!" he shouted. "You know you're stronger and heavier and quicker than your brother! How many times have I told you not to fight him!"

Ned's face was unmarked. The best Patrick had been able to do was beat his arms and his upper torso. Ned glared sullenly at Martin.

"He knocked the ball over the fence into the Cassidys' yard and wouldn't go get it!"

Patrick shook his head, and trying to hold back his sobs, protested, "No, no, Papa. I was goin' to get it, but he hit me before I could even go for it."

Martin slapped Ned a backhanded blow across the cheek. "Get into the house! Go to your room and stay there. You can spend the rest of the day doing some studying. You can use a little more learning, sure enough!"

Chin on his chest, Ned trudged toward the back door, holding his hand to his stinging cheek. He knew Patrick was going to get the ball. He did not understand why he had hit his brother, and pounded him so viciously. What was the matter was that a half hour earlier he had masturbated. And like the good Catholic boy he was, he felt guilt-ridden, furious with himself, and dreaded the fact that he would have to tell Father Boland about it at confession on Friday. He had simply felt he must hit somebody and Patrick was there.

Mike O'Leary had introduced him to the orgasmic pleasures of masturbation two weeks earlier. They were in Mike's room at the O'Leary villa, and Mike took a copy of the latest issue of a pornographic magazine called *Venus Miscellany* from a secret place in his closet. The magazine had been denounced in the *Tribune* as containing articles and stories "worthy of the most vigorous intellect that could be found in the lower regions and illustrations fouler than the most morbid imagination could conceive."

The illustrations of men with substantial penises copulating with naked large-bosomed and sweeping-bottomed beauties stirred the boys. These pictures and others of more perverted acts soon caused them to have erections. Kneeling on the floor with the pages of the magazine opened to an amazing and acrobatic orgiastic scene, Mike quickly unbuttoned his pants and began to stroke himself vigorously, making odd little grunts of pleasure as he worked.

"Come on, come on," he urged Ned. "Get it out and jerk off!"

Ned shook his head, as he stared wide-eyed at fourteen-year-old Mike, who was beginning to look ecstatic.

"No, Mike. I can't. It's a sin," he said uncertainly.

Mike ignored him for a moment, closing his eyes and grinning blissfully. Ned watched him in awe as Mike ejaculated. Mike wiped himself with a handkerchief and sighed. Then he got up and went over to Ned and unbuttoned Ned's fly. Ned's small but erect member sprung out, extending at a forty-five-degree angle, like a rigid pink worm. Mike awkwardly began to masturbate him.

"You think God's got nothing to do but worry about a couple of boys jerkin' off?" he said, as he massaged Ned's small member with his fingers. When Ned's face showed the first signs of pleasurable sensation Mike stopped and took his hand away.

"Do it yourself!" he ordered.

Mike himself had become erect again. He turned the pages of the magazine to a picture of a man sodomizing a woman with buttocks large and round as balloons. Hesitantly, but gazing at the new picture, then at Mike vigorously massaging his larger member, Ned continued to stroke himself. In moments he ejaculated. The sensation was like nothing he had ever experienced before. It sent a delightful tremor through his whole body. But even as he cleaned himself he was overwhelmed by a terrible feeling of guilt.

In the weeks that followed, fighting to resist the temptation each time, he nevertheless had begun to masturbate by himself. Seconds after each ejaculation, he became unbearably disgusted with himself and tortured with guilt.

Oddly enough, over the years, Martin and Kathleen had reversed their outlooks on life. Martin became the worrier, and Kathleen the optimistic, understanding parent.

"I don't know what we're going to do with Ned," Martin said angrily every time Ned got into a new mischief."

"He's a growing lad," soothed Kathleen, "and just like his father, a bit adventurous and with a great fondness for an occasional scuffle. . . . I well remember what a sight you were when I first laid eyes on you, love."

"That was different," said Martin. "I wish he was more like his mother."

Patrick was like Kathleen. Not only in his appearance, with his pale, oval face, his soft, hyacinth-violet eyes, and lustrous, slightly curled brown hair, but in his quiet, soft-spoken manner. And Ned indeed was like Martin, large ears and all, stringy but muscular, strong and aching for a fight every now and again.

Martin's increasingly serious approach to life was attributable to his police work, to the things he saw in the city every day. New York was growing—Martin sensed it was growing out of control. The whole world seemed to be passing its problems on to the city. In Ireland the most devastating potato blight in its history brought famine, disease, and death. A million Irish peasants died between 1846 and 1849. Another million managed to escape across the short span of sea to England. Some went to Australia, but a million more crossed the ocean to North America, and huge numbers of them landed and remained in New York City.

In 1850 alone 117,000 Irish and 45,000 Germans came into the city, and that was not nearly the peak year. Two years later more than a quarter million aliens arrived at the Port of New York. In the decade from 1840 to 1850 the population leaped from just over 300,000 to well over a half million, with no end of arrivals in sight. By 1852 sixty-nine percent of all the paupers in the city were Irish, and more than fifty percent of all criminals arrested were Irish.

In Austria and Germany there was revolution and rioting, and those who could afford it made their way to America, with large numbers settling in New York City. What made the situation extraordinarily difficult was that many European towns, desperate to rid themselves of their sick, their unemployable, and their criminals willingly paid the passage of these unfortunate misfits across the Atlantic, generally about twenty dollars. And again, most of these landed in and remained in New York.

Oh, indeed, the city was growing. From the East River to the Hudson, from the Battery to as far north as Forty-second Street there were homes of every description. Along the East River tenements sprang up; everywhere shanties and shacks were patched together, sometimes cheek by jowl with huge, elegant brick, marble, or granite mansions. The upper west side, called Bloomingdale, was still mainly open country, wooded, lush, and verdant, but even here new homes were being built. More than five hundred people were living in a village called Manhattanville, far north at 125th Street around Broadway. And there were now fifteen hundred people living in Harlem. The more affluent, upper-middle-class Germans had created a *Klein Deutschland,* a Little Germany, which ran along the Bowery from Houston Street on the south to Twelfth Street on the north. Some were moving out to a new settlement called Yorkville at Eighty-fourth Street and Fourth Avenue.

Martin and Kathleen tried hard to do their duty as good citizens in these troubling times. Martin put in longer and longer hours at the Mulberry Street precinct, and frequently on the street with his men. He often worked twelve to fourteen hours a day, seven days a week, taking time out on Sunday only to go to church. Kathleen had become increasingly active in the Ladies' Home Missionary Society. A year after Father Boland died in 1851, the society finally did purchase the Old Brewery, in order, as they said, "to convert it from a pest-house of sin to a school of virtue."

Kathleen suggested the idea that before they proceed with the demolition of the dank, decrepit old building they invite middle- and upper-class New Yorkers and out-of-town visitors to make a tour of the infamous site. At the end of the shocking journey through the stinking, winding halls, the filthy rooms, the secret tunnels and passageways, the visitors were requested to make a small contribution to the society. These funds were used to organize and operate a day school, a Sunday school, and an employment bureau. Kathleen worked in the bureau three afternoons each week.

Indeed she was giving so much of her time to the society and St. Peter's that Martin complained finally that she was neglecting the upbringing of the boys. He insisted she curtail her outside activities and spend more time at home. Kathleen countered that Martin need not try to clean up crime in the city single-handed. She felt he should cut down on the number of hours he spent at work and devote more time to their sons. They were beginning to have many more arguments than they had ever had, and found themselves uncharacteristically short-tempered with each other.

Patrick was really no problem. He had read an article in *Harper's Magazine* about Samuel Finley Morse and his invention of the electric telegraph. The story of how Morse, a struggling, unsuccessful artist, fanatically pursued his dream fascinated Patrick. Since Morse could not buy insulated wire in the mid-1830s, when he originally conceived the idea of the telegraph, he had bought wire in small pieces and soldered it together inch by inch, foot by foot, and mile by mile, and then wrapped it in cotton thread. Of course, it had not worked.

Then, ten years later, he prepared a demonstration of the telegraph machine he was sure would prove successful. He waterproofed two miles of wire with tar, pitch, and rubber and laid it underwater from the Battery to Governor's Island. The newspapers published stories about the upcoming demonstration. A ship's anchor caught the underwater wire, the crew brought it up and cut it, and the demonstration was condemned as an irresponsible hoax. But Morse was not discouraged. Patrick excitedly read the last portion of the article aloud to his mother and brother one evening when Martin was again working late. It told of the day in May 1844, the twenty-fourth, when Morse, having strung a telegraph line from the courtroom of the Supreme Court of the United States in Washington, D.C., to Baltimore, tapped out in code the message "W-H-A-T H-A-T-H G-O-D W-R-O-U-G-H-T."

Patrick was truly inspired by the story. Ever since reading it he had been working as diligently studying the Morse code, and attempting to build a telegraph machine, as on his schoolwork.

Ned pretended to be impressed by the story, but his mind was still full of an incident that had taken place the previous evening. Mike O'Leary, now a dashing, handsome sixteen, had persuaded Ned to accompany him to an establishment on the lower Bowery called the Anatomical Museum. Artist-and model shows were proliferating in some of the Bowery's lesser showplaces such as the Anatomical Museum, Thiers Concert Hall, the Novelty Hall, and the Temple of the Muses. Mike paid the admission price of one dollar each, and he and Ned walked with a crowd of older men toward a doorway inside the theater. A curtain of gauze hung over the open doorway. Behind the curtain four naked ladies danced awkwardly. A guide, giving a lecture on the dance, then led them to another section of the museum where three naked men and three naked women, behind another curtain of gauze, cavorted in execrably executed versions of the minuet and the polka to the accompaniment of a screechy violin and an out-of-tune harpsichord. While the audience was gaping at the shocking scene, six policemen burst into the room, and Mike and Ned barely escaped capture.

Five blocks from the Anatomical Museum they came upon two Negro children, a skinny boy of about ten, and a sad-eyed girl of eight, begging in the street. Mike lifted the girl's long, ragged skirt and clutched at her groin. The boy tried to defend her and Mike beat him savagely. Ned was finally able to tear him away from the black boy, who ran off with the hysterically weeping girl following.

"What the hell'd you stop me for?" panted Mike, glaring at Ned.

"They didn't do anything to you, Mike. No reason you should beat 'em."

"I hate niggers," said Mike. "All of 'em."

11

Because Charley Taylor, the manager of Purdy's National Theatre, was a good friend of Martin's, he took Martin and Kathleen backstage after the performance of *Uncle Tom's Cabin* to meet the players. Kathleen's eyes were still red and moist, and she kept dabbing at them with her kerchief. She thought the melodrama the saddest and most moving she had ever seen. When Taylor escorted them into the dressing room of George C. Howard, Mrs. Howard, and their five-year-old daughter, Cordelia, Kathleen impulsively hugged the little girl, who had played Eva.

"You were wonderful, Cordelia!" she said. "Just remarkable, so sad . . ."

"Yes, she's quite an accomplished little actress," said the flamboyant Mr. Howard, who had played St. Clair. Kathleen nodded and turned to Mrs. Howard, who had portrayed Topsy.

"And you were most moving, too, Mrs. Howard," she said. "You must be very proud, all of you, you're such excellent players."

It was late when they got home to the house on Fortieth Street, and they were surprised to see the light still on in the front parlor. Ned was stretched out on the sofa, awake, hands behind his head, staring at the ceiling when they came into the gaslighted room. He was a tall, gangly thirteen that spring of 1852. He looked toward his parents with a half-frightened, nervous expression as he squirmed around to a sitting position. He rubbed his cheeks with both hands with a vigorous vertical motion.

"I stayed up because I have to talk to you," he said, his voice a little hoarse. Kathleen unpinned her hat and took it and a scarf to a closet, but looked back at Ned. Concern showed in her eyes. Martin stood over Ned and said, "What's wrong, lad?"

"I want to quit school," said Ned.

"You know that's out of the question, Ned," Martin said firmly. "It's important you get a good education. In another year or two you'll be ready for the Free Academy." The academy was the college the new Board of Education had opened on Twenty-third Street and Lexington Avenue. Kathleen sat beside her son on the sofa.

"What's wrong, Ned? What brought this on so sudden like?"

"Mike O'Leary's just bought a brig and is sailing her down to Norfolk on Monday, and I want to go with him. . . . When I get back I'll get a job."

What Ned was not telling his parents was that two young girls, models in the artists-and-models show at Palmo's Opera

House, were going on the voyage. One of them, Tessie Kearns, an extraordinarily well developed girl of fourteen, who used the stage name Fleurette, said she was in love with Ned, and he was madly infatuated with her. Ned was tall for his age, and his large-eared, eager puppy-dog awkwardness had an irresistible appeal to certain young women. Fleurette was a mermaid in the living statue of "Neptune Rising from the Sea," as well as Esther in the tableau entitled "Esther in the Persian Bath."

Martin, weary from the long day, said impatiently and gruffly, "It's out of the question. Get on to bed with you."

"School's a waste of time," said Ned sullenly.

Martin spoke angrily. "Don't make me tell you again, Ned! Get to bed!"

Ned rose and, muttering to himself, walked into his bedroom. That was on a Wednesday. The following Monday he did not come home from school at the time he was due. He had gone to Norfolk with Mike O'Leary and the tableau ladies.

"I'll give him the beating of his life when he comes back!" stormed Martin, when they learned that he had indeed sailed off.'

"It's that Mike O'Leary," said Kathleen. "Ned would be fine—"

"Goddamit! Don't say that, Kathleen. Don't blame Mike or anyone else for his stubborn stupidity. He's got a mind and a will of his own!"

Yet there was nothing to do but hope that he would come back at all. By mid-July Mike and Ned had not returned, nor had any word of them come to either the Morrisseys or the O'Learys.

Martin's professional problems, stemming from the city's unrest, continued. Not only did the slavery controversy intensify but the Morrisseys' own church added new fuel to the nativist fires. Martin and Kathleen were shocked at Mass on the second Sunday in July, when Father Dennehy, the young priest who had replaced Father Boland, preached a new revolutionary line in his sermon. Pope Pius IX had elevated the diocese of New York to an archdiocese and had raised Bishop John Hughes to an archbishop.

Father Dennehy told the congregation that the new archbishop had vowed that the only true church, the Catholic

Church, would convert all pagan nations, including all Protestant nations, even England.

" 'Let it be known,' " Dennehy quoted the new archbishop, " 'that it is our mission to convert the entire world, including the inhabitants of the United States, the people of the cities and the country, the officers of the Navy and the Marines, the commanders of the Army, the Legislature, the Senate, the Cabinet, the President and all.' "

Martin groaned inwardly as he listened to the orotund outpourings of the young priest. Martin considered himself a good Catholic, but he was also an officer of the law. And he knew what the Know-Nothings would make of the archbishop's radical new stance. *God bless Archbishop Hughes*, thought Martin, *and God help the Irish. God help us one and all!* He welcomed the invitation of his old friend Captain Henry Hutchings of the harbor police to come along and bring Kathleen and Patrick for a ride up the Hudson on the new steamboat the *Henry Clay* on Tuesday, July 27. He could use the day off, and Kathleen and Patrick would enjoy it. And, Hutchings told him, it would be more than just a languorous voyage up the river. The *Henry Clay* was to race another of the newer steamboats, the *Jolly Knickerbocker*.

The day of the race was clear and sunny, with the humidity relatively low for late July. They had just passed Yonkers and the two vessels were cutting through the choppy, deep green waters almost prow and prow. Thick, gray-white smoke belched from their stacks, drifting off into the bright, cerulean skies. The *Henry Clay*, running along the New York side of the river, was beginning to fall behind, slowly but steadily. Martin stood at the port side rail, amidship, talking with an old friend, former mayor Stephen Allen, about the plans the city was making for a world's fair the following summer.

"Have you seen the new hotels they're starting to build along Broadway?" asked Allen.

Martin had, and they talked about the St. Nicholas, the Aeolian, the Carlton, and several other of the hostelries on which work had already started. Lines of men to their left and right along the crowded rail commented excitedly on the closeness of the race.

Unconcerned with the contest, Kathleen sat in a deck chair under an awning on the starboard side of the steamboat, totally absorbed in a paperback copy of Mrs. Stowe's *Uncle Tom's Cabin*. She liked the book even better than the play at the Purdy. Using his father's influence, Patrick had received the captain's permission to go down to the engine room. He watched two sweating, muscular crewmen hurling shovelful after shovelful of coals into the maw of the huge boiler. They alternated to an unspoken but even cadence, with the precision of oarsmen in a sculls competition. But what really fascinated Patrick were the monstrous, gleaming engines.

Suddenly the world seemed to blow apart. The massive boiler exploded with a deafening roar. The *Henry Clay* trembled from stem to stern. Flame flashed through the engine room and within moments roared upward through the deck. The forward movement of the vessel and the northerly breeze swept it across the length of the ship. Patrick was catapulted by the blast through a huge jagged hole in the engine room's starboard side, where icy water had begun to spout through. The minute Martin heard the explosion, even before the raging fire burned across the deck, he dashed to the vessel's stern, elbowing, shoving, hurling panicky passengers out of his path. By the time he reached the stern, rounded the bend, and headed up the starboard side where he had left Kathleen, that section of the ship was ablaze. He could not see his wife through the soaring sheets of flame, sparks, and smoke. The air was filled with screams and cries of agony and terror and the crackling of the devouring holocaust. All around him people began to leap from the tilting, burning ship into the waters. Head bent low, his right arm shielding his eyes, Martin charged about like a madman.

"Kathleen! Kathleen!" he shouted, over and over, till he was hoarse. Once, up near the ship's prow, he saw a woman wearing the same kind of broad-brimmed sun hat that Kathleen had worn, but it was not Kathleen. It was a younger woman, having uncontrollable hysterics. Screaming, she clutched at Martin, but he tore himself loose and kept running about, trying to find Kathleen. Finally, choking from smoke, singed by flame, wracked by sobs, he flung himself over the side of the boat. The cold water was a blessed relief. He beat his arms and kicked furiously as he swam about in eccentric circles, shaking water from his eyes, still trying to sight his wife among the bobbing heads and flailing arms around him.

He did not see her, but after long minutes of thrashing about, some ten yards distant, he saw a wild-eyed woman and a small boy of perhaps five clinging to a log shaft of wreckage. Even as he spotted them, the woman's hands slipped from the large, white-painted splinter and she sank beneath the roiling waters. Martin stroked furiously toward the child, and caught him just as his hands, too, lost their grip on the floating, jagged piece of wood. Gasping for breath, Martin saw that he was less than a hundred yards from the New York bank. He struggled to cradle the terrified boy's chin in the crook of his right arm and maneuver him onto his hip. Swallowing so much water he became sick, he nevertheless swam strongly and stubbornly with his free left arm and hard-kicking legs to the shore.

There had been other occasional racing disasters on the river, when a steamboat crew raised excessive heads of steam in their eagerness to win, but the fire on the *Henry Clay* was the most catastrophic the city had ever experienced. Sixty-eight passengers lost their lives and many more were severely burned, injured, or reported missing. It took days before the majority of the bodies were recovered. Stephen Allen's corpse was pulled from the river on the second day. On the fourth day Kathleen's bloated body washed ashore just above Greystone, several miles south of Yonkers. Patrick's body was not found, and there was no word of him.

Max Kessler was the first of Martin's many friends to arrive at the house on Fortieth Street to offer condolences and comfort.

"Would you like me to go to Norfolk to see if I can locate Ned?" asked Kessler. "I can easily take the time off and I need a vacation anyway."

Martin shook his head. He felt a numbness, an emptiness after the disaster, which even precluded concern over his elder son. There was only a vague, unformed resentment that Ned was not here with him now. The Deasys and the O'Learys came to the wake, and Mary refused to take a single drink. She hugged Martin fiercely.

"Life stinks, Martin. You know that," she said in her hoarse whiskey voice. "They're probably better off out of it."

After a half hour, still refusing all offers of the whiskey which flowed freely at the wake, she took Martin aside again.

"I've got to go, Martin," she said and kissed him on the cheek. "I can't stand the smell of the goddam flowers."

Among the many floral pieces was a huge cross of white and red roses from the Ladies' Home Missionary Society. When Mary got home she drank a pint of Irish whiskey and passed out on her bed.

Ten days after Kathleen had been buried, Ned returned from Virginia. Martin had just come home from the Mulberry Street precinct and was sitting in the front parlor, staring dumbly into space, a habit he indulged ever more frequently these pointless days.

Flossie Cassidy, now a buxom, plain-looking young woman of twenty-four, with kind, compassionate gray eyes, had been keeping house and cooking for Martin since the *Henry Clay* tragedy.

"Will pork and greens be all right for supper, Mr. Morrissey?" she called from the kitchen. When Martin didn't respond, she repeated the question in a louder voice.

"Oh, yes, yes, fine, Flossie," said Martin. There was a knock at the door, and realizing that Martin would pay it no attention, Flossie went to answer it. Ned stood there, pale as flour, his eyes haunted and moist. Flossie stepped back and waved a hand toward the parlor.

"Your father's in there, Ned," she said solemnly.

Ned walked quickly to the threshold of the parlor. He stood there for a moment. Martin stared at him, grief and tears shining in his eyes. He shook his head and spread his arms in a hopeless gesture. Ned ran to him and fell to his knees before him. He put his head in his father's lap and began to cry in heaving, choking sobs.

"I—I'm—sorr—sorry, Papa."

Tears streaming down his face, he looked up at Martin. "For—for—forgive me, Papa. Please, please forgive me."

Martin pulled him to his feet and stood up himself. He hugged the boy tightly to him, and Ned, almost as tall as his father, returned the fierce hug. Each patted the other's back, over and over. Their tears blended as they kissed and tried to comfort each other. There were no words for what they were feeling, only the crushing embrace, the tears, and the kisses. Watching from the doorway of the kitchen, tears formed in Flossie's eyes, and she went determinedly to the counter and began chopping the greens.

Ned promised he would go back to school, and asked his father to get him a job for the balance of the summer. Before he and Mike had reached Norfolk, Ned had gone through an experience that altered his outlook on life and, particularly, on romance. He had left New York a young man in love for the first time in his life, and he was under the impression that

Tessie Kearns loved him too. She did, but halfway to the Virginia port town, he discovered that she loved Mike O'Leary just as well. Mike had suggested one night that they change partners; that Ned sleep with Helen Van Wirtz, the plump Dutch girl, who modeled under the name Michelle and who had been Mike's companion, and Mike sleep with Tessie.

Ned was shocked, but when Tessie giggled and clapped her hands and enthusiastically agreed, he was heartbroken as well. However, having no choice, he went along with the swapping arrangement. For many weeks he was uneasy with it, and had difficulty making love to either of the two models. But they were patient with him, and amused. Soon he adopted at least a surface cynicism, and decided he would pursue the same free-and-easy attitude toward females that Mike maintained. With all the seriousness of his thirteen years he vowed he would never fall in love again. In the meantime he began to enjoy the variety of sex the two girls offered with such abandon.

Of course when the brig landed in New York harbor and he learned from a policeman on the waterfront what had happened to his mother and brother, his romantic problems and pleasures vanished entirely. In a strange way he felt that his running away with Mike and his sinful activities had contributed to the tragedy, perhaps had even caused it. *A punishment! A severe punishment from the Almighty!*

At the Smith and Dimon Shipyards on the East River between Fourth and Fifth streets they were building two new clipper ships. Martin had gotten Mickey Mulchahy a job there, and he had no trouble getting them to take on Ned. The relationship between Martin and the boy grew closer and closer. On the first Friday after his return Ned went to confession and shocked young Father Dennehy with an embarrassed and stammering recital of his sexual escapades. Even though he could not see Ned's features in the dark confessional, Father Dennehy could tell from the sound of Ned's voice that he was quite young. He could not resist asking Ned's age. When Ned told him, he expressed shock and surprise.

"You are well on the road to perdition, young man," he said sternly.

It took Ned five hours in bed that night to say all the Hail Marys and Our Fathers the priest decreed as his penance.

Two weeks after Ned's confession, Mike O'Leary came by

the shipyard during one of the dinner breaks and asked Ned to accompany him that evening to a new bawdy house, featuring prostitutes of various colors and nationalities. He would be glad to pay, he told Ned. Ned told him he was going to Niblo's with his father that evening.

"Besides, Mike," he said, "I don't want anything to do with women any more."

"For crise sake, Ned, you can't quit livin', just because your mother and brother died!"

"Get the hell out of here, Mike. Leave me alone!" said Ned. Mike walked off disgustedly.

On a Saturday in mid-August Ned and Martin attended another baseball game at Elysian Fields. They got back to the house on Fortieth Street in the late afternoon. Flossie prepared a supper of roast chicken and dumplings. In the middle of the meal there was a knock at the door. Flossie went to answer it. Ned was saying, "I think Mulrooney was out in that play at third base—"

Flossie's piercing, hysterical shriek interruped his comment. Simultaneously Martin and Ned pushed away from the table and rushed toward the foyer and the front door. Ned beat his father by a step. Flossie was pointing with a trembling hand to two men in the doorway.

"It's—it's—" she stuttered in a high-pitched squeak.

"Godawmighty, lass, git control o' yerself," said a stout, gray-haired man, the older of the two. He grinned at Martin over Flossie's shoulder.

"Brought ye a little surprise, Marty!" he said, and with one brawny arm hugged the young man standing beside him affectionately, and pushed into the foyer. The young man had a livid scar along his left cheek, and the skin on his face was a deep copper color and tight on the ridge of his brown eyebrows, the bones of his cheek and jaw. There was an odd troubled look in his hyacinth-violet eyes. He looked somewhat like a young Indian brave. He was thin, but hard-looking and muscular. He was changed, but there was no mistaking him. Patrick had come back. He grinned shyly at Flossie and Martin and Ned.

"Hello, Papa . . . Floss . . . Ned," he said shyly. Martin, frozen in his tracks with surprise, suddenly came to surging life. He rushed forward and threw his arms around his younger son.

"Praise be to the Lord," muttered Flossie, making the sign

of the cross and wiping the moisture from her eyes. After almost crushing Patrick breathless, Martin finally released him and turned to the gray-haired man who had come with him. He shook the man's hand vigorously.

"God bless you, Jimmy Burns! God bless you! Where on God's green earth did you find this lad"

Ned was hugging Patrick now and the four went into the kitchen, trailed by a beaming, tearful Flossie. She had made a sufficiency of chicken and dumplings and the four men ate and drank copious quantities of Kessler beer, while Jimmy Burns, the captain of the Thirtieth police precinct at 131st Street in Manhattanville, and an old friend of Martin's, told about Patrick Morrissey walking into the precinct house that afternoon. And Patrick himself, haltingly and with some wonder, told them what had happened before that.

12

Patrick had not remembered that he was Patrick Morrissey until early that morning, when he listened to the produce wholesaler in Yonkers. Then it came back.

He had been standing at a rail in the engine room of the *Henry Clay* when the boiler exploded. The roaring boom was the last sound he recalled, but he had no recollection of what had caused the deafening noise. All in a split second an unseen battering-ram force slammed into his midsection, knocked the wind out of him, and drove him backward. The back of his head banged a beam. Boiling liquid seared the side of his face. Then he was miraculously catapulted out of what had been an inferno into chilling water. Instinctively he began to swim. It was blind good fortune that he swam toward the New York shore of the Hudson. He stumbled out of the water, alive and able to move, but with no knowledge of what had happened, no idea where or who he was.

He struggled up a grass bank and walked through a wooded area until he came to a dirt road. His cotton shirt and homespun trousers were tattered and clung to his body. There was a tremendous ache in his head and he could feel the hard bump on the back of his skull and the water-filled blister which seemed to cover the entire left side of his face. His legs seemed to be fine, except for a dull pain at both knee joints. This pain was similar to that which he felt in his shoulders and arms. He thought the discomfort in his joints might be from the distance he had swum.

He was deeply troubled by his total disorientation. He kept walking until twilight. He saw no one and no houses or structures of any kind. When the sun went down he walked off into the woods and collapsed beneath a huge oak tree. He did not know how long he slept. When he awoke the sun was high in the sky, almost directly overhead, so he thought it must be approximately noon. There was still the ache in his head, and he shook it and tried to remember who and where he was, but he could not. He walked through the woods until he came to a small stream. Even through the heavy-leafed trees, the hot sun had dried him. He stuck his head into the stream, washed his face and hands, and drank five handfuls of water.

Soon he found a narrow path in the woods that led to another, broader road. He heard the distant clippety-clop of a horse's hooves, and as he walked the sound became louder. He turned and saw a bearded, red-faced man with a large straw hat and a soiled gray shirt, loosely holding the reins of a sway-backed horse, coming toward him.

He moved over to the side of the road and the man brought the wagon to a halt beside him.

"Where ya headin', son?" asked the man.

Patrick shrugged. "I don't know."

"You lost?" There was genuine concern and curiosity in the man's kindly eyes.

"I think so."

"Climb aboard," said the man, tapping the hard wooden seat beside him. Patrick did, wincing as he clambered onto the seat.

"You're truly a mess," said the man as he flicked the horse's back lightly and made a clicking sound. The horse obediently plodded forward. Patrick just nodded.

"What happened to you?"

"I don't know."

"Are you sick?"

"No. I don't think so. My head just aches some."

"That's a nasty scar on your cheek. Did ya get burned?"

Again Patrick shrugged. "I don't know."

"Where ya from?"

Now Patrick looked embarrassed and troubled. "I—I'm—sorry, sir. I don't know."

"Saints alive, boy! What's your name?"

"I—I'm—not sure. I think maybe . . . Morse."

Between the wound on his cheek and his embarrassment, Patrick's pronunciation of the name sounded like "Mose" instead of "Morse."

"You hungry, Mose?" asked the man.

Patrick realized he was very hungry. He nodded. The man turned the wagon off the road onto a brush-flanked, narrow, hard dirt path, which sloped gently downward. Two hundred yards down the path they came to a two-story wood-frame farmhouse. The man's name was Silas Collins. He was in his midforties, two years younger than his wife, Helga. They farmed twenty acres and their single hand, a strong but lazy Italian, had just left them. Mrs. Collins prepared a huge platter of a half-dozen scrambled eggs and a ham hock and mashed potatoes for Patrick. When he finished the meal they questioned him again, but he apologized and told them again that he simply had no memory of his past.

They asked him if he would like to work on the farm and he accepted enthusiastically. All day as he worked under the hot sun, and half the night as he lay awake in the small spare room in the house, he tried to find some clue as to his identity, but it seemed hopeless. Then on the third day of his stay with the Collinses, Silas took him out to the barn and showed him how to hitch up a sturdy mule. The farmer patted the patient, long-eared animal on his neck, and told Patrick, "This is ol' Ned, Mose. They'll tell ya mules are stubborn, but ol' Ned here ain't nearly as stubborn as most horses, an' he's twice as smart and willing."

The name "Ned" struck a familiar chord in Patrick's brain. The long, hard hours in the clear air and the baking sun, and the hearty farm meals, had already done wonders for him physically. Now he hoped perhaps the shroud that encased his memory might fall away. Maybe his name was Ned, he thought. *Ned! Ned! Ned!* He repeated the name to himself, over and over, as he trudged behind the mule, patiently dragging the plow through the rich soil. In bed that night he had come to the conclusion that Ned was not his name, nor was it Morse or Mose. But Ned was someone he knew, someone who had been very close to him. He wondered if he had a father and mother, and if so, if they were alive. Perhaps he had brothers or sisters.

A week later he was quite sure he had a brother named Ned. He tried to picture Ned in his mind, but couldn't. Then on the following Monday he helped Silas load the wagon with produce, and they drove in to the market in Yonkers, some eleven miles south of the Collins farm. Collins had not been into the town in a month, so he had heard nothing of the *Henry Clay* disaster. But in Yonkers they were still talking about it, and about the persons still missing. Patrick listened with increasing excitement to the produce wholesaler's detailed and vivid account of the incident.

". . . goddam boiler exploded like somebody'd set off a ton o' blastin' powder in the middle o' that fancy boat. Blew two engineers all to hell'n gone. They found pieces of 'em in the river, next two, three days."

Silas Collins stared at Patrick. He was turning pale beneath his deeply tanned face.

"Was you . . . ? Mose? Was you on that steamboat?"

It came over Patrick in a rush. Horror showed on his face and tears formed in his eyes. He nodded dumbly.

"My mother—father—not Ned—my mother and father . . ."

When he told Collins his name was Patrick Morrissey and his father was a New York City police sergeant, they climbed onto the wagon and rode quickly to the northernmost police precinct, the Thirtieth at 131st Street in Manhattanville. Marty's old friend Jimmy Burns was stunned and overjoyed at the sight of young Patrick.

Patrick was devastated when he learned that his mother had drowned. But time and the loving attention of his father and brother gradually eased that grief. Less than two months after the new term began in the ward school, Patrick was again number one in his class. The amnesia he had suffered had cleared entirely. Indeed, he seemed more keenly intelligent than ever.

The same could not be said of Ned. He found it difficult to concentrate on his schoolwork. Having tasted the forbidden fruit so enticingly served up by the accomplished Tessie and Helen, he found it difficult at fourteen to resist the continuing urging of Mike O'Leary to resume their relationships. Nevertheless he was able to do so until one Saturday in late

February, when Mike and he had a date to go ice-skating on a pond near the O'Leary villa.

When they arrived at the pond, Ned was surprised to find Tessie and Helen waiting for them. The four skated for several hours, as the snow fell pleasantly and lightly. Ned, skating arm in arm with Tessie, frequently, sometimes unintentionally, brushing against her firm bosom, realized that her appeal for him had hardly diminished.

"I've missed you, Neddie," she told him, smiling up into his face.

"Well—well—I've missed you, too, Tess. But I've been very busy."

"You're not busy tonight, are you?"

"I—I—why . . . ?"

"Mike has taken a suite at the new St. Nicholas hotel. Have you been there yet?"

"Not inside. I've seen it, but I've never been inside."

When they skated to the shed at the side of the pond, and rested while they sipped hot coffee, Mike took a bottle of rum from the deep pocket of his wool-lined jacket. He poured generous portions into all of their cups. After the second cup of the rum-laced coffee, he told Ned about his plans for the evening at the St. Nicholas.

"They've got room service," he said. "We'll order up a dinner and some champagne and then we'll fuck all night long!"

Ned knew that his father would be attending a police banquet that evening, and that Patrick had a meeting of a science club to which he belonged. He put up a token resistance, but soon persuaded himself that it could not hurt to have one more fling with Tessie Kearns. In late afternoon they climbed into Mike's elegant carriage-sleigh and raced through the streets downtown to the St. Nicholas. Ned had never seen anything like the St. Nicholas hotel. Neither had anyone else in New York City. It ran one hundred feet along Broadway, and two hundred feet through to Mercer Street. It was six stories high, of white Westchester marble in an Italianate mode of architecture.

The hotel manager, standing alongside his assistant, whispered as Mike and the group walked by. "We're going to have to talk to Councilman O'Leary about young Michael. He and his friends are not the most desirable type of St. Nicholas guest."

The assistant manager turned away and grinned cynically to

himself. Alderman O'Leary had saved the St. Nicholas a great deal of money by exerting his influence in eliminating some of their building-code problems. He knew that young Michael would have to create a public riot before the hotel would challenge him.

Ned was ill at ease, but Tessie and Helen gaped in awe at the elegant surroundings. Mike took them into the hotel bar, which was to the left of the reception desk. The bartender hailed him.

"Well, young Mr. O'Leary! What may we serve you and your friends today!"

Ned ordered a Kessler beer and wondered if the barkeep would make an issue of serving him. He not only did not question Ned, but briskly set the whiskies Mike had ordered before him and the girls. After they had several drinks at the bar, Mike led them up a grand staircase, built of white oak, to the second floor, which was the most extraordinary of all the six floors in the hotel. The hall was two hundred feet long, lined on both sides with a succession of mirrors.

Tessie and Helen went into the ladies' parlor, gazed wide-eyed and made awe-filled comments about the ornate décor and furnishings. Finally Mike led them to the private suite on the fifth floor. He swung open the doors. There was an oversized rosewood bed with a white satin canopy. The bed was covered with white lace and satin.

"I'll wager you two little trollops've never been fucked in a bed like that!" declared Mike.

The girls gigglingly admitted they had not. Mike took them into the drawing room. On one wall, near a handsome white oak table and four chairs, was a large pearl button in the center of a dial.

"This is the annunciator!" said Mike.

On the dial in neatly calligraphed letters separated by fine black lines were the services guests could summon: Laundry, Bellhop, Ice Water, Room Service. Mike deftly turned the dial to Room Service, pressed the button, and said, "There will be a French waiter here in a moment to take our order for dinner."

"Gawd's sake!" commented Tessie. "How does it work?"

"You pick your service," explained Mike, "press the button, and downstairs at the deskman's counter a metal disk with our room number and what we ordered flops down. Simple!"

Within ten minutes a stiff-backed, bearded man in livery

arrived to take their orders. He looked French, but he spoke with a decided Irish brogue, and winked knowingly at Mike when he delivered the champagne and the supper some forty minutes later.

Ned did not stay the night. An hour after the repast, slightly dizzy from the champagne, the beer, and the rum, he permitted Tessie, who had stripped, to undress him, and they went into the virginal bedroom. Tessie aroused him quickly and he spent the most exciting half hour he had experienced since his return from Virginia. But as soon as it was over, even though Mike and Helen, both naked, came into the bedroom, and tried to entice him into some orgiastic games, he got up, dressed, and left, ignoring their ribald taunts and making awkward apologies and excuses. Before he was out of the hotel he was consumed with an overwhelming sense of guilt and shame. He hated himself. And he wondered if he could summon the courage to confess to Father Dennehy that he had fallen—no, not fallen, crashed—from grace once again.

Although the St. Nicholas was easily the most elegant, it was by no means the only new hotel in the city. As soon as plans for the Exhibition of the Industry of All Nations, the world's fair, was announced, hotel construction had begun at a mad pace. In addition to the St. Nicholas, numerous other modern hotels were built all along Broadway. There was the Carlton, the Howard, the City, the Union, the Carroll, the Astor Place, the Albion, and the Aeolian. The American was at Broadway and Grand Street, and the Prescott House and the Collamore were on Broadway, both at Spring Street.

However, the building projects that commanded the most attention during this frenzied construction period were the venue, which would house the fair itself, and the Crystal Palace and Latting Tower. The Palace was built directly behind the Croton water system distributing reservoir, on Sixth Avenue between Fortieth and Forty-second streets. It was a replica of the establishment of the same name, which had been built for a world's fair in London in 1851.

Patrick spent a good deal of his free time watching the construction of the Palace. But the building of the Latting Tower fascinated him even more. It was a three-hundred-fifty foot-high iron-and-wood structure, somewhat similar to the Eiffel Tower in Paris. It had been built as an observation tower for visitors to the fair, and was named after its builder,

Waring Latting. It stood directly opposite the Crystal Palace itself. There were a number of observation platforms, on which visitors could use the telescopes supplied by the tower and study the maps of the city and surrounding countryside displayed on walls and tables. What intrigued Patrick was the newly invented screw elevator, which took visitors up to the second level. From there one had to climb a winding staircase to reach the highest platform, which was more than three hundred feet above ground level. If the Latting Tower had been a building its height would have reached some twenty-five stories. It was by far the highest structure in the city.

The fair was scheduled to open on July 14, that year, 1853, and Martin and all the members of the police department had finally been issued uniforms. They were handsome and impressive: blue coat with shiny brass buttons, a matching blue cap, and neat gray trousers.

"Papa," said Ned, when Martin returned home in his uniform for the first time, "you look like an army officer. I think I'll become a policeman!"

Ned saluted his father.

"I await your command, General!" he said, grinning and standing stiffly at attention.

Flossie said, "Mr. Morrissey, if you don't mind my saying so, you're the handsomest figure of a man I've seen in many a moon."

Martin was pleased to be wearing the uniform. So were all the men under his command. He hoped it would have at least some small effect in improving the morale in the department. Graft and corruption on the force were so widespread and blatant that, in desperation, he had often thought of resigning. Occasionally a reform mayor would come into office and launch a clean-up campaign, and for a time the bribe-taking and other mischiefs would slacken. But a year earlier, two new politicians, whom Martin considered potentially venal influences on the force and the city, had arrived on the scene.

One was a handsome, forty-one-year-old man named Fernando Wood, who retired from business with a small fortune and was devoting himself entirely to politics, in which he had been a subtle, behind-the-scenes factor for some years.

The second politician whose budding career worried Martin was William Marcy Tweed. Tweed had gained considerable prestige as foreman of the Americus Volunteer Fire Company, Number Six, and in 1852 had been elected one of the city's twenty aldermen. Martin had heard one report that seemed to indicate that Tweed's eventual graft would make Timothy O'Leary's and John Deasy's considerable earnings seem like small change. Tweed had managed to have himself appointed head of a committee responsible for purchasing land for a new potter's field for the city. He had found some seventy acres on Ward's Island, which were worth a little more than $25,000. He had paid $103,000 of the city's money for the land, and split the difference between himself and the members of his committee.

But even more depressing to Martin than the corruption among the city's politicians was the larceny in the police department itself. It was common knowledge that many captains, sergeants, and patrolmen in a substantial number of the city's thirty-two precincts were on the payrolls of bawdy-house operators, bookmakers, and unlicensed gambling dens. Several worked closely with Isaiah Rynders and the gangs. Martin was quite sure that the chief of police himself, George Matsell, accepted large bribes from various illegal operators, including Madame Restell, who was the city's leading abortionist.

What enabled Martin to continue his police work in the face of the depressing situation was the pleasure he got from struggling to be both father and mother to Ned and Patrick. He spent every spare moment with them. Ned still occasionally seemed a problem. In late April he became edgy and nervous, and was short with his father, Patrick, and Flossie whenever they talked to him. Martin questioned him, but Ned would only say that he thought it might be best if he left school and went back to work in the shipyard. Martin adamantly refused to consider it. He had no idea that what was prompting Ned's unpleasant behavior was the fact that Tessie Kearns had met him coming out of the ward school the third Friday in late April. She seemed distraught as she ran up to him. She walked by his side and after a bit of nonsensical chatter she blurted, "Ned, I'm going to have a baby! I just found out today!"

"Wha—!" gasped Ned. "A baby?! You sure . . . ? You think it's mine?"

"I'm sure, Neddie, very sure."

"What do you want to do?" asked Ned, his voice quaking.

"I want you to marry me, Neddie. I'm working, and you can get a job, and we would get along fine."

"I'm—I'm—I'm not yet fifteen, Tess. I wasn't planning on getting married—"

"I'm only sixteen, Neddie. Age has nothing to do with it. You're more a man than a lot of people twice your age."

"Well . . ." said Ned nervously. "If you really think we should . . . but let me think about it, please, Tessie, please."

She giggled foolishly and patted his cheek.

"Sure, poor Neddie, think about it."

Ned fretted and wondered what his father would say when he told him he was getting—had to get—married. Fortunately Tessie and Mike O'Leary only persisted in the prank for another few days. Then Mike told Ned that he and Tessie had just decided to play a practical joke on Ned and worry him a little. Tessie *was* pregnant, but she did not want a baby, and Mike was paying for her abortion at the finest establishment in the city, Madame Restell's mansion on the northeast corner of Fifth-second Street and Fifth Avenue. Ned was furious, but so relieved, he simply said, "Jeeze, Mike, that wasn't funny. It wasn't funny at all."

Mike slapped him on the back and said, "Little problems like that'll make a man out of you, Ned."

Martin was astonished at the sudden change in Ned. Overnight the boy became his former cheerful, outgoing self, and never mentioned his wish to leave school. When summer came Ned did return to his job in the shipyard and Patrick got a job in the telegraph office on Chambers Street. Martin had the warm feeling that he and the boys were like three very good friends rather than father and sons. They went fishing together, attended the baseball games in Hoboken, went to Niblo's and Castle Garden and back to Barnum's Museum frequently. And they looked forward to the opening of the fair.

A week before the opening Martin had a visit from Tim O'Leary. O'Leary was pale and sweating profusely as he came into Martin's office on Mulberry Street. John Deasy had been killed earlier in the day while crossing Broadway at Fulton Street. The traffic along lower Broadway had been a growing scandal for some time. Martin recalled that the last time he and Kathleen had crossed the wide avenue it had taken fifteen minutes before they could find a relatively safe opportunity to dart across without being run down.

The wake for Deasy was one of the most crowded and boisterous Martin had ever attended. Mary O'Leary became very drunk, and attached herself to Martin and spent most of the long evening telling him in maudlin speeches how much she adored her father and loved Martin. Tim O'Leary ignored her completely and spent most of his time drinking with a group of fellow politicos, and discussing the prevalent rumor that Fernando Wood was planning to run for mayor. The grimmest mourner was young Mike O'Leary. He sat in a chair near the old man's coffin, sobbing quietly and refusing to be comforted by Mary, his grandmother, his father, or any relative or friend. "Just leave me alone, you fucking boob," he growled at Ned when Ned tried to comfort him. Ned had been aware that Mike was fond of his grandfather, but he did not realize how close the two had been. From Mike's earliest years, Deasy had pampered and coddled him, and had given him any money he requested, which Mary or Tim refused to supply. It was almost as though John Deasy were attempting to compensate for the indifference his daughter and son-in-law showed the boy most of the time. Indeed, he left a considerable part of his fortune in trust to his grandson.

Martin took off the Monday, July 14 in 1853, when the fair opened. And Ned and Patrick were excused from their jobs for the day. The three, dressed in their Sunday suits, walked the few blocks over to the elegant glass palace. The American flag flew high over the top of the central dome, and flags of many nations waved in the summer breeze from positions all around the handsome building. They stood in the crush of people and listened to President Franklin Pierce's speech, officially opening the fair.

There were crowds around all the exhibits, ranging from beautiful statuary through English silver, Sèvres vases, Gobelin tapestries, sparkling glass from Austria, and splendiferous displays of silks from India, Turkey, Italy, and France. But the exhibit that interested Patrick most of all was the Telegraph Company booth, at which booklets telling the story of Samuel Finley Morse and the miracle of telegraphic communication were distributed. Martin and the boys were also enormously impressed by a new farming machine, called the reaper, that had been invented by a man named Cyrus McCormick.

At the German exhibit they ran into Max Kessler, who was in deep conversation with his old friend Professor Carl Schoenbrun and a bright-cheeked, blond, blue-eyed girl, whom Max introduced as the professor's daughter, Clara. It was almost dinnertime and Max invited the Morrisseys to join the Schoenbruns and himself at a nearby coffeehouse. At dinner Martin discovered that he and Professor Schoenbrun had a number of mutual friends. The professor was a short, thin man with a gray-blond Vandyke beard and mustache and sad, watery blue-gray eyes. He was president of the German Society of the City of New York, a benevolent organization dedicated to helping impoverished German immigrants who came to the city. The professor was also head of the Volkstheatre in *Klein Deutschland,* and he was a good friend of a number of Martin's colleagues in the police department. The professor spoke English precisely, but with a pronounced German accent. There was a weary sound to his voice. Martin suspected he was not in the best of health. He could be taken for a man of sixty, although Martin realized he could hardly be more than in his midforties.

His daughter, Clara, was surely no more than sixteen. Ned was totally captivated by her. She was so completely the opposite of the Tessie Kearns and Helen Van Wirths he had known that he could hardly believe she was real. She had a round face with cheeks so glowingly pink, Ned thought at first she was blushing. But it was a perpetual blush of vibrant health. The silken, silver-gold blond hair, which she wore in two neat braids, was lustrous and her eyes were a clear deep blue, sparkling with intelligence. She was not shy, but she did not initiate much of the conversation. Max Kessler, who obviously was as proud of her as if she were a sister, a daughter, or a wife, raved about her activities and accomplishments, much to her embarrassment.

"Clara is the choirmaster of the *Klein Deutschland* singing society," he said. "The first woman to hold that position."

Clara looked down at her plate and her eyelids and long lashes covered her eyes. The pink in her cheeks deepened.

"Max, please! You must not! It is only that all the qualified men are too busy to do the work."

She had less of an accent than her father. Max smiled broadly at her protest.

"But more important, Martin," he said. "She is a good deal like your wonderful Mrs. Morrissey. She, too, works for the Ladies' Home Missionary Society—"

"Many ladies work there," said Clara. "They still speak of your wife, Mr. Morrissey. Of the fine work she did when they took over an old building in the Five Points."

Obviously eager to prevent Max from extolling her further, she turned toward Ned and Patrick.

"You young men are in school?" she asked.

Ned was speechless. He merely stared at her. Patrick said, "We're working through the summer. I'm a junior telegrapher and Ned builds clipper ships."

Martin laughed. "Well, Ned works in the shipyard, anyway."

"I'm—I'm going to be a policeman," blurted Ned suddenly.

"Ah, like your father! A fine profession," said Professor Schoenbrun. "A city cannot grow without law and order."

Max insisted on paying the check and the entire group made their way through the crowds to the Latting Tower. Ned could hardly take his eyes off Clara Schoenbrun. They took the screw elevator up to the second level. Professor Schoenbrun was breathing a bit heavily. He moved to one of the telescopes and said, "Please, go on up to the higher platforms if you wish. I will remain here."

"I will stay with you, Father," said Clara.

"And I," said Max

"No, no! Please, Max, go ahead. Go, Clara, go. I am fine."

Reluctantly Clara permitted Max to lead her to the winding staircase, which led to the upper-level platforms. Martin, Ned, and Patrick followed directly behind them. Clara lifted her long taffeta skirt carefully as she ascended. They went all the way up to the highest platform. Almost directly below them they could see people promenading around the broad walk of the pyramidlike Croton distribution reservoir, and over on Fifth Avenue, between Forty-third and Forty-fourth streets, the bulky building of the Colored Orphan Asylum. Martin moved to a telescope and looked southward.

He could hardly believe what he saw. He had lived in the city all his fifty-five years, but not until this moment when he looked at the panorama from this height, first with the naked eye, then through the telescope, did the full impact of the city's growth hit him. In the far distance across the harbor verdant Staten Island could be seen, and the blue-green waters of the Narrows and the Lower Bay. Off to the left the growing community of Brooklyn, and across the river to the right, New Jersey.

From the tip of Manhattan at the Battery all the way to

Twenty-third Street, the city was solidly built from south to north and river to river. Houses and structures of every description, many six stories high, lined every street and avenue. He recalled with a sudden feeling of nostalgia his happy early days at 106 Rivington Street. Rivington then had been largely open country.

He noted now all the modern touches, which had come about so gradually he had hardly given them a thought. The principal avenues were laid with large, square granite blocks. There were gaslights on almost every street corner. The new telegraph poles stuck up like wayward ships' masts at intervals along a number of streets and avenues. There had been talk that the police department was planning to install telegraphic communication between each of its thirty-two precincts and the headquarters at Mulberry Street. That would surely improve the force's capabilities, particularly in the handling of the nativist- and antislave-inspired riots, which continued from time to time.

The built-up section of the city seemed to be laid out in a grid pattern. Somehow, to Martin, it was exciting, in spite of a certain monotonous evenness. The better residential streets all had rows of four-story private brownstone houses, each with the same high front stoop. The most elegant of these brownstones were at Union Square and Fourteenth Street. He turned the scope to his left and looked to the east. Straight across, along the line of Forty-second Street, near the river, he saw the settlement of shacks on Dutch Hill. The shanties looked like battered little houses, which some sloppy giant had carelessly strewn about on the slopes, and the people and goats and pigs and chickens moved about like miniatures in an ugly fairyland.

Martin swung about and looked westward to the Hudson. Here, near the riverfront, was a section of small wooden houses, rickety but not quite as decrepit as Dutch Hill's shanties. They were mainly occupied by Irish and Negro laborers and their families, generally men who had worked on the Croton reservoir and on the first railroad lines. To the north from Twenty-third Street up to as far as the naked eye or the telescope could see there was still mainly wooded area and marshes and meadows, lush in the summer sun. However, a not inconsiderable number of expensive mansions and villas dotted the open countryside. Among these more imposing structures Martin could make out the Orphan Asylum

Society and the Watts Orphan Home buildings, both on Seventy-fourth Street, the latter on Tenth Avenue, and the former nearer the river on West End Avenue. Even farther north, all the way up at Broadway and 117th Street, was the Bloomingdale Insane Asylum.

Turning back again and viewing the lower section of the city, Martin noted busy Broadway and the horse-drawn railroads, moving along the avenues, halting now and then to take on or disembark passengers. The Sixth Avenue line had been completed in 1851; the Third Avenue line was just nearing completion. New lines were planned for Eighth and Ninth Avenues in the next several years.

Martin fell into a reflective mood. It was strange that in spite of fire and epidemic, riots and corruption, swarming immigration, severe depression, the city grew. How much further it could grow he hardly dared guess. Max Kessler backed away from a telescope near Martin's. The view seemed to have the same effect on him.

"It is some city, some fine city, Martin, is it not?"

As he spoke he backed away from the telescope and gently put his arm around Clara's shoulder and moved her toward the viewer. He kept his arm around her in an affectionate, proprietary manner. Ned had made no special effort to get near a telescope. The view he preferred was Clara, although he tried to conceal his single-minded concentration on her by moving about aimlessly, and making some irrelevant comment from time to time to Patrick. A pang of jealousy came over him when he saw Max put his arm around the girl. My God, he said to himself, Max Kessler must be old enough to be her father. Actually Max was twenty-nine, thirteen years older than Clara. Ned was pleased when Clara turned away from the telescope to Max, blushing, and squirmed her shoulder from beneath his arm.

"Please, Max," she said softly. "You mustn't. In public."

She noticed that Ned was staring at her when Max withdrew his arm. She smiled at him briefly before she turned to the telescope. Ned grinned idiotically.

PART FIVE

William Kessler

Detective Edward Morrissey,
Police Telegrapher Patrick Morrissey

Mike O'Leary's *Wicked Lady*

Mayor Fernando Wood and the City's
Two Police Departments

The Colonel and the Blackbirders

Abraham Lincoln Comes to New York

Fort Sumter Falls

"Fernando Wood, instead of occupying the Mayor's seat, ought to be on the rolls of the State Prison."

—Philip Hone, former mayor of New York, 1850 diary entry

"News of the attack on Fort Sumter and the flag at Charleston Harbor, S. C., was received in New York City late at night and was immediately sent out in extras of the newspapers. . . . I bought an extra and crossed to the Metropolitan Hotel, where the great lamps were still brightly blazing. . . . For the benefit of some who had no papers, one of us read the telegram aloud, while all listened silently and attentively. No remark was made by any of the crowd, which had increased to thirty or forty, but all stood a minute or two, I remember, before they dispersed. I can almost see them now, under the lamps at midnight again."

—Walt Whitman, *The Brooklyn Eagle*, April 14, 1861

"The peace faction was particularly strong in New York City, which from the elections of 1860 to Appomattox provided moral support to the Confederacy and more opposition to the war than any other important section of the North."

—*A Short History of New York State*

13

Ned Morrissey, just past eighteen and one of the youngest members of the new Metropolitan Police force, still tended to strut. He did not like the dark navy frock-coat and plug-hat uniform as much as he did the blue-coated, brass-button outfit of the old force, but the gleaming badge on his chest gave him a sense of pride and importance. At noon on this scorching, humid day in the third week of June in 1857, he was walking along Broadway, sweating contentedly, when he saw a tall, thin, scruffy-looking man dart out of a doorway. The man scampered up to a middle-aged lady carrying a parasol, and snatched her purse, which hung from her left arm. The lady screamed as the force of the purse being ripped from her arm whirled her about, and almost whipped her to the ground. The thief raced down Broadway and Ned dashed after him. Darting in and out among the languid pedestrians on the crowded street, Ned soon was within a few feet of the culprit, when just a short distance beyond the man, he saw another policeman, a member of the Municipal force. As Ned accelerated, the tall hat flew from his head. That was the trouble with the plug-toppers.

Ned dove and tackled the purse-snatcher firmly around the knees. As he pulled the panting, snarling man to his feet the Municipal policeman, at least ten years older than Ned, trotted up and clutched the miscreant by the shoulder.

"I'll take care of this scum!" he said authoritatively, and began to march the man along the street. Ned grabbed the policeman's wrist and yanked his hand off the thief's shoulder.

"You'll do no such thing, sir!" he yelled indignantly. "I captured this man!"

He grabbed the thief by an arm. The Municipal officer, a beefy, broad-shouldered Irishman, shoved Ned backward with such force that he lost his grip on the prisoner. A small crowd gathered around the two policemen and their prize. Furious, Ned swung at the other officer, and soon the two were wrestling awkwardly. The skinny purse-snatcher burst through the crowd, and knocked down an old lady as he dashed to the corner, and quickly around it into Houston Street. Before

Ned and the Municipal patrolman could disentangle themselves the culprit was gone.

Several in the crowd around them made ribald and nasty remarks about the stupid police rivalry. This was not an altogether unusual incident. In the city the police were at war with the police, and the criminal element was taking full advantage of the unprecedented situation. Political corruption and competition had brought about the existence of the two vying police departments. William Marcy Tweed and Fernando Wood had attempted to outdo each other in using every city department to enrich themselves and their cohorts. Both were Democrats, but Tweed was a growing power in the Tammany wing of the party, while Wood controlled the Mozart Hall group, so-called because that was where they held their meetings. Both participated in every form of graft, and struggled for power within the party.

In 1854 Wood won out, and was elected mayor, with the strong help of Isaiah Rynders and the city's gangs, the saloonkeepers, and whorehouse operators. Wood had run a moderately honest administration in his first term, but this was just a smokescreen for the outrageously corrupt schemes he inaugurated when reelected. In his second term he brought bribery and graft to new peaks. Every city bill was padded and the Wood group kept the overcharges.

In the police department, corruption reached new heights. Illegal enterprises of every description flourished as they happily paid policemen and their superiors not only for overlooking their activities but also for protecting them against the efforts of the honest officers in the department to shut them down. By early 1857 Martin was ready to resign and take his chances on finding some other means of earning a livelihood. He was talked out of it by his friends George Walling, captain of the Twentieth Precinct, and Max Kessler.

"Goddamit, Martin," said Walling, "there're few enough honest cops in the department. You *can't* quit! Somehow, sooner or later, we'll get rid of the thieves."

Max, who had connections not only in the city but also in Albany, gave him more concrete reason to stand fast.

"I'm not sure of this, Martin," he said one night at supper at the Morrisseys, after he had returned from a trip to the capital, "but I think the state legislature is working on a plan to create an entirely new police force in the city."

"How can they do that?"

Max shrugged. "I believe they have the power to disband the present force. At least that's what I hear. It's a Republican administration up there, and they're sick and tired of Wood's bleeding the city."

Max was right. Less than a month after his discussion with Martin the legislature passed just such a law. It created a completely revised police district, composed of the counties of New York, Richmond, Kings, and Westchester (which included the section of the city later called the Bronx). Five police commissioners were appointed to oversee the new force. The mayors of New York and Brooklyn were made *ex officio* members of the commission. Frederick Tallmadge became the superintendent of police. This new force was named the Metropolitan Police. Mayor Wood was ordered to disband the old city Municipal force.

Wood refused. He insisted the state's act was unconstitutional. He called for a vote of the members of the Municipal police to determine which force they chose to serve. Martin, George Walling, and other honest members of the department were not surprised at the results. Of over a thousand members voting, eight hundred of them, all loyal Democrats and graft participants, on however petty a scale, voted to remain with the Municipal force. Close to three hundred, Martin and Walling among them, elected to join the new Metropolitan Police.

The state set up headquarters on White Street and began a frenzied effort to recruit members to add to the nucleus of three hundred with which they were starting. With the depression deepening by the day they had little trouble signing up new officers. The shipyard, where Ned had been working since finishing ward school, had shut down and Ned leaped at the chance to become a policeman. Martin was promoted to captain, and worked out of the new White Street headquarters.

When Wood refused to disband the Municipal force, Captain Walling, armed with a warrant, was assigned to go to City Hall and arrest the mayor. The fearless captain was driven off by the overwhelming number of Municipal policemen, whom Wood had stationed all around the City Hall. It finally required the National Guard to break through the mayor's Municipal protectors and arrest Wood. He was released on bond immediately and never did come to trial. But in the weeks that followed his arrest, while the courts wrestled with the issue, the city went through one of the most ludicrous and crime-ridden periods in its young history.

The two police forces were almost of equal strength and they fought each other at every turn. The ridiculous, anarchistic condition prevailed until the Supreme Court finally found in the state's favor and Wood had no choice but to disband the Municipal force. Unhappily its eleven hundred members joined the city's growing mob of more than forty thousand unemployed, who were becoming desperate over their plight.

Long before the city suffered the idiocy of the rival police departments, Max Kessler had developed his brewery into the second largest in New York. He employed fifty-six people in the thriving plant at Rivington Street. Of these, fourteen were Negroes. Max was completely without prejudice. Not only did he train and hire competent free Negroes, but he was one of the most active officers of the American Anti-Slavery Society. He spent many evenings in meetings with other officers of the society laying plans to further the abolitionist cause, and occasionally to arrange for his own participation in helping slaves escape via the Underground Railroad.

This activity cost him a certain amount of business, since a number of the brewery's customers were fanatically proslavery and hated Negroes generally. Max's competitors had little trouble persuading such establishments to boycott the Kessler Brewery. The loss of such customers did not bother the energetic thirty-three-year-old Max. The quality of his brew and his prices were such that the majority of saloons, taverns, brauhauses, and hotels in the city disregarded his participation in the antislave movement.

With Max serving as catalyst the Morrisseys and the Schoenbruns had become good friends. Max had no reason to suspect that this could ever lead to problems. He was in love with Clara Schoenbrun and she with him, and he took it for granted that in due time they would marry. However, Frau Wilhelmina Schoenbrun, who was the professor's second wife and Clara's stepmother, conducted a relentless campaign to turn Max's romantic interest away from Clara and toward her daughter, Ilka. Ilka was eight years older than Clara, and only five years younger than Max. There was no question she would make some lucky man a most excellent *Frau*. She loved to cook and sew. She had tailored cotton work shirts for Max, his brewmaster, and his six delivery men with the words "Kessler Brewery" embroidered across their broad backs. She also did excellent needlepoint and knitting. She was short and plump with a small pug nose, round pink cheeks, and merry gray eyes. Max liked her hearty manner and cheerful disposition. He considered her a good friend, and she felt the same way about him. She also liked Clara, and happily sang under Clara's direction in the choir. But her mother, Wilhelmina, a stiff-backed, aristocratic-appearing woman, had quite different ideas.

Professor Schoenbrun's first wife had died during the time of the riots against the Prussian king in Berlin some nine years earlier. Wilhelmina's first husband, Hans Horsmann, director of the Berlin opera, died a month after the first Frau Schoenbrun. The Horsmanns and the Schoenbruns had been fast friends, and a year after Horsmann's death, Professor Schoenbrun married Wilhelmina. She lost no opportunity to convey to Max, subtly most of the time, rather directly when it seemed appropriate, that women who spent all their time working with the dirty, diseased people in the tenements, and attending abolitionist meetings and lectures on women's rights preached by shameless troublemakers like Mrs. Elizabeth Cady Stanton—such women could hardly make a man a proper wife. Clara, of course, was increasingly involved in all these pursuits. Frau Schoenbrun also persistently found occasion to comment on the inadvisability of men marrying women who were far younger than they.

She carried on this campaign in such an artful manner that Professor Schoenbrun himself was unaware of it. Max frequently understood the purpose of her preachments, yet, tongue in cheek, he agreed with her, pretending to be unaware that her comments were meant for him specifically. Clara was annoyed by her stepmother's plotting but, secure in the knowledge that neither Max nor Ilka were interested in each other romantically, she ignored it. Ilka herself was occasionally irritated by her mother's efforts to push her on Max. However, she was much too good-natured to do anything but protest mildly now and then when she was alone with her scheming parent. Frau Schoenbrun was becoming increasingly frustrated when the Morrisseys—and young Ned Morrissey in particular—arrived on the scene.

She quickly became aware of young Ned's interest in Clara Schoenbrun. It appeared nothing more than a light and platonic relationship, and although she learned that Ned was two years younger than Clara, she felt that with some adroit encouragement, the relationship might be converted into a romantic one. She encouraged the tall, gangly young man to join in the songfests that she, Ilka, and Clara often performed after supper. She played the piano, while Clara and Ilka sang German *Lieder*.

Max was so fond of Ned, and so totally oblivious to the possibility of any romantic feelings between Clara and him, that he was often responsible for throwing them together. On several occasions when he had tickets to a play, a concert, or a lecture but could not go because of a sudden business or abolitionist emergency, he asked Ned to escort Clara to the event.

Clara enjoyed Ned's company, and of course, he never made even the slightest amorous advance toward her. He concealed his true feelings by adopting a humorous, almost clownish attitude when he was with her. She considered him a good young friend and a pleasant, frequently amusing relief from Max's unfailingly mature and serious manner. As a member of the police force, Ned developed the same contacts with entertainment entrepreneurs as his father, and with increasing frequency, when Max was busy or out of town, he would take Clara to a theater, a new museum exhibit, or a concert. Frau Schoenbrun never missed an opportunity to remark on what a lovely young couple they made. The fact that none of the Morrisseys, nor Max Kessler, seemed to attach any significance to Clara's relationship to Ned bothered her. Had she been able to peer into Ned's secret heart, she would have been encouraged. He was quite certain that Clara would marry Max Kessler one day despite the fact that (in Ned's opinion) Max was too old for her. But he loved her dearly, and he hoped against hope that, by some miracle, she would decide she loved him, and marry him instead of their old friend.

Martin's and Patrick's interest in visiting with the Schoenbruns was quite different from Ned's. Patrick was an excellent chess player, as was Professor Schoenbrun, and he and the professor played long, challenging contests. Martin particularly enjoyed the discussions of local and national affairs with Max and the professor. On the last occasion, when the Schoenbruns had supped at the Morrisseys', they had inevitably drifted into an exchange of opinions on the overwhelmingly dominant issue of the day, slavery. Max simply took the position that slavery was inhuman. The professor had additional and somewhat unorthodox reasons for supporting abolition, but under controlled conditions.

"One must oppose slavery not because it is inhuman," he said. "After all, slavery is just one instance of social immorality. How about the starving tenant farmers in Ireland, Martin? What of the sick children, slaving in factories and mills for pennies a day? What, indeed, of the people, young and old, living in abominable conditions in our own tenements, many of which are owned by some of your most rabid abolitionists, Max?"

"Well, for whatever reasons one opposes it, it must be abolished!" said Max.

The professor nodded.

"True enough, Max. For even the Southern plantation owners cannot continue to profit from slavery indefinitely. The unholy power over human lives that it gives them must corrupt them sooner or later to the detriment of their peace of mind, and the eventual loss of their immortal souls."

"They will never see that!" grumbled Max.

"And you abolitionists will never see that hurtling into freeing the slaves, helter-skelter, may prove calamitous. The Negroes have lived in dependency on their masters so long that it will take many years before they can be educated to perform at their full capacities."

"I don't have any argument with what they do in the South," said Martin. "But I'm concerned with people who break the laws of the city and the nation. Do you know that the blackbirders are more active than they have been in years?"

"Blackbirders?" queried the professor.

"They're the scoundrels who smuggle Negroes into the country from Africa. The slaves bring high prices these days, so high the smugglers call them 'black ivory.' "

"Do our police try to prevent such smuggling?" asked Max.

"No," said Martin, "but we work with the Federal agency, which does."

The Federal government had passed the original law against importation of slaves almost fifty years earlier, in 1808, but it was not until 1820 that a special agency was set up to cope with the smugglers. The agency was becoming hard-pressed to do its job in these days when Southern slave owners were replacing escaped slaves with newly imported Negroes.

Ned had gone for a walk with Patrick, Clara, and Ilka on the night that the older men discussed the slavery issue, but almost a year later he himself became involved in a major blackbirder episode. It actually began on a September evening when he and Clara came out of Burton's Metropolitan Theatre. They had just seen Edwin Booth, the most popular actor in America, as Petruchio in *The Taming of the Shrew.*

In the lobby, as they were leaving the theatre, Ned was making a comment on the play. He threw out both arms, simulating a Petruchio gesture. The back of his left hand accidentally hit an elegantly dressed young lady sharply on the bosom. She squeaked and reached for the feathered hat threatening to topple from her high coiffure.

"Oh, excuse me, please," said Ned, turning to the woman. Then, "Mike!" he exclaimed as he saw the handsome blond man who was the lady's escort.

"Bumbling as ever, aren't you, old Ned!" said Mike O'Leary. "This beauty you've struck is Miss Nellie Shaw. Perhaps you've seen her in the show at Niblo's."

Nellie Shaw was indeed a beauty. And an expert in the art of makeup. Her gray-green eyes were delicately shadowed, the lashes darkened; her cheeks rouged and lips carmined to perfection.

"I've had boys steal a feel before," said Nellie Shaw, touching her full and firm bosom daintily with gloved fingers, "but never with the back of their hand, and never so roughly."

Ned blushed and apologized again.

"Stop stammering, Ned, and introduce us to this fascinating young woman."

Ned introduced Clara.

"We're headed for Sweet's," said Mike. "Come along. It's been a long, long time, old Ned. I've heard you've become a copper."

"I was sorry to hear about your grandmother," said Ned, after they had ordered (champagne for Mike and Nellie Shaw; coffee for Clara and a Kessler beer for Ned). Anne Deasy had died six months ago.

"Just as well," said Mike, "the poor old girl was never the same after my grandfather went. Took her a long time, but she just grieved away."

Mrs. Deasy, as had her husband, left a considerable fortune to young Mike. Now in his midtwenties he was a wealthy young man. Right after Anne Deasy's death he had gone into business with his father (or his mother's husband, at any rate). For some strange reason, he and Timothy O'Leary got along far better in their later years than they ever had while Mike was growing up. Ten months earlier he had gone into the cotton-and-tobacco brokerage business with Timothy. In his midsixties, just three weeks ago, O'Leary had retired.

Mike was running the business and was extraordinarily successful. He made many trips these days to the South, particularly Georgia and Virginia, where he had business arrangements with a number of the largest planters.

"What are you two doing this Saturday and Sunday?" he asked Ned when he observed that the young women were growing restless listening to his recital of his business ventures.

"I believe my fiancé and I are attending a lecture at Cooper Union Saturday night," said Clara politely.

"Your fiancé!" exclaimed Mike. "You mean you're actually engaged to marry this foolish policeman?"

Ned pinked and said, "No—no—I—I'm—"

Clara patted Ned's hand on the table.

"Ned and I are just good friends," she said. "I'm betrothed to another."

"Max Kessler," said Ned. "I think you may know him."

"I've never met him," said Mike, "but he owns a brewery, doesn't he?"

Clara nodded.

"And"—Mike smiled at her—"isn't he one of those—er—ah—abolitionists?"

"He and I are both abolitionists," said Clara defiantly.

"I don't understand all this fuss over the niggers," said Nellie petulantly. "Why don't they let them be?"

Mike smiled at Clara again.

"I was asking about the weekend because I wanted to invite you to a party aboard my yacht."

"Your yacht?" said Ned. "You've bought a yacht?"

"Just a ninety-five-footer. A couple of feet bigger than that brig we sailed to Norfolk with Tessie and Helen. Remember, Ned?"

Ned's cheeks reddened again.

"They'll be aboard this weekend too. I promise it will be a grand party," said Mike, grinning at Ned.

"If you can't have a good time on the *Wicked Lady*," said

Nellie, sipping her fourth glass of champagne, "you should have yourself examined to make sure you're not dead."

"Well—" began Ned, and then he heard a wheezing sound growing louder behind him. The wheezing sound and its producer, a very short, very round man in a white linen suit, waddled by him to Mike O'Leary's chair across the table.

"Uhhh—uhhh—pardon," grunted the obese man between wheezes.

He placed his pudgy left fist over his large left breast as he spoke. Mike took the plump right hand, nodded, and said softly, what sounded to Ned like, "Caljay . . . jaysee."

The fat man's thick lips widened, his mustache and eyebrows lifted, and his beige, piglike eyes twinkled as he smiled and bobbed his round head up and down enthusiastically. Mike stood up and said to Nellie, Clara, and Ned, "Excuse me, just a minute."

Mike and the waddling round man walked to a door at the rear of the room, opened the door, went through, and closed it behind them.

"What—what was that?" asked Ned.

Nellie shrugged and poured herself another glass of champagne.

"Mike knows some strange people," she said.

Out of curiosity and yet another unsuccessful effort to resist temptation, Ned had gone to the party aboard the *Wicked Lady* that weekend. It had been as bacchanalian and lewd, as shamefully exciting and pleasurable as Mike and Nellie had promised. Again Ned suffered manifold tortures before and during his confession to Father Dennehy, who had come to look forward to hearing of Ned's occasional lurid escapades.

Some six months later Ned was largely responsible for having the short, fat man sent to a Federal prison for three years. He was a notorious blackbirder, and on that evening at Sweet's when Ned had seen him for the first time, the fat man had chartered Mike's yacht, the *Wicked Lady*. He arranged a voyage to the Congo and brought back three hundred and sixty-two slaves, only eleven of whom had died in the hold on the way across the seas. When the *Wicked Lady* dropped anchor in the middle of the night in a cove on one of the Sea Islands off the Georgia coast to disembark the cargo of black ivory, a half dozen armed men from the Federal Agency Against Slave Importation met them, arrested the captain, the crew, and the mastermind of the operation, self-designated Colonel James Joseph Armbruster, known to his friends as Old Jimmy Jo.

The episode had several notable consequences. It shed further light on the existence of a powerful secret society called the Knights of the Golden Circle, a fanatical and quasimilitary proslavery organization, of which both Armbruster and Mike O'Leary were members. Their code for identifying each other was a series of gestures and passwords built around the name of South Carolina's fiery Congressman John C. Calhoun. The Federal men suspected that New York's mayor, Fernando Wood, was the head of the Knights, and that Mary Deasy was actually attempting to set up a woman's auxiliary, to be called, of course, Ladies of the Golden Circle. Her efforts were being violently opposed by leaders of the Knights themselves, but she was a stubborn, aggressive, and wealthy old biddy.

Mike O'Leary was able to escape punishment in the case, except that he lost his membership in the exclusive New York Yacht Club, where he moored the *Wicked Lady*. He did, however, make up his mind never again to have anything to do with Ned Morrissey.

"After all I did for the son of a bitch!" he cursed. And they did not see each other again until several years later.

Ned's work came to the attention of the superintendent of the force, Frederick Tallmadge, who made it a point to congratulate not only the young officer but also Martin, on his son's exceptional intelligence effort. Ned's undercover investigation in the Armbruster case was largely responsible for his promotion, some time later, to the rank of detective. There were only seven plainclothes detectives in the entire department at this time, and Ned, at twenty, was by far the youngest. Those days, Martin, too, tended to strut. He was proud of his sons, both of them.

14

Ned's promotion and Patrick's joining the police department occurred within months of each other. Patrick had completed his studies at the Free Academy (which was to become the City College of New York) and was taking special science courses at Peter Cooper's new college, the Cooper

Union for the Advancement of Science and Art. He had become a telegraphic expert, and when the police department installed telegraphic communication among its thirty-two precincts, they were in desperate need of men proficient in this technology. The headquarters had been moved to 300 Mulberry Street, and it was here that the central controls of the system were set up. Patrick signed on as both an operator and one of the bureau's most capable maintenance and repairmen.

"I'm sure glad Patrick's with us," Jim Crowley, superintendent of the telegraph bureau, told Martin a week after Patrick joined the force.

The police adoption of telegraphic communication was only one sign of New York's continuing growth. Immigrants continued to pour into the city at such a rate that the population was now well over three-quarters of a million. Castle Garden had been converted into an Immigration Control Center. William Cullen Bryant, the editor of the New York *Evening Post*, who also wrote poetry, had been campaigning for years for a large city park, similar to those to be found in and around London. He editorialized that the pressures of daily life in New York had become such that the people required a quiet, well-designed rural place where they could relax and meditate. In 1856 the City Council authorized the creation of such a retreat, to be called the Central Park. Seven hundred and sixty acres lying about a mile and a half north of Forty-second Street, extending some two and a half miles farther north, and about a half mile wide from east to west, were chosen as the site.

Frederick Law Olmsted, a civic-minded man who had lived in England and studied London's parks, and who had also traveled extensively in the South for the recently founded *New York Times*, was appointed architect for Central Park, and work began on it in 1857.

The O'Learys and Max Kessler were among several hundred affluent New Yorkers who made substantial contributions to yet another important construction program. Despite Martin Morrissey's fears, Archbishop John Hughes's aggressive declarations that he intended to convert every soul in America to Catholicism had not attracted the attention of, nor stirred up the ire of, too many non-Catholics. Anti-Catholicism, like every other issue of the day—nativism, women's rights, temperance—had been pushed into the background of the public consciousness by the continuing bitter arguments over extending slavery into free states and territories. So the archbishop had been able to raise over two hundred thousand dollars to build a new St. Patrick's Cathedral. Some two hundred wealthy Catholics, including the O'Learys, had contributed one thousand dollars each to the cathedral fund. Max Kessler had given Martin Morrissey one thousand dollars and requested that he donate it to the archbishop. He made Martin promise that he would not reveal the source of the money.

"That's very generous of you, Max," said Martin, "but I think the Catholic community should know you made the contribution."

"No! No, Martin! Please! It's little enough I can do. Do you know how many of my saloon customers are Irishers? But it would appear a condescension if they knew I was making such a donation. Say just that the money is being contributed by you and your friends in the police department."

The Morrisseys were among those present at the groundbreaking ceremonies. Indeed, it was the first occasion on which Patrick brought his new friend, Fiona Lafferty, to the Morrissey home.

Fiona was a seventeen-year-old art student at Cooper Union and an ardent advocate of women's rights. She attended church at the old St. Patrick's with the Morrisseys that morning, and after the groundbreaking ceremonies, joined them for dinner and spent a pleasant afternoon with them. She and Patrick seemed very fond of each other, and Martin was pleased to see that his eighteen-year-old son had finally found a female friend.

Max Kessler himself was busy that Sunday at a secret abolitionist meeting at the Kessler Brewery on Rivington Street. The previous afternoon he had had an angry discussion with a banker with whom he had done business for more than ten years.

"You've got to be realistic, Max, for God's sake," said the stern-faced, bearded Wall Streeter. "Right here in New York City we bankers have somewhere between a hundred million and two hundred million dollars invested in the South. You simply cannot abolish slavery."

"We must," insisted Max vehemently. "People were not meant to be slaves."

"But these are niggers, Max. They're not like you and me.

I warn you that if slavery is ever abolished the ships will lie idle in the harbor, and Wall Street and Broadway will become ghost streets. It will mean the end of New York as we know it."

That attitude was prevalent among the speculators and the moneylenders, and Max expected it. What was more upsetting to him was the fact that the city's newspapers seemed to be leaning toward the proslavery side. As the argument grew more heated with each passing month, even the most responsible of the city's journals came out against the abolitionists.

More and more it became necessary for Max and his abolitionist colleagues to plan their activities in closed meetings. And matters grew worse. Fernando Wood was elected mayor for a third term to begin in 1860.

The pro- versus antislavery argument so dominated the day's issues that the New York papers carried full reports on a series of debates between two United States senatorial candidates from the free state of Illinois. Horace Greeley of the *Tribune* had even sent a reporter to Illinois to cover the debates in person, rather than depend on local correspondents. One of the candidates, a thin, gangly lawyer named Abranam Lincoln, was the most outspoken opponent of slavery of any man seeking government office.

"A house divided against itself cannot stand," said Lincoln. "I believe this government cannot endure permanently, half slave and half free. . . . Either the opponents of slavery will arrest the further spread of it, and place it where the public mind shall rest in the belief that it is in the course of ultimate extinction, or its advocates will push it forward till it shall become alike lawful in all the states, old as well as new, north as well as south."

Seven debates were held between Lincoln and his opponent, Stephen Douglas, between August 21 and October 15. Douglas defeated Lincoln for the Senate seat by eight votes, 54 to 46, but Lincoln had become a nationally known figure. Max Kessler was one of his greatest admirers and staunchest supporters. Max had joined the newly formed Republican Party, and was particularly active in a group called the Young Men's Republican Union of New York City. The Republicans were planning to nominate William Henry Seward as their Presidential candidate in the 1860 elections, but Max and the Young Republicans were eager to have Lincoln run.

He had never made an appearance in the East, so the

Young Republicans arranged for him to come to the city to make a speech at Cooper Union Hall on Monday, February 27, in 1860. There were rumors that some fanatic members of the quasimilitary, Negro-hating Knights of the Golden Circle were plotting to assassinate the lawyer from Springfield, Illinois, should he dare come to New York. Police Superintendent Fred Tallmadge decided to supply an unobtrusive plainclothes bodyguard for Lincoln during his New York stay.

Ned Morrissey fitted in well as a member of the escort group of Young Republicans. He and a veteran plainclothes detective named Gustave "Dutch" Winckler were assigned to stay close to Lincoln at all times and keep a sharp eye out for suspicious characters. Max Kessler, at thirty-six, was the oldest member of the Young Republican escort group, and he was pleased that Ned and his older partner had been assigned to protect their controversial guest.

They all met Lincoln at the Astor House, where he was staying, on Monday morning. Ned and Max were impressed with the soft-spoken, gentle man from Illinois.

"I surely appreciate you gentlemen taking the time to show me the city," Lincoln said after being introduced to each member of the group by Max. He put his scruffy beaver topper on his black-haired head as they left the hotel.

"Could we stop at a hatter's?" he asked. "My old beaver hardly seems fit for the occasion."

They crowded into a coach they had rented for the day and took him to Knox's Great Hat and Cap shop at Broadway near Fulton. They dashed into the hatter's. Knox's hobby was collecting politicians' hats, so he traded Lincoln a fine new silk topper for his old beaver. Ned and Dutch Winckler led the way out of the hatter's, looking warily up and down the street. A steady rain had reduced pedestrian traffic on Broadway to a minimum. They rode the coach to Matthew Brady's Photo Studio at 643 Broadway. Lincoln had promised his political advisors to have some statesmanlike photos taken while he was in the city.

By early evening the temperature had dropped. The rain had turned to snow and the streets were covered with slush. Nevertheless more than fifteen hundred people struggled to reach Cooper Union Hall and paid twenty-five cents each to hear Lincoln.

"Good luck, Mr. Lincoln," Ned said as he started for the door leading down to the main floor of the great hall. Lincoln smiled at him and said, "Thank you, son. Thanks to you and your colleagues for everything."

From a backstage wing, Ned had watched the people make their way into the hall and seat themselves in the revolving maroon leather chairs. There was Fernando Wood and his brother, Benjamin, publisher of the *New York Daily News*, Mike O'Leary with his mother, Ned's father, his friend George Walling, and Max Kessler, with Clara Schoenbrun and her father.

The buzzing of the audience intensified as William Cullen Bryant strode to the podium at the center of the stage. He held up a hand for quiet and then introduced Lincoln. There was tentative and scattered applause as the tall, bearded man walked toward the podium. He was pale and beads of moisture showed on his high forehead. His high, thin voice quavered as he thanked Bryant for the introduction and began his speech. But in less than five minutes he became a changed man. His voice steadied and took on a timbre that captured the total attention of everyone in the hall. He spoke with great feeling about the wickedness of slavery.

Lincoln had been speaking for some forty minutes when Ned saw Mary O'Leary's mouth moving in agitated spasms. He saw her pudgy fingers snap open the silk purse in her lap, and watched as her right hand reached into it. The gaslight caught the gleam of the barrel of a small pistol as she withdrew it from the purse. Ned started to dash toward the O'Learys when Mike grabbed his mother's wrist with his right hand and snatched the pistol from her grip with his left. Quickly he stuffed the pistol into the pocket of his coat. Ned reached him just as he withdrew his empty hand.

"I'll take the gun, Mike," he whispered tensely, leaning over to O'Leary. Mike grinned at him and shook his head. He reached out and patted Ned's arm.

"Nothing to worry about, old Ned. Mama just got a little excited."

Mary O'Leary glared at Ned, her face florid, her lips compressed, fire in her eyes. Her full bosom heaved with emotion.

"Fucking nigger lover," she muttered sullenly.

Ned did not know whether she meant him or Mr. Lincoln, but he was disturbed by the manic look in her green eyes. Mike patted her hand, and turned to Ned, grinning again.

"I guarantee no trouble, Neddie... not now... not tonight."

Ned moved to the wall, remaining close to the O'Learys. He began to concentrate again on what Lincoln was saying. He felt a sense of relief as he noted the appeasing nature of the Springfield man's words.

"Let us have faith that right makes might, and in that faith let us to the end dare to do our duty as we understand it."

There was a tremendous burst of applause. Most of the audience rose to their feet as Lincoln completed his talk. Ned had been keeping a watchful eye on Mike and Mary O'Leary, and he followed their movement all the way up the aisle as Mary angrily elbowed her son on the way out of the hall. Later he told Dutch Winckler about Mrs. O'Leary taking the pistol from her purse. Winckler nodded, a grim expression on his face.

"Some of these proslavers hate Lincoln with a vengeance. Did you see the dandy sitting next to old Fernandy?"

"Yes. You know who he was?"

"Sure. John Andrews, a goddam rabble-rouser from Virginia. I'm pretty sure he's one of the leaders of those crazy Knights of the Golden Circle."

Lincoln's speech was an enormous success, but bitterly resented by the proslavers. On May 16 at the Republican convention in Chicago, Lincoln won the nomination on the third ballot over Senator William Seward of New York and Senator Salmon Chase of Ohio. Senator Hannibal Hamlin of Maine was nominated to be Lincoln's vice-presidential running mate.

The news reached New York the following day. Max Kessler came bounding into the Schoenbrun house on Twelfth Street shortly after noon. Clara had just served her father a bowl of chicken soup and was preparing to leave for her regular Thursday afternoon food-distribution visit to the tenement district.

"He won! He won!" shouted Max. He danced Clara around the kitchen, then stopped suddenly and went to Professor Schoenbrun. Even though it was a warm, sunny day the professor was wrapped in a heavy wool robe. He placed his soup spoon in his plate and smiled wanly at Max.

"Congratulations, Max," he said feebly. "You worked hard and I am happy for you."

On the wet and bitter night of Lincoln's Cooper Union speech, the professor had come down with a cold that had developed into a serious case of influenza. It had taken him most of the balance of the winter and spring to recover, and even now he was in a weak condition and subject to frequent attacks of uncontrollable coughing and alarmingly high temperatures.

"Thank you, Professor," said Max, joining the older man at the table. There was a mischievous sparkle in his dark eyes as he looked over his shoulder at Clara at the washtub. He smiled and turned back to the professor.

"And now," he said, "I must ask you a question you have no doubt been expecting me to ask for some time."

The professor nodded weakly, waved a feeble hand at him, and grinned, "Of course you have my permission to marry Clara," he said. "I presume you have decided to wed to celebrate Mr. Lincoln's nomination."

Clara went to her father and hugged and kissed him. Max shook the professor's hand so vigorously he winced.

"As usual you are right, my dear father," he said. "We would like to marry on the second Monday in June."

It was the first Jewish wedding ceremony the Morrisseys had ever attended. Ned's eyes were moist as he listened to the rabbi intone the vows. He considered Max Kessler one of his best friends and respected him as much as he did his own father. But he loved Clara, and he could not help feeling sorrow over the fact that she was lost to him forever. However, he managed to conceal his disappointment well. To all at the elegant postnuptial reception at the St. Nicholas Hotel, he seemed to be the most joyous member of the party. One member of the wedding who did not hide her displeasure was Frau Schoenbrun. As she stood beside the professor in the Shearith Israel synagogue, listening to the rabbi's sonorous tones, she grumbled sotto voce, "He is much too old for her, Carl. We will live to regret this day."

The professor looked annoyed and began to reply. He was overcome with another coughing attack. The wedding party glanced toward him sympathetically, but his wife stared stonily at the backs of the bride and groom. Ilka stood at the professor's right. At her right was a middle-aged man, as large and robust as she. He was Fritz Himmelfarb, proprietor of Himmelfarb's Hofbräu at Tenth Street and the Bowery. Himmelfarb was a moderately prosperous man, but not nearly as wealthy as Max Kessler, nor nearly so involved in civic and national matters. He had the same jolly attitude toward life as Ilka, and was the musical feature in his Hofbräu. He had a rich bass voice and his greatest pleasure was singing with the Hofbräu's German band. Ilka realized she loved Fritz the first time she had heard him sing, "Nach Lauderbach hab ich mein Herz verlorn." She and Fritz planned to be married on September 1, Ilka's thirty-first birthday. Frau Schoenbrun was not too happy about it, but she considered it better than Ilka remaining an old maid.

Max and Clara allowed themselves only a brief one-week honeymoon. They rented a cottage on the Long Island shore at Hempstead and spent an idyllic seven days reading, swimming, fishing, walking along the beach in the moonlight, and making love. When they returned to the city Clara set about adding some feminine touches to the living quarters on the third floor of the building on Rivington Street. Max divided his time between running the brewery and organizing the Young Republican campaign in the city for Lincoln's bid for the Presidency.

Late in October Professor Schoenbrun, Wilhelmina, and Ilka and her husband, Fritz, spent a pleasant Sunday with Max and Clara. While the women were in the kitchen preparing supper, the men sat in the parlor discussing the upcoming election.

"What do you think of Mr. Lincoln's chances, Max?" asked the professor.

"I believe they are good," said Max. "It may be a close contest, but we are counting on the Democratic vote being split between Northern and Southern members of the party."

"Douglas did beat Lincoln in Illinois," reminded the professor. "He's a very able man, and well liked."

"Yes, but the Southern Democrats are pushing John Breckenridge."

"I think maybe it would be better if Mr. Lincoln does not win," said Himmelfarb. "He seems to be dividing the country over the nigger slaves."

"There must be no slaves, Fritz!" said Max. "No man can own another."

"Ach, you make a fine beer, Max, but you know nothing about people," scoffed Fritz. "People whose business depends on slaves will have them. In the South they will never give up their niggers."

"I'm afraid Fritz may be right, Max. A number of Southern

states are insisting they will secede from the union if Lincoln is elected."

The Democrats did split, yet in November Lincoln got more electoral votes (one hundred and eighty) than Breckenridge and Douglas combined. Breckenridge got seventy-two and Douglas only twelve. And almost immediately a number of Southern states seceded. Just five days before Christmas the South Carolina legislature met and led the way by passing a resolution stating that "the union now existing between South Carolina and the other states, under the name of the United States of America, is hereby dissolved."

By the first of February, Mississippi, Florida, Alabama, Georgia, and Louisiana had followed South Carolina's lead.

Most New Yorkers were shocked and dismayed. James Gordon Bennett's *Herald* said, "Just as Lincoln once split rails, so is he now splitting the union."

The nation was divided, and New York City was possibly the most violently torn asunder of any major community. Mayor Fernando Wood professed to speak for the segment of the population that favored the Southern position. Indeed, the new year was just a week old when Wood sent a message to the City Council urging that New York City also secede and declare itself a free city. He insisted that the dissolution of the union was inevitable.

"What the scoundrel is after," Max told Martin Morrissey the day after Wood's startling pronouncement, "is all that money in custom duties that is collected in New York harbor and goes to the Federal government."

Horace Greeley denounced the mayor in the *Tribune*. "Fernando Wood evidently wants to be a traitor. It is lack of courage only that makes him content with being a blackguard."

On Saturday night, the thirteenth of April, Max and Clara, indulging themselves in a rare evening of pleasure, attended the opera at the Academy of Music on Fourteenth Street. When they exited from the theater, a young boy in tattered clothes with a bundle of newspapers under his arm was racing up and down the street.

"H'uxtra!" he shouted. "H'uxtra! It's war! *War!* South fires on Union fort! Read all about h'it! H'uxtra!"

Max took his copy, and he and Clara, along with several other people, hastened across the street to the front of the Metropolitan Hotel, where the great gas lamps burned brightly. The spread newspaper trembled in Max's hands as he read the account. He turned pale. Clara, reading along with him, squeezed his forearm and made a choking sound as she fought to hold back the tears. Max shook his head and cursed.

"They have done it! The goddam fools! They have done it!"

Early the previous morning South Carolinian and other Southern naval forces had fired on Federal Fort Sumter in Charleston harbor. They had blasted away at the Union stronghold for thirty-four hours and captured the fort. There had been a black comedy of a civil war between New York's two police forces, but now the nation itself was launched upon an internecine struggle of such horrific dimensions as not even the most bloodthirsty of the doomsayers could have predicted.

Over the next several days, as word of the Southern attack spread, New York City expressed its outrage by converting abruptly and almost totally to the Union cause. Secession was one thing, but firing upon brothers, trampling the flag of the United States was something else again. Within a week the city was an armed camp. A circle of cannon formed around the Croton fountain in City Hall park. Barracks were set up in the park, at the Battery, at Atlantic and Flatbush avenues in Brooklyn, and on Riker's Island and Staten Island. Frederick Law Olmsted was appointed general secretary of a newly formed Federal Sanitary Commission and sent to Washington. Work on Central Park, St. Patrick's Cathedral, and other nonmilitary projects came to a halt.

Martin had been arguing with Ned and Patrick since news of Sumter had reached the city. The young Morrisseys insisted they must enlist, but Martin, George Walling, Jimmy Burns, and other senior members of the force convinced them that it was far more important that they remain in New York and continue their police work. There would be greater need than ever, they told Ned and Patrick, for strong law enforcement in the city.

On Wednesday, the twenty-fourth, Max came home from a meeting of the Committee for Union Defense.

Clara was at the stove, basting a beef roast. Max walked up behind her and put his arms around her waist. He kissed her ear.

"I have enlisted, Clara," he said quietly. "It is ridiculous for a strong, able-bodied man like me to serve on nonmilitary committees."

Clara put down the bowl, but held the wooden spoon as

she turned to face Max. She put her arms around him. She saw immediately that there was no point in trying to dissuade him. A fanatical fire burned in his dark eyes. He was thirty-seven years old and in splendid physical condition.

"I will miss you, Max," she said, and kissed him softly. He pressed her close to him and she felt the strength in his arms. He kissed her mouth, her cheeks, her neck, then her mouth again, long and passionately. When she could catch her breath, she looked up at the spoon in her raised right hand and said, "Your suit, Max. I am dripping on your suit."

He reached behind him and touched the large spot of greasy water that had dripped from the basting spoon. He took the spoon from her hand and tossed it toward the sink. He lifted her in his arms, and kissed her neck again as he carried her toward the bedroom.

"Max!" she exclaimed. "The roast!"

When they finished making love that Wednesday evening Clara lay quietly beside Max. Her heart was racing. A sudden chill ran through her. She had an inexplicable and terrible premonition that she would never see Max again. She turned to him and embraced him and kissed him hungrily and he responded. They made love again, fiercely this time, almost desperately. It was as though Max, too, felt he might never see Clara again. When she felt the smooth heat of his explosion inside her, she dug her fingers into his muscular back and pulled him down upon her. She groaned and sighed. When they married they had decided they would not have children for a year or two. Now, breathing hard, holding each other close, neither of them said anything. But Clara silently prayed, "Please, God. If he doesn't come back, let me have his child. Let a part of him stay with me."

15

Ned Morrissey sat across from Clara Kessler in the Kessler parlor on the third floor of the house on Rivington Street, bouncing eighteen-month-old William Kessler on his knee. The child giggled and squealed happily. Ned, holding him under his arms, said, between breaths, "I've already looked, Clara.... Down the whole list.... No Kesslers!"

Clara continued to scan the copy of the *Tribune* spread on

the low tea table in front of her, biting her lower lip, tracing each name on the casualty list with a trembling finger.

Kabelsky . . . Kadell . . . Kagelein . . . Kane . . . Kaplan . . . Kartez . . . Kaylor . . . Keane . . . Kennelly . . . Kiley . . . King . . .

She went back to be sure there were no other *Ke*'s. Ned halted his knee horse and William protested and kept bouncing on his own volition. Ned said, "No news is good news, Clara. The War Department is very conscientious about casualty lists."

"I suppose so, Ned, but why hasn't Max written?"

"The postal service in time of war is almost nonexistent. Any day now, Max will walk in."

They had been through similar dialogues a number of times in the past two years. The newspapers, of course, published the alphabetical lists of dead and wounded as soon as the War Department released the names after each battle. Now on July 10 of 1863 the list of casualties of the three-day battle at Gettysburg, as well as the names of the dead and wounded at Vicksburg, were published. Clara had, naturally, been gratified over the fact that Lee had been driven out of Pennsylvania, and that thirty thousand Confederate troops had surrendered to Grant at Vicksburg, but she was always most eager to learn if Max had been involved. As much as she dreaded the idea that he might have been killed or wounded, she still believed it would be best to know if he had.

Since the April day in 1861 when Max had gone off to the war, Clara had had just three letters from him. One within ten days after he left the city. It came from Washington, D.C., and expressed his unhappiness over having been assigned administrative duties in the Quartermaster's Department rather than a place with a unit heading for action on the front. He told her how much he loved her and missed her. A second letter came a month later. It was even more bitter than the first.

"I was always philosophical about the graft and corruption in the city government," he wrote, "but it sickens me to see the way high-placed officials in the Federal government and the military enrich themselves and the profiteering suppliers, while other men die fighting in a noble cause."

He was pulling every conceivable string to get out of his quartermaster's post and win assignment to a fighting unit. Again he told her how dearly he loved her and how much he missed her. The third letter was by far the happiest of the three. It came in late September of 1861. It was dated July 19. He had finally been assigned to a combat company, and spoke hopefully of seeing action in the near future, although he could not, of course, say where. He told her how much he adored her and missed her. She had replied promptly to his first two letters, telling him that everything was going well with the brewery. Friedrich, his *Braumeister,* and Willie Simpkins, Friedrich's Negro assistant, were doing an excellent job. She herself was having no trouble keeping the accounts, and business was thriving. The war seemed to be making New Yorkers thirstier than ever. She was also enjoying working with the Women's Central Association of Relief. Her father and stepmother and the Himmelfarbs and all the Morrisseys sent their love.

In Max's third letter he had told her he would write again soon and give her an address to which she could direct her communications. That was the last she had heard from him in the more than two years that had passed. After several months without word from him, she wrote him again at the Washington, D.C., address. Her letter came back marked "No Such Person at This Address." She wondered if he had gotten in trouble for speaking out against the thieves he had encountered, and had been arrested and jailed or worse.

But for more than a year she continued to write, hoping against hope that somehow the letters would find him. She did not tell him she was pregnant, when she learned she was in the third week in June of 1861, after she had missed two menstrual periods. She decided it would only add to his frustrations. And she felt it would be a wonderful surprise for him if the war was indeed short (as everyone said it would be) and he arrived suddenly at Rivington Street. As month after month passed she continued to write, but said nothing of being with child. But she had to tell someone. It was significant that she chose to tell Ned Morrissey, rather than her stepmother or her stepsister, or any of the ladies in the association, or even her ailing father. She felt a closeness to Ned and was convinced that he would help her in any difficulty. She had felt this way about her gangly young Irish friend for some time.

By mid-July of 1861 it had become plain to anyone who troubled to notice that Clara was pregnant. Frau Schoenbrun lost no time in stating her opinion to her husband.

"I told you, Carl! I told you that Morrissey boy and Clara have been carrying on."

The professor was suffering in the oppressive summer heat. He was irritable and lost his temper with his wife.

"I forbid you to say such wicked things, Wilhelmina! I'm certain Clara conceived before Max left. You have a filthy mind. Do not let me hear you spreading such malicious gossip!"

"You are blind, Carl!" said Wilhelmina sullenly, and of course she disobeyed his orders about spreading the story as she believed it to be. A number of Clara's neighbors on Rivington Street began to gossip about Mrs. Kessler and the young Irishman. The probability was that in the bitter cold January of 1862, when William Kessler was born, Professor Schoenbrun would have been stricken with the influenza bug again without the agitation he suffered over Wilhelmina's nastiness. In any event, just a month after William was born, on February 7, the professor died of his most recent and severe influenza attack. Clara was devastated. She still had not heard from or about Max, and now her father was gone. Her baby, however, was strong and healthy, and she thanked God for that.

For two whole years she had lived with anxiety and dread. Her nerves were raw and it often seemed to her that the only reason she was able to retain her sanity and health was the knowledge that baby William needed her. That, and the devoted manner in which Ned Morrissey shared her concern and constantly reassured her that Max would come back one day, and William would grow up proud of his father's heroic deeds in the war.

Ned, edgy himself from lack of sleep and the pressures of his job, spent two or three evenings a week with her, and was a major force in enabling her to get through the difficult times. More often than he liked, he thought about the possibility that Clara's premonition might be justified, that Max would indeed never come back. He was ashamed of the secret pleasure he found himself taking in that possibility. To conceal it he made certain that he gave no one, least of all Clara, the idea that he was in love with her. His every action went to make clear without question that the relationship was purely platonic. Sometimes when he played with young William, he thought how wonderful it would be if the boy were his. His and Clara's. But he hated himself for having such thoughts. He loved Max Kessler like a favorite uncle, and in his heart he hoped Max was well and would return soon. He had managed to live with his secret love for Clara Kessler for many years, and would surely be able to do so for the rest of his life.

When Professor Schoenbrun died, Wilhelmina sold the house on Twelfth Street and moved in with Fritz and Ilka Himmelfarb in their two-story frame house in Yorkville. Clara visited them only on a few special occasions such as birthdays and holidays. Ned accompanied Clara on two of the visits. Wilhelmina's attitude was cold and standoffish with both Clara and Ned, but Ilka and Fritz were warm and welcoming.

Fritz, outgoing as ever, considered the war a great foolishness, and paid little attention to its progress. Business was good at the Hofbräu; he was in excellent voice; Ilka was a most satisfying wife in bed and kitchen. Even when the Federal Draft Law went into effect he was not disturbed. The law stipulated that all able-bodied males between the ages of twenty and forty-five years of age were liable to service, but provided that any man who chose not to serve could buy an exemption by paying the Federal government three hundred dollars. Fritz promptly paid it.

New York State itself had passed a weaker conscription act than the Union law sometime earlier. Nevertheless on July 4, 1863, just a week before the first names were to be drawn in the New York City draft, New York's Democratic Governor, Horace Seymour, made an Independence Day speech in the city. Incredibly enough, he challenged the Federal government's right to draft citizens. Martin, Ned, and Patrick Morrissey were in the crowd in the steamy Academy of Music that afternoon, which heard him shout: "Remember this! Remember this! The bloody, treasonable and revolutionary doctrine of public necessity can be proclaimed by a mob as well as by a government!"

Crime and violence in the city were rampant. In the year 1862 one out of every ten of the 800,000 New Yorkers had been arrested on one criminal charge or another. Police records showed that more than 75,000, the great majority men, but a surprisingly large number of women and children, were full-time, unregenerate lawbreakers.

The war, of course, had exacerbated the situation. Profiteering was widespread. Prices had soared. The poor, and even the middle-class laborer, could hardly buy enough food to subsist, or wood or coal to keep warm in the bitter winters. More than 400,000 inhabitants were foreign-born, and of those, more than 203,000 were Irish. Many had voluntarily enlisted and had made notable contributions, and given their lives to bring about the resurgence of the Union forces after the early Confederate victories. But of those remaining in the city, most considered the war a rich man's war. The draft gave them reason to believe they were right. Few of them, even those employed, could raise the three hundred dollars to buy exemption. And many Northern copperheads, eager to reach any agreement with the South and end the war, constantly added fuel to the fiery discontent of the masses. The most insidious element in perpetuating the restiveness was the secret society, the Knights of the Golden Circle.

There were only 2,297 men in the entire police force, including those on desk duty in the thirty-two precincts and the Mulberry Street headquarters. They had all they could do to attempt to prevent the robberies, assaults, rapes, homicides, and scores of lesser crimes in the city's twenty-two wards. But by putting in sixteen- and eighteen-hour days and nights, seven days a week, Ned had made a continuing investigation of the Knights a personal crusade, while contributing his share to tracking down routine killers and other gangsters and thugs. Mike O'Leary had warned him on several occasions to desist in his efforts to keep abreast of the Knights' activities.

"You're playing with fire, old Ned," Mike said. "One day you'll get burned."

Patrick was putting in the same kind of time and effort in the telegraph department since the constant and immediate communication between each precinct and headquarters was essential to enabling the police to keep criminal activity under reasonable control. And Martin was working as long and hard and worrying more than either of his sons. Now on this still and humid Independence Day evening he mopped the sweat from his face with a large kerchief. He took a long swallow from his beer mug. Pat finished reading a printed flyer that Ned had just given him. He shook his head, and handed the sheet to his father.

He asked Ned, "Where did you get this mad manifesto?"

Ned said, "A printer friend of mine who works at the *Daily News* gave it to me yesterday."

The document was headed, "Declaration and Protest of

Liberty Against Usurpation and Tyranny." It denounced the Lincoln administration in most vicious terms.

" '. . . The Federal government has become a filthy hybrid; a monster smeared with the bloody sacrifice of its own children; a detestable compound of crimes and vices; a despotism which cannot be fitly described in decorous language . . .'

"This is a goddam outrage," blustered Martin, as he read on.

" '. . . Should the Confederate Army capture Washington and exterminate the herd of thieves, Pharisees, and cutthroats which pasture there, defiling the temple of our liberty, we should regard it as a special interposition of Divine Providence in behalf of justice, judgment and mercy.' "

Patrick grinned at Martin, who was muttering more and more angrily as he read.

"Quite an arraignment, isn't it, Papa?" he said. Martin was just coming to the declaration's final charges.

" 'Abraham Lincoln and his administration must be condemned for the tyrannies, bloodshed, widespread defraudings, robberies, panderings and desolations, wastes and cruelties they have perpetrated!' "

Martin read the signature at the end of the article.

"Who the hell is this 'Spirit of '76'?"

"Just another name for the Knights, I'm guessing," said Ned. "They've been distributing it all over town today."

Three days later on Tuesday, July 7, the *Tribune* published the diatribe. It appeared under a head that said, "Pro-Rebel Attempts at Revolution," and was prefaced by Greeley's editorial comment:

> That the more determined sympathizers with the Slaveholders' Rebellion have for months conspired and plotted to bring about a revolution in the North, which should place the whole tier of Free States bordering on the slave region in alliance with and practical subordination to the Rebel Confederacy, is just as certain as that we are involved in Civil War. Had Meade been defeated at Gettysburg—as the Copperheads had no doubt he would be—they would have been ready to raise the flag of rebellion and proclaim McClellan the head of a provisional government. Here follows one of their recent manifestoes.

* * *

Then appeared the "Declaration and Protest" in full.

It was after midnight on that night of the seventh before Ned got home. He had just completed the rounds of several establishments where he had reliable informants. The first day for drawing the names in the New York City draft was scheduled for Saturday, the eleventh. All the detectives had been ordered by Sergeant John Young, the chief of detectives, to see what they could learn about the mood of the people as the draft day neared. In a tavern at Second Avenue and Twentieth Street, the big-bellied proprietor, Fitzhugh Higgins, whispered to Ned that a secret-society band intended to raid the Union Steam Works at Twenty-second Street and Second Avenue or the New York State Armory on Twenty-first and Second. The Steam Works had been converted into a factory for the manufacture of carbines, and the armory was stocked with substantial quantities of weapons and ammunition. Higgins's description of the man he had heard discussing the plot fitted John Andrews, the Virginian Ned and Dutch Winckler had seen at Cooper Union during Lincoln's first address in the city.

Ned also checked in at several whorehouses. Tessie Kearns worked at one, and she had heard nothing of any consequence.

"You look so tired, Neddie," she said. "Why don't you come to bed with me and relax a bit. Free for old friends."

He thanked her and continued his search. At Windust's Restaurant a German waiter said he had heard a group discussing a raid on the *Tribune* building on Printing House Square. Windust's was just a few blocks from the *Tribune* building, and many proslavers resented Greeley's editorial policies. Ned dutifully took descriptions and made notes of all these rumors. Actually the city seemed even quieter than usual, and he found it hard to believe that the draft would bring any real trouble.

At home Martin and Patrick were still up. Martin was working over some papers at a table in the kitchen, a glass of beer at his elbow, and Patrick was at a desk in the parlor, with a map of the city marked with the telegraph lines running out from the Mulberry Street headquarters to each of the thirty-two precincts. Even this late at night the air was heavy and humid. Pat poured beers for the three of them and Martin said, "How does it look, lad?"

Ned shrugged. "I don't know. All kinds of rumors, but I'm not too sure anything serious is going to happen."

"Some of the Federal enrollment officers canvassing the Five Points, the Fourth Ward, and the Bowery were threatened," said Martin, "but the only arrest we made was over in the Ninth District. A provost marshal named Ehrhardt was set upon by a bunch of roughnecks at Broadway and Liberty. Otherwise it was just another hot summer night."

Pat said, "That's one of the biggest problems, I think. This insufferable heat. Drives people crazy. And why they decided to begin the draft on a Saturday morning I'll never understand."

"What difference does that make?" said Ned. "One day is like any other."

Pat shook his head. "Not quite. More of these thugs and laborers spend more time in the saloons on Saturday and get drunker than on any other day of the week. And all the saloons have been staying open all day Sunday. With nothing to do over Saturday and Sunday except stand around the bars and drink and complain about the draft, these people could be ready for a little rioting by Monday."

"Could be," said Martin. "We'll just have to be ready."

Pat said, "We're checking every line in the city. One thing you can depend on: We'll get and spread word of any trouble, anywhere in the city, as fast as it happens."

The next evening, Friday, the tenth, the draft also became the subject of conversation in the Kessler parlor at Rivington Street. Having checked out the latest casualty lists, Clara went into the kitchen, brewed fresh coffee, and brought two cups into the parlor. Ned had resumed bouncing baby William on his knee, and when Clara reentered the room he stopped again.

"Willie Simpkins left at noon today," said Clara, as she placed a cup on the end table beside Ned. The baby began to protest the inaction of Ned's knee.

"He was terrified," continued Clara. "He said gangs with clubs and lead pipes were roaming Leonard and Baxter streets all last night, threatening to hang some of the Negroes who live there. He's worried about his wife and two little boys."

"Some of these brainless brutes just get their pleasure out of plaguing the coloreds," said Ned, "but the area's well patrolled. I don't think there will be any real trouble."

"Willie said the Irish are blaming the Negroes for the war and the draft."

"I know," said Ned.

On his thigh William suddenly sat very still. He puffed out his baby cheeks and his face reddened. He made a small grunt.

"I told Willie to bring his family here if he felt it was getting too dangerous to stay on Leonard."

Ned felt warm moisture through his pants on his thigh, where the baby's diapered bottom rested. An unpleasant odor drifted to his nostrils. William gurgled happily, squirmed once and again began making sounds to indicate he wished his steed reactivated.

"I . . . I . . . don't think he's in any condition to continue his ride," said Ned, lifting William gingerly from his thigh and holding him out to Clara.

Clara ran to him and took the baby.

"Oooh, I'm sorry, Ned," she said as she fetched a blanket, placed it on the brocade sofa and placed William upon it.

Ned stood beside her and watched her clean and change the baby. Despite the mess and malodor he found the scene touching. He had an impulse to put his arm around Clara's shoulder, but he resisted it.

"I've got to go, Clara, " he said abruptly. "Don't worry."

She followed him to the door with the freshly diapered baby in her arms.

"Ned! Ned, where will you be when they begin the draft tomorrow?"

"I'm assigned to the Ninth District office over on Third Avenue and Forty-sixth Street. I'll be mingling with the crowd, keeping an eye out for troublemakers. We'll have a number of uniformed constables there."

She looked at him with a worried expression. She reached out and touched his cheek, and then lightly kissed the place she had touched. William reached out a pudgy little hand and clutched his ear, just as Clara began to move away. He lost his grip on Ned's ear and squealed a protest. Clara said, "Be careful, Ned. Please be careful."

He grinned at her.

"Not to worry, Mrs. Kessler," he said. "Detective Edward Morrissey is indestructible!"

But Clara had another premonition. As the door closed behind Ned, she said to herself, *Clara Kessler, you are a fool! Nothing but dire anticipation of doom! All nonsense, I am sure! It is only that you have been too long without Max.*

Then she took William into the bedchamber and placed

him in his crib. On his back he kicked and punched the air, and gurgled happily. She prayed aloud.

"Please, God, please bring Max back to us. And please, please do not let anything happen to Ned." She leaned down and kissed William's cheek.

PART SIX

*
**

John Andrews

The Willie Simpkins Family

Colonel Fred Van Gelder

Othello Jones and His Captain

Objections to the Draft

Colored Orphans and Arms

The Brewery Under Siege

Free Apparel at Brooks Brothers

"The fire now became fearful and incessant, merged into a tumultuous chorus that made the earth tremble. The discharge of musketry sounded upon the air like the rolling thunder of a thousand distant drums."

—Felix de Fontaine (Southern war correspondent), July 1862 report on the Battle of Antietam

"Governor Seymour, whose partisans constituted the rioters and whose partisanship encouraged them, has been in New York City, talking namby-pamby. This Sir Forcible Feeble is himself chiefly responsible for the outrage."

—Secretary of the Navy Gideon Welles, diary entry, July 1863

"I have been hurt by reports that you are rioters. You cannot imagine that I could hear those things without being pained grievously. . . . When these so-called riots are over and blame is justly laid on Irish Catholics, how can I claim with any pride that I was born in Ireland? Ireland, that has been the mother of heroes and poets, but never the mother of cowards. . . . If by any chance on your way home you should meet a police officer or a military man, why, just—look at him!"

—Archbishop John Hughes, speech to a crowd of thousands gathered before his home, Friday, July 15, 1863. The archbishop had just returned from Europe, where he served as emissary for President Lincoln.

"This is a nice town to call itself a center of civilization!"

—George Templeton Strong, distinguished New Yorker, comment on the rioting, late July 1863

16

The shirt sticking to his back, the odor of his own sweat unpleasant in his nostrils, Ned was nevertheless whistling a merry tune when he arrived home about seven o'clock on the evening of Saturday, July 11. Martin and Patrick had reported for duty at dawn that day, and were now taking the evening off.

"How did it go, son?" asked Martin.

"Surprisingly well," said Ned. "There was a little grumbling and cursing here and there, but they drew more than a thousand names and nobody threw a single brick."

"Was there much of a crowd?" asked Pat.

"The draft office itself was packed. Maybe a hundred, hundred and fifty people, and maybe another couple of hundred outside, but peaceable enough—they even made jokes every so often about some poor fellow whose name was called."

Martin mopped his brow.

"I just wish this goddam heat would let up."

"I wish the saloons could be closed down till Monday," said Pat.

"Soon as I have a little supper and wash up, I'm going out to make the rounds," said Ned. "Sergeant Young assigned us to a couple dozen saloons each. We're to lift a few with the boys and see if there's any agitation going on."

"Don't get too drunk," said Pat, chuckling.

Martin said, "They brought in fifteen or twenty hoodlums during the day. The thugs were chasing and clubbing Negroes over on Leonard and Baxter."

"That's still going on, is it?" said Ned. "Clara told me Willie Simpkins was worried about his family."

By Sunday night it was plain that there might indeed be cause for concern. In virtually every saloon he visited Ned found one or more loud, aggressive characters denouncing the draft, cursing the rich who were pushing the poor Irish workingman to go out and die for a bunch of niggers. In Sweet's Restaurant, where he went for a solitary dinner on Sunday, he saw Mike O'Leary at a secluded table with the Virginian John Andrews and a group of other well-dressed men. There was a decidedly conspiratorial air about them. Mike came over to Ned's table and slapped Ned on the back.

"You ready for a little discontent, old Ned?" he joshed. "I hear tell there's going to be a proper rebellion tomorrow."

"You and your friends wouldn't be organizing it, now would you?" asked Ned lightly.

"We're sure as hell not going to do anything to discourage it, old Ned," said Mike. "Keep your powder dry."

He walked with nonchalant arrogance back to his companions.

Ned went back to look in on Clara late Sunday night. Willie Simpkins had brought his wife and his young son and daughter to the house and Clara had turned the second bedroom over to them. Ned cautioned them to be careful, and Clara again urged Ned to take care of himself. She did not sleep at all Sunday night. Ned did not sleep that night either. He had not slept well Saturday night. For that matter few, if any, in the city were able to sleep comfortably. The heat was more than oppressive. It made the simple act of breathing difficult. The humidity plastered people's clothing to their skins and caused irritating rashes in crotch and armpits, and surly, disagreeable thoughts in their minds. Except for the hundreds of drunks in the saloons and the stinking ghettos, who were either stupidly giddy or merry or mean and bellicose, thousands of New Yorkers sweated sluggishly through the unrelenting moist and scorching days and nights. Almost any distraction would be a relief from their misery. It was as though nature itself were setting a stage, creating an atmosphere for disaster.

At dawn on Monday, a sullen sun inched over the horizon and set about reheating the breezeless air into steam. The police department's Sunday–Monday night shift came off their weary rounds at six A.M. and the day shifts reported. All three Morrisseys left the house after the break of day. Martin and Pat boarded the horse-drawn streetcar to head downtown, while Ned walked wearily over to Broadway. They were all startled to see a substantial mob of ragged, sweating people—men, women, and children—straggling along Broadway. Some carried sticks or clubs or iron bars; others bricks, rocks, and cobblestones. They were shouting and cursing. Most of the men, and some of the women and even a few children, seemed quite drunk.

"Looks like there'll be some trouble after all," said Martin.

"They're obviously from the Lower East Side," said Pat.

"You think they could be heading for the enrollment office over on Third and Forty-sixth?"

Martin frowned.

"Enrollments begin this morning in another office on Broadway," he said. "Maybe they're headed there."

Ned eased himself into the tail end of the boisterous band at Forty-sixth Street and marched along with them as they headed west to Eighth Avenue. Here some turned north, while others continued toward Ninth Avenue. They came together again at the south end of Central Park. Despite the war, the attractive circular paths, the vast expanse of verdant lawn, now showing sere patches, the colorful flower beds, shrubs, and trees of the park had been completed as far north as 102nd Street. A second reservoir for the Croton water system had even been constructed in the park. Now at Fifty-ninth Street Ned saw men pushing through the mob distributing placards on long wooden sticks. Soon here and there, throughout the noisy assemblage, the placards were raised and waved drunkenly.

"NO DRAFT," they read in awkwardly printed large black letters. The crowd congregated in clusters around various speakers. Some stood on tall rock outcroppings, some on hillocks. All were obviously haranguing their milling listeners. On a grass mound beneath a maple tree Ned saw John Andrews shouting exhortations, waving his arms.

Ned squirmed and elbowed his way out of the herd at Lexington Avenue and walked rapidly to the Nineteenth Precinct station house on Fifty-ninth Street near Third Avenue. His clothes clung to him, but he was totally oblivious to either his discomfort or his weariness. The adrenaline flowed in his veins as he identified himself, and Captain Porter of the precinct put his message on the telegraph to Mulberry Street headquarters. He gave a succinct description and an estimate of the number of threatening rioters, which he thought might be between five thousand and eight thousand. He informed the central office that the mob had persistently added to its numbers as it staggered forward, by drawing workers out of shops, factories, or warehouses, sometimes by persuasion, sometimes by force. When he completed his message he requested further orders from Sergeant Young, the chief of detectives. Young replied:

PROCEED TO 677 THIRD AVENUE DRAFT OFFICE. REMAIN WITH MOB. REPORT FURTHER WHEN ABLE AND NECESSARY VIA TELEGRAPH FROM NEAREST PRECINCT OR RETURN PERSONALLY TO HQ IF VITAL.

At headquarters the superintendent of police, John A. Kennedy, read Ned's report with some concern. He decided to send Captain Porter and a contingent of sixty men to the Third Avenue draft office, and to send Captain Fred Speight and about the same number of patrolmen to stand guard at the second draft office on Broadway. He also telegraphed all precincts. Pat Morrissey and his operating colleagues sent the superintendent's instructions:

TO ALL STATIONS IN NEW YORK AND BROOKLYN. CALL IN YOUR RESERVE PLATOONS AND HOLD THEM AT STATION HOUSE SUBJECT TO FURTHER ORDERS.

Ned rejoined the mob just as it was approaching Third Avenue. It was now nearly nine o'clock. There was continuous shouting and screaming and cursing, but the splinter groups seemed to be operating spontaneously, without direction from any leaders. Ned had no idea what they were up to, but it was obvious they were bent on creating havoc in one way or another. What they were up to was soon learned at Mulberry Street as one telegraph report after another clacked into the basement where Pat and a half dozen other operators sat at their machines and tensely wrote out the messages they were receiving.

"Armed mob halting railway car at Fourth Avenue between Thirty-second and Thirty-third streets. Unhitching horses. Have shoved car off tracks and overturned it. No passengers hurt. Many joining rioters."

"Crowd, consisting mainly of women, many apparently under influence of alcohol, led by half dozen known Dead Rabbit gangsters, ripping up tracks with crowbars at Harlem and New Haven Railroad right of way near Forty-seventh Street."

"Three hardware stores, two gunsmith shops on Fifth Avenue looted by rioters."

One report coming in from Captain James Bogart at the

Thirty-first Precinct on Eighty-sixth Street and Bloomingdale Road was interrupted before it could be completed.

"Citizens report mob chopping down telegraph poles and cutting wires at—"

As the day wore on Pat Morrissey and his colleagues in the telegraph bureau's central control in the basement became increasingly frustrated and furious as connections between Mulberry Street and one precinct after another were cut off. Most, in these early stages, were precincts north of Fifty-ninth Street, but Martin was certain that it would not be long before the mob would attempt to disrupt the entire system.

"It seems a reasonably well organized riot, sir," he told Superintendent Kennedy as the reports continued to come in.

Trouble was indeed brewing. The swarming rioters had gathered at the Third Avenue office, where names were still being drawn from the lottery drum. Ned watched and listened tensely. He was surrounded by five brawny members of the Black Joke Volunteer Fire Company, a renegade group known for its bullying roughneck ways. They were drunk and still drinking, passing a bottle of amber whiskey from one to another. Their black shirts were wet with sweat, and moisture rolled down their faces from beneath the leather firemen's hats they wore.

Ahead of them, blocking the mob from the draft office, were Captain Porter's sixty policemen, locustwood nightsticks at the ready.

"Why don't ya go fight the fuckin' war yerself, ya stinkin' copper!" bellowed one of the Black Jokes. Suddenly from somewhere to the left of Ned a pistol shot sounded. It was as though the shot were a signal. The mob surged forward, swinging fists, clubs, and iron pipes, hurling stones and bricks. Ned ducked as a policeman's nightstick swung by his head. When he looked up he saw jagged, geometric-shaped holes appear in the draft-office windows as bricks and cobblestones shattered them. Screams, curses, roars, and shrieks of fury and pain filled the air. The police had no choice but to fall back before the overwhelmingly superior numbers of the mob.

Inside the office the provost marshal and his aides piled together the enrollment lists and raced out the back door with them. Fighting the enraged mob as they retreated, the men from the Nineteenth Precinct backed into the office and made their escape through the same door the Federal people had used. Only a few members of the mob chased them. The rest set about destroying the draft office. The lottery drum, the tables and chairs were smashed, supplying new clubs for some of the unarmed. Three men with axes banged away at the marshal's iron safe, but could not break it open. A burly, sweating bearded giant bellowed, "Outta the way . . . we're gonna burn 'er down!"

As the rioters near him leaped out of range, he splashed turpentine over the wreckage in the office. Two other men and a woman did likewise. The resinous odor of the turpentine blended with the stale smell of sweat and blind malignity as the bearded man shouted, "Everybody out!"

He led the way to the front door with dozens of wild-eyed rioters preceding and following him. Twenty others charged out through the back door. The bearded man lit a newspaper and tossed it into the middle of the room. In moments the draft office was ablaze from wall to wall. Ned, struggling to get through the mob and back to the precinct, discovered that the frenzied congregation had grown to monstrous proportions. It stretched north and south of Forty-sixth Street along Third Avenue. He was fighting his way south, and had almost reached the end of the southern edge of the mass of crazed rioters, when he saw a strange sight. *A small army was advancing on the crowd.* Ned guessed there were about fifty men. They were dressed in the uniforms of a dozen or more different Union regiments. Some had one arm; some walked with the aid of a crutch; some wore eyepatches. They were all armed with muskets with affixed bayonets or sabers. At their head limped a middle-aged man with a dark mustache and beard and fierce eyes. Ned, Pat, and Martin had attended the first drill of the Invalid Corps not too long ago. They were soldiers who had been wounded in the war, and having returned home, organized this brave band of the disabled. Normally they served as guards at military or war production installations. Since no other military forces were available in the city—all New York regiments had been rushed to Pennsylvania to join the Union forces at Gettysburg—Superintendent Kennedy had called upon the Invalid Corps for help.

Ned recognized the limping man at their head. He was Lieutenant Abel Reade. Ned heard him shout at the mob to halt, under threat of fire. Ducking low, Ned charged into a nearby doorway. The mob kept advancing. The Invalid Corps fired a volley. Ned noted they had raised their muskets and fired into the air. The charging mob kept coming. Those in front seemed intimidated by the warning shot, but the drunken, angry men and women behind them forced them forward. Once more Lieutenant Reade gave the order to fire. This time the crippled soldiers fired point-blank into the onrushing crowd. A shirtless, heavyset man with a hairy chest, leading the mob with an iron bar in his upraised fist, staggered to a sudden stop. A surprised look came over his face. He gasped as blood turned a deep pink in the sweat-soaked hair on his chest. He sat, then toppled over backward. Five other men in the vanguard of the mob fell to the Invalids' musket balls. But the crazed crowd came on, mindlessly trampling its leaders.

Ned watched in helpless horror as the rioters swarmed all over the soldiers. He saw more than a dozen lose their bayoneted muskets and sabers to savage maniacs, too drunk to know fear. He saw two of the Invalid troopers beaten to the ground, hammered, slashed, stabbed, and stomped to death. He was suddenly aware of intense heat and smoke, and a quite different pandemonium behind him. He turned and saw that not only was the building at 677 burning from ground to roof, but the tenements flanking it at 675 and 679 were ablaze too. Courageous firefighters from volunteer companies—who had miraculously made it to the scene—were desperately trying to get their engines and equipment into position to gain control of the blaze. But the mob beat them off. Ironically, some members of the Black Joke Volunteers were among the most aggressive in hampering the efforts of their saner, duty-bound fellow firefighters. Ned realized it was hopeless, the three buildings were surely doomed to destruction.

The Twenty-second Precinct was at Forty-seventh Street between Eighth and Ninth avenues and he decided to try to make his way there to telegraph another report to headquarters and urge help from whatever sources might be available. Fighting his way through the mob he heard a blowsy, sweating Irishwoman, armed with a table leg, scream, "Pass the word, ya buggers . . . pass the word . . . t' the nigger orphanage . . ."

In a clearing off to her left a gaunt man on a horse, his shirt in tatters, a wild look in his eyes, waved a saber and shouted,

"Everybody! Everybody! Listen, ya brave and bloody fools! We're gonna take the orphanage . . ."

Ned realized he would not have time to get to either the Nineteenth or Twenty-second precinct. He battled his way out of the mob until he reached Fifth Avenue. Here he saw a coachman, standing beside his coach outside a greengrocer's shop. He rushed up to the man and showed him his detective badge and identification card.

"Come on, man! The rioters are headed to the orphan asylum! Come on, damn you! Let's go!"

The pudgy coachman stared at him stupidly.

"I can't, officer. My lady's in—"

Ned clambered up on the high seat of the coach, grabbed the reins, whipped the single sturdy horse, and bolted off. Behind him the coachman roared in protest. The Colored Orphan Asylum was home for two hundred and thirty-three boys and girls, all under thirteen years of age. It was a handsome brick building, set in grassy grounds dotted with elm, oak, and maple trees and thick shrubbery. William Davis, the superintendent, answered Ned's frantic pounding on the front door. Davis had already heard of the rioting and was preparing the children for a quick departure. The fifty-three employees of the asylum were helping the boys and girls get together their few belongings. In the near distance the roar of the oncoming mob sounded like rumbling thunder.

"Better barricade the doors," urged Ned. All the doors except one in the rear were bolted. Tables, chairs, desks, and other furniture were piled against the doors.

"Let's get the children over to the Nineteenth Precinct for now," said Ned. "We can make it to Madison. The omnibuses are still running."

Terror showed in the dark eyes of the children. Some whimpered and cried. But obediently, holding hands, they marched out of the rear double door of the orphanage, and headed toward Madison, led and flanked by Ned, Davis, and the asylum workers. They staggered along fearfully. The angry, demented clamor of the crowd grew louder. As Ned got on the last of the omnibuses with Davis and some twenty-six of the children, he held the hand of a kinky-haired boy of nine, who was sobbing uncontrollably, and muttering something Ned could not understand. He put his arm around the boy's shoulder and tried to console him.

"Lu—sss—sisss—lu—" the boy cried as the horses pulled

the omnibus up the avenue toward Fifty-ninth Street. Ned looked back and saw thick smoke and flame soaring into the sun-baked summer sky from the windows of the orphanage.

"What's your name?" Ned asked the boy.

"Lu—Lucius..." he said, sobbing. "But Lu—my sisss—my sister, Lucinda... she lef' behind."

Over the clatter of the iron wheels, the sharp cracking of the horses' hooves, and the frightened muttering of the children, Ned shouted to Davis, seated two rows before him.

"Mr. Davis! Is Lucinda—this boy's sister, Lucinda—is she here?"

Davis looked around at the children in the omnibus.

"I—I—I don't see her, Mr. Morrissey," he said. "Maybe she's in one of the other buses."

Lucius shook his head and wailed loudly.

"No—no—she hide under de bed. I tell her come out, but she hide..."

The omnibus was approaching Fiftieth Street. Ned was flung to his knees as he leaped off. His trousers were ripped and both knees and the palms of his hands were skinned. Nervous pedestrians gaped at him and cleared the way, as he raced back to the orphanage. The insane mob had surrounded it. They were singing and dancing and roaring obscenities, as sparks and flame and smoke twisted out of the building's windows. Ned elbowed and shoved his way through the rioters to the back door. The door had been scorched and it gave immediately as he slammed his shoulder against it. Crawling on hands and knees, keeping low where the heat and smoke were minimal, he squinted his eyes and looked around the large room. His eyes stung and tears rolled down his cheeks. His nose itched and he coughed in short, hacking barks as he inhaled the drifting smoke.

Then he saw the small figure of a child. It lay to his left in a section of the room that had not been touched by the fire. He crawled toward the child. Through stinging eyes, blurred by tears, he saw the battered head, the crushed face, the blood dried on the thin naked body. He reached out and touched the little girl's cheek just below where the cheekbone protruded. Despite the heat, the cheek was cold, the body rigid. Ned crawled back to the door and out. He gulped a breath of the humid, ash-laden air and charged toward the mob. A tall young man, filthy with dirt and sweat, was waving a club in his right hand and greedily swallowing whiskey from a bottle in his left. Ned rushed toward him, ripped the bottle from his grasp, and, as the man began to bellow a protest, smashed it into his face. The man screamed, dropped his club, and held both hands over his bleeding face. Three men near him shouted at Ned. One reached for him. Holding the broken bottle by its neck, Ned jabbed it at the reacher, and picked up the club his victim had dropped. Stabbing out with the jagged-edged bottle in his left hand, swinging the club with his right, he charged his way out of the mob like a madman. No one tried too hard to stop him. Most of the rioters had no idea what had happened. They thought the sheer ecstasy they felt over the devastation they were wreaking and a touch too much whiskey had made one of their own a mite crazy. Some even applauded and cheered him as he jabbed and swung and cursed his way through them.

He had no idea how long it took him, nor how he got there, but he found himself back at headquarters at Mulberry Street. They had already heard the news of the firing of the orphanage via telegraph from the Nineteenth Precinct, where two hundred and thirty-two of the two hundred and thirty-three children had arrived safely. Arrangements were being made to ship the orphans to Blackwell's Island as soon as a protective force could be assembled to accompany them.

At Mulberry Street it was bedlam. Scores of citizens who had been burned out of their homes nearby had come to the station. Close to a hundred Negro men, women, and children were huddled in rooms on the second and third floors of the massive stone building. Most of them had barely escaped being maimed or murdered by the mob. Sergeant Young had set up a commissary where coffee and sandwiches were dispensed. Ned did not feel like eating. He reported to Young and then joined a long line of patrolmen who were having their various wounds attended by four busy doctors. A young aide to one of the physicians cleansed the dirt out of his palms and scraped knees, dabbed them with an ointment that stung, and bandaged them loosely. He changed his torn and filthy trousers and shirt, and went to his father's office. A young sergeant told him that Martin was down in the basement in the telegraph room. He found his father rushing from one operator to another, frantic and red-faced. He joined Martin at Pat's desk.

"Is it word from Kennedy, Pat?" Martin was asking anxiously as Ned stood beside him. Sweat dripping from his face, Pat shook his head.

"No. Another report from the Eighteenth," he said, speaking as he scrawled out the message. "The entire block from Twenty-fourth to Twenty-fifth Street on Third Avenue is burning."

Martin became aware of Ned, standing at his elbow.

"Oh, thank Christ, son! Are you all right?"

"Fine. Just a few scrapes. They're going mad out there, Papa!"

"I know. I know. The superintendent, damned fool, left over an hour ago. Had to make a personal inspection. Insisted on going all by himself. Drove off in his light carriage. We haven't heard a word from him since."

Pat cursed sharply.

"Goddammit! Another line down!"

A patrolman came clumping down the stairs and ran across the broad basement to Martin.

"Captain! They got a body outside in a wagon. Claim it's Superintendent Kennedy!"

Martin led the way up the stairs with Ned and the patrolman close behind. Outside in front of the headquarters building stood an open wagon, with a small crowd gathered around it. A half dozen policemen had climbed into it, and were staring down at the body of a man. A dirty tarpaulin cover had been thrown aside. Ned scaled himself nimbly onto the wagon bed, wincing at the pain in his hands. He helped Martin aboard. They both gasped as they looked down at the mutilated body. Martin knelt and held the bloody wrist.

"The driver says it's Superintendent Kennedy," said one of the policemen. "Claims he saw the mob kill 'im. When they left 'im for dead, he thought he better bring 'im in."

Martin felt a slight pulse. The man was not dead, not quite. But it was impossible to tell if he was Kennedy. The face had been battered and smashed; the body slashed with a score of deep knife wounds. The head was lumped and cracked. The clothes he wore were ripped and tattered and covered with blood and mud. Martin held the wrist and looked at a ring on a mud-caked finger. He wiped the finger and the ring. The gold initials *JK* showed. It was the ring the officers at headquarters had given Kennedy when he became superintendent of the Metropolitan Police Force.

"It's the superintendent," said Martin, grimly. "Get him over to Bellevue. . . ."

The task of supervising control of the rioters fell to the Metropolitan Board of Police Commissioners. One of the three, James Bowen, had recently been appointed a brigadier general and had left for active duty. A second member lived in Brooklyn and said he believed he should continue to direct activities there, even though no extensive rioting had broken out in that community yet. Thus it was left to the president of the board himself to take over. He was Thomas Acton, a founder of the Union League club and a strong, well-respected civic leader. However, he was a stockbroker with little practical police experience. He immediately met with Mayor Opdyke and urged the mayor to call upon the harbor garrisons and every available militia unit for help.

He then met with the senior officers at 300 Mulberry Street. Martin suggested that all the reserves from every precinct in the city be rushed to the Twenty-fifth precinct headquarters.

"The other station houses can be guarded by small forces of men," he said.

"I think you're right, Captain. There's every indication that the rioters have some kind of intelligent and aggressive copperhead leadership. We can anticipate an eventual assault on the headquarters here."

A patrolman came into the meeting room, and handed a telegraph to the commissioner.

It was from Captain John Cameron of the Eighteenth Precinct at 163 East Twenty-second Street.

HAVE RELIABLE WORD STATE ARMORY AND UNION STEAM WORKS SCHEDULED FOR MOB ATTACK. HAVE STATIONED GUARDS BOTH LOCATIONS. URGE ADDITIONAL FORCES SOONEST.

Sixteen men from Mulberry Street were rushed to the armory, a wooden warehouse on Second Avenue and Twenty-first Street. They took along carbines, in addition to the pistols and nightsticks they normally carried. They joined the men from the Eighteenth, guarding the entrances and positioning themselves inside at every window of the three-story armory and the carbine-manufacturing facility, which was formerly the steam works. Martin himself led the group defending the armory.

Ned, continuing his assignment to mingle with the crowd, picked up a large band of drunken rioters near Third Avenue at Tenth Street and learned that they were, indeed, on their way to the armory. By the time this group joined the main body of the rioters on Third and Nineteenth Street, the crowd seemed to fill the streets in every direction as far as the eye could see. Ned had no way of estimating the size of the mob, but later guesses placed it at near ten thousand.

Whatever the number, it was more than enough to overwhelm the fifty or sixty police defenders of the armory. Still, the policemen, occasionally firing their carbines over the heads of the milling throng, kept them from attempting to storm the building for more than an hour. The mob had assembled before the armory a little after two-thirty, and they boiled restlessly in their own sweat under the blistering midday sun, but somehow could not bring themselves to charge the building.

Squirming and muscling his way closer and closer to the front, Ned saw the blond Virginian John Andrews recklessly ride a tan and brown horse into the crowd, waving a saber and urging them to storm the armory. Then, some fifteen yards to the right of Andrews, he saw Mike O'Leary holding an American flag high on a pole. Beside Mike, gray-streaked orange-red hair hanging wetly down to her shoulders, staggered his mother. Mary O'Leary reeled and wildly waved a pistol in her right hand, all the while screaming something Ned could not make out in the general cacophony.

It took more than an hour of frantic exhortation on the part of Andrews, Mike O'Leary, and other leaders to convince those at the head of the mob to break into the armory. Finally a giant of a man with scraggly rust-colored hair, standing beside Mike, led the charge. The policemen at the wide double doors fired their carbines directly at the onrushing rioters. The giant fell, and so did a dozen others, but Ned saw Mike stab the foot of the flagpole into the face of one of the policemen, drop the flag, and, waving both fists in the air, roar into the building. His mother stumbled after him, brandishing her pistol and shrieking. The mad mob stomped over their fallen comrades and soon were bursting into the armory by the scores. Police firing did not deter them. Ned was carried along with them. He managed to get his own pistol out of its leg holster. He knew Martin was in the building, and if the opportunity arose for him to protect his father, he surely would. In the meantime, of course, he risked being shot by one of the policemen, who might not know him, or by any of the rioters who might recognize him. But he had been aware of those paradoxical and unhappy possibilities when he took on the infiltration assignment.

He saw that Martin and a knot of some twenty police, realizing the hopelessness of their position, had chopped a hole out of the rear wall of the armory. Martin and the survivors of his band from the headquarters precinct then made their way back to the Eighteenth Precinct and telegraphed the news that the mob had taken the armory. Commissioner Acton, in the meantime, had directed the regrouping of the squads of police who had been beaten off at Third Avenue. They joined Martin's men, and now, numbering a few more than a hundred, the combined band of grimly determined policemen rushed back to the armory.

The mob still outside, though huge, was mainly drunk and disorganized. The police scattered them quickly. Some ran into the armory, shouting that an enormous police force had returned. Pandemonium broke out inside the armory as rioters raced to get out. But Martin and his men were at every exit. As the confused rioters poured out, the police clubbed any who were armed, and ignored the unarmed, who fled down Second Avenue. Ned saw a drunken man splashing turpentine out of a can onto the wooden lockers, cabinets and all over the floor. He dashed for the door himself, his pistol back in its holster, and ran the gauntlet of club-swinging police. He managed to get away with nothing more than an aching forearm, where one nightstick had struck him.

A half block from the armory Ned stopped and looked back. The fire was spreading fast. He saw men and some women leaping from the second- and third-floor windows. A tall, handsome blond young man lifted a third-floor window and fired a carbine wildly down into an area where police were battering escaping rioters. It was Mike O'Leary. When Mike reloaded for the fourth time, Ned saw a huge sheet of flame, pale yellow and gold in the sunlight, flare up behind him. Then the sheet of flame diminished, and was replaced spectacularly by dozens of fiery brilliant bursts and jagged streaks of incandescent golden-greens, radiant orange-scarlets, gleaming ice-white silvers. It was as though Mike O'Leary's body had suddenly become the center of an extraordinary fireworks creation. Ned realized that a cache of ammunition, cartridges, powder, whatever, had exploded, probably directly below the window where Mike O'Leary stood. Then Mike, his body outlined in a nimbus of flickering fire, his flaming arms high and wide over his haloed head, fell forward into the street.

The next day Ned learned from Martin that Mike, flying face down from the third floor, had impaled himself on the upraised bayonet of one of the rioters. It had pierced his stomach and exited at his back, and the impact of his fall had knocked over the bayonet holder so forcefully that the rioter's skull was cracked when he hit a low stone wall. Twenty-nine other jumping rioters had also died, but none as freakishly as Mike O'Leary. Forty-six were badly injured. It was almost six o'clock before the mob was finally driven off. But the rebellion Mike had promised was not yet over.

Darkness brought no relief from the oppressive heat and humidity. When night fell Pat Morrissey and a fellow telegrapher left their posts and rode about the city, dressed as coachmen, repairing downed telegraph lines wherever they could without being discovered by wandering, bloodthirsty rioters.

At eleven o'clock Martin was asleep on a cot in his office at headquarters. Ned lay on a cot beside him, listening to his father snoring heavily and occasionally moaning in his sleep. He was so weary and full of aches he could not sleep. He worried about Martin's blood pressure. He wished his father had retired a year earlier.

The picture of Mike O'Leary falling from the armory window flashed in his mind. And Mary O'Leary, brandishing her pistol and screeching through the mob like some wild Irish banshee. He was wide awake now, and he thought about Clara. He wondered where Max was; whether he was still alive; whether he would ever return. Poor Max-less Clara. She worried about him, just the way she worried about Max. But here he was, indestructible Edward Morrissey. Aching, but indestructible.

17

Clara and the baby were safe. Thank God!

He lay on the brocade sofa in the parlor, wearier than he

had ever been in his life, but still unable to sleep. He got up, feeling somewhat clownish in Max's robe. It was far too short for him, the hem inches above his knees, and far too broad, so that its shoulders slumped halfway down his stringy but muscular upper arms. His own drenched clothes, wrung out, were hanging on an improvised line over the wood and coal stove in the kitchen. He walked to the window and stared at the welcome and continuing deluge. The glass panes wept a thousand tears. The room was becoming stuffy, so Ned opened the window two inches. Rain bounced off the sill and small splashes stained Max's robe and cooled Ned's bare legs.

Clara and the baby were alive, but the tension, fear, and grief here on the third-floor living quarters of the brewery were palpable. Faintly from the north-facing bedroom Ned could hear Willie Simpkins's wife, Sarah, sobbing quietly.

When Willie Simpkins had answered Ned's prearranged knock (three, then a pause; two and another pause; and finally one; repeated till answered) Ned's heart almost stopped at the look on the gaunt young Negro's face. He was certain something terrible had happened to Clara and the baby.

"Is—is Mrs. Kessler—"

"She all right, Mr. Ned," said Willie in a thick, grief-stricken voice. "It's my brother, Samuel. . . . They hang him—and burn 'im."

Back on the third floor Willie had hastened to the bedroom, where Sarah was trying to comfort their eleven-year-old daughter and eight-year-old son. Clara, her blue eyes bloodshot, her silver-gold hair stringy and damp, came out of her own bedroom, where William had just fallen asleep again. She told Ned what had happened. Willie Simpkins's brother was one of the waiters in a restaurant called Crook's. Since all the waiters in Crook's were Negroes, a mob had decided to go there, wreck the restaurant, and hang the waiters. Two had escaped, but Samuel Simpkins had not been so lucky.

"You knew Mrs. Gillicuddy, Ned, did you not?" said Clara, sitting on the sofa beside him, holding his hand in both of hers. Ned nodded.

"I arrested a young colored man who raped her daughter. It was just before the war, about three years ago. He was hanged."

"She was the leader of the mob," said Clara. "Did you know her daughter had a baby?"

"No, it must have been when Dutch Winckler and me were over in New Jersey, after a band of thieves who'd robbed Tiffany's."

"The baby was colored. The girl killed the child—a little boy—and herself . . . with a kitchen knife."

"I remember that case. I didn't know it was the Gillicuddy girl."

Clara nodded sadly.

"Mrs. Gillicuddy has been demented ever since. For years she's been cursing and threatening every Negro she sees in the street. Now I'm afraid the poor woman believes her day has come."

Ned thought of Mary O'Leary. Sisters at arms, fighting the war against the black infidels, she and Mrs. Gillicuddy. Clara suddenly began to shiver, although it was warm in the room. He put one arm around her and drew her close to him. She put both arms around him and kissed him lightly on the cheek.

"I'm so glad you're here, Ned. I was so afraid something terrible would happen to you."

"Just a few scrapes," he said, holding her tightly in both arms, ignoring the stinging sensation in his now unbandaged palms, and the fact that they were no doubt soiling the back of her cotton nightdress.

"I wish you could stay with us, Ned," she said with a sigh, and kissed his cheek again.

"I do, too, but I've got to leave at dawn. We need every man at Mulberry Street. The rioting's far from over."

She raised her head and kissed him softly on the lips. They lay close together on the sofa. A deep and complex need, long denied, possessed them both. Just before Ned's arrival Clara had nursed baby William for the eighth time that evening. The tense atmosphere around him seemed to stimulate the baby's appetite and his craving for the comfort of her breast. The nursing had aroused sexual stirrings in her. She had been so long without Max. Who a better surrogate than Ned, dear Ned. He represented goodness in this berserk and evil world; goodness and protection for herself and William, the Simpkinses and their children.

Ned's desire for Clara had been smoldering inside him for years. At this moment, after being a participant in and eyewitness to a day of wholesale, mindless murder and mayhem in the city itself, after more than two years of news of brave men dying in a bloody war, it became an urgent necessity that he lose himself in Clara's embrace, her moist, hot, openmouthed kiss.

Somehow by an instinctual cooperative series of twists and turns, Max's robe had slipped from Ned's body and Clara's nightdress had fallen to the floor beside the sofa. He drew her closer to him and caressed her back, her waist, her buttocks. Even the stinging pain of the raw palms of his hands became part of the ecstatic joy he felt. They made love hungrily, yet tenderly; gently, yet with intense passion. All too soon they reached a shuddering, simultaneous orgasm.

Clara moaned and sighed and turned from her side onto her back. "Max," she gasped and moaned again, and repeated her husband's name. She rested her silver-blond head on Ned's heaving chest. Ned was puzzled, and for an instant, resentful, but he was sated and exhausted, and said nothing. Except for the steady sound of the rainstorm beating against the weeping windowpanes, and Ned's and Clara's heavy breathing, there was silence. In a few moments they were both asleep.

The Morrisseys were a peculiar-looking trio as they sat around Martin's desk, drinking black coffee. Martin's gray-streaked hair was tousled. His eyes were bloodshot. He was unshaved and a salt-and-pepper stubble showed on his gaunt face. The purple and scarlet blood vessels in his puffy cheeks, like river and road lines on a map, seemed more vivid than usual. His liver-spotted hands trembled as he held the *Tribune* in front of him. Ned noted that a fat vein in his temple on the right side throbbed. Pat looked rakish with a heavy white bandage around his head, covering the entire skull and all of one ear, but tilted to leave the other ear exposed. The turbanlike wrapping, along with the cheek scar from the *Henry Clay* fire, gave him the look of a weary pirate.

Before going off to their individual assignments, Ned and Pat were exchanging tales of the previous day's happenings with their father. They were all particularly shocked by Mike O'Leary's death, but Martin and Pat were glad that Clara and her child were safe. Martin asked Pat about Fiona and the Laffertys. They had gone over to New Jersey, and were staying with relatives there. Pat had spent the night sloshing around in the rain, repairing cut telegraph wires. They were working in the backyard of a saloon on Forty-ninth Street near Ninth Avenue, when five burly drunken men with clubs and iron pipes charged out of the noisy establishment and set upon them. They fought the attackers off and managed to get back to their coach, but not before Pat had suffered a severe gash in the top of his head, and almost had an ear torn off. Charlie Towne had a shattered cheekbone and a broken arm. And that was the end of their night's work, but it was almost dawn and they would have had to stop anyway. Towne was already in the basement, manning his post with bandaged cheek and one arm in a sling. Pat was almost finished with his second cup of strong coffee, and though his head ached, he was ready to get back to his telegraph table.

Ned, his clothes dirty and wrinkled but dry, his cheeks hollow, and his eyes red-streaked and deep in their sockets, nevertheless seemed incredibly energetic and fresh. When he had awakened it was still dark, but the rain had stopped. Clara had left him alone on the sofa. He had been sleeping so soundly that he had not even awakened when she left him. He slipped on Max's ill-fitting robe and went into the bedchamber and saw that both she and the baby were fast asleep. He touched her cheek gently with the tips of his fingers, careful not to wake her. He dressed and walked briskly to Mulberry Street. Dawn was breaking and many people were apparently rushing to get out of the city. He knew the ferries would be crowded, and he already had seen wealthier families, their coaches and carriages piled high with belongings, heading northward.

Now in his father's office at headquarters he disgustedly dropped the copy of *The Daily News* he'd been reading on the desk. Martin nodded aggressively and said, "Greeley knows what he's talking about. Hear this!"

In a voice hoarse with fatigue, he read, "'. . . The nucleus of the true mob is a hardened corps of about three hundred miscreants who had a previously understood purpose. They carried out their atrocities by the aid of a certain amount of rough discipline. No person who carefully watched the movements of this mob, who noticed their careful attention to the words of certain tacitly acknowledged leaders, who observed the unquestionably preconcerted regularity with which they proceeded from one part of their infernal program to the next; and the persistency with which the "rear guard" remained and fought off all who dared to check any part of the destruction that everywhere marked their work, can presume to doubt that these men are acting under leaders who have carefully elaborated their plans, who have, as they think, made all things sure of their accomplishment, and that they are resolved to carry them out through fire and blood, this day's crimson work fully attests.'"

Ned nodded somberly. Well, he reflected, they lost one of their leaders when Mike died. Maybe today John Andrews could be taken . . . or killed.

Commissioner Acton came into the office, looking as haggard as Martin Morrissey. He waved copies of *The Daily News* and the *World* angrily.

"These scoundrels should be tried for treason," he said vehemently.

The same papers lay open to their editorial pages on Martin's desk. The Morrisseys had already cursed the Wood-owned-and-controlled publications. The *News* had drawn comparisons between the rioters and the Union soldiers at Gettysburg. "The men who have gone from among us to the war," it proclaimed, "who today guard the Capital and hold Lee and his men at bay among the Maryland hills, are just such men as those who have struck terror through our peaceful streets, of like passions, swayed by like motives, to be kindled with the same patriotic fire. Will the insensate men at Washington now at length listen to our voices?"

The *World* showed great understanding toward the rioters. "Does any man wonder that poor men refuse to be forced into a war mismanaged almost into hopelessness, perverted into partisanship? Did the President and his cabinet imagine that their lawlessness could conquer, or their folly seduce, a free people?"

Martin swept the papers from his desk.

"They're just what we need to keep the bloody mobs marching!" he exclaimed bitterly.

"I assume all the arrangements have been made for the guards around the City Hall this morning," said Acton. "We never know what that fool of a governor will say."

Governor Seymour, who had all but urged the citizens to riot not so long ago, was coming in from his vacation home in Long Branch, New Jersey, to make a pronouncement this morning.

"He'll be well protected, Commissioner," said Martin.

The forces stationed at City Hall could ill be spared. The day was hot, although not as humid as Monday, and it soon became apparent that the rioters, in large and small mobs, all over the city, were intent on continuing the rebellion. Only a minimum of military assistance had been forthcoming, largely due to a misunderstanding and a power struggle among Harvey Brown, brevet brigadier general of the Federal army and military commandant of New York City; General Charles Sandford, whose New York National Guardsmen had broken up the gang riots in 1857; and Major General John Wool, a hero of previous wars, but now almost eighty and commander of the Military Department in the East.

The governor made a mild and conciliatory speech. He appealed to the crowd as his friends to maintain the law, return to their jobs, and cease the rioting. He told them he had sent his personal adjutant general to Washington to plead to have the draft discontinued. He believed it would be. The crowd, sweating and restless, grumbled and cursed the police and the few militia units standing guard with rifles at the ready, but attempted no violence.

Ned had continued infiltrating the larger mobs of rioters, finding his way to Second Avenue and Thirty-fifth Street where he was amazed to see an army of more than a hundred and fifty men marching into Second Avenue from Thirty-fifth Street. They were the Eleventh New York Volunteers, a newly formed regiment, and not only were they uniformed and armed, but they were supported by a detachment of artillerymen, who wheeled two six-pounder cannon into the avenue. Ned watched as the mob, in confusion, turned away from the police attack on their southern fringe to face the military force advancing on them from Thirty-fifth Street.

The officer leading the regiment ordered the lieutenant at the head of the artillery force to fire the cannon. Ned paled as he watched the most horrible episode of the rebellion he had yet seen. The six-pounders fired a half dozen rounds of canister and grape, one after another, into the panicking rioters. Bloody, mutilated bodies of men, women, and children were everywhere. Finally the mob broke and those who were able escaped hysterically into side streets and dashed madly east and west.

When Ned returned to the Mulberry Street headquarters in early afternoon, Chief of Detectives Young was in consultation with Commissioner Acton, three inspectors, Martin, and several other senior officers. A number of telegraphic reports had indicated that the larger mobs were breaking down into smaller groups, many consisting of younger men, totally undisciplined and seemingly without any other objectives than to loot and plunder.

Ned was weary when he returned. He collapsed on a cot in the basement and fell asleep to the clatter of the telegraph machines and the grim but subdued hubbub of the tense telegraphers.

It was dark when Martin shook him awake.

"You feel up to one more brouhaha today, lad?" asked Martin.

Ned sat up and rubbed his eyes with his knuckles.

"Sure, Papa. Where we going?"

"There's a mob of lunatics robbing the Brooks Brothers clothing store on Catherine Street. We don't have too many able-bodied men left who can still stand on their feet. I'm taking a squad over there. Shouldn't take us too long to roust them."

It was nine o'clock when they headed toward Catherine Street in the police wagons. The city was dark except for eerie luminous patches in the black sky, here and there where fires still burned. Even the streets, which would normally be lighted by gas lamps, were dark, since many of the lamp posts had been knocked down and carted away. But as Martin, Ned, and a dozen other policemen leaped from the wagons at Catherine Street they saw that the Brooks Brothers building was brightly lit. Every gas jet in the three-story clothing emporium was burning. The display windows were shattered. Men and women stood in the upper-story windows, tossing shirts, ties, stockings, underwear, coats, vests, and trousers down to their companions in the street.

As the police charged across the street and into the building, the plunderers in the street scattered with their arms full of fancy apparel. Inside the store the looters were busy on every floor.

When the police attacked, the rioters began firing guns and swinging clubs and iron pipes, trying to fight their way to the front door. Ned stood several feet in front of and to the left of Martin in the middle of the ground floor. He clubbed several looters as they tried to run past him, arms laden with clothing. Then he saw Mary O'Leary come bursting out of one of the dressing rooms halfway down the east side of the store. At first he did not recognize her. She was dressed in a black wool man's suit, complete with vest. Under the vest she wore a white silk shirt and a bright crimson cravat. Apart from the fact that it was extremely tight around her upper torso, the suit fitted her well.

Ned only realized it was Mrs. O'Leary when she dashed past him and he saw, in a flash, the wild look in her green eyes. Her long, reddish hair, streaked with gray, hung wetly down to her shoulders. Her face was flushed and red with sweat. Ned did not notice the small pistol in her right hand. It was the same one she had taken from her purse the night of Lincoln's first speech in New York City.

Out of the corner of his eye he saw Martin, a surprised look on his face, staring at Mary O'Leary as she rushed toward him. Ned gasped as he saw Mrs. O'Leary, almost in Martin's arms, fire her small pistol directly into Martin's chest. Martin fell to his knees, clutching his breast. Ned saw the blood seeping between his father's fingers and watched in horror as Martin toppled forward on his face, arms outstretched at either side of his head. He ran to his father and knelt beside him. He was trying to turn him over when he saw Mary O'Leary bend and snatch the police pistol from Martin's limp hand.

"You're such a brave one, Martin, such a brave one," she cooed drunkenly, kneeling beside him. And then, before Ned could move, she put Martin's pistol to her temple and pulled the trigger. She toppled forward onto Martin's body. In the stifling July heat in the store, she reeked of sweat and alcohol.

There was little time for wakes or mourning. Martin was buried the next day, along with sixteen other policemen who had fallen in Tuesday's rioting, in a special cemetery the department had set aside in a field near the new, yet-to-be-completed St. Patrick's Cathedral. Ned and Pat returned to Mulberry Street immediately after the burial services. Pat manned his telegraph table and Ned reported to Chief Young for his next assignment.

It was only then that he learned that the Kessler Brewery on Rivington Street had been wrecked and set afire; that Willie Simpkins, his wife, and children had all been killed; that Sarah Simpkins, as well as her young daughter and Clara Kessler, had not only been bludgeoned, stabbed, and slashed, but raped as well. Somehow the murderers had spared, intentionally or by oversight, baby William Kessler. He was presently in the care of Chief Young's wife, who had improvised a nursery and child-care center on the third floor of the headquarters building.

Ned took William Kessler up to the Yorkville home of Ilka and Fritz Himmelfarb. There was weeping and wailing and oaths to Christ that the Himmelfarbs would care for him as if he were their own.

Ned did not cry. He was beyond tears. A total, chilling numbness possessed him. Shortly after midnight of the day Martin and Clara died, Mayor George Opdyke received a telegram at his temporary quarters at the St. Nicholas Hotel. It was from Secretary of War Edwin M. Stanton.

"Sir," it said. "Five regiments are under orders to return to New York. The retreat of Lee now becomes a rout, with his army broken and much heavier loss of killed and wounded than was supposed. This will relieve a large force for the restoration of order in New York."

The irate feeling against the rioters was intensifying. A fierce editorial in Horace Greeley's *Tribune* concluded, ". . . give them grape and plenty of it!"

About midnight Wednesday the first troops of the 74th Regiment, which had fought at Gettysburg and many of whose members died on Cemetery Hill, disembarked from the ferry from Jersey City, ready to battle the rioters. Later Zouave troops returned to the city. At four o'clock Thursday morning the 7th Regiment of the New York National Guard landed at Canal Street, and six hours later the 65th New York Regiment and the artillery battery of the 8th arrived. Later in the afternoon still another proud and powerful regiment, New York State's German-American Excelsior Brigade, marched into the city.

At ten minutes to eleven Thursday morning four of Ned's fellow detectives, Dusenberry, McCord, Radford, and Farley, arrested John Andrews. They found him in bed with his Negro mistress.

By Thursday night the rioting was completely under control, and the city once more settled down to the task of cleaning up and rebuilding itself. All day Wednesday and Thursday Ned and Pat went about their duties like zombies. Only when he heard of the arrival of the Gettysburg troops and the German-American brigade did it pass through Ned's mind that Max Kessler might possibly be among them. Even that thought stirred no particular feeling in him. He cared nothing about the riots. Even less about the war. He felt like a dead man, going through the motions, efficiently enough, but with absolute indifference.

18

Time, twenty-one months of it, from the July Thursday in 1863 when the riots ended to the second week in April of 1865, had at least partially healed Ned's grievous emotional wounds. Time and his absorption with and success in his work. In November of 1864 desperate Confederate spies had set fires in a number of the city's hotels, and even one in Barnum's museum, and Ned had been instrumental in tracking down and capturing three of them. The newly formed Metropolitan Fire Department, all of whose members were paid, extinguished the blazes before any of them did significant damage.

Time, his work, and the psychological adjustment he made in connection with baby William Kessler all contributed to his resurrection. Within weeks after his father's and Clara's deaths, he had decided that William was his one link to the woman he loved so deeply. He began to make regular visits to the Himmelfarbs, bringing William some simple toy, a top, a ball, and once, when William was almost four, a handsomely carved figure of a Union soldier on a horse, brandishing a saber.

"That's your father, William," he told the boy. "He is a brave soldier, and he will come home soon."

Frau Schoenbrun heard him, and said curtly, "You should not put such nonsense and false hopes in the boy's head, Ned Morrissey!"

Ned had long since come to realize that Frau Schoenbrun believed William was his illegitimate son, but he chose not to discuss the matter with the cantankerous old woman. He also realized that there was, indeed, little possibility that Max would ever return. Less than a week after the end of the rioting a tall, blond, curly-haired Union officer with a neatly trimmed blond mustache had come to the house on Fortieth Street. The man, a colonel in the 132nd Pennsylvania Regiment, which had been dispatched to New York to help put down the riots, introduced himself.

"I'm Fred Van Gelder," he said. "I'm looking for a Martin Morrissey."

In the parlor, over brandies, Ned told Colonel Van Gelder who he was and informed him that his father had been killed in the rioting.

"My father will be most unhappy to learn that," said Van Gelder. "They were the best of friends."

His father was Christopher Van Gelder. Christopher was sixty-eight years old and still lived in Buffalo. Colonel Van Gelder's twin brother, Ned, had died in the fighting at Kernstown, Virginia, early in the war, when the Union forces defeated General Stonewall Jackson in the first battle of the Shenandoah Valley campaign. They talked about other members of the family. Ned told the colonel about Pat, and Van Gelder told Ned about his sister, Laura, who had married a doctor in Buffalo, and was active in a woman's group that operated a canteen for soldiers, rolled bandages, and otherwise worked in the war effort. Laura had three children, all sons; the colonel himself had two, a son and a daughter.

"Did you, by any chance, ever come across a soldier named Max Kessler?" asked Ned.

Much to his surprise, the colonel said, "I did, indeed. Essler was one of the fiercest, most reckless fighting men I've ever known."

"Essler?" repeated Ned.

"Essler—we all called him that. He told me his name was Kessler, but the volunteer office where he enlisted apparently got it mixed up. He complained bitterly that he never received any mail because of the incompetence of the people in New York and Washington, and the postal service in general. It was the only thing I ever heard him complain about."

Ned nodded.

"His wife wrote him for years and never got a reply."

He told Van Gelder what had happened to Clara.

The colonel shook his head sympathetically.

"Seems as brutal a war at home as in the field. . . . I don't know if Essler—Kessler—is alive or not. Did you read about the fighting in the cornfields and woods around Sharpsburg, Maryland, the Antietam bridge? It was almost three years ago."

Ned nodded solemnly.

"We read a great deal about it. Wasn't it the bloodiest battle of the entire war so far?"

"I think so. Far worse than Gettysburg, bad as that was. In less than twelve hours more than twenty-two thousand of our men and theirs died. That's where I ran into Mack Essler."

Ned recalled going over the seemingly endless list of casualties with Clara at the time. No Max Kessler. Of course they had not looked under the *E*'s.

"Was he with your regiment?" he asked the colonel.

"No, but it was pandemonium. Troops from New York regiments, Wisconsin regiments, God knows which other regiments, were mixing together in the murderous maelstrom. There'd been fierce hand-to-hand fighting since dawn, and artillery blasting both sides. About noontime our lookouts spotted a number of Confederate units in a narrow sunken road and the real massacre began."

He paused and sipped his brandy, wincing at the memory of the scene.

"I think the newspapers called it the Battle of Bloody Lane. It was bloody all right. We charged and trampled over dead and wounded bodies, as if they'd been used to pave the road. That was when I saw Essler. In one frantic whirl he bayoneted a charging rebel, somehow managed to withdraw his steel and club another, who was about to shoot one of our boys. How he survived that encounter I'll never know.

"We were victorious in that brief siege, and we took a respite. I happened to sit with a group of men, which included Essler. I complimented him and we talked quite a while. He was the kind of man who made you feel like you were an old friend almost immediately. I never met a soldier who understood the cause for which he was fighting so clearly and was so dedicated to it. It was almost religious, fanatical.

"Later we went back into the fray. I was riding at the head of a force and I saw him charging across a farm yard with a forward group, toward a Confederate position in the woods. There was a church there, a Dunker church, I recall. Just then fragments from a shell from a rebel gun ripped into one of the farmer's beehives. I don't know how many hives, dozens at least, scores probably, maybe a hundred. Those bees were deadlier than the Southern fire. God knows how many thousands of them there were. Clouds of them swirled around the men. Even over the sounds of the battle you could hear their buzzing. They swarmed all over those poor troops. I looked back as I raced away from there and saw Essler. His entire head and upper body were covered with bees. And so were many of the men around him. That was the last I saw of Essler."

"Kessler," said Ned.

"Kessler. He was certainly a fighter."

Later Ned asked several of the police doctors whether a man could die from bee stings. He was assured it was entirely possible if there were enough bees. He told Pat the story when Pat returned home. When no further word came from or about Max in the next twenty-one months, Ned was almost certain that Max was dead, either of a multiple-bee assault or Confederate sword or bullet.

Ned had never given any thought to what a person risen from the dead might look like. But never in his most horrific nightmares (and he suffered many) could he have envisioned the appearance of Max when he returned to life and New York City. It was on April 10, 1865, almost two years after the draft riots. The city was in the most jubilant mood it had enjoyed since long before the beginning of the war.

Word had reached New York that General Lee had surrendered the army of Northern Virginia to General Grant at the courthouse at Appomattox, Virginia. For all practical purposes the war was over, although thousands more were yet to die. It was a Sunday. Ned had just returned from church and he sat in the backyard with a glass of beer, reading the *Tribune*. Pat and Fiona were boating in Central Park and Flossie had gone to visit an ailing aunt.

There was a knock at the door and Ned opened it and saw a strange pair standing there. One was a broad-shouldered Negro tall as Ned himself, with a gaunt, hollow-cheeked face, short, kinky hair, a nose that seemed to have been broken and flattened on the face, thick lips, and soft, mahogany eyes. The other was a squat and ugly white man with sunken cheeks, a large, eaglelike nose, and eyes as fierce as that bird's. Thick, dusty-gray eyebrows accentuated the impression of fierceness. The dark pupils darted from side to side, even as he looked up at Ned, as though he feared being set upon by some unseen enemy. What made the face uniquely unattractive were the small, glossy bumps on hollow cheeks, jutting jaw, and forehead, like hillocks on a barren plain. The man had broad shoulders, but they seemed narrow because they were arched, bowlike, to the front. His upper torso was slightly twisted to the right. Both wore Union army uniforms, but the white man's fitted him awkwardly. His peaked military cap seemed a size too small for him.

"You have grown a bit older, Ned Morrissey," said the white man.

Ned said, "Who—who are—who are you?"

The squat, stooped man pushed him aside and stalked into the foyer, strode boldly on into the parlor, and sat down in Martin's favorite Russian leather chair. The tall Negro followed, but stood at his side. Ned, baffled and beginning to get angry, walked silently behind them.

"Who—" he started to say again, but the ugly little man barked, "Sorry about Martin! Was a fine man, Martin!"

He took off his cap with his left hand and dropped it to the floor beside him. His head was completely bald and contained small bumps similar to those on his face.

"I am Max Kessler," he said curtly, and laughed. The sound seemed more a bark than a laugh. "I have changed, Ned, have I not!"

"Max!" exclaimed Ned, recognizing now the hooked nose, the dark eyes. He rushed toward Max and grasped his right hand. As he shook it he felt that there were no whole fingers, just four stumps and a thumb.

"Tha—thank God you're alive, Max!"

Max laughed the barklike laugh again.

"What is left is alive!" he said. "Who killed Clara, Ned?"

Ned took the chair opposite him and spread his hands, palms upward.

"I don't know, Max. No one knows. It was some of the rioters."

"At Rivington Street they told me it was Irishers. Burned the brewery and killed them all. Raped, too, they told me."

Ned nodded.

"I'm sure they were Irish, Max. But there were thousands of them. We never knew. I tried to find out, but there was no way."

Max indicated the tall Negro with a toss of his fingerless hand.

"This is Othello Jones, Ned. Good man. Since Fort Pillow I cannot get rid of him. He is my adopted son."

The tall Negro grinned and nodded enthusiastically. His

teeth were worse than Max's. Max's eyes moved restlessly from left to right, twice, thrice, then stared at Ned.

"At Rivington Street they told me I have a son. They say you took him when Clara was killed."

Ned told Max that William was being cared for by the Himmelfarbs.

"You will take me there!" ordered Max.

"Sure."

On the horse-drawn streetcar Max shook his head and muttered bitterly about the flag- and bunting-decorated buildings.

"Jefferson Davis is a stubborn man. There will be more dying. There is nothing to celebrate."

The Himmelfarbs and Frau Schoenbrun were shocked at Max's appearance, and had great difficulty concealing their reaction. Max frowned when he shook hands with Fritz, who had gained more than fifty pounds since Max had last seen him.

"When one lives off the fat of the land," he said, sneering, "one becomes fat . . . enormous . . . like a prize pig at the fair."

Fritz managed a feeble laugh and ignored the insult. Max's fierce, darting eyes made him nervous.

"We are happy you are home, Max," he said in a quavering basso. Ilka went into the bedroom and brought four-year-old William out in her arms. He had been taking his nap.

"Your father, Willie," she cooed, handing the child to Max. "Your father is home from the war."

William started to cry as soon as Max took him. Max held him tightly to his convex chest and kissed his cheek, which made the child scream in terror and wail louder. He reached desperately for Ned, who stood beside Max.

"Unc'a Ned! Unc'a Ned!" he begged pitifully.

Max's shifty eyes became moist, and he handed the boy to Ned.

"Yah, Willie," he said. "To be sure. To be sure. A handsome policeman—even one with such big ears—is nicer than a stinking, crippled soldier!"

Ned held William and patted his back gently.

"Don't cry, Willie, lad," he said. "It's your father. He is a brave soldier who won the war for us."

"Bullshit!" said Max crisply. "Come, Othello."

And he walked out of the ornately furnished Himmelfarb home with the tall Negro trailing him obediently.

Fifteen days later, on Monday, April 24, Max and Othello knocked on the Morrissey door once again. Ned, Pat, Fiona, and Flossie were all dressed in their finest to pay their respects to the President. Ten days earlier, on the fourteenth, an actor named John Wilkes Booth had shot Lincoln during a performance of *Our American Cousin* at the Ford Theatre in Washington, D.C. Lincoln died the following day. His body had been brought to New York City, where it was to lie in state for twenty-four hours before being shipped to Springfield, Illinois, for burial.

"We will make a final visit to the great man together, Ned," announced Max flatly. "Do you remember when we escorted him about the city and to the Cooper Union Hall?"

Ned nodded somberly.

The city was draped in black. At City Hall more than a hundred thousand people stood in long lines and slowly followed each other up the circular stairs to the room where Lincoln lay in his silk-lined coffin. Max was ahead of Othello, Ned, Pat, Fiona, and Flossie in the queue. He stopped at the bier, and for a moment his crippled body seemed to force itself erect. He saluted smartly with his fingerless right hand. Flossie and Fiona wept bitterly as they made the sign of the cross over the dead body and walked on. Hours later they all stood at the curb on Broadway and watched the funeral procession march by on its way to the Hudson River Railroad depot. Afterward Max demanded that Ned accompany him and Othello to the Himmelfarbs again.

"Perhaps if we visit together for a time, the boy will learn to accept me," he said.

"I'm sure he will," said Ned.

It took a long time, but almost a year later, the deep, possessive love Max felt for him reached the child's heart. Despite Max's bizarre appearance, William gradually progressed from cautious acceptance to fondness, and toward the end of the year reached the point where he looked forward to visits from his father. Ned's constant reiteration of the fact that Max was a war hero, and his vivid tales of Max's deeds of derring-do scaled to the capacity of the bright five-year-old to understand, also helped young William learn to respect and love his father. He never told the stories in Max's presence, of course. And they came directly from Ned's imagination, and were fairy-tale versions of his reading of accounts of the battles of the war, plus what Colonel Van Gelder and Othello Jones had told him.

One day when Max left Othello with Ned at the Fortieth Street house, while he went off to a meeting with the construction people who were rebuilding the Rivington Street brewery, Ned had loosened Othello's tongue with brandy.

"Were you in the army with Mr. Kessler, Othello?" asked Ned.

"Not *mistuh*, Mistuh Ned," said the Negro in the strange, whisperlike voice caused by his damaged larynx. "*Cap'n!* Cap'n's what Mistuh Mack Essler be! Cap'n, an' the bes' goddam cap'n de army ever see!"

He swallowed the brandy in his glass and Ned refilled it.

"He save my life, do the Cap'n. We the first colored troop fightin' fer the Union. You know they wouldn't take none o' us colored in the Fed'ral army till the war nearly two year old. We holdin' this Fort Pillow on de Mississippi an' along come these rebel bastids. I hear tell dey gen'ral a Memphis slave trader, an' he one mean sumbitch. Dey outnumber us bad; dat river turn red wid de blood of almost all us coloreds. One dem rebels 'bout to slice mah head off, when Cap'n shoot 'im dead."

He shook his head and emptied his brandy glass once again. Ned refilled it once more.

"We lose de fort an' de cap'n an' me an' maybe sixty udder colored so'jers we captured an' dey ship us to prison called An'sonville. Asshole o' the South! Nothin' but sand plains, piney woods, an' swamplan'. Dat An'sonville one stinkin' hellhole. Men die by de hun'reds ev'y day. Either starve t' death 'r die o' scurvy or some udder disease. Rebels make us dig big, long trench an' dey throw the bodies in an' we gotta shovel dirt over 'em."

He paused and stared at Ned.

"You know how de cap'n lose dem fingers?"

"No."

"Guy grabs a piece o' meat fum me, an' I rassle 'im fer it. We all the time hungry. We eat rats, fat bugs, anythin' we kin cotch. Dat piece o' meat a prize. Ah drop it inta de dirt. Cap'n reaches t' git it fer me. 'Nuther guy chops at 'is hand with a hatchet. Gits all four fingers. Ah thought de cap'n gonna die fer sure. But he tough!"

He shook his head in admiration.

"Sure tough, dat man! Come November we hear Sherman be marchin' through Georgia. This An'sonville in Georgia. We 'scape, the cap'n an' me. Don't think nobuddy else ever 'scape An'sonville. We 'bout ta freeze t' death, when we come on some Union so'jers near Milledgeville. Know what dey doin'?"

He gave a hoarse chuckle.

"Dey burnin' Confed'rate money in dey fires t' cook and keep warm. Yassuh, Mistuh Ned, he some man, dat cap'n."

"What happened to his back?" asked Ned. "Did he injure it at Fort Pillow or in Andersonville?"

Othello shook his head vigorously.

"Naw. Friend o' his tell me at Fort Pillow de cap'n not long outta hospital. Got a minnie ball right near 'is spine. Dat a mighty big ball, dat minnie ball."

Ned knew from his police ballistics studies that the bullet Othello referred to was the minié ball, named after the Frenchman who invented it. Some of the minié balls measured .69 of an inch in diameter, a size that could cause considerable internal damage.

"Where was he hit? In what battle?" asked Ned.

Othello shrugged.

"Ah dunno, Mistuh Ned. Cap'n never say. Kin ah have a li'l more dat whiskey?"

Max had no financial worries. Indeed he was quite wealthy. When he enlisted he had a considerable fortune in several banks in Wall Street. Upon his return to the city he had decided not to go back into the brewery business. He reconstructed the brewery on Rivington Street into a fine five-story tenement and purchased the two tenements flanking it. In mid-1866, he gave Fritz and Ilka Himmelfarb one thousand dollars and told them William had finally agreed to come to live with him.

"Is that enough?" he asked Fritz Himmelfarb.

"Well," said Fritz, "it's been since the summer of sixty-three we've cared for the boy. Prices were very high, Max."

Max took out a roll of bills and peeled off another five hundred with the stump of his index finger and his thumb.

"Enough?" he asked.

"Oh, of course, of course. We did not take the boy expecting to be paid. It was a pleasure to have him."

"Yes, Fritz," said Max. "Now it is time the pleasure should be mine."

Two days later Ned accompanied Max, Othello, and young William to the new quarters on Rivington Street. Max had set aside the entire ground floor for his own use, and had given Othello an apartment in the basement. He had hired a motherly, middle-aged Jewish widow named Rebecca Horowitz, whose husband had recently died, to keep house and look after William. That night after Ned, Max, and Mrs. Horowitz had put William to bed in his bright new room, surrounded by more toys than he had ever seen, Ned and Max settled down in the comfortably furnished parlor. Max poured a beer for Ned. There was no glass on the table beside his chair.

"Aren't you drinking, Max?" asked Ned. "It's a night to celebrate!"

Max's eyes darted left and right and he shook his head.

"Stomach! Bad stomach!" he said. "I cannot drink beer, any alcohol."

"Well." Ned lifted his glass. "To William," he toasted.

Max nodded and grinned.

"To William," Ned repeated, "and to his brave father!"

"Bullshit!" said Max. He watched Ned drink.

"You know, Ned," he said, "Willie does not look very much like me, thank whatever gods there be."

The boy had Clara's silver-blond hair and her blue eyes. Only his somewhat large nose, evident even at so early an age as five, seemed a legacy from Max.

"He looks a lot like Clara," said Ned.

"Do you think his ears are a little large?"

Ned looked at Max. He finished his beer. Then he smiled and said, "His nose, Max. Not his ears."

Max did not return his grin.

"Tell me, Ned," he demanded. "Did you ever fuck my wife?"

Ned looked directly into Max's restless eyes.

"No, Max," he said quietly. "She loved you more than any woman ever loved a man. Always."

Max's bad teeth showed as he chortled happily, but perhaps, thought Ned, with a touch of irony. His pupils searched right and left a dozen times.

"That's what I told Frau Schoenbrun," he said pleasantly. "I told her if she didn't stop her malicious gossiping I would kill her. She believed me, I think. And she is right. I never liked her. Even Ilka has become a sow and Himmelfarb is a gross abomination! Have another glass of beer, Ned!"

PART SEVEN

Malka Roitman

Joseph Wilensky

Martin and Kevin Morrissey

Lilly Welcome and Hannah Weiss

Bridget and Sal Lombardi

Howard Borsum and Anna Van Vorst Borsum

Harry Kessler

Dr. Charles Parkhurst and Clarence Lexow

Jacob A. Riis and Theodore Roosevelt

Corruption and Reform

An Adventure on the Subway

"At the end of the year 1888, when a regular census was taken for the first time since 1869 . . . there were 32,390 tenements with a population of 1,093,701 souls. Today we have 37,316 tenements, including 2630 rear houses, and their population is over 1,250,000. A large share of this population, especially of that which came to us from abroad, crowds below Fourteenth Street, where the population is already packed beyond reason."

—Jacob A. Riis, *How the Other Half Lives*, 1890

"The Tenement House Commission called the worst of the barracks 'infant slaughter houses,' and showed, by reference to the mortality lists, that they killed one out of every five babies born in them."

—Jacob A. Riis, *The Battle with the Slum*, 1902

"When finally, upon the wave of wrath excited by the Parkhurst and Lexow disclosures, reform came with a shock that dislodged Tammany, it found us wide awake, and, it must be admitted, not a little astonished at our sudden access of righteousness."

—Jacob A. Riis, *The Battle with the Slum*, 1902

"New York is the electric city. It is probably the most brilliantly illuminated city in the world. . . . The most remarkable single tract of night illumination lies in Broadway from 34th to 46th Streets. This glittering trail along upper Broadway, the 'Great White Way' is celebrated all over the world."

—*The New York Herald Tribune*, September 22, 1906

19

In two hours she had gone from joyous if somewhat nervous anticipation to despair bordering on terror. *Could he possibly not come? Could he have changed his mind and decided he did not wish to marry her after all?*

Don't be such a fool, Malka Roitman, she scolded herself, trying to bolster her spirit. *Would a man come all the way to Prosnica and pay a shadchen so much money to make a match for a seventeen-year-old Polish girl who knew only how to cook a little and keep a house clean and mend and sew?* Not only had Mr. Wilensky traveled to the poor village all the way from America, and paid Chaim Plotnik, the elderly matchmaker, twice what anyone had ever paid for finding a wife—no, not only that! Mr. Wilensky (he had asked her to call him Joseph, which he said was the style in America, but she could only think of him as Mr. Wilensky)—Mr. Wilensky had even given her ailing widowed mother a handsome gold brooch inlaid with a shining stone. And he was a religious man. He had given the rabbi a substantial contribution (ten American dollars) toward the money needed to build the new synagogue. Her mother was not feeling well enough to make the long journey across the ocean, but Mr. Wilensky had even promised to send her the money to come over as soon as she was feeling a little better.

The only reason he had insisted they be married in America, in New York City instead of Prosnica, was that he wanted an elegant wedding with all his important Jewish and American friends present.

"A beauty like you, my dear Malka, must have a big wedding like a show," he had said. "With Joseph Wilensky nothing is too good for his bride."

She blushed when he said that. She stared at him with her dark bright eyes, and as she felt her cheeks burning, lowered her lashes and clasped her hands in her lap to control her excitement. She was awed by him. He was ten, maybe fifteen, years older than she and so forceful, such a commanding manner. And dressed so fine in a checked wool suit with a gold watch hanging across his solid paunch, and a white silk shirt with a high starched collar. He was stocky and broad-shouldered, and had thick black hair, parted on the side and slicked to his head. He had a heavy mustache, curled at the ends. At first his eyes bothered her. They had a strange glint, calculating it seemed, but then she realized she was being foolish. To be so successful, so rich in America a man would have to have such shrewd eyes. Even a seventeen-year-old Polish girl from the Pomeranian region should know that!

But now as the minutes stretched into hours, sitting on a scarred bench outside the large, though battered Barge Office, which was the city's Immigration Reception Center, she didn't know what to think. Mr. Wilensky knew the ship on which she had made the four-week journey across the ocean. He himself had bought the steerage tickets for her.

She herself had been so excited at being here in America that she had endured the questioning of the immigration officers (the young Polish interpreter seemed to be undressing her with his eyes), and the examinations of the doctors and health inspectors, for whom she actually had had to undress, and all the lesser ordeals of her arrival, blushing mightily, but without even a thought of complaint. The whole procedure had been humiliating, noisy, disorganized, and chaotic. It was indeed more disorganized than New York City immigration reception had been in the recent past or would be in the near future. It was the summer of 1891 and the influx of foreigners—Italians and Jews from eastern and southeastern Europe were now beginning to represent the greatest numbers—had long since proved too heavy for proper handling at the Castle Garden Center. New, modern, and much larger facilities were under construction at Ellis Island, but in the meantime the center was at the Barge Office at the Battery. It had always been the landing place for immigrants arriving from the steamship piers on their way to nearby Castle Garden, and now, temporarily, all foreigners were being processed here.

Malka had arrived about four o'clock on this warm afternoon in late June, and it was now nearly suppertime. She had not eaten since early morning, and then only a piece of black bread and weak tea, and her stomach was growling, but her concern over Mr. Wilensky's failure to appear overrode her hunger pangs. Some of the immigration personnel were leaving the building and they looked at her curiously. The young Polish interpreter came out and stopped before her. She had lowered her head scarf to her shoulders, and now she clutched it tightly over her bosom. The dark blue belted cotton peasant dress she wore was high-necked and ankle-length and fitted loosely, but the young man ran his eyes up and down her young, well-developed body. He asked her if she would like to have supper with him. Nervously she thanked him and said her husband-to-be would arrive any minute, she was sure.

Later a burly middle-aged Irishman, one of the guards, came to her and asked her if he could help. But she understood not a word of English, only Polish, Russian, and Yiddish, and she shook her head in confusion. He shrugged and went on his way.

Another half hour passed. She was sorry she had not asked the Polish interpreter how she might go about finding Mr. Wilensky, but the young man's lustful manner had frightened her. Maybe she could find a policeman who might be able to find him. Just then a hackney cab drawn by a single horse came to a halt at the curb across from the wide front doors of the Barge Office. A stocky man with slicked-down black hair stepped out and looked toward the building. Malka got to her feet. He looked like Mr. Wilensky. He was not wearing a wool checked suit, but brown trousers and a yellow cotton shirt, open at the neck. Malka hesitantly waved at him as he looked in her direction. He strode purposefully toward her, and she smiled with relief. It *was* Mr. Wilensky, but as he came nearer she was taken aback to note that he was not returning her wave or her smile. Indeed he was looking grim. As he reached her a porter came from a corner of the building with a small cart. He wheeled the cart toward Malka's heavy trunk. Wilensky brushed him away with a pudgy hand.

"No! No! Never mind!" he said. "We need no help!"

Malka could not understand the English words, but she gathered by Mr. Wilensky's gesture and tone that he was dismissing the porter. He reached for the scuffed leather handle at one end of the trunk and, in Yiddish, said gruffly to Malka, "So pick up that end already, Malka. You are a strong, healthy girl. We do not waste money on porters!"

Together they got the trunk onto the rack of the coach, while the driver stared at Malka admiringly. He admired his passenger's choice in young women, but he also knew Wilensky was a poor tipper, and he would not condescend to help. When they were settled inside the coach, the perspiring, hairy-chested Wilensky looked at Malka critically. In Yiddish he said coldly, "You look tired and dirty. We will have to clean you up."

This was hardly the reception Malka had anticipated.

"Mr. Wilensky," she said timidly, "I was—I was becoming worried. I thought maybe you would not come."

"I said I would come, did I not!" he said angrily. "When Joseph Wilensky says he will come he comes. I was busy and could not come earlier. I am a very busy man!"

She was so upset and confused by Mr. Wilensky's hostile reception that she was only vaguely aware of the buildings and storefronts on both sides of the street as they rode up Broadway from the Battery.

"What—what is wrong, Mr. Wilensky? Have I done something wrong?"

He took a long black cigar from the pocket of his shirt, bit off a tip, spat it onto the floor, and stared at her over the flame of the match as he lit the cigar. He blew out a small cloud of thick, pungent smoke.

"No. Never mind. I have had a bad day. When we clean you up you will be fine. With a little rest the bloom will come back in your cheeks."

Malka had hoped for something a bit more romantic, at least friendly, but she was relieved that he was not angry. She looked out the window of the coach as the driver made a turn into a narrow side street. Soon she saw such a congestion of people that it made the broad avenue they had just left seem sparsely populated. And she knew by their appearance, most of them swarthy and olive-skinned like herself, the women in head scarfs and shawls and long, loose dresses, many of the men bearded, some with yarmulkes, that she was in a Jewish neighborhood. She would have known even if the signs on most of the storefronts were not written in Hebrew, and even if all the names were not obviously Semitic.

The milling, noisy throng filled the sidewalks on both sides of the street. Outside the stores, protected from the sun by canvas awnings, there were rows of pushcarts with every conceivable kind of merchandise: fruits and vegetables, and fish and sausages and clothes and hats and shoes. Clusters of people sat on the stoops and on iron extensions attached to the sides of the buildings. Malka had never seen fire escapes. Here and there clothing hung on lines extending from one fire escape to another.

Malka forgot about her rude welcome and stared spellbound at the frenetic scene. The hackney stopped finally at a three-story brownstone building with a high stoop, flanked on both sides by five-story tenements. Mr. Wilensky nudged her upper arm and pushed her toward the door.

"Here. We are here, Malka. Your fine new home!"

He chuckled as he followed her out. She stood dumbly in the street as he paid the hackney driver, who said something plainly sarcastic to him. Two young boys in ragged clothes and caps rushed up and spoke to Wilensky in English. He patted one on the head and nodded and they took Malka's trunk into the house. When they came out he gave each of them a coin, and patted the second boy on the behind. Wilensky then grabbed Malka by the wrist and dragged her through the bustling throng, up the stoop, and into the foyer of the house on Allen Street. She thought there must be a celebration, a party going on. For a fleeting moment she let herself believe it might be a party to welcome her to America. Mr. Wilensky had been behaving gruffly so that the celebration would come as a total surprise. Then as she halted and stared into the large parlor to the left of the foyer she realized that the young girls and the men assembled there were not gathered to welcome a prospective bride. Inexperienced and naïve as she was, she knew that young ladies dressed in silk robes and kimonos, drinking, laughing, chatting coquettishly with affluent, well-dressed men, were not awaiting Mr. Wilensky's Polish girl.

This early in the evening there were only two men and they sat with two of the prettier young women at a marble-topped, claw-legged table, drinking champagne. The women giggled at a ribald story one of the men had just told. More than a dozen other attractive young girls—none seemed much older than Malka—sat in small groups of three or four on elegant overstuffed sofas, talking idly among themselves. A tall, dark-haired lady in Oriental dress was serving them tea. Malka just had time to notice a huge painting hanging over the mantel of an ornate fireplace. It showed three plump, naked women being chased through a sylvan glade by a satyr. She also got a quick impression that the carpet, the drapes, the furniture, all the appointments in the large parlor were expensive and elegant.

Wilensky gripped Malka's arm and in English bellowed orders Malka did not understand.

"Wei Chang! Come! Now! Quick! Quick!"

The tall Oriental woman promptly set the teapot on a serving table and with mincing steps hurried to Wilensky and Malka. In the glow of the overhead gas chandelier Malka saw that the left side of the woman's face was slick, pinkish scar tissue from her black hairline to the collar of her high-necked crimson silk blouse. The left eye had no pupil and was obviously sightless. The left corner of her mouth was scarred a slightly deeper pink than the skin above and below it.

"This is Malka," said Wilensky sharply. "Take her now to thirty-one. She needs to be cleaned and fed."

An expression of fear seemed to be fixed permanently in the Chinese woman's slanted right eye. She nodded vigorously and took Malka by the wrist. Malka tried to pull away, but Wei Chang's bony fingers held her tightly.

"Who—Mr. Wilensky—please—who are all these ladies? Who—" pleaded Malka.

"They are my wives, Malka dear," said Wilensky, grinning. "Just like you. Go now."

"But—" protested Malka.

Wilensky cuffed her across the cheek with the back of his pudgy right hand.

"Go when I tell you!" he ordered. "I want no disobedience."

The Chinese woman led her up two flights of stairs to the third floor of the house and down a long hallway to a paneled wooden door with the number 31 painted on it. The room was small, but clean and attractively furnished. There was a double bed with freshly laundered white sheets and two pillows. Small tables with glass kerosene lamps with floral decorations flanked either side of the bed. A dressing table with a large ornately framed mirror was on one side of the room. The mirror reflected the image of the bed. On the table was a large porcelain basin filled with clean water, a small pile of towels, and more than a dozen bottles and jars. On the opposite side of the room was an alcove in which four dresses and three white silk kimonos hung on hooks. Also hanging from hooks in the alcove were several leather whips and three-foot lengths of link chains attached to wooden handles. Floor-length scarlet velvet drapes hung at the only window. An odor unfamiliar to Malka, of perfume and dried perspiration, filled the airless room.

Malka was startled when the Chinese woman spoke to her in Yiddish with a distinct Oriental accent and phrase structure.

"You remove clothing. Wei Chang will cleanse you."

"No!" Malka protested. "I can wash myself."

Wei Chang shook her head.

"I must do. I must clean private parts. Medicate and perfume. All girls clean. All the time."

Malka was a strong young peasant girl and she resisted, but Wei Chang had a wiry strength and used strange holds to force Malka into submission. When Malka finally sat on the edge of the bed, dressed in one of the white silk virginal robes, weeping, Wei Chang said, "I do not wish to hurt you, Malka. But I must prepare all girls. Mr. Wilensky cruel man when disobeyed."

Her genital area stinging from Wei Chang's treatment, Malka looked at the Chinese woman and wailed, "Th—this—this is a house of prostitution. I have heard—"

"Is so. Girls get too old, Mr. Wilensky sells. Brings new girls, always young, always from Europe."

Malka stared at the Chinese woman with tear-filled, reddened eyes. She shook her head vigorously. Stuttering and choking, she managed to say, "I will not stay here! I will never be a prostitute. I will kill myself first!"

A glimmer of compassion showed in Wei Chang's good eye. "This is good house, Malka. Girls always clean and eat well. Men better class. Many worse houses, bad houses, girls sick, diseased."

"I will not stay!" screamed Malka. Wei Chang placed a hand firmly over her mouth.

"You must, Malka. There is no way to leave. Many years ago when I am younger than you I try. I get away."

She shook her hand from Malka's mouth and caressed her own scarred cheek.

"Acid!" she said. "Man working for Mr. Wilensky find me on Mott Street. Throw acid in my face. Bring me back."

Malka's sobbing subsided. She looked at Wei Chang with frightened, desperate eyes.

"One Hungarian girl run away last year," said Wei Chang sadly. "They find body in river."

When Wei Chang left the room, Malka heard her turn a key in the lock of the door. She went to the window and saw that it was not only closed but bolted and barred. In the fading twilight she saw a garbage-strewn backyard area with ugly shacks and laundry hanging from lines from the rear windows of the tenements to high poles in the yards.

Wei Chang returned in less than half an hour with a tray laden with a bowl of chicken soup, a plate with a chicken leg and breast, and two large potatoes. Despite her desperation and terror, or perhaps because of it, Malka ate ravenously. She had already made up her mind that she would keep up her strength no matter what. She knew she would find some way to escape despite Wei Chang's insistence that it could not be done. As she ate, her desperation transformed itself into a bitter hatred for Joseph Wilensky. What a lying scoundrel! What a brute! Bride, indeed! She wished him dead as she finished the last of the food on her plate. She prayed that God would strike him dead.

Wei Chang fed her substantial meals for the next two days, but she was not permitted to leave her room. Late at night of the second day she lay on her bed in her white silk robe, wondering what would happen if she should break the glass in the window and scream for help. She had half decided she might try it, when she heard a key in the door and it was opened and Joseph Wilensky came in. He was carrying a kerosene lantern and behind him came a heavyset man in a uniform. Wilensky set the lantern on the dressing table and lighted the two lamps on the tables flanking the bed. Malka lay still, terrified, as she watched him through slitted eyes.

"You are awake, Malka?" asked Wilensky, shaking her shoulder. She pulled the bedsheet up to her neck and sat up. The heavyset man stood beside Wilensky at the side of the bed, grinning down at her. He had a beefy face with heavy black eyebrows over lust-filled, yellow-flecked pale green eyes. He had his hands clasped behind his back and he rocked on his heels and the balls of his feet. Malka did not understand his words, but she sensed that he was saying something lascivious about her. What he said was, "Ach, Joey. This one is a real beauty! She looks like a Lithuanian, a ripe little Litvak. What is her name, Joey?"

"No. Polish," said Wilensky. "Malka."

"Yah, yah, a Polack. They are full of fire. Polacks I always like."

Wilensky spoke in Yiddish to Malka.

"This is Hermann Mueller, Malka dear. He is a captain of the police and he tests all my wives to make sure they are suitable. I wish you to be extremely nice to him."

Mueller reached a rough, sausage-fingered hand to Malka's cheek, and as she recoiled, he lowered the hand and ripped the bedsheet out of her grasp. He pulled it back so she was completely uncovered. The hem of the robe had slid up to her upper thigh and she quickly reached down to tug it to her ankles. The bedside lamps highlighted the curves of her body. Malka crossed her hands over her bosom and tried to slide up in the bed, away from the burly man, who was now beginning to perspire. He reached down, and grabbing her wrists, tore her hands away from her breasts. With a quick motion he ripped the buttoned robe so that her firm round breasts were exposed. Malka screamed and Mueller slapped her sharply across the cheek. Wilensky laughed and said, "Those robes are expensive, Hermann."

"Deduct it from my hundred this week, Joey," said Mueller, not taking his eyes from Malka. He sat on the bed and pulled her roughly to him. Holding her firmly in his thick arms, he tried to kiss her, but she twisted her head so that his full lips and brushlike mustache landed high on her cheek. He held her tightly with his right arm, and with his left hand grasped her chin and turned her face to his. He kissed her wetly and fiercely on the mouth. His breath smelled of stale beer and tobacco. Wilensky chuckled and said, "Please, Hermann. Not too many bruises. I wish the new Mrs. Wilensky to be prepared to receive guests tomorrow if possible."

Mueller reached down and yanked the robe up above Malka's waist. Holding her so tightly she thought he would crush her ribs, he looked over his shoulder at Wilensky and said, "She will be a little sore for a day or two, Joey."

He pushed Malka flat on the bed and began kissing her neck and squeezing her right breast as though he were kneading dough. Malka tried to scream, but the pressure of his mouth against her throat choked off the sound. She tried to beat him off with both fists, and kicked and squirmed. But he was far too heavy and too strong for her. She was faintly aware of Wilensky opening and closing the door. She tried to scratch at Mueller's eyes, but he turned his head and she raked his cheek. In the struggle the robe had slid all the way up to her navel. Mueller knelt between her legs and pinned both her outstretched arms to the bed. Sweat dripped from his chin onto her stomach. He was panting. Somehow he had managed to unbutton his pants. Malka caught a glimpse of the thick, erect penis and turned away. She concentrated so fiercely on fighting off unconsciousness that she could not even scream.

Wei Chang came in with a pan of water and a syringe almost immediately after Mueller left her. Malka lay face down in the soiled and blood-stained bed, sobbing hysterically.

"Captain Mueller brutal man," said Wei Chang with quiet compassion, as she put the pan on the bedside table and filled the syringe. A new fear possessed Malka.

"Wha—what—what are you . . . doing?"

"Must do," said Wei Chang. "If no do, you maybe with child. Mr. Wilensky makes abortion. Kills baby."

Malka stared at the Oriental woman in shocked disbelief. Wei Chang explained the absolute necessity for the douche. She told Malka that all the girls learned to douche themselves properly very quickly. Occasionally one would become careless and find herself pregnant, and Wilensky would send her off to a man he called the butcher to have the pregnancy aborted. Wei Chang told Malka that several times, the girls had died in the course of the abortion or shortly afterward. When Malka finally understood she not only submitted willingly, but eagerly. The idea of being impregnated by the bestial Captain Mueller and being forced to abort a child horrified her. Not only did she permit Wei Chang to treat her, but she determined to learn quickly how to douche herself most effectively, so she would never become pregnant in these horrible circumstances.

It took a full week for Malka to heal after Mueller's brutal deflowering. Even after she had begun to bleed he persisted in his assault. He was merciless and insatiable. For the first three days her physical agony was so great and persistent that she prayed for nothing but relief. Wilensky himself never used her. It was only later, after many months, that she learned he was a pederast and kept a steady succession of young Jewish boys coming to his rooms. Wei Chang ministered to her, and some of the girls were permitted to come up to talk to her, one at a time. The friendliest and brightest of these was Maria Wozniak. Maria came from Kolobrzeg on the Baltic Sea, not too far from Prosnica. She was two years older than Malka and had been in Wilensky's house for three years. She held Malka's hand and said, "You must accept the life, little Malka. It is the only way. Otherwise Wilensky will send you the animals, the men like Mueller, who will destroy you."

Malka shook her head. As the physical pain lessened, she was sick to her soul over the realization that she was trapped into being used by men in every brutal way imaginable.

"I cannot do it, Maria," she said. "I will kill myself."

"No, no, Malka. This is a better class house. Most of the men who come here are not cruel. Believe me, there are many worse ways of earning a living in this city."

Maria's evaluation of the brothel's clients proved correct. None of Malka's first patrons were abusive. In a paradoxical way Mueller's bestiality enabled her to accept their relatively subdued use of her without losing her sanity. She serviced them in passive despair, and soon an unconquerable part of her was determined to find some means of escape.

As the degrading days and weeks and months passed Malka began to concentrate her entire being on her escape plans. She talked to the other girls, all of them Jewish, from various southern, eastern, and southeastern European countries. There were four Russian girls, three from Austria-Hungary, two others from Poland, three Rumanians, one Serbian, and one from Greece. Mrs. Krimsky, the madam in charge of the house, was a Russian-Jewish woman in her fifties, who was related in some way to Wilensky. Malka could hardly believe it, but all the girls seemed resigned to the life. Some even talked admiringly of Wilensky and his important friends. He was on intimate terms with judges, police inspectors, city councilmen. Captain Mueller, it seemed, was one of the lesser personages with whom Wilensky had connections.

Malka and Maria Wozniak became close friends. Although Maria seemed intelligent and spirited, she, too, seemed resigned, if not completely contented, with the life. Malka discovered Maria had a dream.

"One day," she told Malka, "a fine, rich gentleman will find me so desirable that he will wish to marry me. Then I will arrange with Wilensky for him to purchase me, and I shall live in a big mansion uptown and wear beautiful gowns and go to balls and concerts. I think I will miss the variety of fucking, but one cannot have everything."

"How did you learn to speak English?" asked Malka.

"The third week I was here a German-Jewish schoolteacher came in. He spoke English well and I told him I wished to learn. He brought me books, and each time when we were finished fucking, he would spend a little time teaching me. I studied the books very hard. It is good to know English in America."

"Do you have the books?"

"Yes, and I will teach you. It is an interesting language,

and when you get Irish politicians or Jewish lawyers or any customers who speak English, you will get bigger tips if you can speak English with them."

Most of the girls were permitted to leave the house one day a week. Only the two who had arrived in the months just before Malka, and were still sullen and rebellious part of the time, were not allowed out. Wilensky had told Malka that unless she learned to behave far better than she had, she might never again see the outside world. One day Malka asked Maria if she had ever considered escaping.

"It would be foolish, Malka," said Maria. She told Malka the terrible story of the Hungarian girl whose body had been found in the river. She pointed to Wei Chang, who was at the opposite side of the parlor, and asked Malka whether she knew what had happened to the Chinese woman. Malka said yes.

"You do not know what a hard life the people here have, Malka, especially here in the ghetto. Only the rich, who live uptown, have enough to eat and drink and fancy clothes. If I left here without a rich husband, I would just have to compete in the street with a thousand diseased whores who fuck for a piece of bread. I would soon catch the pox myself. Better you should stay here, Malka, until a rich man comes along who wants to marry you."

Malka did not believe a rich man would come along and pay Wilensky to take her out of this life of prostitution. She had seriously considered killing herself. One night in the third week, after Captain Mueller had returned and used her again—although less abusively this time because she did not resist—she actually had begun a suicide attempt. First she had opened the jar of medication that Wei Chang used to protect her against disease. It was a thick, pungent jelly. She was certain that if she could swallow some of it, it would kill her. But when she scooped out two fingersful and lifted it to her mouth, the odor sickened her and she wiped it from her hands and put the cap back on the jar.

Then she considered breaking the window and slashing her wrists with a piece of glass. But she decided against that too. Finally she took the sheet from the bed and began to roll it together tightly, trying to make a rope with which to hang herself. Halfway through rolling the sheet, a cold fury filled her. This sickening life was making her crazy. *Why do you want to kill yourself, you stupid girl!* she asked herself. *Mr.*

Wilensky is the one you should kill! She unfurled the sheet, and smoothed it out on the bed. Then she sat on the bed's edge and swore to herself that someday she would kill Joseph Wilensky.

In the middle of the seventh month of her imprisonment, Wilensky came into her room with Mrs. Krimsky. The madam was a short, stout, but hard-muscled woman with a mole on her chin, and a faint black mustache.

"One of our most honorable guests has taken a fancy to you, Malka, my dear," said Wilensky. Malka sat on the stool in front of her dressing table and said coldly, "This is the first man you've announced personally since Captain Mueller."

Wilensky chuckled.

"No, no, Malka. This one does not enjoy beating beautiful young girls. He prefers that beautiful young girls beat him."

Malka had often wondered about the presence of the whips and chains in the alcove closet. She had assumed they would be used to punish her if she went beyond certain bounds in creating trouble. But now Mrs. Krimsky walked toward her with one of the whips.

"The judge likes to be lashed," she announced in Yiddish. She flicked the whip, making a cracking sound. "So!"

"Ninotchka has been servicing him," said Wilensky, "but the last time he was in he saw you in the parlor, and he said he wished to have you flagellate him on his next visit. He is downstairs now."

"I will not do it!" said Malka firmly.

"Would you rather have Mrs. Krimsky whip you?" demanded Wilensky harshly.

"No, but I will not do that. I cannot!"

Wilensky nodded at Mrs. Krimsky, and the Russian madam took a step forward and slashed the whip across Malka's left shoulder. The sting made her cry out.

"Shall we have the judge come up, Malka dear?" asked Wilensky.

Tears streaming down her cheeks, Malka rose from the chair and backed away from Wilensky and the madam.

"No! No!"

Mrs. Krimsky moved toward her again, whip raised, but Malka jumped up on and ran across the bed. Then ensued a chase, like some bizarre game, with Wilensky and the madam trying to catch Malka. They did, finally, huffing and puffing with exertion. Sweating and furious at being made to exert herself so mightily, Mrs. Krimsky whipped Malka until the blood seeped through and showed in thick pinkish stripes on the back of the white silk robe.

"Stubborn goddam Polack bitch!" cursed Wilensky as they strode from the room and locked the door behind them. Malka, lying across the bed, sobbing uncontrollably, her back afire, renewed to herself her promise to kill Joseph Wilensky someday. But hours later, when she finally fell asleep, she dreamed that a rich man came to the house, shot Wilensky dead, took her out of the house, and married her. The man looked like her father, with a luxuriant mustache and dancing eyes. He had died when she was twelve.

20

In early March of 1892 a rich and distinguished man visited Wilensky's and selected Malka from the collection of girls in the parlor. He was dressed plainly and there were no outward signs that he was rich and distinguished, but Malka had an instinctive feeling that he was. He was in his midforties and had wavy, light brown hair with early traces of silver, and a square, hard-jawed face with keen blue eyes. His mustache and beard were grayer than his hair. Possibly it was his erect bearing, his manner, more than anything else, that created Malka's impression of him. He had come into the house with two other men. One was older, perhaps fifty, slim with a thin, serious face, a Vandyke beard, and glasses. The other was younger, perhaps in his early thirties. He seemed much more at ease in the parlor and in the way he talked with Mrs. Krimsky than the two older men.

When they got to her room, Malka's guest seated himself stiffly in a chair. Malka sat on the edge of the bed.

"May we talk a bit, Malka?" said the man.

"But yes," she said. "It is your half hour."

She had learned to speak English quite well, though of course with a pronounced accent. Indeed she could even read the language. Far into the night when her unhappy work was done, she devoured the copies of the newspapers that were left in the parlor. Her favorite papers were the *Evening Post* and the *Evening Sun*. She especially enjoyed the writings of a reporter on the latter paper. His name was Jacob A.

Riis and he frequently wrote tragic stories of people in the east-side tenements. The stories confirmed what Maria Wozniak had told her. Malka herself had not yet been permitted to leave the house.

"You do not seem at all like the rest of the girls here, Malka," said the man.

Malka shrugged.

"I—I think we are—are all the same."

The man shook his head.

"You seem exceptionally intelligent. How long have you worked here?"

"Nearly one year . . . nine months, one week, four days."

"It is plain to me that you did not choose this, er—ah—profession."

"Profession? What is pro—fession?"

"This way of life."

"No, I do not choose."

"Would you like to get out of it?"

Malka looked around.

"Please—please to lower your voice, sir," she said. "The walls are thin."

A loud groan came from the adjoining room, followed by a burst of raucous laughter.

"As you hear."

The man pulled his chair closer to the bed. With a quiet intensity he said, "The tall man with the glasses, with whom I came in—you have no idea who he is, of course?"

Malka shook her head, looking puzzled.

"He is a minister, a reverend of the Madison Square Presbyterian Church. He is also president of the Society for the Prevention of Crime."

"Pa—Pockhust?" exclaimed Malka.

The man looked surprised.

"Yes, the Reverend Charles Parkhurst. How did you know?"

"I—I read in newspapers about him. He makes sermon in church. Last week what you call grand jury and mayor say he lies . . . about police . . . and houses like—like this. Mayor is angry with him."

The man nodded.

"Yes, but everything the reverend said in his sermons about the corrupt police, the houses—"

"What is . . . co—cohrup?"

"Wicked. Dishonest . . ."

Malka nodded vigorously.

"Yes. Is all true. About houses. About Mr. Wilensky and police. A captain, Mueller by name."

The man's blue eyes brightened. He leaned forward and took her hand.

"Would—would you give us an affidavit, Malka?"

"What—what—what is ahfidavid?"

"Sorry... Excuse me. Affidavit means you tell about Wilensky and the police. All you know. We write it down. You sign—"

Fear showed in Malka's dark eyes. She shook her head.

"No! No!" she said in alarm, looking about her as though Mr. Wilensky or Mrs. Krimsky might be in the room. "I cannot. They will—they will kill me!"

"We would protect you, Malka. This time when Dr. Parkhurst makes his charges we will have many affidavits as proof. No one will hurt you."

"No, I cannot do. I pray to God you will hang Mr. Wilensky and the police captain, Mueller... but I cannot help you."

The man spent another forty-five minutes trying to convince Malka that she could testify safely, but her fear was too great. Finally he thanked her for her time and her help. He gave her a ten-dollar tip. Along with it a card.

"If you should change your mind, Malka, if you think you can help us, come to see me."

When he left she studied the card.

"Howard Borsum," it said. "Counselor at Law." And it confirmed her suspicion that he was a rich and important man. The address was on Fifth Avenue. That was where most of the rich lived. She wondered about the numbers in the lower right-hand corner of the card. If she had known they were Borsum's telephone number, she would have been doubly certain he was wealthy. Only the rich had the new telephones. Malka was later to learn from newspaper accounts that the man was a descendant of a distinguished Dutch family. His great-great-great-great-grandfather was an attorney and prominent statesman, Johannes Borsum, and his great-great-great-great-grandmother was Frederika deVries Borsum. It was not mentioned that Frederika was the illegitimate daughter of a less distinguished Dutchman, Willem Van Gelder.

The same week that Howard Borsum had selected her from among the Wilensky girls, another rich man took her to her room. She did not guess this one would turn out to be rich. Anything but! He was dressed in decent enough clothes, but they were ill-cared-for, unpressed, and even slightly soiled. He was younger than Howard Borsum and had blond hair and sad, soft blue eyes and a large nose. His manner was the precise opposite of Borsum's. Where the attorney was self-confident, authoritative, eloquent, this young man was shy, awkward, apologetic. He said his name was Walter Klein. Like Borsum, however, it turned out that on his first visit he, too, wanted only to talk.

Once when he halted in his stammering, embarrassed narrative, she thought, from the hungry look in his eyes, perhaps he wished to use her. She began to slip off her robe, but he said quickly, "No! No! Please, Malka. There is no need for you to undress!"

She only guessed that he must be wealthy because Wilensky charged by the half hour, and on his first visit, Walter Klein talked with her for more than five hours. And left her a five-dollar tip. He came once a week for the next two weeks, and then twice a week, and always spent the entire time in conversation. And left her the five-dollar tip. He talked much about his father. He told her his father was a prosperous dry-goods merchant, and that he worked in his father's business, although he had no interest in it. His father was strict and erratic and it was plain that Walter feared him.

"I am an artist," he told Malka shyly on his ninth visit, "but I am not certain I have any genuine talent."

All he knew was that he loved to paint and hoped someday to become successful at it. He got no encouragement at all from his father. Indeed the father usually ridiculed his work. Only his good friend, an older lady who had taught for years at the Art Students League, believed in him. But he thought she was probably wrong. Malka's quiet, attentive, and compassionate attitude toward his ramblings encouraged him finally to talk about intimate details of his private life. He told her about his terrible difficulties with women. He was thirty years old and had never had intercourse with a woman. Once in another brothel he had tried, but had been unable to achieve an erection and the whore had laughed at him. He told Malka, blushing fiercely and with stuttering embarrassment, that he abused himself sexually and derived satisfaction from it, but had contempt for himself for doing so.

He did not talk about himself exclusively. He pleaded with

Malka to tell him about herself, her life before she came to Wilensky's. Malka had very mixed, confused emotions about this strange young man. He seemed as imprisoned by his erratic, domineering father as she was by Wilensky. Her heart went out to him, but at the same time she began to speculate on the possibility that he might be the means of her escape from the brothel. She told him how she had been deceived into coming to America, how she had been entrapped, and how bitterly she hated the life.

"Some day, Walter," she said seriously, "I will kill Mr. Wilensky."

The young man paled.

"No, no! You must not think that way, Malka. There must be some other way for you to get away and lead a new life."

She waited for him to say perhaps he would marry her, but all he did was urge her not to do anything violent.

"Believe me," he said, "there will be a better way."

Partially because he seemed so genuinely interested, and partially because she thought that if she created a sympathetic and wholesome picture of herself he might decide to marry her, she told him about her childhood in Prosnica. The town was only about sixteen kilometers from the Baltic Sea, and she told him about the summer Sunday visits she and her mother and father made to the seashore. And about how her father had drowned on one such Sunday trying to rescue a ten-year-old child who had been swept out by a riptide. Her mother was an excellent seamstress, and after her father's death, Malka had learned to sew and she and her mother had earned their living, bare as it was, from sewing.

Her mother and father were Polish, but long before she was born, the Russians had taken over the country, about 1863, and made Russian the official language. Thus her mother and father spoke Russian, Polish, and Yiddish, and she, too, spoke all three languages. And, she added with some pride, now English too.

"Not well," she said, "but understandable, I hope."

"Oh, very well," said the young man.

He continued to dwell on stories about his father, a German-Jew, who had fought in the Civil War and had been wounded. She was baffled by his attitude toward his father. Sometimes he spoke of him with great admiration, almost reverence, but mostly with obvious fear. However the father treated him, she had to believe he paid his son well. He usually stayed at least five hours, and she knew that was costly. He also left her a five-dollar tip each time he visited, except two or three times when he simply forgot.

They did not always talk of personal matters. Late in March, when he had begun coming three times a week, they spent a good deal of time discussing the newspaper accounts of the events following Dr. Charles Parkhurst's shocking sermon on Sunday, March 13. The Reverend and one of his parishioners, a wealthy lawyer named Howard Borsum, had spent several weeks visiting a broad variety of the city's more disreputable establishments. They had hired a private detective named Charles Gardner, and paid him six dollars a night to serve as their guide and escort. Gardner had hired four other investigators, who turned in reports on scores of places. Malka vividly recalled the visit of Parkhurst, Borsum, and the man she now realized was the private detective, Gardner. She told Walter Klein about her talk with Borsum.

"I am sorry I did not agree to affidavit," she said. "The minister, he has many, but perhaps none to hang Mr. Wilensky."

Parkhurst, Borsum, and Gardner, along with the other investigators, had visited more than two hundred saloons, bawdy houses, gambling emporiums, and other places where vice was rampant. Some of the brothels featured girls of specific nationalities. Just as Wilensky's offered East European Jewesses, there were houses in the Negro district around West Houston and Sullivan streets where the harlots were all colored girls. On the southern edge of Washington Square in Greenwich Village was Frenchtown, with girls from Marseilles, Paris, and many smaller villages in France. On Forsyth Street they found a lively German bordello.

The papers quoted Parkhurst as being most shocked by an establishment called the True Enchantment Club, where young men and boys, heavily rouged, with carmined lips and shadowed eyes, spoke in high-pitched feminine voices, called themselves by exotic girls' names, and giggled and screamed as they indulged in aberrant sexual behavior with male customers in small, boxlike private rooms. In a gambling den in Chinatown the Reverend and Borsum watched white men and Chinese at fan-tan tables, and saw a number of Chinese men and white girls in bunks, smoking opium pipes.

On March 13, Parkhurst had made a full report and preached a fiery sermon in his jam-packed church. He waved a thick sheaf of papers at his parishioners, and told them that these were sworn affidavits testifying to the vice and corruption he and Borsum and the investigators had witnessed. He declared that these dens of iniquity were able to operate only because the police department was utterly corrupt. He insisted that DeLancy Nicoll, the district attorney, and Mayor Hugh Grant take action and force the courts to close these establishments.

Remarkably enough, despite the affidavits, Parkhurst's charges brought no action. Worse than that, some of the newspapers ridiculed the Reverend, charging him with being a blatant publicity-seeker. The *Evening Sun* went so far as to insist that Parkhurst's effectiveness as a man of the church had been nullified by his participation in these obscene activities. One newspaper reported that he had played leap frog with a group of naked whores in a "Tight House" (a place where women wore colored tights and performed outrageous dances) in the Tenderloin district. Soon cynical New Yorkers were singing a ditty on the theme, to the tune of a popular song.

Dr. Parkhurst on the floor
Playing leap frog with a whore
Ta Ra Ra Boom Dee Ay!

Reading the latest reports during one of Walter's visits, Malka said, "They wish to make fool of Parkhurst, but with all the affidavits, do you not think they will close the houses, Walter?"

He shook his head sadly.

"I think not, Malka. My father says that Tammany Hall controls the district attorney, the mayor, and all the judges. The politicians profit greatly from all these places."

"The police, also, yes?" said Malka bitterly.

Walter's father was right. Months passed and the stories about Parkhurst's fight against vice disappeared from the newspapers and nothing changed. Walter continued to visit Malka three evenings each week. In late spring he asked if she would mind modeling for him.

"I would be pleased, Walter," she said. "But would Mr. Wilensky . . . Mrs. Krimsky, would they permit it?"

"Yes, I have talked to Wilensky," he said. On his next visit he set up an oblong of mounted canvas on his easel and began to freshen up the paints on his palette. They had lighted the lamps on each side of the bed and Malka lay on her side with her head resting on two white silk pillows. Her normally sleek raven hair had lost some of its luster, but it hung gracefully over her shoulders, and touched the curve of her breast just above the chocolate-colored nipples. Her normally rose-tinged olive cheeks were pale, but her dark eyes sparkled brightly and there was a sheen on the silken olive skin. The lamplight cast shadows and highlights on her lush body. After such a long time in Wilensky's house, she was completely unselfconscious about her nudity.

Walter looked at her, sketched a few strokes on his canvas, looked back at her and sketched again. As she watched him, she smiled seductively. She knew he was being aroused. She was not sure she had fallen in love with him, but since he was the only male with whom she shared intelligent, even intimate conversation she had at least become extremely fond of him. Beyond that she still saw him as her potential means of escaping Wilensky. When he had asked her to pose, she had welcomed the opportunity. Several times previously, she had asked him gently whether he would like to make love to her. He had always rejected her offer with embarrassed thanks. When he asked if he could paint her, she did not even inquire whether he meant to paint her in the nude. She suspected it was his foolish, awkward way of arranging to see her naked.

His glances toward her between sketching became more and more extended. Finally he stopped marking the canvas and said hoarsely, "You are so beautiful, Malka. So beautiful. Like a goddess."

She smiled at him.

"Come here," she said softly. "Please to come here, Walter."

He put down the charcoal and wiped his hands on a cloth, then on the seat of his pants. He walked to the side of the bed and gazed down at her, idolatry and desire bringing tears to his eyes. She took his hand.

"Sit here by me, Walter," she whispered.

When he sat, timidly, perspiring, she unbuttoned his cotton shirt. He took off his shoes and socks and when she unbuttoned his trousers, she saw that he was erect and rigid. But when he was entirely naked and lay in the bed beside her, she felt him soften and become limp.

"I—I'm sorry, Malka. It is terrible. But I—I can't!"

She put her arms around him and gently pushed his head down upon her breast. She stroked his hair. She felt his tears slide down her breast.

"It's all right, Walter. It is only that you cannot . . . in a place like this!"

Even as she spoke the words, she did not know whether the thought had come to her because she really did love him, or for another, more pragmatic reason. She was aware as she spoke that if she could convince him he could not perform like a man *only* because he was in a house of prostitution, he might well find some way to get her to another place. Nevertheless she tried with all the techniques she had learned in a year at Wilensky's to bring him back to rigidity. But to no avail. Finally, he said, "It's no use, Malka. I love you more than I can say, but I just cannot . . ."

And she said again, "In a place like this, it is not surprising that a true gentleman cannot make love."

The very next Friday he came up to her room shortly after she had finished her supper. She had never seen him in such a state of excitement.

"I have good news, Malka. I am taking you out of this house!"

Malka gasped. She could not believe her ears.

"What—how—Mr. Wilensky? Have you talked with Mr. Wilensky?"

"I certainly have."

She rushed to him and threw her arms around him.

"Oh, Walter! How wonderful! How fine! When can we leave?"

"Right now. This very minute! Pack enough clothes for the entire weekend."

She stepped back from him.

"The—the week—you mean today and Saturday and Sunday?"

He nodded happily.

"The *whole* weekend! I am paying Wilensky fifty dollars for each day. It is more than I can afford, but I have saved up some money. It will be worth it. I have made reservations for a room at the Waldorf Hotel. Wait until you see it, Malka. It is the finest new hotel in the city. I will show you the whole city; the parks and the Statue of Liberty and the Brooklyn Bridge and—"

"What do we do on Monday, Walter?" interrupted Malka firmly.

Walter seemed startled.

"Monday? On Monday? On Monday you must come back,"

he said sorrowfully, spreading his hands palms up and shrugging his shoulders.

Her shock, her disappointment were staggering. Somehow she fought off the impulse to curse him for a feelingless idiot. She realized that two days would be better than nothing. At least it was her first opportunity to get out of the house. Perhaps she would not come back. Perhaps he would change his mind and beg her not to go back. Perhaps he would decide he wished to marry her.

He did not tell her, but that was precisely what he had discussed with Wilensky before he had settled for taking Malka away for the weekend.

Mrs. Krimsky had arranged the appointment with Mr. Wilensky. In Wilensky's parlor-office on the second floor, a large room furnished with overstuffed furniture and smelling of tobacco smoke, Walter sweated nervously as he began the conversation.

"Uh—er—this may seem a strange request, Mr. Wilensky, but I would like to marry one of your girls."

Wilensky blew out a puff of smoke from his long cigar. He smiled.

"It is not so strange. It has happened before. Not often, but it has happened. How much are you prepared to pay?"

"Pay? Pay! I don't understand."

"Never mind, you don't understand. You know I have a large investment in these girls. You know how much Malka brings in in a year?"

"Brings in?"

"Brings in!" said Wilensky impatiently. "How much have you alone paid for her company in the last six months? You are not stupid, Mr. Kessler."

It shocked William Kessler that Wilensky knew his true identity. He had never told Malka, certainly not Mrs. Krimsky, nor anyone else in the establishment.

"Don't look so surprised, Mr. Kessler. When comes along a customer so free with money as you, Joe Wilensky makes it his business to find out who he is, this guest. I know that your father is Max Kessler, the wealthy real estate and investment broker."

He drew on his cigar and made self-satisfied smoke rings, while his stare remained fixed on William Kessler.

"So, how much already, would you be prepared to pay to take Malka away and make her Mrs. William Kessler?"

"I don't have very much money," stammered William finally. "I only work for my father. How much would it cost?"

"For you, because you are a nice, honest young man with great artistic talent, only five thousand dollars."

"Five—five thousand . . . ! It is not possible. I could not—"

Wilensky leaned forward. He smiled again and said, "If you convinced your father how much you love Malka, he would maybe give you the money. It is not so much for such a rich man to give to make his only son happy."

William shook his head in bewilderment. When he insisted that under no circumstances would his father give him such a large sum of money, Wilensky suggested the weekend arrangement. And William gratefully accepted it. As he was leaving the office, Wilensky called after him.

"Mr. Kessler, one other thing I should call to your attention. Malka has sometimes proved to be a headstrong, stubborn child. She maybe will tell you she does not wish to return on Monday. She maybe will think she can run away and hide someplace."

He waved his cigar to indicate the idea was nonsensical.

"She cannot. Believe me, Mr. Kessler, she cannot. Other girls have tried to leave Joe Wilensky before Joe Wilensky was ready they should leave. All have had bad accidents. Very bad."

Malka had told William Kessler, alias Walter Klein, about Wei Chang and the Hungarian girl. He stood with his sweating hand on the knob of the door to Wilensky's parlor-office, feeling nauseous as he listened to the burly whoremaster's words.

"And Mr. Kessler," said Wilensky cheerily. "It could be you, yourself, who is severely injured in some way if Malka does not return. You understand that you are responsible for her."

21

A few years after the Civil War, Ned Morrissey, like his father before him, had been ready to resign from the police department. The east-side politician William Marcy Tweed, a whale-shaped man, had become a power not only in the city but in New York State. He and a group of cohorts inaugurated a period of corruption that made Fernando Wood's larceny seem like pilfering piggy banks. Ned knew that on the construction of the new County Court House in sixty-nine and seventy Tweed's ring had stolen almost $10,000,000. The building should have cost less than $3,000,000 but the city paid $12,000,000 for it. Tweed accumulated wealth from every conceivable source. Financial giants Cornelius Vanderbilt and Daniel Drew were battling Jim Fisk and Jay Gould for control of the Erie Railroad, and Tweed backed Fisk and Gould. They won and Tweed's payoff was appointment to the board of directors of the railroad. He also became the Erie's legal advisor at a salary of $100,000 per year. The newspapers claimed that the Tweed grafters had robbed the city of close to $200,000,000 over the years.

Ned often discussed with Max Kessler his bitter feelings over the monstrous new corruption and the growth of the ever more powerful gangs, supported by the politicians, but he got less and less sympathy from his old friend. Max had become increasingly cynical and misanthropic with each passing year. Ned attributed this in some degree to the fact that Max was in constant physical discomfort and often in excruciating pain. He realized that Max had also suffered disenchantments with people he trusted. Ned had no way of knowing how many such instances occurred in Max's complex dealings in real estate and investments, but he did know that Othello Jones and Mrs. Horowitz had both taken advantage of him.

In the years when William was growing up, Othello was employed and paid well to perform two functions for Max. One was to collect the rents from the tenement tenants. He knew most Jews hated the Negroes and it gave him perverse pleasure to force them to give their money to Othello. The tall Negro's main function was to drive Max's coach. The first of May in 1871 Othello, all the rent monies, and the horse and coach disappeared. Max knew that Othello had become a steady and heavy drinker and visited a colored whorehouse on Sullivan Street regularly. He chastised Othello from time to time and the Negro always apologized abjectly and promised to reform. But Max had never expected him to run off with nine hundred and forty-five dollars and his horse and coach. The last Max heard was that Othello and one of the colored prostitutes were seen in Connecticut, heading north. Max cursed Othello, but made no effort to have him arrested and brought back. He simply bought another coach and horse and hired a brawny, newly arrived German blacksmith named Otto Starker as his driver. He paid Starker five dollars a month less than he had paid Othello.

Max could easily have afforded to purchase a mansion uptown on Fifth Avenue, but he continued to live in the Rivington Street tenement he had built. It was his custom to give Mrs. Horowitz a fixed and liberal amount of money each Monday to buy the food, groceries, and goat's milk for the week. He was unable to eat many foods. His stomach was bad, and soon he lost all his teeth. He had a set of dentures made, but they fitted poorly and were not much help in chewing. He existed mainly on mush dishes made up of grains of various kinds and mashed vegetables, finely chopped fowl, and goat's milk.

One day he discovered that Mrs. Horowitz was spending only half the money he gave her for the food and groceries, and giving the other half to her sister, Rebecca Cohen. Rebecca lived with her husband and six small children on the fifth floor of the tenement. The Cohens worked twelve hours a day, seven days a week at machines in one of the tenement rooms, sewing knee pants. Between them they produced an average of about a hundred and twenty knickerbockers each week. Bent over their sewing machines they merely cut and stitched together the pants. Then the garments went to a finisher, an ironer, and a buttonholer. All these workers were given their employment by a sort of contractor, known as a sweater. The sweater took a large part of the seventy cents a dozen that the manufacturer paid for the finished pants. The Cohens' weekly earnings came to approximately eight dollars. Their monthly rent for the two rooms in the tenement was ten dollars. This would not have been too bad, except for the fact that the sweater had work for them only about six months out of the year.

When Max discovered that Mrs. Horowitz was cheating him, he dismissed her and dispossessed the Cohens from the rooms, which he rented to new tenants for eleven dollars a month. He hired Otto Starker's sturdy German wife, Veronica, as cook and housekeeper. He also paid her five dollars a month less than he had been paying Mrs. Horowitz. Ned found the Horowitz incident difficult to understand. He did not know exactly how much money Max Kessler had, but he knew it was a considerable fortune. He knew that Max owned at least ten tenements, some of which he had purchased and some he had constructed. He also knew that Max had bought substantial shares in the Erie at a low price and sold at a peak.

Max had an office in the Drexel Building on Wall Street, the same building in which J. P. Morgan had his offices, and Ned knew Max was on close business terms with Morgan. He was also very active in dealings with the Jay Cooke Investment House, one of the leading firms in the city. Ned had had supper with Max the week the news of the collapse of the financial market become general knowledge and the depression of 1873 began. He expressed the hope that Max had not lost too much. Max laughed his barklike laugh.

"I sold everything a month ago, Ned. Max Kessler is not a fool. Not in matters of money."

Max was also privy to a good deal of political information, since he was a heavy contributor to key politicians' campaign funds. It had been on an evening in the spring of 1871, when Ned sat in the parlor of the Harlem home of his brother and sister-in-law, Pat and Fiona Morrissey, with their family and Max and William Kessler. Pat, as disgusted with the corruption in the police department as Ned, had resigned in 1867 and accepted a position as vice-president of the American Telegraph Company. He and Fiona Lafferty had married that same year, and on this night they were celebrating the first birthday of Martin Morrissey III. Two other children had preceded Martin: Kevin, born in 1868, and Bridget, in 1869.

William Kessler, a nervous nine-year-old who seemed perpetually confused, was in the kitchen with Fiona Morrissey, regal-looking and bright-eyed at thirty. Fiona and Pat, along with Ned, were William's favorite grown-ups, and he looked upon Fiona as a mother. On this birthday evening, over brandies in the parlor, Ned said to Pat and Max, "I don't know if I can stand it any longer. Last week we arrested Larry Houlihan, one of the leaders of the Hudston Dusters, for murder. Open and shut. And this afternoon the district attorney's office threw out the case. Insufficient evidence, they said. God! We gave them—"

"Stand it! Stand it!" interrupted Max gruffly. "Tweed is through and conditions will change! You will make inspector before the year is out."

It seemed uncanny to Ned, but in October of that year two of Tweed's underlings, Sheriff Jimmy O'Brien and County

Bookkeeper Matt O'Rourke, turned against him and supplie the newspapers with concrete evidence of a number of in stances of grand larceny. After a number of trials Tweed wa finally sent to the penitentiary on Blackwell's Island. H escaped and fled to Spain, but was recaptured and died in th Ludlow Street jail in April of 1878.

Ned had indeed made inspector in March of 1872, and ha decided to remain in the department. With his promotion h rededicated himself to his work. He realized there wa nothing he could do about the astonishing changes in the cit The character of the Lower East Side had altered drasticall and for the worse. Over the years the middle-class Germa and Irish had almost all moved uptown, and the Italians an primarily the Jews (some two million between 1885 and 18 alone) poured into the rows upon rows of decrepit tenement which filled block after block. The Italians settled aroun Mulberry Street. A loud, colorful, frequently violent Litt Italy spread out from there, and expanded eventually into th Thompson and Sullivan Street area just south of Washingto Square. Bayard Street, running across the Bowery from Mu berry, led into another, larger, even more overcrowded ten ment district called Jewtown.

Between the two, centered around Mott, Doyer, and Pe streets, was Chinatown, a stark contrast in its clean, uncrowde alleys and byways to the Italian and Jewish slum section Unlike the Italians and the Jews, who lived all their lives the bustling ghetto streets, unless the weather was incleme or unless they were slaving away in a roach- and rat-ridde tenement room, the Chinese carried on all their activiti behind closed red or yellow doors. The neat stores we mainly laundries; some doors led to gambling casinos, othe to opium dens. In too many of the dens, Ned knew, ignoran desperate, unloved young Irish, Jewish, German, and Itali girls, lured into smoking the long pipe of happy dream wasted their pathetic lives. As "wives" to brutally chauvinist Chinamen, they smoked their way to early graves.

It did not help keep the ghetto dwellers calm and conten ed that in this same period some of the most extravagant a elegant mansions in the city's history came into being. A. Stewart's marble palace on the northwest corner of Thirt fourth Street and Fifth Avenue was one, and a Mrs. Ma Mason Jones developed what was called Marble Row, eig imposing mansions, side by side, on the Fifth Avenue blo from Fifty-seventh to Fifty-eighth streets. More than three hundred and fifty brick, marble, and granite residences were constructed, mainly along Fifth Avenue, at the same time that Max Kessler and other real estate speculators and landlords were building tenements consisting of small boxlike rooms, mostly airless and running one into another, and thus called railroad flats. The more modern tenements had one toilet on each floor, rather than a single toilet in the backyard.

Clara lived on in Ned's heart. He never for a moment entertained the thought of establishing a permanent relationship with a woman. His sister-in-law, Fiona, often invited bright, attractive women friends for supper on the same evenings as Ned, but her matchmaking efforts were to no avail. He visited with Pat and Fiona frequently because their children were the true delight of his bachelor life. He loved his nephews and his niece and they adored him.

Being a strong, vital man, he was not entirely celibate. At least twice a month, sometimes more frequently, he visited a whorehouse on Fourteenth Street owned and operated by Tessie Kearns. It was a small, sedate place with only four young girls and Tessie. In the police department it was known that Tessie was Ned's friend, so the local precinct captain excluded her from his list of houses that paid for permission to operate. In her midthirties, Tessie was still a lushly beautiful woman. Her jolly attitude toward life had stood her in good stead. Ned often told her his troubles and her invariable reply was, "Oh, Neddie, you just take life too seriously."

She paused and poured him a whiskey and sat on his lap. She ran her fingers through his hair and laughed.

"Do you remember when you got me pregnant?"

"I do, I do, you vixen. You took five years off my life. You and Mike O'Leary."

He swallowed his whiskey and Tessie got off his lap and began to undress him. He raised one arm after the other to make it easier for her to take off his shirt. Then she removed his heavy shoes and socks.

"Stretch out your legs, Neddie," she ordered. When he did so, she pulled off his trousers and quickly tugged off his underwear. He still had a hard, flat belly. She took him by the hand and led him to the bed in the feminine, pink-accented room. She pushed him down on the bed.

"You know, Tessie," he said, lying comfortably on his back,

hands clasped behind his head, "I worry about William. Old Max grows stranger by the day."

Tessie knew all about the Kesslers. Ned had discussed them on numerous occasions.

"Oh, forget the old money-grubber," she said, and let her pink silk robe fall to the floor. She was naked. She stood before Ned and caressed her breasts, flicking the nipples with the tips of her index fingers. She smiled wickedly as she saw him become moderately tumescent. She climbed nimbly into the bed and knelt between his spread legs.

"You need to relax, Neddie, my love," she said, and stroked his member. Almost immediately it grew rigid and she took it in her mouth.

Ned did worry about the Kesslers. He learned from Shimon Levine, the butcher on Rivington Street, that Levine supplied Max with a gallon of beef blood each week. Max kept it in an icebox and had a large glassful with his supper every day. He was convinced it gave him strength. The beef blood had been recommended by a Dr. Hans Guttman. Max was in constant pain from the injuries to his spine and back, and Dr. Guttman also supplied him with a thick, brown liquid medication, which Ned was certain contained either opium or morphine. He also prescribed another medicine, which Ned was convinced was one hundred-proof alcohol, sugared and tinctured with something which gave it a bluish color. Over the years, as Max resorted to these medications in increasing doses, he became alarmingly unpredictable. One minute he could be an understanding and compassionate if curt friend, and the next a snarling, bitter denunciator.

This erratic behavior affected his relationship with everyone, but the most pathetic victim of it was young William. In his pain-free pleasant periods he would overwhelm his son with affection and give him money or whatever presents he thought William might enjoy. Then without warning he would curse him viciously, accuse him of being unmanly and lazy, and often slap him and kick him and order him out of his sight.

William spent more and more time with Ned and Pat and Fiona Morrissey and their children. Although he was six years older than Kevin, and eight older than Marty, he seemed younger and far less mature than either of the boys, or even Bridget. He was a nervous, insecure twenty-one on the Thursday, May 24, in 1883, when he joined the entire Morrissey family at the festive opening of the Brooklyn Bridge. He seemed more childishly awestruck at the sight of the great span than the Morrissey children. Max had decided against attending the festivities.

Fiona stared wide-eyed at the graceful strands of steel cable spanning the magnificent bridge.

"It's so beautiful," she murmured. "I must paint it!"

William, seated beside her, whispered urgently, "May I try, too, Mrs. Morrissey?"

She smiled at him and patted his hand.

"Of course," she said. "Perhaps Sunday we can bring our oils and see if we can capture part of this glorious structure in some small way."

Fiona was the only female teacher at the Art Students League and William had been studying with her for almost four years.

"It's the greatest engineering feat in history," said Ned.

"As great as the Suez Canal," said Pat. "John Roebling gave his life for this bridge, and his son Washington almost lost his. They are great men."

He turned to fifteen-year-old Kevin, seated beside him.

"Did you know that it took thirteen years to build this great bridge, Kev? You were just two when they started."

But Kevin was tugging at Marty's sleeve.

"When we come again on Sunday," he said, "I'll race you across."

"Me, too," said Bridget.

When William returned to the tenement on Rivington Street from the bridge celebration, he found Max in the parlor, reading the *Evening Sun* with the large magnifying glass he used. With great enthusiasm William began to tall his father about the wonders of the Roeblings' achievement.

"You should see it, Father!" he said. "Perhaps you would like to join Mrs. Morrissey and me on Sunday. We're going to do paintings of the bridge."

Max put down his paper and slammed the magnifying glass on top of it. He glared at William.

"You spend altogether too much time with the Irishers!" he barked. "And altogether too much time with your foolish painting. Better you should go back to the City College and take some extra courses in economics and finance. How will you ever be able to run the business when I die?"

"But Father, I—I'm just not good at business. You know—"

Max's bark became louder.

"Don't tell me you are not good. At painting you're not good! If I thought you were, I would have no objections to all the time you waste with it."

William reddened and lowered his head.

"Mrs. Morrissey believes I have some talent," he muttered. "She thinks—"

"Mrs. Morrissey is a mediocre painter herself. What does she know of talent?"

He took a cardboard-covered account book from the table beside which he had placed his newspaper. With his left hand he waved it angrily at William.

"Seventeen tenants are already four months or more behind in their rents, William. What do I have to do to convince you you must be firmer with these *goniffs*. You want it to be known all over the East Side that good-for-nothings can live free in Max Kessler's buildings?"

To William the most distasteful of all his duties with his father's real estate and investment firm was collecting the rents each month.

"They'll pay, Father," he said sullenly. "It's just that in some cases the children are sick, or there is no work. Last month Kolodnik on Ludlow Street died. They had to bury him in Potter's Field."

"So Kolodnik died! People die all the time, William! Till they die they must pay their rent! Do you understand!"

William nodded wearily. The following Monday Max came down into the basement, where William had his own living quarters and studio. William was putting some touches on the painting he had done, working all the previous day at Brooklyn Bridge with Fiona. His father craned his neck forward and stared at the canvas in the yellowish gaslight.

"That is good, William," he said, "quite good. But I want you to clean up and come with me. We have a meeting at the office with Weintraub. He has six lots on the West Side he wants to sell. I think Weintraub likes you. Maybe we will pick up a good bargain."

So it went. Raging abuse one day; pleasant, even complimentary remarks the next. But with each passing year Max's suffering and the potent, mind-altering medication transformed him into an ever more insensitive misanthrope. He hated people in general, but most of all he seemed to have developed a special bitterness toward the Morrisseys, and toward Ned Morrissey in particular.

In the spring of 1892, at fifty-two, Ned was not the most contented of men himself. After a reform wave and a period of relative honesty and efficiency in the city government following Tweed's downfall, political and police venality seemed rampant once more. A dynamic Democrat named Richard Croker had taken over the leadership of Tammany and ran the city. To Ned it seemed that each succeeding political boss learned from the swindling techniques of the previous leader, and added new, more outrageous refinements to the corrupt practices. And this time, for Ned, it was far worse than it had ever been. His own nephew, Kevin, was involved.

Three years earlier Kevin had quit City College over the vociferous objections of his parents and his uncle, and joined the police force. For several years he was an earnest and dedicated young patrolman. Then he was assigned to the newly developed theatrical district, the Rialto, often called the Tenderloin, which went from Twenty-third to Forty-second streets and from Broadway west to Ninth Avenue. Not only was it the heart of the entertainment area now, but it was also a center of vice and crime of every sort. Kevin met a beautiful nineteen-year-old actress named Lilly Welcome, who was appearing in a play at the Casino Theatre, and Kevin was smitten with her. She liked fancy restaurants, fine clothes, and jewelry, and Kevin supplied them. He bought himself a sergeancy by the simple expedient of paying one of the Tammany bigwigs twenty-five hundred dollars. He raised the money by emulating many other policemen he knew, who were collecting from gambling and opium-den operators, whorehouse madams, and even from some legitimate businesses—for "protection." As a sergeant he was able to command even greater bribes. He also developed a taste for high-stakes gambling.

He and the vivacious, shapely actress moved into an apartment in the elegant new Dakota on Central Park West and Seventy-second Street. Kevin's parents were shattered by his behavior. They and Ned tried to persuade him to give up his wicked ways; they pleaded, cajoled, threatened, but all to no avail. Miss Welcome's appeal was stronger than all their petitionings. Kevin was a self-confident, cocky, amoral young man of twenty-four, and loving every minute of his flamboyant, exciting life. His brother, Marty, also pleaded with him to correct his ways. Marty had graduated summa cum laude from City College, completed law school, and was in the process of taking his bar exams.

"To each his own, kiddo," Kevin replied to Marty's pleading. "You keep your nose in your books, and out of my business. All right?"

"You're breaking Mom's heart," said Marty.

"She'll adjust, kiddo. Lilly'll win her over."

Bridget was still another worry to her parents and to Ned. Six years earlier, when she was seventeen, she thought she was in love with William Kessler. To her he seemed a struggling young artist. His helpless, confused, brooding manner appealed to her maternal instincts. But after a little more than a year of attempting to bring some sunshine into his life by permitting him to escort her to concerts, the theater, for walks and boating in the park, she realized that it was beyond her powers to cure his perpetual melancholy. Twice she had teased him into kissing her, but he acted as though he had ravaged her and apologized for hours afterward. The kisses were so awkwardly and hastily implanted that to passionate young Bridget, William's penitent reaction seemed unbelievably ludicrous.

On March 12 in 1888 she had foolishly decided to visit a girlfriend on 101st Street, despite the surprising snowstorm that had suddenly burst upon the city that morning. A robust nineteen-year-old, she knew a little snow would not hurt her. But she would have perished on the way to the friend's house in the raging blizzard, which seemed to develop within minutes, if a young man in a produce wagon had not chanced upon her. She was staggering around beneath the loop of elevated track on 110th Street called Angel's Curve. She was trying to search out a doorway in which she might take shelter, but saw no such haven through the slashing sheets of white ice.

Suddenly out of nowhere a man with a snow-covered dark wool cap pulled low over his ears, just above his ice-coated eyebrows, appeared beside her in the foot-high drift. In the howling wind she could not make out what he was saying through his frozen mouth, but he put an arm around her and dragged her to a wagon about six feet behind them. With the single dray horse pulling the wagon, skidding and sliding in the deep, icy snow, it took more than two hours before the man was able to deliver her at her house on 117th Street in

Harlem. She insisted he come in for hot coffee before he ventured forth again.

As a matter of fact the blizzard had become so severe, travel by any means was impossible. Pat and Fiona insisted the young man stay overnight. His name was Salvatore Lombardi. He was a curly-haired, dark-eyed man of twenty-five. To Bridget, he was like one of her favorite storybook characters, Sir Galahad, come to life. His father owned a wholesale-produce business on Catherine Street. After that frigid but romantic meeting beneath the icicle-laden Angel's Curve elevated tracks, during the worst blizzard in the city's history, Bridget married Sal Lombardi in June of that year.

In March of 1889 their first child, a boy, was born. They named him Anthony after Sal's father. In July of 1890 their second child, a girl, arrived. At Bridget's absolute, stubborn Irish insistence they named her Fiona. Sal's mother, Rosa, was furious that the girl was not named after her. Her displeasure only added to the enmity she had displayed toward Bridget from the first day they met. She would have hated any woman—even an Italian girl—who took her son away from her. This thick-headed Irish wench she despised.

Bridget's problems with her mother-in-law were only one of her parents' and uncle Ned's worries. Another was that Sal was short-tempered and, not infrequently, beat Bridget. Pat and Ned and Kevin and Marty had all told Bridget they would kill him one of these days, but she loved her Sir Galahad. She did not tell her family, but after beating her, he almost always apologized by making passionate love to her. She merely told her kinfolks to stay out of her domestic affairs.

Ned's work had become his life. He had reached the point where he accepted as inevitable the cycle of reform and corruption that seemed to recur in the city like the ebb and flow of the tides. Now in June of 1893, he sat at his desk one rainy morning and read that a new Grand Jury was being formed. The report said that this Jury would be headed by Henry Taber, an honest, influential and well-respected businessman, and would invite the Reverend Charles Parkhurst to appear before it. Ned had not been surprised when another Grand Jury in March a year earlier had rejected the strong evidence of corruption the minister had laid before it. Croker and Tammany were still riding high and they not only took no action on Parkhurst's affidavits, but actually made him somewhat of a laughingstock.

Now, however, the tide of reform seemed to be ready to flow once again. Pat Morrissey, who served on the city's new Tenement Commission, had formed a warm friendship with an *Evening Sun* reporter, Jake Riis. Riis had told Pat, and Pat told Ned, that the city's Chamber of Commerce was beginning to worry that widespread vice of every description, flourishing under corrupt police protection, was severely damaging the city's reputation. Tourist trade was falling off alarmingly. Ned smiled as he finished reading the story of the formation of the new Grand Jury. Now they might listen to Parkhurst. There was a knock on his door and Captain James Healy came into his office.

"Inspector," said Healy, "I'm afraid your young friend Willie Kessler is jinxed. He's in the hospital again."

"He didn't try—"

"No," said Healy. "He didn't try to kill himself again. This time he was beat up by a bunch of thugs when he left his office on Wall Street last night."

"How seriously is he hurt?"

"Not too bad. Seems a party of men came out of a restaurant nearby in the middle of the assault and the hoodlums beat it. They didn't even have time to rob him."

"Has his father been notified, Jim?"

"We tried to reach him, but his housekeeper said he was on Long Island and wouldn't be back till later tonight."

As soon as Ned finished some overdue paperwork he went to Bellevue. William was sitting up glumly in bed. In his early thirties, his blond hair was already thinning. Unkempt strands of it hung limply at the sides of his bandaged head. One of his eyes was completely closed, his left cheek was bruised and discolored, and his right arm rested in a sling tied around his neck. His upper lip was swollen, but he could speak clearly enough to make himself understood.

"Thank you for coming, Uncle Ned," he muttered. "I should have come to you about this right after I tried to take my life."

He lowered his head, obviously embarrassed.

"You see—it wasn't just—it wasn't just the terrible reaction to my work. . . ."

His one good eye pleaded for understanding.

"I—I love a girl . . . desperately . . . and now she's gone."

Ned listened patiently and even managed to convey a great deal of empathy as William stammeringly, blushing a good deal of the time, told him about having fallen in love with Malka Roitman. He told Malka's story about how she had been entrapped and kept prisoner and how he had paid Wilensky to permit him to take Malka away for an entire weekend.

"It was the most wonderful three days of my life, Uncle Ned," said William. "Malka didn't want to go back. She wanted us to marry and run away."

Ned nodded his understanding.

"But Wilensky told me he would hurt her, maybe kill her if she didn't return. I had to insist she go back. She—she was furious with me. She told me she never wanted to see me again. It broke my heart. I thought, then, about killing myself. Then the exhibition . . ."

Ned waited patiently for William to regain control of himself. Finally William said, "Last Saturday when I got home from the hospital after I tried to kill myself, I went back to Wilensky's. I had to see Malka. I was so surprised and happy when she agreed to see me. And I arranged with Wilensky to take her away for Saturday and Sunday again. I told her about trying to kill myself and how I was saved. But then she finally told me something much worse that had happened to her. She had tried to run away on her own, right after our first weekend, and one of Wilensky's brutes followed her and brought her back. He—he raped her . . . and beat her—"

"That son of a bitch Wilensky should be hanged," said Ned grimly. William nodded, but rushed on with his story.

"I had made up my mind I wanted to marry Malka. She was very happy about it and we decided to talk to my father together and ask him to lend us five thousand dollars to buy Malka's freedom from Wilensky. That's what he wanted—"

Now the uneven tears rolled down William's cheeks again, and he took another moment before he could continue.

"When we were talking to my father, Malka surprised me by saying she was pregnant. It didn't matter. My father refused to lend us the money. Malka ran out of the house in a fury. I tried to run after her, but my father stopped me. When I finally broke loose from him and ran out into the street she was gone. I looked all over the city for her all Saturday night and Sunday. On Monday I went to Wilensky's.

She had not gone back. I kept looking for her all through the week, but she's simply disappeared. Wednesday night I went back to Wilensky's and she still hadn't come back there. Wilensky said he knew I was trying to play some kind of a trick on him. And last night when I left the office—I was working late—these hoodlums beat me. . . . God, Uncle Ned, do you think you can find Malka? If they've killed her, I don't know what I'll do!"

"We'll try, Willie. We'll try to find her," Ned assured him.

He walked back to his office, mulling William's predicament. It was just like the confused, melancholy young man to fall desperately in love with a prostitute. She sounded like a proud young girl with a fiery spirit, highly unusual for one who had lived the life of a brutalized whore for a year. He was sympathetic but had cynical doubts about her story of being pregnant. Most of the prostitutes dreamed of marrying a rich man someday; and many would do anything to entrap a husband, particularly one who could be heir to a fortune. Ned cursed Wilensky. He knew a good deal about the whoremaster. Wilensky not only owned the house on Allen Street, but was part owner of the True Enchantment Club. He also knew about Captain Mueller. Mueller shared his spoils with and was protected by two inspectors in his precinct, and the inspectors, in turn, were protected by one of the police commissioners. Ned cursed the society in which a brutal thug like Wilensky could destroy the lives of helpless young girls and brazenly blackmail and assault good but weak men like Willie.

He called in the chief of detectives and asked that the homicide reports be checked to see if the body of a young Caucasian female fitting Malka Roitman's description might have been found. He also instructed the chief to contact the authorities in Brooklyn and New Jersey.

"It's possible, Chief," he said, "there could be a two-month embryo."

It had stopped raining and Ned walked over to the brothel on Allen Street. Wilensky claimed he knew nothing of Malka's whereabouts and denied any knowledge of the attack on William.

"I know you're lying, you scum," said Ned bitterly. "But I want you to know that Willie Kessler is a friend of mine. If your thugs lay a finger on him again, I'll come by here and kick your brains in myself. You understand, you miserable pimp?"

Wilensky puffed nervously on his cigar, blew out a ragged cloud of smoke, and put the cigar back in his mouth. He bit on it, and spoke with false bravado through clenched teeth.

"Never mind with the threats, Inspector. Joe Wilensky has friends too. *Important* friends!"

Ned was halfway to the door, but he turned and went back and stood over Wilensky, who was seated at his desk.

"Another thing, you low bastard. If we find that girl and she's been killed, I swear you'll hang for it! And fuck your important friends!"

He reached across the desk and tore the cigar from Wilensky's teeth and smashed it back into the middle of his face. There was a small shower of sparks. Hot ash burned Ned's palm, and Wilensky bellowed in pain as he frantically brushed tobacco and burning ash from his cheek and nose with both hands. Ned slammed the door behind him as he stormed out.

He ate a quick, lonesome supper at Clancy's, a restaurant on Mulberry Street frequented by policemen, and decided to go to see Max Kessler. He had not seen Max since William's suicide attempt. The old man's increasingly cold and hostile attitude had bothered Ned, but he was aware of Max's suffering. Max was almost sixty-nine now and Ned felt he had to make allowances for his dyspeptic disposition and erratic ways. Mrs. Starker opened the front door of the apartment for him and told him Max was in the dining room. She attempted to stop him when he headed for the closed French doors.

"Not to go in, Herr Inspector!" she said nervously. "Herr Kessler wants no visitor tonight! He say no one, no one, no matter whoever!"

Ned smiled at her reassuringly and strode to the dining-room doors. He pushed one open. Max sat at the rosewood linen-covered table. It was set for two. In the center of the table was a silver candelabra, holding six burning candles. The gas lamps in the chandelier overhead and on the four walls had not been lighted. The glow of the flickering candles furnished the only light in the room, creating an eerie effect. On Max's plate there was a mound of mashed potatoes, another of mashed carrots. Beside the plate was a tall glass, half full of beef blood, which looked brown in the light. A carafe of white wine stood beside a filled wineglass at the place opposite Max. On a plate beside the glass of wine was a roasted chicken breast with mashed potatoes and diced carrots.

Max's dark, rheumy eyes shifted frantically and glittered in the flickering light as he glared at Ned.

"What are you doing here, Ned Morrissey?" he demanded hoarsely. "What are you doing here on this night? This night of all nights!"

"Don't get excited, Max," said Ned quietly. "I just came by to tell you that Willie had a little accident last night, but he's all right. He's in—"

Max's laugh was a cackle.

"Willie," he repeated, hysterically attempting to imitate Ned's patient tone. ". . . Willie . . . your son, Willie is all right, eh, Ned?"

"Aagh, come on, Max. Don't be foolish."

Max waved a hand at the empty chair across the table from him. His restless eyes darted left and right.

"Tell him, my dear Clara! Tell him that you have told me all! How he fucked you every night all the time I was in the war! Tell him!" he screamed. He leaped up and, like an ugly, demented gnome, banged the table with both bony fists.

"Max, Max," pleaded Ned, walking slowly toward the old man. "Willie is *your* son. Believe me, as God is my witness. Believe me."

"Don't blaspheme, you Irish son of a bitch! Every June fourteenth, on our anniversary, I have supper with Clara, and tonight . . . finally tonight . . . she tells me! *You* are Willie's father. Get out of my house! Out! Out!"

He was bellowing, and he staggered toward Ned, fists upraised. Ned, more than a head taller than the bent old man, took him in his arms, ignoring the feeble beating on his chest. While Max squirmed to break away, Ned held him firmly. Then as Max all but collapsed, Ned held him more gently, and half dragged, half carried him back to his chair. Max began to sob quietly, as he dropped his oddly ridged bald head onto his arms on the table. His left fist was closed tightly. The stumps of the fingers on his right hand twitched. Ned patted his arching back.

"He *is* your son, Max. May God strike me dead on this spot if that is not the truth!"

Max lifted his head and looked up at Ned, tears rolling down his lined, hollow cheeks.

"All right, Ned," he said in a croaking whisper, nodding. "Willie *is* my boy. God help him!"

Ned did not ask Max for his version of the meeting he had had with his son and the young whore. It seemed an inauspicious time. He patted Max's shoulder, and said quietly, "Some hoodlums beat Willie up, Max. Not bad. He's in Bellevue if you want to go see him. He should be home in a day or two. Good night, old friend."

On the way out he sucked at his fingers and the place on his palm where the hot ash of Wilensky's cigar had burned him.

22

On that warm day in April when William had told Malka he had arranged with Mr. Wilensky to take her out of the house, she had been delirious with joy. Escape at last! But then when he had hesitantly told her she must return on Monday, she had been shocked and furious. William was devastated by her angry reaction.

"You understand, do you not, my dearest Malka?" pleaded William for the fifth time. Standing before the mirror in her room at Wilensky's, Malka grimly continued to adjust the billowing skirt of the beautiful yellow taffeta dress William had bought her. She had already secreted a small linen pouch with her hundred and forty dollars in savings inside the pocket she had sewn into her bloomers.

"Yes, William, yes," she said impatiently. He had finally told her his real name and true occupation with his wealthy father. Her mind was racing as swiftly as her heart. When William told her that he must bring her back to Wilensky's on Monday she had pleaded with him, berated him, pleaded again. She brushed aside his insistence that Wilensky would harm her, possibly even have her killed, if she did not return. She was willing to risk that. But when he told her almost tearfully, the terror plain in his eyes, that Wilensky would also have him beaten or killed, she knew she must agree to return. She wondered how she could love this weak, cowardly man, but she was almost sure she did.

She went to him and patted his cheek.

"Yes," she said again, gently this time. "I do understand. Monday I will come back."

But she had not been at all sure that she would.

Those two days and three nights in April were a tense and exciting time in her life, desperate and unhappy as she was. For a young girl who had never been more than twenty kilometers from Prosnica, New York in 1893 was a city of endless wonders. William had hired a two-wheel hansom cab.

Maybe William will leave the horse and cab and I will be able to ride away, thought Malka, but then she saw the boyish enthusiasm in his eyes as he touched the back of her hand. She knew it was unlikely she could risk having him harmed by Wilensky.

"There! There, Malka!" He was pointing. "There is the Tower Building!"

Malka looked up. The building was truly impressive. It was number 50 Broadway, eleven stories tall.

"But it is not the tallest in the city," said William.

Maybe she could persuade William to run away with her, thought Malka. *Out of the city. There must be far places where Wilensky could not find them.*

"That is very interesting, William," she said.

Next William drove them uptown, just beyond Madison Square Park. He stopped to show her Madison Square Garden.

"See that beautiful statue on top," he said. "It is Diana the Huntress. It was sculpted by a great artist, Augustus Saint-Gaudens."

It surprised Malka that they would have a statue of a naked girl for everyone to see, right on top of a building.

"Will I be able to see your paintings, William?" she asked. She had admired his painting of her, but realized she knew little of art, and so could not tell whether it was a truly fine painting or not. She did not think the girl he painted resembled her. She thought the expression on the face overly angelic; the body excessively curvaceous. She thought the painting more a girl William imagined, than Malka as she was.

"Saturday evenings my father always meets with a group of landlords. He is away most of the evening. So tomorrow we will go to my studio," said William.

It irritated Malka that he so obviously feared having her meet his father, but she said nothing. The dusk was deepening and William drove up to Thirty-fourth Street and Fifth Avenue and halted at the elegant entrance to the new Waldorf Hotel. It had been built that year on the site of the Fifth Avenue mansions owned by the Astors. Some four years later it would be merged with the Astoria Hotel and become the Waldorf-Astoria. Malka was stunned at the magnificence of the new hotel. The electric lights in the opulent chandeliers in the vast lobby and in the lamps fascinated her. Although Thomas Edison had established a generating plant on Pearl Street almost ten years earlier, electricity was still not widely used in 1893.

In their small suite on the sixth floor William had champagne sent up. While Malka walked about the parlor, staring at the ornate furnishings, the thick Turkish carpet, the heavy, silk-lined damask drapes at the windows, the intricately carved Chippendale chairs and marble-topped tables, the rich, glowing silk-shaded electric lamps, William filled two glasses.

"Come, Malka, dearest," he said. "I want to make a toast."

He lifted his glass.

"To you, my love, with the earnest hope that one day I will be able to make you my wife."

Malka lifted her glass.

"Are you saying we will be married, William?"

"I am praying we will be."

"If we wish, we can," she said firmly.

He shook his head sadly.

"Wilensky will not permit it."

She put down her glass without drinking.

"Wilensky! Wilensky!" she stormed. "Does Wilensky own me? Am I a slave?"

Even as she said it, she realized that she was, indeed, a slave. In the most abject and degraded sense.

"You yourself told me about Wei Chang and—and the other girls . . ." William said. "Only if I pay him five thousand dollars will he permit you to leave his house. . . ."

Malka stared at him.

"You mean he will not try to make me come back if—if you give him five thousand dollars?"

William put his own glass back on the table, unsipped. He nodded sadly.

"But I do not have five thousand dollars, Malka. My father has been talking with a man who owns an art gallery. It is possible he will present an exhibition of my paintings.

Perhaps . . . if it is successful . . . I will earn a great deal of money. Then, Malka, then . . ."

The unhappy thought flashed through Malka's mind that it was most unlikely people would pay such huge sums for paintings such as William had done of Malka. She lifted her skirt and took the cloth pouch from her bloomers. She threw the small stack of bills on the table.

"Here, William! More than a hundred dollars I have . . . and you have spent much money at Mr. Wilensky's. And—and your father is a rich man, is he not?"

"Yes, but—"

"Borrow the money from him, William. Then if people pay you five thousand dollars for your paintings, you can pay him back. If not—if they do not wish to pay so much, we will pay him back anyway. I am fine seamstress. I can work. You can pay back some of wages your father pays you. We can live where does not cost much."

William walked disconsolately to a chocolate and beige striped sofa and sat wearily. Head in hands, he said, "It is no use, Malka. Never. My father would never give me the money. Never."

She sat beside him and put her arms around him. She kissed his cheek.

"You could, maybe, try, my William. It would be so wonderful. You could ask . . ."

He did not say so, but in the back of his mind was the dread conviction that his father might advance him a substantial sum of money if he were marrying a wealthy girl, but surely not to enable him to marry a prostitute. His father would never permit it, let alone give him the money to make it possible. He had considered the idea of introducing Malka to his father as a respectable seamstress, but he knew his father would not be deceived. His father had an uncanny way of knowing everything he did. He had even known William had gone to the brothel on the occasion when the whore laughed at him. It was almost as though his father followed him day and night.

He did not tell Malka any of this, but finally, in response to her continued pleading, he said, "Perhaps I will talk to him, Malka. I love you. I love you."

She kissed his cheek again, then moved her lips to his, and they embraced and kissed passionately. That night in the airy, beautifully appointed bedroom with a full moon casting a soft, magical silver-blue light upon the wide double bed, William, was gradually, but thoroughly, transformed into a confident, capable, insatiable lover. Malka inspired the transformation. She had urgent dual incentives. Despite her pity, sometimes scorn, for his weakness, she believed she truly loved him. His very timidity cried out to the mother in her. Possibly even more important, she believed that if he felt her deep love, if he experienced the repeated ecstasy of it in their long, frequent, and ardent couplings, he would stop at nothing to marry her and find the courage to take her out of Mr. Wilensky's sordid prison forever. During those three nights at the Waldorf she forsook all the professional, mechanical techniques she had unwillingly learned. She gave herself to him completely and loved him with a wholeheartedness and a natural abandon she did not even know she possessed. After each mutual orgasm, she simply lay in his arms and fell into blissful semiconsciousness.

Saturday night and Sunday night in the Waldorf bedroom were as thrilling and fulfilling as Friday had been. It was almost dawn on Monday when they reached a simultaneous orgasm for the fourth time that night. Malka lay on her side with William's warm body against her back, his arm around her waist, his knees snuggled behind hers. She smiled complacently to herself. In an hour or so, when they had rested a little, she would tell William about her simple plan. During their brief stay at the Waldorf she had found and read several travel booklets, which explained the routes, fares, and other pertinent information about the sea journey from New York to Boston, Philadelphia, and other coastal cities. They could drive their hansom to the waterfront, where they would book passage to Philadelphia. In that thriving Pennsylvania metropolis they would be married. William could change his name once again, if necessary, but not to Walter Klein this time. She would find work as a seamstress and perhaps William could sell his paintings. If not, she was certain he could find employment or earn money in some other occupation, perhaps real estate.

Suddenly she felt William's chest heaving against her back, and he burrowed his face into the curve of her neck and shoulder. He was crying. She twisted quickly to face him.

"What—what is the matter, William?"

He shook his head.

"Noth—nothing . . . only in a few hours . . . our beautiful dream must end. You—you must go back . . . to Wilensky's."

She sat up in the bed and laughed. She held his face in her hands, and bent down and kissed his tear-stained cheeks.

"Do not be foolish, William," she said. "I will not go back. We will be married in Philadelphia, where Mr. Wilensky will never find us."

"Phil—Philadelphia!?"

"Of course. Let us dress now, and leave early. There is boat departs ten o'clock."

William shook his head and sobbed.

"We—we can't, Malka. We cannot do it. . . ."

For two hours Malka used all her persuasive powers, all her charms, in an effort to seduce William into accepting her scheme. Finally she flatly demanded that he take her to Philadelphia and marry her. But he stubbornly refused. His fear for her; his fear for his own safety; his lack of confidence in his own ability to survive, let alone protect her, were insurmountable. Malka began to dress with a grim aggressiveness.

"All right, then, William Kessler!" she said bitterly. "Take me back to Mr. Wilensky. And do not let me look upon your coward's face ever—ever again! Never!"

Having tasted freedom, Malka was determined to escape from Wilensky's on her own, if need be. She could find her way to the dock where the boats left for Philadelphia and would buy her own passage. But first she had to convince Mrs. Krimsky and Mr. Wilensky that they could trust her to leave the house for an occasional morning or afternoon, like the other girls. She forced herself to go to extraordinary lengths to be pleasant and flattering to Wilensky's guests. So much so, that they began to compliment the madam and Wilensky on her behavior and her proficiency in bed. Wilensky was displeased when William Kessler failed to show up following his weekend with Malka. He asked her what she had done to discourage William's visits. Malka shrugged.

"He will come back soon, Mr. Wilensky," she said. "He told me to New Jersey he must go to buy some land there for his father."

In mid-May Mrs. Krimsky agreed to permit Malka to have a whole Sunday free, and out of the house.

"Just be certain you are back here by six o'clock this evening," she said gruffly.

With money in her purse for her fare, her savings in the pouch in her bloomers, wearing the yellow taffeta dress William had given her, Malka walked leisurely to the dock on the East River. It was a hot, humid morning and she was perspiring as she headed toward the window where the tickets for the boat to Philadelphia were sold. She had not quite reached the window when a burly man rushed out of the small crowd of people behind her and grabbed her roughly around the shoulders. There was a strong odor of garlic about him. She had been too intent on finding her way to the dock to notice that the man had been following her from the time she left Allen Street. She screamed and the man clamped a hard, moist hand over her mouth. The smell and the taste of garlic on the hand almost nauseated her.

"She wants to run away—my wife! An' leave me with three bambinos!" shouted the man, in explanation to the startled men and women around him and the struggling Malka. He was powerful and had little trouble dragging her to a hackney cab parked at dockside. In less than fifteen minutes they were back at Wilensky's. Although there were expressions of sympathy and concern on the faces of the girls in the parlor, none dared say a word as the stocky man carried Malka, crying and struggling, up the stairs. Panting, he dropped her to her feet as they entered the room. He kicked the door shut behind him. She ran behind the chair at her dressing table. Her captor was sweating profusely, cursing and sucking at the torn skin on his right hand where Malka had scratched and bitten him. Wilensky came into the room. He laughed when he saw Malka, poised behind the chair, breathing hard, her face smeared with tears.

"So you thought Joseph Wilensky was stupid enough to trust you not to run away, little Malka," he said. "It will cost me a little money, but never mind. You will learn your lesson."

He turned to the thick-chested, black-haired man standing beside him, still panting, and staring lustfully now at Malka.

"Tony," said Wilensky, "would you like to take your pleasure with our little runaway?"

Tony grinned and began to unbutton his shirt.

"She is yours for the rest of the day and the night, my friend," said Wilensky. "But be careful of the face, do not damage her too much. Just enough, maybe, to teach her that Joseph Wilensky's brides do not run away."

He nodded to Tony, smiled at Malka, and left the room. Malka heard the key turn in the lock. Tony, naked and damp, stalked toward Malka, standing at her dressing table. As he advanced, she began to throw bottles and jars and dishes at him. Perfumes and powders splashed against the wall, and made small clouds in the room. Tony came on, hiding behind upraised arms, ducking and weaving, but several of the missiles struck him. He cursed and finally knocked aside the dressing-table chair and grabbed Malka by the hair and shoulder as she tried to twist past him. He lifted her in his powerful arms. She beat at him ineffectually with her fists and kicked and screamed as he carried her to the bed. He dropped her on it and threw himself upon her. The blend of perfume, powder, and garlic was even more nauseating to Malka than the garlic alone had been. Bile rose from her stomach into her throat. Tony twisted her viciously so she lay face down. He raped her anally and when he finished he beat her savagely, then raped her the same way again.

Wilensky was unhappy with his sadistic enforcer because it was a full four weeks before Malka could entertain paying guests. On the day before she was to receive her first patron, Wei Chang brought her the *Evening World* with her supper. She was just beginning to revive her interest in what was happening outside her house of horrors. On the front page of the paper was a story telling of the activities of the new grand jury headed by businessman Henry Taber. Dr. Parkhurst had appeared before the jury and had presented his voluminous affidavits.

In its final findings the grand jury report said, "The city's police department is either incompetent to do what is frequently done by private individuals with imperfect facilities for such work, or else there exist reasons and motives for such inaction which are illegal and corrupt. The general efficiency of the Department is so great that it is our belief that the latter suggestion is the explanation for the peculiar inactivity."

Malka did not understand some of the words, but she gathered that the grand jury was discovering what men like Mr. Wilensky and Captain Mueller were doing. Dr. Parkhurst had continued to sermonize week in and week out against the rampant vice and corruption, and Howard Borsum was mentioned as the attorney representing a number of key witnesses before the jury. Malka put the paper down and tears welled in her eyes. She wondered what would have happened if she had agreed to give Mr. Borsum her affidavit.

In April when she had missed her first menstrual period, she assumed it might be due to the emotional and physical trauma she had suffered since William Kessler had brought her back to Wilensky's. But when a second month, and now a third, passed and she failed to menstruate twice more, she began to worry. She recalled that she had not tended to herself after her coupling with William, although she had douched and medicated herself more thoroughly than ever since her return to the brothel. She talked to Maria about her fears that she might be pregnant. Maria insisted they determine whether she was or not before it was too late safely to have an abortion. To her dismay it was verified that she was with child.

"But I will not have an abortion!" she told Maria firmly. "I will not kill my baby!"

"Do not be foolish, Malka," said Maria. "Wilensky will not permit you to go through six or seven months with a big belly. And what would you do with a child? If you have the abortion soon enough, there is not too great a danger."

"I will not do it!" said Malka stubbornly. She was sorry she had told William she never wished to see him again. There was no doubt in her mind that it was his child. Perhaps if he knew she was carrying his seed, he would marry her. She prayed that he would come back. And God must have passed her prayer on to William. On the Saturday after she discovered her pregnancy he did come to Wilensky's. At first she hardly recognized him. There was a haunted look in his blue eyes, accentuated by deep, purplish-gray crescents beneath them. His complexion was sallow with a bilious green undertone. The bones of the cheeks and jaw seemed ready to cut through the tight skin. With his large nose he looked like a species of sorrowful bird.

"I'm so happy you would permit me to see you, Malka," he said, standing nervously before her in her room. "I love you . . . I need you so desperately."

He dropped to his knees, threw his arms around her thighs, and buried his face in the folds of her silk robe. She reached down and helped him to his feet and guided him to the bed. They sat together on the bed's edge. Her compassion for him pushed her own recent traumatic experience and her dilemma to a corner of her mind. She put her arm around him.

"What has happened to you, my poor William? You look so—not good—sick!"

He nodded and took her hand. He raised it to his lips and kissed her fingers fervently. Then he told her in stammering, tortured sentences that he had tried to kill himself. A week after their rendezvous at the Waldorf, the exhibition of his paintings had opened at a gallery on Madison Avenue. Only one painting had been sold, and that for ten dollars. And it had been purchased by an old lady named Ilka Himmelfarb, who had cared for him when he was an infant. At the end of the long, dismally unsuccessful evening, the gallery owner had told William he would send his paintings back in the morning. Two art experts had told the gallery owner and William himself that the work was hopelessly sentimental, unoriginal, uninspired, and unsalable. William did not know that his father had secretly paid the gallery owner to mount the exhibition and also paid the critics to make the devastating comments. It would never have occurred to William that his father would take such extreme measures to discourage his painting once and for all, and thus force his total attention to their real estate and investment activities.

"I could not bear it, dearest Malka," William told Malka wearily. "I prayed the exhibition would be successful so I could get the money to pay Wilensky and marry you. The next day I tried to kill myself. I sealed the windows in the basement and turned on the gas jets and the stove. But it seems I failed to seal one of the front windows, and the man from the gallery, who was bringing back my paintings, smelled the gas. He broke two windows and kicked down the door."

He sighed deeply.

"They got me to the hospital in time to save my life. As I came back from the brink of death, Malka, I realized that the painting did not matter. Nothing mattered except you. My father was very kind to me while I was in the hospital. And he has been good to me since I returned home two days ago. I think if you will come with me and help me talk with him, perhaps he will lend us the money for Wilensky and . . ."

He lifted Malka's hand to his lips and kissed it again.

". . . and we can be married. I have promised my father I will devote myself to the business with all my heart. I have already burned all my paintings—except the one of you. I think if he meets you, and sees what a wonderful person you are, and—"

He paused abruptly and looked into her eyes with a terrible expression of anxiety.

"Will you, Malka? My God, I did not even ask you! Will you, Malka dearest, will you marry me? I love you. I love you. I need you."

Malka's eyes were moist. She patted his cheek and gently drew his head to her breast. She patted his shoulder.

"Yes, William. I love you too."

As she stroked his hair, she wondered if she should tell William that she was pregnant. Some instinct told her she should not. Not at this time. He seemed too emotionally and physically fragile. After they received Max Kessler's blessing and the loan of the five thousand dollars, there would be time enough to inform William that he was to be a father.

When William told Wilensky he wished to take Malka out that day, Wilensky agreed but with another explicit warning.

"I suppose little Malka has told you what happened when she tried to run away last time, William Kessler. If she is not back here by Monday, her punishment this time will be far worse. And you yourself will meet with an accident. Remember, you are responsible."

On the way to the tenement on Rivington Street William told Malka that Wilensky had told him she had attempted to run away and been punished. He insisted she tell him what had happened. She did, and near the end of her recital, she broke down, fighting back tears.

"Someday, William . . . I have told you before. Someday . . . I will kill that beast, Mr. Wilensky!"

Now they stood on the corner of Rivington and Essex streets comforting each other in a tearful embrace, patting each other's backs, two confused, lost souls. For a desperate moment they were totally oblivious to the stares and the teasing, ribald comments of two nearby pushcart peddlers and their loud customers. When the crowd's laughter became raucous they broke apart in embarrassment and hurried to Max Kessler's tenement down the block.

Most people who saw Max Kessler for the first time, especially now when he was sixty-nine years old, were startled, if not repulsed. Malka sat nervously on the edge of a chair in the parlor and tried not to show any sign that she was shocked by the old man's appearance. She held her hands in her lap and waited for Max Kessler to say something in response to the impassioned plea William had just made for the loan of the money to buy Malka's freedom so they could be married.

"I tell you again, Father. I swear it on all that is sacred," he concluded, "that I will devote myself entirely to the business. If you will permit it, I will return to you half the wages you pay me every week to repay the money—"

"And I will work, too, Mr. Kessler," interrupted Malka, swept up by William's fervor. "I am fine seamstress. I will pay you all I earn."

William said earnestly, "It is most important to both of us, Father. Our very lives depend upon our being together. You *must* give us the money."

Malka was proud of William, proud and greatly surprised by the utter lack of fear, the eloquence with which he had told his father of his deep love for Malka. He had told Max frankly how she had been forced into prostitution, and of her brave attempt to escape and the terrible consequences. Now she held her breath as she watched Max Kessler's restless, dark, and rheumy eyes move from his son to her and back again, over and over.

"I must, Willie? You say I must!" he said finally in his hoarse, cracked voice. "I must give you five thousand dollars so you can marry a whore?"

He grimaced toward Malka, an expression he intended as a smile, but to her it seemed a look of distaste.

"Do not misunderstand me, young lady," he said. "I have nothing against whores. I understand that you were forced into such a life. In this city many thousands of girls are whores. But I do not have long to live. Willie will be the head of one of the most important investment firms in New York City. How can he be married to a whore?"

"But, Father, please . . ." said William.

Malka impulsively decided to reveal what she hoped would be one more, possibly the most important, fact to support the case for their marriage.

"Mr. Kessler," she said, her dark eyes pleading for understanding, "I am carrying William's child."

"Malka!" gasped William, turning pale.

Malka thought the expression on Max's ravaged face was

one of surprise, but she immediately discovered it was contemptuous anger.

"William's child!" he barked. "Now I know you have deliberately laid a trap to catch my Willie! *William's child!* How can you say that! How many men have you fucked? How can you say it is Willie's child?"

Malka's face turned chalk white. She rose from the chair and took two quick steps to reach Max Kessler and slammed her right hand viciously across his cheek.

"Keep your money, you evil old man! Keep your money and your son!"

William tried to put his arm around her as she stood over Max Kessler, who was struggling to get up out of his chair.

"Malka, please—" pleaded William.

Malka brushed his arm from her shoulder, pushed him away from her, and slammed her right hand once again across Max Kessler's cheek. She turned and ran from the room and out of the building. William began to go after her, but Max had managed to get to his feet and threw his arms around his son. With unexpected strength he held William, weakened by his recent hospitalization and the debilitating trauma of the confrontation between Malka and his father.

"Let her go, Willie," barked Max. "She is a lying whore! She is trying to force you to marry her!"

William's face turned red with anger and effort. He broke loose from his father's grasp and pushed him savagely back into his chair. He charged out into Rivington Street, but Malka was nowhere to be seen in the typically chaotic activity among the crowds of people up and down the street. He asked a fat lady on the stoop of the tenement next door if she had seen a young girl running by. The lady shrugged and spread beefy palms upward.

"A girl—a running girl . . . ?" she said. "Why would I see a girl running? Here everybody is running all the time."

He asked a pushcart peddler and a young boy, but no one had noticed Malka. He went back into the tenement and got into a violent argument with his father. It was the first time in his life he had ever challenged the old man. Max gasped in the middle of one of his most bitter denunciations of William, and clutched at his chest.

"You—I know, Willie—you are trying to—to kill me!" he barked, between desperate breaths. William fell to his knees at his father's chair.

"No! No, Father I am not— Where is your medicine?"

Max indicated the bottles on a tray on the buffet at the side of the room.

"The—the blue . . ."

William uncorked the bottle and brought it to him quickly. Max drank. His heavy breathing eased and in five minutes he seemed to have recovered.

"I'm sorry, Father. But I love Malka. I must marry her. I know the child is mine. I know she would not—"

Max glared at him and waved his fingerless hand.

"Don't start up again, Willie. For God's sake, show some common sense for once in your life!"

William spent all of that Saturday afternoon and night looking for Malka. Foolishly enough he went to the Waldorf, but of course she had not checked in there. Finally he went back to Wilensky's, but she had not returned to the brothel. On Sunday, Monday, Tuesday, and Wednesday he wandered aimlessly about the city, trying the places they had gone to on their first weekend. Wednesday night he went back to Wilensky's and discovered she had not returned. Mrs. Krimsky told him Wilensky wished to see him.

"Never mind telling me you are looking for little Malka, Mr. Kessler," Wilensky snarled at him. "You take Joe Wilensky for a fool? I know you have her somewhere and you wish to make me believe she has run away." He blew an angry cloud of cigar smoke.

"I have told you, Mr. Kessler, you are responsible that she has not come back!"

And the next night the hoodlums attacked William as he left the office on Wall Street, where he had gone to try to catch up on his neglected work. When he got out of Bellevue after recovering from the attack, his father was nicer to him, but still insisted that it would be a mistake for him to marry such a girl as Malka.

"You see what happens when you consort with whores, Willie!" Max told him. William ignored his father and went to the Mulberry precinct to see Ned Morrissey.

"Have you found any trace of her, Uncle Ned?" he asked, desperation showing in his blue eyes.

"Not a sign, not a sign, Willie," said Ned sadly.

23

When Malka ran out of Max Kessler's tenement on Rivington Street she stumbled on the top step of the stoop and would have crashed to her hands and knees on the sidewalk had she not bumped into a short, stout, bearded man walking by. He grumbled a sharp Yiddish complaint, but held her up. She tore out of his arms and blindly raced west along Rivington. Tears of bitter disappointment and fury streamed down her cheeks. After running through the crowded streets for some distance, out of breath, her bosom heaving, she flopped onto a chair outside a "concert garden" called Norton's Paradise. The chair was one of a dozen a Negro janitor had stacked on the sidewalk while he cleaned up inside. He came out and saw Malka on the chair, head back, eyes closed, cheeks wet with sweat and tears, mouth open, gasping for air. Broom in hand, he shuffled toward her.

"You all right, lady?"

Malka looked at him and nodded.

"Yes. In one moment. If I can rest . . . just for one minute."

"Sure, sure. Don't need those chairs for now. Gotta wash up the floor."

"Thank you," Malka said.

Passersby stared at the sweating, panting girl on the chair. Malka ignored them. She opened her purse and deftly bit loose a thread of the interior lining. In the brief time she had been trying to compose herself the thought had come to her. *Howard Borsum!* He had told her to come to him if he could ever help her. She would not return to Wilensky's if it cost her her life. She surely would not ever see William Kessler again. She had sewn Howard Borsum's card inside the lining of the purse, and now she took it out. She was studying it when a policeman suddenly stopped before her. He was a middle-aged, red-faced Irishman.

"That's hardly a proper place fer a young lass t'be sittin'," he said. "I'll have t' ask ya t'be movin' on."

Malka's only experience with policemen had been with Captain Mueller. She looked at this burly officer nervously and held out the card to him.

"Please, sir," she said, "can you tell me, please, how I can get to Mr. Borsum's house?"

"Ho," said the policeman, studying the card, "that's one o' them mansions on Fifth Avenue. About Fifty-eighth Street if I know me house numbers."

He began to tell her how she might get there by omnibus and horsecar.

"Is it possible I can walk, sir?" interrupted Malka. She felt she needed time to think what she would say to Mr. Borsum.

"Oh, t'be sure," said the policeman. "It's maybe three miles or thereabouts from here. You just walk north . . ."

A liveried butler, bald and portly, opened the imposing dark oak door as Malka timidly used the glittering brass knocker several times.

"Yes?"

Her hand trembled slightly as she handed him Howard Borsum's card.

"Mr. B—Bor—sum . . ." she stammered. "He said I should come to see him. I am Malka. Malka Roitman."

The butler did not close the door, but he said, "Wait one moment, please," and walked back into the house. Borsum himself came to the door almost immediately.

"Come in, come in, Malka," he said, extending his hand. He led her through the ornate foyer into the most elegant parlor Malka had ever seen, and then into a small room near the rear of the house. It was his study. Borsum held a wing chair at the side of the desk for Malka.

"Please sit down, Malka," he said. He stared at her as he walked to his own chair behind the desk.

"You—I'm sorry to say, Malka—you do not look well. You have aged since I saw you. I see . . . much pain in your eyes."

Tears formed in Malka's dark eyes, but she clenched her teeth, breathed deeply through her nose, determined not to cry. Finally she said, "I am all right, Mr. Borsum. Now I am all right. I have come to make affidavit for you." She looked at him anxiously. "You still wish affidavit . . . ? I have much to tell."

"Oh, yes, indeed, Malka! Yes, indeed!" He spoke fervently. "The day of reckoning is near for the corrupters and the vice lords of this city . . . and for the politicians and police who have shielded them. On Monday I will bring a stenographer here and you will tell her all you know and we will have a typewriter put it all on paper and . . . But for now, please tell me what *has* happened to you, informally, at your ease. . . . Would you like tea, perhaps?"

Malka nodded shyly. He pressed a button on his desk and as if by magic a young girl about Malka's age, with straw-colored hair and a placid face, came into the room. She curtsied toward Borsum and looked at him inquiringly.

"Helga, please bring us a pot of tea and a platter of Mrs. Kouwenhoven's cakes."

The girl curtsied again and left the room. Malka noticed she walked with a limp.

Night came and Borsum switched on the electric lamp on his desk as Malka finished telling him everything that had happened to her since Borsum's visit to Wilensky's. *Almost* everything. She told him about William and the attack upon him, but she said nothing of her meeting with Max Kessler, nor of her pregnancy.

"Are you and William planning to be married?" asked Borsum.

"No, I think not. I have decided he is not the man I wish to marry."

"Do you think William would be willing to testify as to his experience with Wilensky . . . that Wilensky wanted five thousand dollars for your freedom?"

"I do not know. Perhaps not. He has not so much— He is not so brave a man. His father tells him what he must do."

Borsum nodded.

"I know Max Kessler," he said. "A very strong-willed man. Peculiar and eccentric and most strong-willed."

"Mr. Borsum, could I ask . . ."

"Of course, Malka, anything."

"Will you send me away, somewhere where I will be safe from Mr. Wilensky and Captain Mueller, when I make affidavit?"

"Malka! You have nothing to fear! Believe me! I not only need your affidavit. I'm certain Wilensky and Mueller and that brute who beat you when you tried to escape will all be indicted. We will need your testimony on the witness stand when they are tried."

A puzzled and fearful look came over Malka's face. She did not understand many of the words Borsum was using, but she got the gist of what he was saying. He explained, slowly, using simpler words, until she fully understood.

"And till the trials are over and these dastardly criminals are jailed, you will live here. We will employ you as a maid.

Mrs. Borsum has been saying the work is a bit much for Helga. Would you mind working as a maid?"

"Oh, no, no, Mr. Borsum. I will work hard, very hard. I will be fine maid. Also I am fine seamstress. . . ."

Borsum smiled. He rose and extended his hand and Malka timidly took it, and returned his smile.

"It is all arranged, then," said Borsum.

He looked at the wood-framed marquetry clock on the wall.

"Anna will be home any moment now. She works most days at the Nurses' Settlement on Henry Street."

Anna Van Vorst Borsum was a tall, thin woman in her early thirties. She had sleek blond hair, slightly touched with silvery gray, and parted in the middle. Her eyes were blue-gray and sparkled with intelligence and warmth. She compensated for the fact that she and her husband could not have children by devoting a major portion of her time to the Settlement on Henry Street. The Nurses' Settlement was the first nonsectarian visiting-nurse program in the United States and was founded by Anna Borsum's best friend, Lillian Wald. Both Lillian and Anna had done much work with the poor in the East Side tenements before Lillian founded the Settlement.

Mrs. Borsum treated Malka more like a friend than a servant, just as she did Helga, Franz, the butler, and Mrs. Kouwenhoven, the cook. This, however, only made Malka determined to work twice as hard. Malka's tireless insistence on keeping the Borsum house sparkling became a pleasant in-house joke between Howard and Anna Borsum, which often relieved the pressures under which both worked. It took four full days before Howard Borsum was completely satisfied that Malka's affidavit contained every morsel of information that could help assure the indictment of Wilensky, Mueller, and Anthony Roselli. Borsum had learned that he was the thug who had captured and ravaged Malka when she had tried to escape. Then it became a matter of patience. The Lexow Committee finally scheduled its first hearing for March 9, 1894.

Malka had arrived at the Borsums in mid-June of 1883, and when she was told in late July that the hearings would not begin for another eight months, she panicked. She estimated that her baby would be born sometime in January, or maybe even February. She wondered how the Borsums would react when they discovered she was pregnant. She was just beginning to show, and she knew Mrs. Borsum, if not Mr. Borsum, would soon realize she was carrying a child. She thought she had better tell them before they discovered it themselves, but she could not bring herself to do so. She feared their reaction.

On the Fourth of July, Anna Van Vorst Borsum's cousin, Arnold Van Gelder, his wife, and three children, a girl and two boys in their late teens, came from Pennsylvania for a visit. The Borsums had an Independence Day supper party, and in addition to her cleaning and dusting duties Malka had helped the cook, gray-haired, cheery, and rosy-cheeked Mrs. Kouwenhoven, in the kitchen all day. Then she had assisted Franz, the butler, in serving the meal. Late in the evening when the guests and Mr. Borsum had retired, Mrs. Borsum asked Malka to come into the parlor. When Malka entered, Mrs. Borsum closed the French doors behind her and walked to a richly embroidered blue damask sofa. She sat and patted the place beside her.

"Please sit down . . . here, Malka," she requested quietly.

Malka sat, hands folded in her lap. She stared nervously at Anna Borsum.

"I think you are working too hard, Malka," said Mrs. Borsum.

"Oh, no, no, Mrs. Borsum. I enjoy to work for you and Mr. Borsum. You are so good to me. I do not work too hard."

"When a young lady is carrying a child, Malka, she must be careful," said Mrs. Borsum firmly.

Malka's hand went to her open mouth, then to her stomach. "You—you know? It shows already, Mrs. Borsum?"

"Just barely, Malka. But you must be careful not to strain yourself. You must stop trying to do Helga's and Mrs. Kouwenhoven's and Franz's work as well as your own."

"Then—then it is all right that I will have a child?"

"It is more than all right. It is God's greatest gift to a woman that she may bear children." She paused. She knew of Malka's experience as a prostitute. She took Malka's hand.

"Do you know the child's father, Malka?" she asked softly.

"Oh, yes. I know, I know! He is a man I love, but I cannot marry him."

"Would you like to tell me why?"

Malka shook her head as tears came to her eyes.

"Please, Mrs. Borsum. I cannot tell you. If you will help

me when the baby comes, I will take care of him—or maybe her—myself. I will not be a trouble to you and Mr. Borsum. When it is safe I will move away with my child."

Anna Borsum put her arm around Malka's shoulder and drew her close.

"You do not have to move away. We will help you. . . ." She sighed and released Malka. "Now off to bed. And remember, do not strain yourself."

Malka was never happier in her life. Suddenly, miraculously, at twenty-one she felt a sense of security, of being with people who genuinely cared about her. It was the first time she had felt this way since she left Prosnica.

The day after her comforting talk with Mrs. Borsum, she wrote a long twelve-page epistle to her mother. She assured her mother that everything was fine with her. She said that upon her arrival in America she had learned that Mr. Wilensky had died (oh, how she wished it were true!). But, she wrote, she had immediately secured employment with a distinguished attorney and his wife. She agonized over whether she should tell her mother of William and her pregnancy, and finally decided against it. She described the incredible sights she had seen in New York City, and told her mother she was saving her wages and would soon be able to send her passage money, so her mother could join her.

She took advantage of Anna Borsum's order not to work too hard, by borrowing books from Howard Borsum's extensive library, and reading far into each night. She read every kind of work, novels and history books and even law books, especially those relating to real estate. Of special interest to her was a book Mrs. Borsum suggested she read. It was called *Antietam Journal*, and its author was a Colonel Fred Van Gelder, who was the father of Anna Van Vorst's cousin, Arnold Van Gelder. It told of Colonel van Gelder's experiences during the Civil War, with an emphasis on the Battle of Antietam. Arnold, who was now the publisher of the local weekly newspaper his deceased father had founded, and Arnold's family had been the Borsum guests Malka had served during their July visit.

The *Antietam Journal* was fascinating, but three books by Jacob A. Riis impressed Malka most of all. They were *How the Other Half Lives*, *A Ten Years War*, and *The Battle with the Slum*. All three of the volumes dealt with the terrible conditions in the East Side slums and Riis's efforts to improve them. The books were affectionately autographed to Anna Van Vorst Borsum. Mrs. Borsum explained modestly to Malka that she and Mr. Riis had worked together in the Children's Aid Society, which was dedicated to helping the children of the tenements. Whenever Malka had difficulty understanding portions of a book, Mr. or Mrs. Borsum helped her. They were not only kindly employers and friends but also willing tutors. Franz, Helga, and Mrs. Kouwenhoven were as warm and understanding about Malka's impending motherhood as were their master and mistress. They actually began to baby her. She felt as though they were her family, and she prayed nightly and thanked God for her good fortune.

Then in the third week in December a letter came from Prosnica. Franz handed it to her.

"From your mother, no, Malka? It must be a long time since you have heard from home."

They were in the large downstairs kitchen and Malka tore open the envelope with eager fingers. She read as Franz and Mrs. Kouwenhoven watched her with smiles on their faces. Their smiles turned to puzzled frowns and then to expressions of sheer alarm as they saw Malka's hands, holding the pages, tremble. The blood drained from her face and she managed one agonized cry before she collapsed to the floor. The rabbi had written that her mother had died in August of typhoid fever.

That night Malka suffered some vaginal bleeding and Mrs. Borsum summoned the family doctor, Peter Wolphertsen. The doctor urged complete bed rest for at least a week. He estimated that Malka was seven or eight months pregnant and would risk a stillbirth if she exerted herself unduly. She mourned her mother in the small but neatly furnished bedroom on the third floor of the mansion. She was tearfully grateful for the tender care she received at the hands of the Borsums and the other servants. Yet she felt guilty about not being able to do her share of the work. Helga brought her meals. Mr. and Mrs. Borsum brought her books and visited her at least once each day, as did Franz and Mrs. Kouwenhoven.

Before the week was out she felt not only guilty but edgy and restless. The Borsums were giving a large party on Christmas Eve for a number of friends, members of both the Van Vorst and Borsum families, many of whom were coming from Albany and Boston as well as Pennsylvania. Dr. Parkhurst and John Goff, the man who was to be chief counsel for the

Lexow Committee, were also expected. Three days before the party Malka insisted she was completely well. She begged Mrs. Borsum to permit her to help with the preparations. Her belly was so enormous that Mrs. Borsum told her she would only be allowed to help Mrs. Kouwenhoven in the kitchen. All through the morning and afternoon of December 24 she happily assisted the plump, energetic Dutch cook. Mrs. Kouwenhoven saw to it that she did most of her work sitting down. As Malka sat on a high stool before the kitchen counter, Mrs. Kouwenhoven teased her.

"You look like the Humpty Dumpty."

She kept Malka busy for several hours pasting the gold and silver leaf on the Saint Nicholas cakes she had baked.

When the guests began to arrive Malka retired to her room. She did feel weary. She lay down on the bed and began thinking sadly of her mother. She placed her hands over her taut, balloonlike belly and felt the baby kicking. She had no way of estimating time, but soon the sharp pain came again. And again. And then, again and again at briefer and briefer intervals. More frequently and severe. It was almost unbearable. She cried out and before the next stab of agony came, Mrs. Kouwenhoven waddled into the room, holding a candlestick with a flickering candle. As she switched on the electric light, lame Helga limped anxiously up behind her. And in less than five minutes Mrs. Borsum, followed by Mr. Borsum, entered. Malka, trying to keep from screaming, bit her lower lip till it bled as the invisible stiletto plunged into her abdomen again and again.

"I think she is ready to deliver child," said Mrs. Kouwenhoven anxiously. Mrs. Borsum took one look at Malka's tortured face, beaded with sweat, and rushed from the room. In her own bedroom was a telephone. She called Mrs. Goldstein, the ablest midwife in the city, and then Dr. Wolphertsen. The child was born less than five minutes after the Jewish midwife rushed into Malka's bedroom, panting from climbing the three flights of stairs. Mrs. Borsum and Mrs. Kouwenhoven had prepared boiling water, brought in a small mountain of clean towels, and made other preparations for the midwife's arrival. There was a look of awe on Mrs. Goldstein's face as she held the squirming, blood-and-tissue-covered figure upside down by the feet. With two fingers she smartly flicked the slick bottom, no larger than a small plum. The infant wailed thinly. As she wrapped him, she said in a gentle voice, filled with wonder, "Never—never in a hundred births and more, have I seen a smaller bubulah! But thank the good Jehovah he seems to be whole!"

Dr. Wolphertsen, a businesslike, matter-of-fact man, frankly told Anna and Howard Borsum that he was not at all sure that either the baby or Malka would live. He prescribed a diet and treated Malka to prevent gangrene and solemnly left the anxious household.

24

Malka's indomitable will and the concern and love of those around her brought her through the days and nights when she lay near death after the premature birth of her child. As she regained her strength, she began to nurse the scrawny, plucked-chicken infant. And ounce by ounce he began to add to his three pounds, and soon proved as indomitable as his mother. By the end of February both mother and child were out of danger. The boy was named Harry after Malka's father, and was circumcised. Malka began to work a few hours each day, then added more and more working time to her schedule. Again Mrs. Borsum warned her not to overdo, to remember that she must remain healthy to nurse and care for her delicate son. On the first day of March Howard Borsum asked Malka to come to his study.

"How do you feel, Malka?"

"Good," said Malka. "Good and full of thanks to you and to Mrs. Borsum."

He waved away her appreciation.

"You know the Lexow hearings begin in a little more than a week," he said.

"I know. I have been reading in newspapers."

"I'm sorry you won't be able to testify."

"Why...? Why...will I not? I must, Mr. Borsum! I must!"

"Dr. Wolphertsen does not think you are strong enough yet. It will be quite an ordeal."

Malka's hollow-cheeked face paled. She looked puzzled.

"Or—deal? What is ordeal?"

"Hard. Upsetting. Perhaps later in the year, Malka—"

"No! Now! Early—soon as possible I wish to tell about Mr. Wilensky."

The following day Dr. Wolphertsen paid Malka another visit. Howard Borsum came into her bedroom with the doctor. Wolphertsen completed his examination and said, "You are making excellent progress, young lady."

"Then why should I not testify at Lexow hearing in first week . . . as was arranged?"

"Well . . . there is really no point in rushing matters, Malka."

"*Is!* Is much point! Longer I do not tell about Mr. Wilensky, more chance he runs away!"

They argued and Malka finally convinced the doctor it would be more beneficial to her health, at least her mental health, if she testified, than if she were prevented from doing so.

Malka was the fourth witness on the second day of the hearings. She was also the first prostitute to take the stand. The committee and its investigators and counsel had had great difficulty in persuading any of the women to testify, even those who had given Parkhurst and Borsum affidavits. A number had even recanted their earlier statements. The whoremasters and madams had threatened them with severe injury or death if they made an appearance. But after the stories of Malka's testimony (given in part in five trying hours with two rest periods on the first day) appeared in all the city's newspapers, seventeen other prostitutes volunteered to testify.

Malka's story created a sensation. It had an immediate impact in hundreds of homes throughout the city. Suddenly scores of police inspectors, captains, and city officials tendered their resignations, claiming ill health, business abroad, and other reasons. Many operators and madams of brothels, concert gardens, gambling dens, and other illicit businesses deserted the city. Howard Borsum had arranged for the arrest of Joseph Wilensky, Captain Herman Mueller, Anthony Roselli, and Mrs. Krimsky early in the afternoon of Malka's first day of testimony. They had no idea Malka was still in the city, let alone that she would suddenly turn up at the hearings.

Martin Morrissey, who was a legal aide to John Goff, the Lexow Committee chief counsel, arrived late at the Dakota apartment of his brother, Kevin, and Lilly on that first day of the hearings. He came shortly after seven with his fiancée, twenty-year-old Hannah Weiss, who was a typist in the district attorney's office. Marty and Hannah planned to be married when the Lexow hearings were completed. Kevin and Lilly were having a family gathering to celebrate the beginning of a six-month tour of a theatrical company, organized and managed by Kevin, and starring Lilly. She had not yet become quite as popular a star as Sarah Bernhardt, Maude Adams, or Anna Held, but she had her own sizable following in many towns and cities across the country.

Kevin, thanks to consistent warnings from his well-positioned brother about the inevitable effectiveness of the Lexow Committee, had resigned from the police department five months earlier. He had spent much time around the theater with Lilly and had developed many contacts with theater owners, particularly the powerful Klaw and Erlanger combine. He was glib and had a pleasing, outgoing personality. He was certain he would be as successful a manager as Anna Held's husband, Flo Ziegfeld, or even Charles Frohman. Since his retirement, however, he had lost most of his money at gambling, but Lilly had sold all her jewelry and furs to finance the purchase of scenery, costumes, and other requirements of the new Welcome-Morrissey Players.

As Kevin had predicted, Lilly Welcome had completely won over Fiona Morrissey and the rest of the family as well. She had grown up an orphan and immediately upon meeting the Morrisseys had told them all that she had married Kevin only so that she could have a family.

"Not that I ever expected such a glorious, wonderful family as you Morrisseys," she enthused to Fiona. "How could I when I married the only no-good in the tribe?"

She told Ned, upon their first meeting, that if she had known he was a bachelor, she surely would have married him instead of his nephew. And when she met Kevin's brother, Marty, she carried on about the cruel fate that had caused her to meet Kevin before she met Martin. She loved Bridget like a sister, and Bridget's children adored their beautiful and flamboyant Aunt Lilly. She was given to buying gifts for everyone in the family, on their birthdays (of which she kept a meticulous record), on any special occasions, and often on no occasion at all, but just for the pleasure it gave her. And when Kevin's unlucky streak at the fan-tan, poker, and dice tables left them penniless, she unhesitatingly and without a word of complaint sold her possessions to raise the money they needed. Kevin swore he would never gamble again, but he had taken that oath before, and Lilly did not expect him to live by it indefinitely.

When Marty and Hannah arrived at the apartment, Pat, Ned, and Kevin all cornered him immediately after the greetings to hear how the first day of the hearings had gone. He told them about the spectacular testimony of Malka Roitman.

"I don't know who she is, but she is one spunky young lady. Looked like she was dug up from a grave, but she told her story with so much fire she had the committee spellbound."

"What did you say her name was?" asked Ned.

"Malka Roitman."

Ned punched his fist into a palm.

"Yes! Yes! It must be! It's the young whore Willie Kessler wanted to marry. She disappeared last summer. I thought that bastard Wilensky had her killed. . . . Where's she been? Did you find out?"

"It seems Howard Borsum's had her hiding out at his place. You know Borsum?"

"Yes, he's Parkhurst's friend," said Ned. "A good man."

Max Kessler had had two heart attacks since the day in June when Malka had slapped him and run from his house. A relationship even stranger than had existed before developed between the misanthropic old man and his son from that day on. William hated his father, but at the same time still feared him and loved him. He felt an undeniable filial duty to the pathetically ill and increasingly helpless invalid. When Malka disappeared, William totally neglected his work with the investment company. He hired a private investigator to help him find Malka and spent most of his spare time following up on unpromising leads the man turned over to him. He drove his uncle Ned to distraction, nagging him for information about Malka. The police found no trace of her.

Several times William went to see Wilensky, but he finally became convinced that Wilensky was telling the truth when he denied any knowledge of Malka's whereabouts. And Wilensky, in turn, became convinced that the desperate young man had not helped Malka escape, that he knew as little about her disappearance as Wilensky himself. Out of sheer pique he considered having William assaulted again, but Inspector Morrissey's warning was still fresh in his mind, and the blisters on his face had barely healed.

On the morning after Malka's first day of testimony before the Lexow Committee, William came out of his bedroom, went into his bathroom, dressed, and walked down the long hall to the parlor. He knew by the absolute quiet in the house that Mrs. Starker was out. He gasped as he saw his father lying on the floor on his stomach, alongside his chair, crablike, arms akimbo, skeletal legs bent at the knees. The twisted features of the left side of Max's face showed the final quick agony he must have suffered. William ran to him and knelt by his side. His hands, his face were already cold and darkening. Although William knew immediately that it was futile, he called Dr. Hirsh. He thought about lifting his father back into his chair, but could not bring himself to do it.

Conflicting emotions tore at him. Shock and grief, yet some measure of relief. Almost pleasurable anticipation at the thought of a new life, unhampered by his dictatorial, erratic father. At the same time there was an aching sense of loss and a nagging fear of being on his own. If only he could find Malka! She always made him feel strong, confident, capable. Thinking about her evoked the feelings of anger he had felt when his father had driven her from the house with his insults. He wondered for the ten-thousandth time where she was, if she had borne the child she carried. William had always thought of it as his child.

He made himself a pot of tea and sat on a sofa in the parlor, sipping the brew, waiting for the doctor. It was twenty-five minutes before Hirsh arrived, and another fifteen before the ambulance he had summoned pulled up before the tenement and quickly attracted a morbidly curious crowd. William stood alongside his father's body as a burly ambulance attendant lifted the fragile remains of Max Kessler and lowered him onto a stretcher held by two others. It was then that William became conscious of the fact that his father had toppled forward onto the newspaper he had been reading. A headline on the front page caught his eye.

ENSLAVED PROSTITUTE
NAMES POLICE CAPTAIN,
BRUTAL BROTHEL OWNER

Malka Roitman Lured
From Home in Poland

William knelt and picked up the paper as the ambulance people took his father out of the house. Dr. Hirsh, standing over him, said, "What is it, William? What are you doing?"

William ignored the doctor. Spellbound, breathing heavily, he read the entire lengthy story, still kneeling beside the chair.

"It's Malka!" he gasped finally, looking up at Hirsh.

The newspaper report said that Malka would continue her testimony the following morning. There was an excited crowd outside the County Courthouse at 52 Chambers Street a little after nine A.M., when Howard Borsum stepped out of his carriage with Anna Borsum and Malka. William Kessler was among those in the crowd who were being held back by policemen. He tried to push his way forward.

"Malka! Malka!" he shouted. "It is me. William!"

Malka looked back as she walked up the courthouse steps between the Borsums. She was pale and did not smile or wave. She thought she had heard William's voice, but could not be sure in the general hubbub. The public was barred from the hearing room on the third floor, but William bribed a security guard to permit him to sit on a bench across the corridor from the hearing-room door. It was three-thirty in the afternoon when the door opened and people began to emerge. A small, rushing horde of men, reporters covering the hearings, led the way out of the room. Then came three older men, and finally Malka, walking between the Borsums again. She was even paler than when she had arrived in the morning. William rushed to her and threw his arms around her.

"Malka! Malka! Thank God I have found you!"

Howard Borsum grabbed William's shoulder and tried to tear him away from Malka, but Malka said, "No! It is all right, it is William!"

The small crowd in the corridor and those emerging from the hearing room were startled at the strange sight of the gaunt young man with the large nose hugging the lovely, wan prostitute who had just completed her startling testimony.

"Please, sir, please! May I ride in your carriage with you?" begged William as he trailed behind the Borsums and Malka in the street. Borsum looked inquiringly at Malka. There were tears in her eyes. She had sworn to herself that she would never see William Kessler again. But the recent death of her mother, her own struggle for life after the premature birth of the baby, and tiny Harry's survival had all softened her attitude. The quietly triumphant feeling she experienced in having told her story to the committee added to her inclinations toward magnanimity. And especially now that William was here, now that he had held her in his arms again, she realized that she loved him in spite of his weaknesses. He was the father of her child. And somehow he seemed to have changed. She nodded acceptance to Borsum, and William climbed in after Mrs. Borsum and Malka, followed by Howard Borsum.

As they drove uptown toward the Borsums' Fifth Avenue mansion, William apologized to the Borsums for his unseemly behavior.

"I am William Kessler," he said. And then, as though feeling the revelation would explain everything, he added, "My father, Max Kessler, he died yesterday of a heart attack."

"I'm sorry," said Borsum.

Malka was startled by William's announcement. William turned to her, a pleading look in his blue eyes.

"I hope you will forgive him, Malka. He—he was a sick man."

Malka said quietly, "I, too, am sorry, William. I do forgive him. He did not understand—"

"What—what happened to—to our . . . what happened to our child, Malka?" stammered William.

Malka smiled.

"He is two months and two weeks already. A beautiful boy, but a little small."

William beamed, then looked shyly at the Borsums, and back at Malka.

"After—after the funeral . . . when my poor father is laid to rest . . . then Malka . . . can we be married?"

His face reddened as he spoke. It never even crossed his mind that she might have married someone else. The Borsums smiled at each other. Anna Borsum's eyes were moist. Malka said, "Is it all right, Willie, if I go to the funeral services with you?"

He reached out and took her hand, and again looked at the Borsums as though asking permission. Then he kissed her hand, blushing furiously.

They did not marry, however, until after the trials and

sentencing of Wilensky, Mueller, Roselli, and Mrs. Krimsky in late November of that year. Two other witnesses for the prosecution joined Malka in testifying at the trials. Maria Wozniak, inspired by Malka's example, proved a devastating witness. She knew a great deal about the murder of the Hungarian girl and the maiming of Wei Chang, and testified freely about both those crimes. In the course of the trials one of the young deputies in the district attorney's office fell in love with Maria, and they were married early in January. He was not as rich a man as Maria had hoped for, but he loved her and they lived in a nice cottage in Richmond.

William also took the stand and fearlessly detailed his experiences with Wilensky. On Malka's final day of testimony against him, Wilensky created a scene in the courtroom. As Malka left the stand and walked down the aisle toward the witness room, Wilensky leaped from his chair at the defense table and grabbed her fiercely by the shoulders.

"Never mind, you dirty Polish whore!" he cursed. "You'll pay for this!"

Two burly bailiffs rushed forward, tore him away from Malka, and shoved him back into his seat.

Since William had agreed to be a witness he was not allowed to attend the trial sessions, but he heard about the threat later from Marty Morrissey. He expressed grave concern to Malka when he next saw her.

"Do not worry, Willie," she said. "Mr. Wilensky will be in prison for some time."

Malka was right. Wilensky was sentenced to ten years, Mueller and Roselli to seven, and Mrs. Krimsky to three.

Malka and William's wedding, and the festivities that followed afterward in a large banquet room at the Waldorf, seemed to put Wilensky's threat, the trial, all of Malka's horrendous days, and William's difficult years behind the happy couple. At the wedding party were all the Morrisseys, except Kevin and Lilly, who were on the road; the Borsums and all their household employees; Maria and her fiancé, Solomon Kleinman; and scores of William's business friends and associates and their wives and families. William, of course, had inherited his father's considerable fortune. In the interim between the time he had found Malka, after her initial appearance before the Lexow Committee, and the day they were married, William had visited Malka regularly at the Borsums. He idolized his now healthy and growing infant son, and brought him all kinds of ridiculous gifts, far beyond the baby's capacity to enjoy.

They were married on December 24. Four days later, on the twenty-ninth, the Lexow Committee completed its work. The convictions of Wilensky, Mueller, Roselli, and Mrs. Krimsky were only a few of the many the committee had made. It had held more than 70 sessions and heard 678 witnesses. More than 10,000 pages of testimony were taken and 9,500 of these dealt with corruption in the police department. The scale of payments, all the way from the cost of becoming a policeman up to promotions to the level of inspector, was revealed.

A $300 payment to a Tammany politician was necessary to get on the force. A cop paid $2,500 to buy a promotion to sergeant. Captaincies were bought for anywhere from $10,000 to $15,000; and to make the jump from captain to inspector required a payment of $15,000 to $20,000. Saloons paid cops $20 to $40 per month for the privilege of staying open beyond the legal time of one A.M. and all day and night on Sundays, when the law stipulated that they should be closed.

Legitimate businesses also paid off the police and their political protectors. Any dealer or distributor, be it of beer, whiskey, food, cigarettes, cigars, who sold to the police-protected brothels, paid a fee to the police for being allowed to do business with the whorehouses. Even pushcart peddlers paid cops three dollars a week to protect them from petty thievery. The Lexow Committee was a broom, which substantially swept crime and corruption out of the city for a time. Indeed it seemed to be a period when the forces of good government and social improvements dominated the New York scene.

A new mayor, William L. Strong, a Republican and a highly respected dry-goods merchant, was elected with a mandate to clean up the police department. His first move was to dismiss every member of the Board of Police Commissioners. He then appointed Theodore Roosevelt president of the new board.

Roosevelt set about his new job with characteristic vigor. He set up an extensive training program for recruits. A telephonic system of communications between all precincts to supplement the telegraphic system was installed. And an aggressive campaign was launched to persuade Jewish men to become members of the force.

* * *

Over the next decade the means of getting around changed as drastically as the city itself. The horse-drawn cars were gradually replaced by electric cable and trolley cars. But there were still substantial numbers of horse-drawn hacks, hansom cabs, broughams, and barouches. But then, two years before the turn of the century, New Yorkers were startled by the sight of the first horseless carriages. The following year there were enough of the strange, new electric-, steam-, or gasoline-driven vehicles to cause the legislature to pass a law prohibiting their use in Central Park.

On a sunny day in 1900 Malka and William Kessler and their good friends Marty Morrissey and Hannah Weiss attended the first national automobile show at Madison Square Garden. Marty wanted to marry Hannah, but her mother was a fanatically orthodox Jewish woman who said her heart would be broken if Hannah married a gentile. Much to Marty's irritation Hannah decided they must wait. In the meantime she spent as much time helping Marty with his political career as if she were not only his wife but a full-time assistant. William had contributed substantially to Marty Morrissey's campaign fund when the young attorney had run for the city Assembly in 1898, and both William and Malka, as well as Hannah and all the Morrisseys and Lombardis, had worked hard to get him elected. On display at the show was the old gasoline-powered Duryea, built in 1893 by Charles and Frank Duryea of Springfield, Massachusetts. It was simply a regulation carriage with four large wooden wheels, handsome stretched leather top, oil lamps, even a token whipsocket. But instead of reins there was a tiller for steering, and it was powered by a one-cylinder, four-cycle motor with electric ignition and spray carburetor. It could attain speeds up to ten miles per hour.

There were more modern Benzes and Daimlers and the increasingly popular Stanley Steamer. The Kesslers and the Morrisseys watched the hill-climbing demonstrations on the specially constructed incline on the roof of the Garden. They were as greatly impressed as all the other New Yorkers in the crowd who witnessed the steering contests. Skilled and fearless drivers handled the tillers of the elegant new horseless carriages so expertly that they wove in and out of a barrel-strewn obstacle course without accident. William talked about buying one of the automobiles, but Malka argued against it.

She did not think they could afford the six or seven hundred dollars it would cost.

Right after their marriage William had asked Malka whether she would like to live in a house farther uptown, perhaps even in Harlem, where many affluent Jewish people were moving, but Malka was against it. She liked living on Rivington Street, near the people in the Lower East Side tenements, whom she spent so much time helping. William was relieved that she felt that way, since, in truth, the Rivington Street flat was truly home to him, too, despite his often difficult days there.

Despite their wealth, Malka invariably tended to be frugal when it came to spending money on what she considered to be frivolous things. Conversely when it came to supporting causes such as the Nurses' Settlement on Henry Street, the Children's Aid Society, or almost any organized charity, or contributing campaign funds to worthy political candidates, she was extraordinarily generous, even extravagant. She never said so to William, nor to anyone else, but she felt that spending in good causes was the least she could do to thank God for the miraculously happy turn her life had taken. But that day at the auto show William still stared longingly at one new model after another.

"If you do buy one," advised Marty, "buy an electric. They're far easier to drive and control, and they're quiet and they don't stink like the gasoline-powered autos."

"I like the Stanley Steamer," said William.

"Maybe later when they do not cost so much, Willie," said Malka firmly.

At that time there were indeed more electric motor cars among the eight thousand in use throughout the country than either steam or gasoline autos. One reason more people did not purchase any automobile was the fact that there were less than one hundred and fifty miles of paved road on which to drive.

The same year the automobile show was held, construction was begun on the city's first subway. Four years later, on October 24 in 1904, all the Morrisseys, including the Lombardis, along with Malka and William, and Maria and Solomon Kleinman, attended a celebration of the opening of the subway.

Two weeks after the opening of the subway, Ned's body was found in an alley between two tenements on Stanton Street, just a block north of Rivington. Intensive police investigation indicated that one of the Jewish East Side gangs had been ripping the lead and brass piping out of tenements in the process of being remodeled, as well as out of new buildings, and selling the metal to neighborhood junkyards. Through reformed gang members now working with Ned at the Henry Street Settlement, he had apparently learned the identity of the members of the gang who were doing the vandalizing. The police theory was that he had arranged a meeting with them on this frigid night in November and they had killed him. The junkyard dealers and the ex-gang members, fearing for their own lives, denied any knowledge of the vandalizers or the murderers, so the perpetrators were never arrested.

Ned's brother, Pat, and his nephew, Marty, as well as Malka and William Kessler, all felt a vague sense of guilt along with their deep grief as they joined the rest of the family and Ned's many police friends at the wake. Pat had been a member of the Tenement Commission for years. The commission was largely responsible for the passage of a new Tenement House Law in 1901, which had led to the modernization of many of the buildings. Marty, as a member of the Assembly, had fought hard for the bill's passage. And it was Malka and William who had complained bitterly to the police and to Ned about the vandalizing that was going on in the building at Rivington Street and a new building they were putting up on Madison Street. The most tearful mourner at the funeral was a handsome old woman named Tessie Kearns.

Malka had spent the first six years of their marriage exclusively as a mother and housewife. She hardly dared let Harry out of her sight. But when he started school, she hired a young Swedish nurse, Liv Berens, to serve as a full-time governess, and she began to devote much of her time to working in the real estate and investment business with William. She was a shrewd trader. She also spent much time at the Henry Street Settlement, the Children's Aid Society, and soliciting votes in political campaigns for Marty Morrissey and other liberal and socialistically inclined candidates. She and William did not neglect young Harry, nor did they lack for entertainment.

On Saturday afternoon, March 19, in 1904, the "Greatest Show on Earth," the Barnum and Bailey Circus, gave its first performance at Madison Square Garden. And not only Harry but his parents and an elegantly dressed crowd of New Yorkers gazed in openmouthed awe at every dazzling attraction from the "Spectacle" which opened the show to the daring bicycle riding of Auilotti, who looped the gap in a death-defying display near the end. This was a loop from which the top had been removed. The Spectacle represented the Durbar at Delhi, when Edward VII was proclaimed Emperor of India by Lord Curzon. It featured a cast of hundreds, scores of riders on horses and elephants. Humans and animals were caparisoned in the most colorful silks, satins, and armor the audience had ever seen. In between the exotic Durbar and the cycling daredevil were sixteen other displays, featuring clowns, trapeze artists, acrobats, jugglers, bareback equestrians, and wild animals and freaks.

Another delight of all three Kesslers were the new moving-picture and vaudeville shows. In 1896 Malka and William had attended the first moving-picture show at Koster and Bial's Music Hall. The moving-picture program featured two brief terpsichorean turns, the Butterfly Dance and the Skirt Dance, a short boxing match, and Kaiser Wilhelm reviewing his German troops.

The Kesslers were also avid theatergoers. They frequently attended the People's Theater on Second Avenue. It was a Yiddish playhouse and Kevin Morrissey introduced them to the theater's stars, Jacob Adler and Boris Thomashevsky, and to the playwright, Jacob Gordin. Tomashevsky made Malka uneasy with his flamboyant flirtatiousness, while he made William jealous.

Malka and William enjoyed the American theater even more than the Yiddish. The theatrical section of the city had moved on up to Forty-second Street. The marquees of the new playhouses and hotels were so brilliantly lighted with hundreds upon hundreds of electric bulbs that people were calling the area the Great White Way. Going up from the Lower East Side was like visiting an enchanted futuristic metropolis. Malka and William both became devoted fans of Lilly Welcome. Kevin also introduced them to a young Irishman, who was not only an actor but also a songwriter and playwright. Son of a veteran vaudeville family, George M. Cohan won their everlasting admiration with his performance in *Little Johnny Jones* in 1904. For weeks after they saw the musical, William went about the house humming or whistling *Give My Regards to Broadway*. Cohan, of course, was a special favorite of all the Morrisseys.

Indeed, through the decade after the end of the Lexow

hearings and up until the winter and early spring of 1905 the Kesslers led an interesting, fulfilling, and happy life. Young Harry, in one school year after another, proved the brightest boy in his class. After a visit to the Statue of Liberty, he wrote a composition that his English teacher, a Miss Blumstein, declared was the best she had ever read by any student. She predicted that Harry would be a fine and famous writer someday. And then one night in May he disappeared.

25

Malka rushed down the long hall to Harry's bedroom as soon as they got home. William trotted along behind her, a tolerant, loving smile on his face. Malka had been fretting all through the play, and had absolutely refused to attend the opening-night party afterward. All day long, as a matter of fact, she had insisted to William that she had a premonition that something terrible was going to happen to Harry. William tried to chide her out of her mood.

"You've just been working too hard, Malka dear," he said. "You're letting your imagination run away with you."

But now he paled when he heard her scream as she entered the semidark moonlit bedroom. He followed quickly and put his arm around her shoulders. He could feel her trembling as they both stared at the empty bed, the rumpled, twisted sheets, the pillow on the floor. There was still a faint, sweetly sickening odor, perhaps ether or chloroform, in the room, even though the rear window was wide open and a soft spring breeze wafted in. They had had the entire building remodeled, and when William flicked the electric switch and the overhead light came on, Malka saw the sheet of paper on Harry's bedside table, alongside the copy of *The Red Badge of Courage* he had been reading. The lamp on the table had been placed over a corner of the paper.

Malka lifted it and saw that the letters and some words had been clipped out of newspapers and pasted crookedly on the slightly soiled sheet to make the message. Her hand shook so badly that William had to hold her wrist with one hand and the edge of the paper with the other to steady it enough so they could read it.

WE HAV BOY. IF U GO TO POLICE HE WILL BE KILLED. SAY NOTHING. NO 1. WE WILL FONE U WED. MORNING 9. LIKE WE NEW TONIGHT U NOT HOME, WE NO ALL. EVERY MOVE U MAKE WE NO. REMEMBER. YOU TELL POLICE OR ANY 1 WE KILL BOY.

At the bottom of the page was a crude drawing of a black hand, which looked more like a mitten.

Together, with Malka reading and rereading the clumsy note again and again, they walked into the parlor. William headed for the telephone on the desk at the side of the room. As he reached for it, Malka said frantically, "No! No, Willie! We cannot call anyone!"

She dropped wearily to the sofa and stared at the note again. Tears ran down her cheeks. William came and sat beside her. He put his arm around her.

"It is not the Black Hand, William."

In the nearby Italian neighborhood around Mulberry Street there had been talk of a secret criminal organization that called itself the Black Hand. The newspapers had carried occasional stories about their criminal activities, but most of the crimes they committed were in the Italian ghetto.

"They have done kidnappings," said William soberly. "You do not think we should call the police . . . or maybe Marty . . . or Kevin . . . or maybe Mr. Borsum?"

Malka shook her head vigorously.

"No! We do not dare! It is not the Black Hand. It is Mr. Wilensky! He will kill Harry. Perhaps he will kill Harry anyway, even if we do not call police—but we must wait!"

She dabbed at her eyes with a kerchief and took William's hand.

"And pray," she said quietly.

Later as they sat in the parlor, drinking coffee, staring at the telephone, and discussing the desperate situation, William was heartsick.

"I should have listened to you, Malka. I should always listen to you."

He clutched her hand and lifted it to his lips.

"But please, please, dearest Malka. I know he will be all right. They will want money and we will give it to them and they will give Harry back to us."

"Please, God, let it be so," she said. She sighed heavily.

"But I know it is Mr. Wilensky. It is ten years since he went to prison. He is an evil and vengeful man."

Dawn filtered grayly through the east windows and they still sat, holding hands and waiting. Then a bright sun rose higher in the sky and presently the clock on the wall showed five minutes to nine. They stared at it as though hypnotized. They were bone-weary, but too worried to notice or care. The clock's hands seemed frozen.

"It has stopped!" said Malka. "The clock has stopped."

"No. It is moving."

And it did move, each second seeming like an eon, each minute an eternity. Yet promptly at nine, when the phone rang, it startled them both. Malka lifted the receiver from the hook. William leaned closer to her, pressing his ear to the receiver, alongside Malka's head. Malka, in a quavering voice, whispered, "Huh—huhlo. Here is Malka Kessler."

A heavy voice with a distinct Italian accent, slightly muffled as though talking through a cloth, said, "Put Mister Kessler on da phone, lady!"

Malka shakily handed the phone to William and pressed her own ear against the receiver against his head. Leaning over, she clutched William tightly to her with one arm as he spoke.

"This is William Kessler. Where is Harry?"

There was a heavy, muffled chortling.

"We been watchin'. We glad ya was smart enough not t' call da cops," said the voice.

"Where is Harry?" repeated William.

"Da boy is still alive," said the voice ominously, "an' if ya do like we tell ya, ya'll get 'im back alive. Ya unnerstan'?"

"Yes."

"Lissen t' this, ya hear? Maybe ya wanna write it down. Ya got a paper an' pencil?"

Malka pulled open a drawer of the desk and took out a sheet of paper, and handed William a pencil from a cup on the desk.

"Yes," said William. "Go ahead."

"T'ree o'clock tomorrow morning. Dat's t'ree hours past midnight, right?"

"Right! Yes. Go ahead."

"At t'ree o'clock ya be at the sout' end o' da uptown side, da Fourteenth Street subway station. Right? Ya got dat?"

"South end, uptown, Fourteenth Street, yes," said William, scribbling.

"Ya bring da money wit ya in a suitcase. Twenny fi' thousan' in hun'red-, fifty-, twenny-, 'n' ten-dollar bills."

"I—I don't know if I can fit that much in a suitcase."

The caller laughed.

"So it'll be a big suitcase. It'll fit. If ya have t', use mos'ly hun'reds."

"How do we know you'll give Harry back to us unharmed if we give you the money?" asked William. He was perspiring now and finding it hard to talk without gasping. The voice turned angry.

" 'Cause I'm tellin' ya we will! Don't ya trust us, f' crise sake! Who ya tink ya dealin' wit'?"

Malka could hold back no longer. Desperation, frustration made her furious. She leaned toward the phone's mouthpiece and demanded, "When—when will we get him back? And where? When and where will we get him? You must tell us! You must!"

There was a grunting sound and a loud, undistinguishable remark and more grunts and squawks on the other end of the phone, as though two persons were arguing. Then another voice spoke. Whatever cover had been used on the mouthpiece seemed to have been removed. The new voice was clear and cold and loud.

"Never mind when and where, Malka Roitman!" it said. "Do as my friend says. Bring the money or your boy will be dead!"

Malka backed away from the phone. The blood drained from her face.

"I knew! I knew! It *is* Mr. Wilensky!"

William watched her, his mouth open in shock. He, too, had heard the guttural voice. After ten years in prison it still retained much of its East European accent. But now the heavier, Italianate voice was back.

"Kessler? Kessler? Ya dere?"

William said hoarsely, "I'm here!"

"T'ree o'clock tomorrow morning. Sout' end, uptown side. Wit da money. An' come alone or ya'll find yer boy in pieces."

"Yes, yes," said William and there was a click in his ear as the caller hung up.

"Good God!" gasped William. "Sixteen hours we must wait, Malka."

"My poor Harry," wailed Malka. "What will they do to him in all that time? You know, Willie—you know about Mr. Wilensky and young boys?"

William stared at her, puzzled.

"He—he—when I was in Allen Street, he always used young boys."

William took her in his arms. He stroked her hair.

"Now he is interested only in the money, Malka. And we will give him the money, and we will get Harry back unharmed. You will see. They want only the money."

William shaved and changed his clothes, and Malka washed her face with cold water. When she came back into the kitchen where William was drinking still another cup of coffee, William said, "I think, maybe, we should go to the police anyway, Malka. Or at least talk with Marty Morrissey or Mr. Borsum."

"We cannot, Willie. There are people working with Mr. Wilensky. Otherwise how did he know we went to the theater? How did they know Mrs. Starker would not be here?"

William nodded sadly.

"Is it not odd that none of the neighbors have come to tell us about hearing or seeing anything? How did they get into the house, and how did they get Harry out without anyone seeing anything?"

Malka shrugged.

"Such people have keys to open doors. Maybe Harry was asleep already, and they drugged him to take him out. I smelled a strong odor in the room when we came home."

"But you think we should not go to anyone for help?"

"We cannot risk it, Willie," said Malka grimly.

With her mind in a turmoil, her heart beating painfully and irregularly, Malka wandered aimlessly about the house while William went out to gather the twenty-five thousand dollars. She took William's composition out of his schoolbag and read over his homework. *Such a bright boy, and such neat penmanship*. She was so proud of him. In the bedroom she picked up the copy of *The Red Badge of Courage* and sat on the edge of the bed and read a few pages before she realized she was not absorbing a word of what she was reading.

In the parlor she stared, as though hypnotized, at a framed family photograph on the mantelpiece. It was taken when Harry was six. He stood manfully beside his seated father, chin held high, a serious look on his innocent, hollow-cheeked face. Malka was behind them, beaming proudly, with one hand on William's shoulder, the other on Harry's. She held the framed photograph to her breast, then kissed it and replaced it, fighting back a fresh impulse to cry.

"Please God, keep him safe. Please protect him. He is such a good boy."

William was gone until late afternoon. He went to three different banks and to his broker to sell some bonds to put together the ransom money. He also bought a suitcase, and discovered that while it was a snug fit, he was able to pack the money into the case. When he returned, Malka set the table and served the meal she had prepared. Neither of them ate a bite. They drank many cups of coffee and talked while the food got cold. Malka did not even clear the table. They went into the parlor with fresh cups of coffee and debated endlessly and futilely whether or not they should call the police or Marty Morrissey or Howard Borsum. The hours dragged slowly by and they continued to reassure each other that Harry would be safe.

"I will take the carriage and go myself," said William finally. "That way as soon as I give them the money I can pick up Harry and bring him right back."

Malka insisted that she would go along, but for once William was firm and adamant.

"No, Malka!" he said. "I will not permit it. It will be less dangerous for Harry if I go alone. They might think we are up to some trick if they see two of us."

Malka did not argue. She decided that she would let William leave, and then walk up to Fourteenth Street by herself afterward. She finally asked, "How will you do it, Willie? Will you give them the money before they bring you to Harry?"

"I will insist! They cannot expect me to give them the money until I see Harry and know that he is all right."

They decided that William would give himself plenty of time so that he would be sure to be at the designated place on the Fourteenth Street station platform at precisely three o'clock. When William started out, he could readily understand why the kidnappers had chosen this hour. The streets were absolutely deserted. It was a clear night, unusually cool for May. William drove off at two A.M. He wanted to leave at two-thirty, since it would hardly take him more than fifteen minutes to ride from Rivington up to Fourteenth Street, but Malka insisted he take the extra time.

"Just in case you run into an unexpected delay of some kind," she said.

She wanted him to leave so much earlier so that she herself would have enough time to walk up to the Fourteenth Street site and easily arrive before three o'clock.

William actually reined the carriage to a halt at the corner of Fourteenth Street and Lexington Avenue at ten minutes past two. There was a full moon and myriad stars in the ebony sky. He looked up and down the silent streets. Not a soul was in sight. The quiet was eerie. He looked at his pocket watch and began to pace restlessly. He walked to the corner of Fifteenth Street and back to Fourteenth. He went over to Union Square and sat on a bench nervously for a time, praying silent prayers. He looked at his watch again and saw that only twenty-five minutes had passed.

Just about that time Malka reached Fourteenth Street and Lexington. She saw their carriage with the horse tethered to a post, and then she saw William, head down, coming along on the opposite side of the street. She hastened into a dark doorway. William walked slowly, as though he were in a daze. Finally he reached their carriage. She watched him open the trunk at the rear with a key and lift out the suitcase. It seemed heavy. It pulled his shoulder lower as he carried it to the uptown entrance to the subway. His steps echoed in the still night as he descended the stairs. In another ten minutes Malka heard a horse's hoofbeats cracking along a cobblestone street and soon she saw the horse and a wagon turn into Fourteenth Street. The wagon passed her and from her hiding place in the doorway she saw there were two men sitting on the board seat. She could not recognize them from the distance, but in the moonlight she could make out the block lettering on the side of the closed wagon. Firenza Brothers, it said. And beneath, in smaller letters, Beef, Pork, Fowl.

She watched as the wagon pulled up some twenty feet behind the Kessler carriage. A squat, heavyset man dropped to the street closest to the curb away from the driver's side. She knew immediately that it was Wilensky. He was heavier than when she had last seen him, but he still moved in that aggressive, arrogant way he had. For a moment, as he headed toward the same subway entrance William had used, she had a glimpse of his face. A bit beefier, but with the same thick, curled mustache. He disappeared down the stairs and Malka waited.

In a few minutes the driver of the wagon leaped to the ground. He walked slowly to the Kesslers' carriage and began to walk around it, inspecting it carefully. When his back was to her, Malka dashed quickly from the doorway to the rear of the meat wagon. Even in her distraught and frightened state she reasoned that if Mr. Wilensky and the Italians, whoever they were, wanted to get the money and have the matter over with, they would want to deliver Harry back to the Kesslers quickly. *And alive,* she prayed!

As she had walked up from Rivington Street she had thought it out. If they killed Harry, they must realize that she and William would obviously report it to the police and the criminals would be hunted until they were captured. If they released Harry unharmed, Malka would persuade William not even to report it. They could afford the money and it would be well worth getting rid of Mr. Wilensky and his fellow criminals once and for all. As long as they got Harry back unharmed. That was all that mattered.

And she prayed now that they had brought him along in this wagon *(alive, please, please God!),* so that as soon as William gave Wilensky the money, they could take Harry out of the wagon and give him to William to take home in the carriage. The meat wagon had rear double doors, which were unlocked, and a step halfway up to the floor of the wagon's interior. Malka opened the door, quickly stepped up into the wagon, and shut the door behind her.

It was dark in the wagon, but she heard something move, just ahead of her. The something was making sounds. For a second she thought it might be a snorting, grunting pig, but she forced herself to reach forward and she touched skin, then thick, damp hair. The grunting continued and her hand found a thick cloth, tied tightly beneath what her sense of touch told her was a nose. A large nose, a nose she loved. It was Harry.

As her eyes adjusted to the darkness, she could make out the trussed form of her son in the slab of moonlight slanting into the wagon's interior through a square window behind the driver's seat. She felt, as much as saw, that he was securely bound around the ankles, just below the knees, around the thighs. His hands were tied behind his back. He was still in his nightshirt, and she could smell the dried urine, blending with the odors of dead animal carcasses and congealed grease and blood. She unknotted the filthy rag they had tied across his mouth and around his head. He tongued and spat a dirty, balled-up kerchief from his mouth, and breathed deeply, over and over, and finally began to whimper. Malka pulled his head to her breast and stroked his sweating, mucus-smeared cheek.

"It's Mama, sweetheart," she cooed. "It's Mama. You are all right now. Papa is coming and soon we will take you home."

Harry sniffled and squirmed to press himself against his mother. She hugged him tightly to her.

"Don't be frightened, my brave boy. Mama is here."

And then she became aware of footsteps, and the wagon tilted slightly to the left, as the burly man climbed into the high seat.

"Mama!" wailed Harry loudly. "They hurt me. One man—"

Malka clamped her hand over his mouth.

"Sshhh . . . shhhh, sweetheart," she whispered desperately. But the wagon tilted once more and she heard the heavy footsteps again, this time walking alongside the wagon, obviously heading toward the rear doors. She held Harry tightly to her breast and stared desperately around the gloomy, stinking interior of the meat wagon.

When William went down the subway stairs he felt in his pocket for a nickel to go through the turnstile. There was no one on the platform on either the uptown side or across the dull, gleaming rails on the downtown side. The air was damp and chill and a perpetual hum sounded as though somewhere far away the electric trains were hurtling through the dark tunnels.

William walked down toward the south end. There was no one there. He looked at his pocket watch again. It was only twenty minutes to three. He placed the suitcase at his feet and paced short distances back and forth away from it, looking expectantly in the direction of the stairs he himself had just descended. After what seemed like hours he heard heavy steps coming down. A stocky man with a thick mustache, wearing a peaked leather cap, scaled over the turnstile. He stopped and looked in William's direction. William thought the man looked like Wilensky, but he wasn't certain.

He waited. The man strode determinedly toward him. When he was ten feet away William saw that it was indeed Wilensky. The dark hair at the side of his head and his thick mustache were a dirty gray and his heavy eyebrows were snow-white. His black eyes were shiftier than ever in his heavy-jowled face.

"So we meet again, young Kessler," he said coldly. "And you finally married that Polish whore!"

He saw the suitcase and quickly knelt and placed it on its side. William reached down and grabbed his shoulder.

"Wait a minute, Wilensky. Where's Harry?"

Wilensky slapped away William's hand. He released the suitcase's latch and flipped it open. His eyes gleamed greedily as he saw the stacks of bills. William grabbed him again, this time with both hands. Wilensky snapped the suitcase shut and drove both elbows sharply backward into William, as William dragged him up to his feet.

"Goddam it, Kessler! Let me go!" he bellowed angrily. "You'll get your son. Joe Wilensky trusts nobody! I had to make sure you brought the money."

"Where is Harry, Wilensky!" William demanded again, almost hysterical now. The underground tunnel's perennial humming sound intensified and crescendoed into an advancing rumble with a hammering metallic undertone. Wilensky picked up the suitcase. He raised his voice now so William could understand him over the noise of the oncoming train.

"You go back upstairs, Kessler. In the street you will see a meat wagon. Harry is in that wagon. Alive and—"

He looked eagerly in the direction of the now roaring, clattering sound as the subway train approached the south end of the station. William grabbed his arm.

"You come with me, Wilensky. You take me to that wagon where Harry is—then you can have the money."

Wilensky swung at William's head with his free fist.

"Let go of me, you dumb bastard!" he screamed. "Joe Wilensky is getting on that train! The man in the wagon will give you the boy!"

His fist landed alongside William's cheek, but it was a glancing blow. William hurled himself at Wilensky and threw his arms around him. He began to wrestle him to the ground. Wilensky was far stronger than gaunt, slight William Kessler. He held onto the suitcase even as he twisted and elbowed and squirmed and kicked and tried to wrest his free arm out of William's desperate grip.

The two men whirled and staggered about like demented dancers, grunting, cursing. The sound of their struggle was lost in the thunderous clatter of the train, thundering ever nearer to the south end of the station. Wilensky managed to break William's hold, but William dove at him. His shoulder smashed into Wilensky's chest. Still holding the suitcase, his free arm flailing wildly, Wilensky stumbled backward to the edge of the platform and fell just as the train roared into the station. William's heart almost stopped as he saw Wilensky's body slammed through the air a dozen feet in front of the train. The suitcase tore out of his hand and opened. A storm of paper money fluttered around and under and over the moving train as its iron wheels slashed Wilensky's body in half. William thought the screeching sound he heard was coming from his own throat, but it was the scream of the wheels on the iron tracks as the motorman applied the brakes.

As she heard the handle of the rear doors of the meat wagon being turned, Malka looked wildly about her, still holding Harry tightly. There were meat hooks suspended from the ceiling on both sides of the wagon, and racks and shelves along each side, bloodstained and greasy where animal parts had been stacked upon them. On the rear wall beside the window behind the driver's seat was a thick wooden slot in which a cleaver and two long, sharp butcher knives rested. Beneath the window was a chopping block, bolted to the wall. The door swung back and in the moonlight Malka could see the black-stubbled, coarse, and heavy face of the man. It was Tony Roselli.

By some trick of cloud-tattered moonglow his face seemed to take on the same expression she recalled on that day many years ago when he had ravaged her. Roselli placed one foot on the step and began to climb into the wagon. His eyes were not accustomed to the interior darkness.

"What da hell ya doin'? How'd ya git outta dat—"

Malka pushed Harry aside. Sobbing, he rolled over onto his stomach, his face against the slime of the floor. Malka reached up and took the cleaver from the slot. In that moment Roselli's eyes had adjusted just enough so he could see a moving form. He crawled into the wagon, then cursed and raised his hands as he saw the dull glint of the cleaver arcing toward his head. He was too late. The cleaver split the front of his skull and halved his nose and his thick upper lip.

Malka was untying the last of the rope from Harry's ankles. She had untied his hands, but his fingers were too numb, his arms too paralyzed from lack of circulation, to help her. The rear doors of the meat wagon hung open, and William, looking green in the moonlight, stared in, and it slowly dawned on him that he was seeing his wife and son behind the sprawled corpse of a man, whose brains were oozing onto the floor out of a split in his head. Neither William nor Malka nor Harry said a word as William helped them out of the wagon. The Seventeenth Precinct police station was at First Avenue on the corner of Fifth Street and they drove there in the carriage.

The sergeant on duty at the front desk was dozing, dreaming pleasant dreams of the cabin near the lake to which he would retire permanently in another four months. He was startled when William woke him. In his many years on the force he had seen a shocking sight or two, but these three ghastly, bloodied, stinking, sweating apparitions were something out of a nightmare. Frozen horror gleamed in their eyes. They were incoherent. It took the sergeant and the sole detective on duty, whom he called in, almost two and a half hours before they could make any sense out of the story the pale, gaunt man, his catatonic wife, and their shivering, sobbing ten-year-old son, talking in broken, disconnected segments, told them.

PART EIGHT

Mike Morrissey

Commissioner Nathan Wertheim

Dorothy Wertheim

Miriam Ehrenberg Kessler

Isaac Kessler

The Lilly Pad

A New Friendship Between Mike and Harry

"The way a man feels about New York gives a pretty fair indication of the way he feels about humanity. If he loves people then he loves the city; if he is indifferent to human beings he'll grab the first train to the suburbs. It's not just that the city is teeming with human specimens of every description. It also happens to be the most improbable, flawed and intensely human creation ever imposed by mortal intelligence on an unsuspecting and unwitting corner of this earth. Those witty snobs who suggest we sell Manhattan back to the Indians are expressing their fundamental hostility to the human spirit. But those of us who stand by this town, with all its faults, show our basic confidence that in the final analysis mankind is going to turn out all right."

—Harry Kessler's first "My New York" column, *The New York Herald Tribune*, January 22, 1926

"Beneath the exterior of a pleasantly easy-going urban existence, of neighborhoods keeping an older scale and a traditional way of life, was a city grown rotten with corruption and bled white by a long period of public abuse. It was a city . . . in which every man had his price. Money passed from hand to hand mysteriously at the highest levels when a contract was given or an office procured. Intimidation made its way through the affairs of the small shopkeeper, through the police force threatened with political retribution, through the largest industries willing to pay for 'protection.' The finances of New York were in desperate condition, with not enough money to pay for routine services except as a group of bankers allowed special funds to be paid out. Of its seven million inhabitants, one out of six was unemployed and in need."

—Description of New York City at the beginning of Mayor Fiorello LaGuardia's administration, January 1, 1934, August Heckscher with Phyllis Robinson, *When LaGuardia Was Mayor*

26

Nathan Wertheim exuded strength and confidence. Like other successful fifty-year-old men he had experienced occasional setbacks in his lifetime, but he had a talent for obliterating them from his memory. In his own mind he was undefeated and unconquerable. Today, in the fall of 1935, he was at the peak of his career in city government. He was New York's planning commissioner under a new mayor who was going to take the city into a new era: a mayor who was determined to deal once and for all with the problems created by the Great Depression, which had begun in 1929. There would be radical forward steps in relief and welfare, in education and recreation, in the arts and in housing. He knew that Fiorello LaGuardia was capable of creating a totally new and unprecedentedly favorable relationship between the nation's leading urban community and the Federal government under President Franklin Delano Roosevelt.

And he, Commissioner Nathan Wertheim, would play an important role in creating the *new* New York! His pet project at the moment was Rivington Village. It would be the most attractive, most progressive example of urban reconstruction New York or any other city had ever seen. Down would come whole blocks of dilapidated tenements. In their stead would rise modern buildings, interspersed with parks and trees and flower-flanked pathways and sparkling fountains. *Wertheim municipal sorcery!*

It was an early evening in mid-October and the lights had been turned on in many offices in the Chrysler Building, where Wertheim had his headquarters. Twenty-eight-year-old Mike Morrissey scratched the back of his neck as he gazed skyward to the southwest out of the sixty-seventh-floor window and watched the light flicker atop the hundred-and-two-story Empire State Building. Inexplicably, and somewhat to his surprise, the dilemma of the moment washed out of his mind, replaced by flashing random thoughts about the recently completed world's tallest building. *Someday he would design and supervise the construction of such a skyscraper.* He recalled, for no apparent reason, that the building occupied the site of what had been the Waldorf-Astoria Hotel, and before that the mansion of the Astors. His studies in architecture had made him an authority of sorts on New York City's buildings, old and new. These reflections took less than a half minute. The current consideration reclaimed his mind.

Could he get out of talking to Mrs. Kessler?

Commissioner Wertheim's strong bass voice turned him around.

"A problem, Mike?"

"Not really, sir . . ."

Wertheim lifted the monogrammed tumbler in his well-manicured hand and held it out to Mike.

"Well then, son. Pour us one more before Dorothy gets here."

Mike Morrissey walked to the desk, took the glass from the commissioner's hand, and moved across the thick carpet to the built-in bar at the side of the plush office. He always felt oddly ill at ease in Commissioner Wertheim's presence. He was acutely conscious of the fact that his unruly light brown hair kept tumbling down across his forehead. As was his custom toward the workday's end, he had opened the collar of his button-down shirt and loosened his tie. He realized that his pepper-and-salt wool suit was not as sharply pressed as it might have been. Even his black shoes lacked the high gloss of Wertheim's expensive Florsheims, propped on the edge of his leather-surfaced mahogany desk.

Wertheim had been in the office since eight o'clock that morning, and except for a slight shadow of beard on his cheeks and jowl, he looked as immaculate and well-groomed as when he had arrived. Every curly prematurely silver hair on his noble head was in place. His Sulka tie was crisply knotted. He might have donned his white silk shirt and custom-tailored suit ten minutes, instead of ten hours, ago. Mike put ice cubes in both his and the commissioner's tumblers and poured the Chivas Regal. Handing one drink to Wertheim, he said, "It's just that she's such a fine lady, Commissioner. I hate to try to force her to—"

The commissioner sipped his drink.

"Nonsense, Mike. I know she's a fine lady. Fine and *stubborn*! You don't have to force her to do anything. Persuade her with your silver tongue. Charm her with your Irish-Jewish blarney. It certainly has worked wonders with Dorothy!"

He sipped again.

"And you've known the lady from the time you were a tyke. Correct?"

Mike shrugged, and half-nodded an acknowledgment. He touched his Scotch to his lips.

Wertheim said, "I never should have sent Markham to talk to her in the first place. He can set forth the facts, but he has the manner of a hemorrhoidal gorilla."

Seated in the chair alongside the commissioner's desk, Mike stared at his drink for a moment, then looked up at Wertheim.

"The house means a lot to her, Commissioner. She and her husband lived there all through their marriage. They could have afforded to live anywhere, anywhere at all, but they stayed there on Rivington Street. Her husband was born there and died there. Her son, Harry, spent his entire childhood there."

"How is Harry? Have you seen him lately?"

Nathan Wertheim was very much aware of the importance of the press. Harry Kessler wrote a daily column in *The New York Herald Tribune*, called My New York.

Mike sipped, then answered Wertheim's question.

"Not since my father's funeral, almost three years ago. Mrs. Kessler and Harry both came to Georgetown for the services. I don't know either Mrs. Kessler, or Harry, all that well. She and her husband and my mother and father were good friends in the old days before we went to Washington. And Harry must be thirteen, fourteen years older than I. We were never close."

Wertheim smiled a benevolent smile at Mike. His full lips, spread across gleaming white teeth, smiled well, but his gray eyes, the color of two-day-old sidewalk snow, never seemed to join in the smile.

"I have every confidence in you, Mike. After all, we'll pay her well to sell us that old building of hers. And she must realize how much better it will be for the whole neighborhood."

Mike finished his drink.

"Thanks, Commissioner. I'll try."

"By the way, son," said Wertheim. "I went over those preliminary sketches you did for the World's Fair."

He finished his drink, wiped the bottom of the tumbler with his pocket kerchief, and put the glass on the desk.

"Very good!" he said heartily. "Very, *very* good. You're a

little young, but I think there's a chance you may wind up chief architect for the fair."

Mike beamed. It was the immediate goal of his life. He would sell at least part of his soul for the assignment.

"Thank you, sir. I would give anything—"

Wertheim waved away his speech.

"You do your job here, my boy, and everything will fall into place. After all, the fair's a couple of years off yet."

A rhythmic knock—*ta*, ta, ta—*tah! tah!*—sounded at the door.

"There's Dorothy," said Wertheim, and called loudly, "Come in, Pumpkin."

It was sheer coincidence that the girl who came into the office was wearing an orange-colored angora sweater, indeed, almost pumpkin-colored. There were several brownish stains beneath the left breast, as though she might have spilled some coffee on it. Mike Morrissey had never learned why her father called her Pumpkin. She said cheerily, "Hi, N.W." and walked eagerly to Mike, stood on her toes, and kissed his cheek.

"How're you, lover?" she greeted him.

Mike never did know why she called her father N.W. either. As far as he knew, no one else did. And she always said it in an affectionately sarcastic tone, teasing him for his tycoonishness. Dorothy Wertheim was a healthy, aggressive twenty-five; five feet four, almost a foot shorter than Mike Morrissey's six two. Her mother was a fashion designer and was always as impeccably groomed as her husband. In each of the past two years, she had been declared one of America's ten best-dressed women.

Dorothy, in obvious open rebellion, was a slob. She had her sleek black hair cut short, with bangs hanging across her forehead just above her never-plucked full black eyebrows, in a style more suitable to a gangster's moll of the late twenties than a distinguished family's daughter in the mid thirties. She had her mother's dark, bitter-chocolate-colored eyes and an olive complexion, but her father's Roman nose and his full lips. She was some twenty pounds heavier than she should have been, with a full bosom, an amazingly narrow waist, and sweeping hips. Her legs and arms were chunky. She never wore makeup of any kind. A green plaid wool skirt, the pleats of which could have used a pressing, clashed deafeningly with the loose orange sweater. She wore flat-heeled brown shoes and pink knee-high stockings, which made an even worse match with the green skirt than the pumpkin sweater. Her father had grown accustomed to her outlandish, tasteless style of dress and considered it a lovable eccentricity. Her mother could hardly bear to look at her. To Mike it made no difference at all.

"What's on the program for you two tonight?" asked Wertheim, as Dorothy gave him a peck on the cheek, almost toppling him over in his chair. She shrugged.

"The momentous decision has yet to be made," she said. "Morrissey insists on seeing that dumb Billy Rose thing at the Hippodrome and I want to see the new Odets play, *Awake and Sing.*"

"Your mother and I saw *Jumbo* on opening night. It's magnificent! Spectacular! The Rodgers and Hart score is lovely and Durante must be one of the funniest people who ever lived."

"Hallie saw it," said Dorothy. "It's a mishmash. An old-fashioned circus with clowns and half the animals in Africa and a foolish book by Hecht and MacArthur. They ought to be ashamed of themselves."

"It's also the last show you'll ever see at the Hipp," said her father. "They're tearing it down to build a new—"

"Good riddance!" said Dorothy.

She worked for Hallie Flanagan, who supervised the Federal Theater Project, which was an activity of the Works Progress Administration. All through the depression the WPA had kept thousands of the nation's theater people, actors, directors, writers, choreographers, lighting and set designers from starving to death. Mike grinned and said, "Last Monday you dragged me to *Porgy and Bess*. I think you owe me one."

"You dumb architect. You and the critics are both crazy," said Dorothy. "One day that show'll be recognized as a classic!"

Mike Morrissey and Dorothy Wertheim had little in common. Their only mutual interests were jazz and sex. Dorothy concerned herself with the struggles of the masses; Mike with architectural visions and his career. Dorothy was a sexual young animal and most evenings they spent together culminated in lovemaking either in Dorothy's scruffy apartment in Greenwich Village (she had moved out of her parents' Westchester mansion at eighteen) or in Mike's bachelor apartment in a brownstone on West Seventy-third Street.

It was not that Mike was in love with Dorothy. She had majored in political science at Sarah Lawrence, belonging to more young socialist organizations than Mike knew. She attended many meetings, and talked about their plans to change the world. This bored Mike mightily. He was close to being totally apolitical. He had seen enough of politics during his father's (Martin Morrissey III) terms of office, originally as an assemblyman in New York City, and later as a New York congressman in Washington, D.C. He was blindly dedicated to making his way as an architect. He intended to become the best architect not only in New York City but in the entire country. Someday he would have his own firm and design the most impressive, beautiful, even spectacular edifices the nation had ever seen. He considered his staff position with Commissioner Wertheim nothing more than a stepping-stone along the path to the establishment of Michael Morrissey Associates, Inc.

He was fond of Dorothy Wertheim, but he thought about marrying her (as her mother and father had both made it plain they hoped he would) only if it would further his career. As, for instance, by Wertheim designating him chief architect for the planned New York World's Fair.

"Well, let's go eat, and fight it out over a steak," he said now.

"A lobster!" said Dorothy. "All that bloody red meat's not good for you. Let's go to the Gloucester House."

It turned out she had already acquired house seats for *Awake and Sing*, so after dinner at the seafood restaurant they saw the Odets play. After the play they had some drinks at the Low Note, a tacky cellar jazz joint. Then they went to Dorothy's apartment and played some Bessie Smith records. Dorothy finished her fourth glass of wine and another cigarette, and finally said, "I'm horny, Morrissey. Let's go to bed."

When they finished making love, she lit another cigarette, and lay back on her pillow. Mike didn't smoke at all. He sighed heavily, thinking about his upcoming meeting with Malka Kessler.

"What's the matter, lover? It wasn't good?"

Mike turned to her and grinned.

"Oh, sure. Great."

He told her about his distasteful mission.

"I don't know what I'm going to say to her," he said.

"If she doesn't want to do it, leave her alone. Hallie and her friend Lilly Wald know Mrs. Kessler well. They say she's done all kinds of good for the people over there. If she doesn't want to get out, leave her alone. Put the stupid village someplace else."

"I don't think your father would like that."

"Screw N.W.," she said, and crushed her cigarette into an ashtray on the bedside table. She threw her arm across Mike's chest and nibbled his earlobe.

"Or would you rather screw his daughter one more time?" she said, giggling.

Malka Kessler was happy to see young Mike Morrissey. She ushered him into the parlor, to an overstuffed damask-covered armchair, which had been Harry's favorite. She insisted on making a pot of tea. Mike followed her into the kitchen and watched as she set the kettle on to boil. A handsome woman, she moved as though she were thirty, rather than in her early sixties. Her dark, silver-streaked hair was combed flat on her head and parted in the middle and braided down the back. Her face was lined, but her olive skin was clear, and her mahogany eyes, bright, warm, and alert. Her bearing was erect, and she moved about with easy grace. Only the liver spots on the backs of her veined hands were signs of her true age.

"So, Michael," she said, when he was back in Harry's chair, tea cup and honey cakes before him. "To what do I owe this pleasant surprise? You are still working in Commissioner Wertheim's office?"

Mike felt himself blushing. He nodded.

"I must tell you the truth, Mrs. Kessler. That's why I'm here. Mr. Wertheim asked me to come to see you."

"You wouldn't have come otherwise? Ever? We are old friends, Michael. You were even my little boy once, for a while. Your mother, Hannah, was my best friend."

"I know . . . yes . . . thanks . . . sure I would've."

Malka Kessler had made it no easier by evoking memories of his mother. His Wertheim mission was buried momentarily by a flood of images that flashed, unbidden, through his mind. It was 1918. He was eleven years old. The influenza epidemic was ravaging the nation. People walked around like bandits, wearing surgical masks, but it did not help. He hardly ever saw his father, who was working with Bernard Baruch on the War Industries Board. Mike was eleven and in February of that year, his favorite aunt, Bridget Lombardi, succumbed to the killer disease. He had gone to New York with his mother and father for the funeral. He remembered seeing piles of bodies stacked against building walls in some New York City streets in the poor neighborhoods. Two hundred people a day were dying and there weren't enough coffins to bury them. Later he learned that a half million people died of the flu in forty-six states before the epidemic ran its course.

In December, he and his mother had both come down with it. He had survived, but his mother had died. His father never caught it at all. Nor Mrs. Kessler nor her husband, William. They came to Georgetown for his mother's funeral. And Mrs. Kessler stayed and took care of him for five weeks after the funeral, until his father could find a satisfactory housekeeper and surrogate mother. Harry Kessler was twenty-three at the time. He had been a young police reporter on *The New York Tribune*, but he had enlisted in the army a year earlier, as soon as America entered the war. He was presumably somewhere in France, but his parents had not heard from him in many months. Mike remembered Mrs. Kessler telling him how nice it was to have a young boy to take care of again.

Malka Kessler was smiling at him now.

"You said Commissioner Wertheim sent you, Michael?"

He willed the memories from his mind and forced himself to get to the business at hand.

"Yes, he wanted me to talk to you about vacating the building so we can tear it down with the rest of the block and—"

"Drink your tea," she said. "Before it gets cold. Have a cake."

Mike obediently lifted the cup to his lips.

"You know," said Malka, "that Mr. Markham was here already."

"Yes, I know."

"I explained to him. I will explain it to you. I will explain it to Commissioner Wertheim if it is necessary."

Mike put down his cup and waited politely.

"It is not only that this house, this building, means a great deal to me, Michael. It does, it does. I would not deny it.

But it is more than that. Always, when my Willie was alive, and after he died, we kept the building so it would be a model for all the other tenements. Even when the depression was the worst, and I lost all the other buildings and properties, this one I kept. And this one I have continued to improve always and keep in fine condition. That's why still most of the buildings on this street are the cleanest, the most sanitary, the most up-to-date of any of the streets on the East Side. Why should they all be torn down? Mr Markham said the new buildings would be much better. Better light, better ventilation, better toilets, all kinds of modern improvements. But how do I know my tenants, my friends, will be the ones to live in the new buildings? How do I know they will be able to qualify? How do I know if they will be able to afford them? And where will they go while the wrecking and the new construction goes on? Where will they go? How long will it take?"

She looked at him anxiously.

"Your tea is getting cold. Have another cake. I made them myself."

Mike picked up a cake, but before he put it to his lips he said, "I think we can work something out."

Malka Kessler continued as though he had not spoken.

"I know Commissioner Wertheim's heart is in the right place—anyway, I think so. He wants to create a beautiful community in Rivington Village. But why can't he go to other sections of the Lower East Side? Many are much worse than Rivington Street. Much, much worse. Many *should* be torn down, and a new village built."

Mike did not really know any of the behind-the-scenes political and economic reasons why the building commissioner had laid out the area he had, with Rivington Street running right through its center. He had enough experience with politics to realize there were financial and other considerations that were not too visible to the naked, unsuspecting eye, and it would be folly to question Wertheim about the reasons. He had brought copies of the layout of the village. It was most attractively sketched, showing shrubs and trees and fountains, and low, three-story garden apartments and a shopping center. Bumbling uncharacteristically, he tried to explain the geographic and economic reasons for the selection of the specific site.

Malka listened patiently. When he was finished, she said,

"I know it will be wonderful, Michael. I think it will be even more wonderful a little to the east, or to the west, or the north or the south. We do not lack for ugly, neglected tenements to demolish, Michael. Tell the commissioner, please, I am sorry. For you, if not for the city, I would like to do it. But it is wrong. I cannot. I will not turn over my building."

Mike said he was sorry and thanked her for her time and the tea and honey cakes.

"Harry was here for dinner last Monday," she said, as he was leaving. "He was asking about you. Why do you not call him sometime at the paper? Or I could give you his home number."

"Thank you. I will, Mrs. Kessler. How is he . . . and his family?"

"Fine . . . I think," she said. "Call him."

When Mike Morrissey left, Malka Kessler felt suddenly weary. She sighed heavily and walked into the rear bedroom, which she had converted into a sort of library-study, somewhat like Mr. Borsum's. Just as seeing her again had evoked memories for Mike Morrissey, his visit stirred vivid recollections of the past in her mind. More than that, it turned her thoughts back to a project she had worked on intermittently and without a clear purpose ever since William had died in 1919. Ironically, he had lived through the murderous influenza scourge, though many of their friends had died, and then on Christmas Eve, as the epidemic neared its end, he had died of a heart attack in his sleep.

It was one of the saddest times in all her life. Harry had enlisted in the army almost immediately after America had entered the war in 1917. A week before William's sudden death, they had a letter from Harry, saying he was in a hospital outside Paris (perhaps the news had sparked William's cardiac arrest). Harry assured them he was not seriously wounded, just some damage to his left knee. He expected to be out of the hospital in six months, and told them that if the war was over, or he got an extended leave, he planned to stay in Paris for a while.

Malka wrote him, insisting he tell her more about where and how seriously he had been wounded. She did not tell him of his father's death. She felt he had enough troubles. He was always reluctant to complain, and she was not at all sure that he wasn't much more seriously hurt than he said. Maybe he had even lost a leg!

The funeral services for William were attended by Mike and her old friend, his father, Martin Morrissey III, and Kevin Morrissey and his beautiful wife, Lilly, and Sal Lombardi, and many of the Kesslers' other friends. Sal's wife, Bridget, had also died in the flu epidemic, and a month after her death, he received word that his son Anthony had been killed. He and Anthony had parted bitterly in 1912, when Anthony had joined the Marines. And now, before he ever had a chance to ask Anthony to forgive him for his stubborn insistence that Anthony work in the produce business, his son was gone. And Sal's daughter, Fiona, was somewhere in Europe, serving as a Red Cross nurse, and he had not heard from her in almost a year. It was a terrible, terrible time.

Malka had gone to night school for several years and learned to write quite fluently, and now in the long, lonesome nights, when she could not sleep, she began to write about her life. She did not know why this compulsion to tell the story had come over her. Surely it was not for the purpose of, let alone the hope of, publication. She realized as she wrote that she was trying to make a convincing argument that a person, perhaps especially a young girl, a woman, could lead a life of sin and shame and commit unspeakable crimes because fate so ordained it; because she was entrapped and there was no way out. And that she might kill to protect someone she loved.

She had written almost every night for two or three months after William's death, and had then put away the pages. And it was not until Harry returned in early 1920, limping as he would for the rest of his life, and married Miriam Ehrenberg in 1933, and they had their first child, little Isaac, that she began writing again. She still did not know why, although there was some vague notion in the back of her mind that she owed it to Harry (and yes, even Miriam, with whom she did not get along too well), and certainly to her little grandson, Isaac, to tell them why she had done the things she had—in case they ever heard about her time as a prostitute and the murder of Tony Roselli. Most of the time she was quite sure they never would find out about those things, and she would never show them these sad, lurid pages, but she kept writing anyway.

She had stopped again about a month ago. But the night Mike Morrissey visited her, she took the pages out of their folder in the top drawer of the desk, read them over, and then began to write again. With a pen, on clean white sheets of paper, slowly, thoughtfully, laboriously, she wrote, ". . . I did kill the man, but when I did it, it seemed the right thing to do. The only thing. No other thing could I do. Was it because of what he did to me years before—more than ten years before—or because he mistreated and threatened the life of my Harry? I do not know. But I did kill the man, and I have prayed many nights, and pray often still, that God will forgive me."

27

Commissioner Wertheim was disappointed and angry when Mike reported his lack of success with Malka Kessler.

"Goddam it, Mike!" he roared, pounding his desk, "I will not have the stubborn old witch stand in the way of the project!"

Mike said dejectedly, "I'm sorry, Commissioner, but I don't see what we can do about it."

Wertheim's eyes brightened suddenly with a fresh thought. "Did you read Harry Kessler's column this morning?"

"No, why?"

"He wrote about the Dakota, that ancient, weird-looking apartment building over on Seventy-second and Central Park West."

Mike frowned.

"I don't think it's so weird-looking, Commissioner—if you don't mind my saying so. It was designed way back in the 1880s by Henry Hardenburgh, and I think it's one of the most interesting buildings in the city. Matter of fact, my uncle Kevin and his wife lived there for years. . . . But what's that got to do with Rivington Village?"

"Maybe nothing. But Kessler writes about New York buildings every once in a while. Certainly a beautiful garden layout like our Rivington Village is as interesting as an ancient apartment house full of actors. Why don't you get together with him and show him our plans. Maybe you can persuade him to talk to his mother. Maybe he'll even do a column on the project."

Mike smiled. It was strange. Mrs. Kessler, who opposed the project, and the commissioner, who was frantically determined to execute it, were both urging him to talk to Harry Kessler. He had always liked, more than liked—admired, Harry Kessler. He was pleased when Mrs. Kessler told him Harry had asked about him. He would certainly enjoy seeing him again.

"I'm not sure he'll approve, any more than his mother, Commissioner," said Mike, "but I'll give it a try."

"I'm counting on you, son," said Wertheim. Mike thought his tone was a little more ominous than was necessary. But as Mike reached the door of his office, Wertheim called after him, jovially,. "Do you know why they called it the Dakota?"

Mike turned back and shook his head.

Wertheim said, "Because in 1884 Seventy-second Street was so far uptown nobody who was anybody lived there. They said it might as well be in Dakota territory."

The following evening Mike met Harry Kessler in the Oak Room bar at the Plaza Hotel. Harry was slouched comfortably in one of the large maroon leather chairs at a table for two. He was nibbling a handful of peanuts and finishing his fifth Beefeater on the rocks when Mike came into the room. He got to his feet and waved at Mike, and when Mike reached the table, he held out a pudgy hand, then pumped Mike's hand vigorously.

"I'm glad you called me, Mike."

He waved the younger man to a chair alongside his. "What're you drinking?"

Mike had just had three brandies to finish off a dinner with Dorothy.

"B and B, please," he said. "It's good to see you again, Harry."

Harry Kessler was about five eight, short and stocky like his grandfather. At forty-three he was bald with a fringe of grayish black hair at his temples and around his ears. He had a deeply furrowed forehead and a large nose and interesting eyes beneath shaggy, black brows. The expression in the eyes was chameleonlike. It seemed a soft blue mix of suffering, compassion, and cynical humor, any three of which elements could predominate depending on his mood and the situation of the moment. The look was magnified by the thick lenses of the horn-rim glasses he wore. A polka-dot bow tie seemed incongruous beneath his heavy, square jaw. His herringbone tweed coat was snug on his broad shoulders and his gray wool trousers seemed tight around his paunch.

"You haven't changed much, Mike," said Harry when their drinks came.

"Neither have you," said Mike, lifting his glass. Harry patted his navel. "I've put on some weight."

He sipped his gin. "I can't tell you how often I think of you Morrisseys, Mike," he said. "I hear around City Hall that you're Wertheim's fair-haired boy."

Mike shrugged. "He's a tough man to work for."

"So I hear. But he knows talent. That's why he brought you in. I understand you've put together some nice little models for his urban redevelopment schemes. I also understand you're way up on the list for the World's Fair job."

Mike looked into Harry's eyes. "Has your mother talked to you . . . about Rivington Village?"

Harry smiled. He had a warm, pleasing smile. "Yeah. She won't stand for it."

Mike nodded. "I don't want to be cute, Harry. That's why I wanted to see you." He felt his face redden, and shook away his tactless remark. "No, no. I don't mean I didn't want to see you anyway. Your mom suggested I call you, and I've been meaning to . . . ever since I saw you again at Pop's funeral. But something always seems to come up."

Harry swirled his gin around in his glass.

"Don't be embarrassed, kid. I know how those things are. Wertheim sent you to ask me to see if I could talk Mama into going along with the village plan."

Mike nodded. "Yes, but—like I said, Harry—I would have—I wanted to—"

Harry finished his gin and waved to the waiter for a refill of both their drinks. He sighed.

"This is a helluva situation, Mike. I think Mama is crazy, insisting she has to hang on to that old Rivington Street building. I've been trying for years to get her to move out to a nice place on Long Island, or up in Westchester—out in the country, kind of. But I also understand her feeling about wanting to stay there. She's the angel of Rivington Street, and she likes that."

"Yeah, I understand too," said Mike.

"I also know how fanatical Wertheim is about the village,"

said Harry. "And I figured he would get around to asking you to turn Mama around."

The waiter set down the fresh drinks and Harry immediately took a long sip of his. He was beginning to feel mellow. The look of suffering blended with the look of compassion in his eyes, and the cynical cast was gone.

"Our families go back a long way, Mike," he said sentimentally. "I don't know if you know how far back. A lot of it was before your time."

Mike nodded.

"Before you were born, kid, when I was about ten or eleven, your mom and dad took care of me, while my parents were going through hell."

Mike looked at him questioningly.

"Some thugs kidnapped me—believe it or not. And Mama killed one of them, and the other guy fell in front of a subway train while he was rasslin' with my father. The cops and the D.A.'s people tied my parents up for weeks and weeks. One antisemitic deputy D.A. was pushing to indict my father on a murder charge. Mama was in no condition to take care of me and run the house, and Papa wasn't in much better shape. Your mom, Hannah, saw me through a couple of months there when I didn't know if I was going to live or die."

He gulped another swallow of his gin.

"*Nightmares!* Jesus Christ! I thought I'd never stop having them! Night after night I'd wake up screaming! Scared the neighbors half to death. If it wasn't for your mom, I don't know what would have happened to me."

"I never heard a word about that," said Mike.

"Yeah. Hannah Morrissey and Marty, God bless them. They were right there! And did you know that when I got out of journalism school at Columbia, your dad got me my first job in the Washington bureau of the *Trib*? A gofer I was, but it was the foot in the door. And then, when they gave me a crack at covering a beat, your dad tipped me to many a good story."

"I had no idea," said Mike. "But Pop knew talent when he saw it too."

Harry stared into his gin glass as though it were a crystal ball.

"And your uncle Kevin, poor bastard, you remember all he did for me? Him and your aunt Lilly?"

"I remember you around the Lilly Pad," said Mike. "I

remember you came in the night Uncle Kevin and Aunt Lilly and Pop gave me a big birthday party at the Pad. Sixteen, I was . . . and you gave me that portable radio. What a present! Nobody had a radio then. You know, I took it with me when I went to Georgetown. And some rat stole it right out of my room."

Mike paused and his eyes moistened.

"I sure loved Uncle Kevin and Aunt Lilly! Christ, they were fun!"

When Prohibition came in, in 1920, Kevin Morrissey had soon gone into rum-running. He was fifty-two and Lilly was forty-seven and Kevin had taken to gambling again, and Lilly was getting a little long in the tooth for an actress. Particularly since she was never quite skillful enough to make it in character parts. The rum-running led to the opening of a speakeasy, which then became a nightclub, called the Lilly Pad.

It was one of the most successful clubs of that wild twenties era, and Lilly rivaled Texas Guinan as the day's most beloved, uninhibited, happy-go-lucky hostess. Kevin had conceived the idea for the club. The tabletops were all in the shape of lily pads, and on each one squatted a ceramic frog with an unbelievably charming and comic expression on his wide-lipped face, and a lascivious wink, one eye closed, the other bulging and wide open. The dance floor was glazed to look like a pond, and was dotted with pads, which were dark-green-tinted mirrors. The mirrors reflected soft, moonlight-like recessed lights in the ceiling and the bottom portions of the dancers. The naughty girls who wore no panties were teased mercilessly.

The clientele of the Lilly Pad consisted of an assortment of celebrities: Broadway stars, racketeers, show girls, society people, and a sprinkling of out-of-town buyers on unlimited expense accounts. Most of them spent the early evening and night at the Pad before proceeding uptown to the Cotton Club. Lilly greeted them all with a boisterous "Come on in, you bacchanalian bums!" and hugged the men and kissed the women warmly on the cheeks. The waitresses in the Pad wore lily-pad bras with small lecherous, winking and grinning frogs at the nipples, and green tights with another, slightly larger frog over the pubic mound. The waitresses were all young and attractive and had no trouble selling champagne and Scotch at $25 a bottle; $10 for a pint of rye; $2 for a pitcher of water; ginger ale for $1.50 per glass. They also sold grosses of rag dolls for $5 per doll.

"You wanna buy a doll for your baby doll, don'cha?" they cooed to the macho escorts, and the men did. The big spenders also bought their babies paper gardenias or magnolias for a dollar each, or for $5 a boutonniere of tiny real roses.

Kevin was as hospitable, boisterous, and lovable a host as Lilly was a hostess. It was said that he knew more bawdy jokes and stories than anyone in the city. Kevin and Lilly gave Mike a saxophone for his birthday, a very expensive and sweet-toned alto. Mike had been goggle-eyed with excitement. He even thought he was in love with one of the waitresses. Three weeks after the birthday celebration, when Kevin and Lilly got into their Packard touring car outside the club one morning about four-thirty, and Kevin turned on the ignition, there was a tremendous explosion. Kevin and Lilly and the automobile were blown to pieces. The blast even knocked the glass eye out of the winking frog on the Lilly Pad's canopy. No one ever did find out whether the perpetrators were people with whom Kevin had gambling troubles, or rivals from his rum-running days, or what.

Now Mike took a long drink of the B & B, and shook his head, and said again, "They were more fun than anybody I ever knew."

Harry nodded vigorously and caught a waiter going by and ordered another round.

"You're goddam right they were, Mike. Fun, and they helped everybody. When I got back from the dumb war, limping a little, the paper wanted me to work on the city desk in New York, reading copy. I couldn't stand an inside, desk job. I finally persuaded them to put me back on the police beat, and inside of a week I broke one of the hottest stories of the year. You know who tipped me to it?"

"Sure," said Mike, picking up his fresh brandy. "Uncle Kev! He knew everybody. I wish they'da caught the sonsabitches who killed him and Aunt Lilly."

"He steered me to more racket stories than any ten reporters in the city ever broke. I got three raises and five bonuses in one year."

He paused and shook his head.

"Sometimes I think maybe he and Lilly were killed because of one of those tips he gave me."

Mike said, "Don't be silly, Harry. He was much too smart for that." He drank a long drink of his B & B, and put down his glass with a sharp crack.

"I hate those goddam hoodlums! Did you know my great-uncle Ned was killed by some punks down on the East Side? He was retired, an inspector in the P.D."

Harry was staring into his crystal ball again. There was less than half an inch of gin left in the bottom of the glass. He nodded somberly. His words were beginning to slur.

"An' your uncle Sal," he said.

Bridget Morrissey's husband, Sal Lombardi, had been killed nine years earlier, in 1926, at age sixty-three. Two thugs waylaid him as he left the produce market one night. One held him, while the other ripped out his jugular with a savage swipe of a baling hook. He had been resisting a racket-dominated union. Those two murderers were caught and wound up in Sing Sing.

"Poor Fiona," muttered Mike, recalling his uncle Sal's death. Fiona was the only surviving member of that branch of the Morrissey family. Harry finished his gin and waved the glass at the waiter.

"You know I wanted to marry Fiona?" he asked Mike.

Mike looked startled. "I didn't even know you knew her. Didn't you just meet her at the funeral?"

"Yeah," said Harry. "But I fell in love with her right away. I waited almost a month after her father died, then I called her for a date."

"Oh. I was probably back at school by then."

"Yeah, you were. I think you and your dad went back to D.C. the day after the funeral."

Mike nodded.

"We began to go out a lot, " said Harry. "She was the only person in the world I could ever talk to about the goddam war. You know she was a Red Cross nurse."

"Yeah, I know. I think she saw as much action as most of the guys."

"Sure did!" said Harry, and sipped at his gin. "She was one of the nurses in the field hospital at Saint-Mihiel. Christ! What a mess! But she must'a got there just before or right after I was discharged. We never could figure it out. There was no way of keeping track of the days. Anyway, about a year after we began dating I asked her to marry me."

Mike drank brandy and waited.

"She was nursing at St. Vincent's then, and going to school at night," said Harry.

"Oh," said Mike. "I didn't know she was going to school. At . . . let's see . . . thirty, thirty-five, seems a little old to go back to school."

"Still going," said Harry. "I think she's due to finish up in a year or two. She's going to be a doctor. That's why she didn't want to get married. To anybody. Not just me. Anybody."

"Good girl!" said Mike. "Always was."

"She was about eighteen when your great-uncle Pat died of cancer . . . and then her mother passed on, two, three months later. She took care of both of them in their last days. She made up her mind then to be a nurse. In France, later, she decided she was going to become a doctor."

"Jesus Christ, Harry! You know more about my family than I do."

Harry finished his Beefeater. His words were definitely slurring now, and his eyes were wet behind his thick glasses.

"I told you, Mike. I owe a lot to you Morrisseys."

Mike was drunkenly embarrassed on two counts: that Harry did, indeed, know so much more about his family than he; and that he, Mike, was now in the position of asking Harry a favor, which Harry might feel he must grant to pay for the Morrisseys' kindnesses to him—none of which Mike himself had bestowed.

"How's your family?" he asked, to turn the conversation away from the Morrisseys and the depressing stories they had found themselves recalling. Harry stared at him long and sadly. The cynical expression subtly changed the blue of his eyes.

"I waited less than a year after Fiona said no," he said. "An' then I married Miriam. You know Miriam?"

"Dorothy mentioned her to me a couple of times. They're friends, right? She sculs—er—scluptts?"

"Yeah, she's a sculp'er," said Harry. "A lousy one, I think, though Christ knows she spends enough time in her goddam studio in the Village. She an' Dorothy belong to some of those pinko groups together."

He gulped his gin, and said, "You and Dorothy Wertheim have been seeing a lot of each other, I hear. Anything serious?"

Mike shrugged. "Not too. I don't know. Wertheim encourages us a lot."

The cynical cast in Harry's eyes deepened. "Could cinch the World's Fair assignment, maybe?"

Again Mike shrugged. "Wouldn't hurt, I guess." He drank brandy. "You have a little boy, too, don't you?"

"Yeah," said Harry. "Isaac. Cute little bugger. But he's being brought up by a goddam French governess. His mother is too fucking busy sclup'ing and saving the world... and fucking. She's got a thing going with some bearded phony on *The Daily Worker*."

He sighed. "And his father... well, his father ain't much of a father."

"How old is Isaac?"

"Seven. Maybe I'll straighten out and we'll be pals when he gets older."

"Sure," said Mike.

"I'll talk to Mama, Mike," said Harry abruptly. "I don't know if I can convince her to go along with Rivington Village, but I'll try. It makes sense, and... I know it'll help you.... And I sure as hell owe the Morrisseys."

"Not me, Harry," said Mike. "You don't owe me a thing. You don't owe any of us, but I'll appreciate anything you can do."

Harry reached into his pocket to pay the check, but Mike held him by the wrist.

"On me, Harry. On the city of New York."

They rose unsteadily from the table. Harry put his arm around Mike's waist, and Mike put his arm around Harry's shoulder, and rocking and heaving—Harry a bit more so because of his limp—they made their way out of the bar. Outside Mike asked the doorman to get them a cab. Harry said, "Mike, did you know that Miriam's father, Walter Ehrenberg, made his fortune in toilet paper?"

Mike said, "No shit? No connection intended."

"Yeah," said Harry. "During the war. We used a lot of it over there."

The answer was no! Four days after their liquid night at the Plaza bar, Harry called Mike at his office.

"I'm sorry, kid. I truly did everything I could. I reasoned, I begged, I said it meant your whole future, but no. Mama loves Rivington Street, and that's it. I'm really sorry."

"Thanks for trying, Harry. Let's get together when you have time."

"I always have time. When?"

"Lunch? Friday?"

They had lunch at Fraunces Tavern, but Mike was uneasy all through the meal. Nathan Wertheim had come up with some very sketchy, but scandalous, information about Malka Kessler's earlier years. He insisted that Mike search out the fullest details.

"If it's what I think it is," said Wertheim, "the *Journal*, the *News*, or the *Mirror* will be glad to run it. Maybe we can still force the old lady to come around."

Mike had expressed surprise and shock at the idea that Wertheim was willing to blackmail Mrs. Kessler, and the commissioner had made it very clear that Mike do the deed or else! Or else no World's Fair! Or else, also, no job! Or else, also, maybe no job ever with a top architectural firm in the whole city of New York!

"There's also black*ball*, young man, if you're so touchy about black*mail*," he said bluntly. "Who the hell wants a man you can't depend on!"

At the lunch, when Harry asked Mike how badly his failure to deliver Mrs. Kessler would damage him at the office, Mike shrugged.

"It's not going to help, Harry. But I know you tried, and I appreciate it."

He spent the next two full days in the morgue of *The New York Times* making profuse notes on Malka Kessler's testimony before the Lexow Committee, and at the trial of Joseph Wilensky, Anthony Roselli, and Mrs. Krimsky. He also noted the full details of the deaths of Wilensky and Roselli. The Lexow hearing reminded him of the recent hearings conducted by Judge Samuel Seabury, which exposed the worst political and police corruption the city had ever known, resulting in the resignation of the playboy mayor Jimmy Walker.

The thirty-year-old Roselli-Wilensky kidnapping and deaths stunned Mike. No wonder Harry had nightmares! And he found it difficult to believe that Malka Kessler had actually been a whore.

After his second long day at the *Times* he met Dorothy for dinner at the Gloucester House.

"Wow!" said she, halfway through the meal. "You sure are mute and sullen tonight, lover. And if you don't stop drinking, and eat a little of that sole, I'll have to carry you out of here."

"I don't feel like eating! And I don't feel like talking! And if you don't like it, you can go fuck yourself!" he said angrily.

People at nearby tables stared at them. It was what Mike really felt like saying to Wertheim, but his career meant far too much to him. He was trying to tell himself that Mrs. Kessler was just being too stubborn and unreasonable, and surely when he told her they would reveal her sordid past if she did not cooperate, she would go along with them. He finished his sixth Chivas Regal on the rocks and said to Dorothy, "After it's done, she'll be glad she did it. It'll be a great development, and she'll enjoy living there, or maybe out in the country."

"What the hell are you talking about, Morrissey?" said Dorothy. He stared at her stupidly, and waved his hand, and got up from the table and said, "You don't mind finishing dinner alone, do you, Dorothy? I gotta see a woman about a murder and some whoring!"

He bumped a couple of irritated diners on his way out of the restaurant. He took a cab up to his apartment on Seventy-third Street and spent the night organizing his material on Malka Kessler's dark past.

28

Malka Kessler's chin quivered and her eyes were wet, but she drew a deep breath and held back the tears. She took another deep breath and clenched her hands before she said, "It means this much to you, Mikey? You would do this to me for Commissioner Wertheim?"

Mike Morrissey was just drunk enough to have total control of his voice and actions, and still maintain a spiritual numbness. His appointment with Mrs. Kessler had been for seven o'clock this Tuesday night, and he had left the office at five and gone around the corner to P. J. Moriarty's and had a number of drinks. Now the notes he had made from the 1905 copies of *The New York Times* lay on the long marquetry coffee table in Malka Kessler's parlor. They were a bit scattered but all still more or less in chronological order. Malka had not gone through all of them, but she knew from those she had read carefully that Mike had done a very thorough job.

"Not for Wertheim," Mike said now, sounding gruffer than

he intended. "For Rivington Village. For the finest planned urban redevelopment project in the nation."

A voice inside his head said, *Morrissey, you're full of shit!* but he ignored it. Malka Kessler said nothing of the kind. She said, "It will not be a good thing for Harry to learn all this. Miriam, she might like it, she might gloat a little. And for Isaac, when he grows a little older, maybe even now, it will be very bad."

"Harry knows all about Wilensky and Roselli," Mike said, sounding a little less gruff. "After all, he was the one that was kidnapped."

Malka shook her head. "Not that I was a whore, he doesn't know."

Having no answer, Mike began to reassemble the papers on the table. He made them into a neat, even-edged pile and put them back into the large manila folder he had brought along. He put the folder into his leather briefcase.

"Don't make me give these to the newspapers, Mrs. Kessler,"he said coldly. The voice inside his head said, *How can you be such a prick!* Still he ignored it.

"You go along, Mrs. Kessler," he said, trying to sound like a nephew, giving advice to a not-too-bright old aunt, "and when it's all over, you'll see that it was the right thing to do. You'll be proud of Rivington Village. You can say to yourself, 'I—I made it possible.' "

She stared at him as though she felt very sorry for him; sorry for both of them. She nodded and said, "You leave me no choice, Mikey. I cannot have these terrible things printed for all the world to know. For Harry and Isaac and his children to be ashamed forever."

Nausea swirled in Mike's stomach, but he said, "It's a wise decision, Mrs. Kessler. You won't regret it."

He started to rise, but she came to him and placed her hand gently on his shoulder.

"Sit a minute . . . please," she said. "Excuse me."

She went toward the rear of the flat and returned in a few moments with a large envelope. She handed him the envelope.

"Please read this, young Mike. I care about you. I care what you think of me. I want, if it is possible, that you should understand why everything happened."

He took the envelope and slipped it into his briefcase. He bowed to her and walked to the door. When he opened it, he looked back at her. She was still holding back the tears.

"You'll—you'll be glad, Mrs. Kessler," he said, and suddenly felt as though he were going to cry himself. "When it's all over, you'll be glad."

He decided against dinner. He did not feel like eating. He took a cab from Rivington Street back to his apartment. In his liquor cabinet he had an uncorked fifth of Chivas Regal. He went to the refrigerator and took out some ice cubes and poured himself a long Chivas on the rocks in a tall highball glass. And he filled it to within an eighth of an inch from the top.

Well, you did it! said the voice in his head. *Proud of yourself?* Mike not only ignored the voice but with a defiant stride went to the phone on his desk and called Wertheim at his Park Avenue home.

"All done, Commissioner," he said. "Mrs. Kessler will go along!"

Wertheim chuckled. "Congratulations, son!" he said. "I knew you would deliver!"

"Thanks, Commissioner."

"And by the way, Mike," said Wertheim, "I had a dinner meeting with four of the members of the World's Fair committee. You're it . . . but don't say anything yet."

For some reason the triumphant surge Mike had anticipated did not come. Instead the voice in his head spoke again, with cutting sarcasm. *Yeah! Congratulations, shithead! So what if you wreck the life of one mule-headed old lady!*

Again Mike ignored it. "Time to celebrate!" he told himself aloud.

He put on an Oscar Peterson record. The man's delicate and tasteful pianistics did nothing at all for him. He lifted the tonearm and turned off the phonograph. He sat down in a chair by the window and stared out into the darkness of Seventy-third Street. Mike took a long swallow of his drink and pushed himself back up out of the chair and went to the desk and took out the envelope Mrs. Kessler had given him.

He turned on the floor lamp beside his reading chair and began to read the pages. The handwriting was Old World, but attractive and readable, with wide margins and plenty of space between the lines. He was halfway through the two hundred and sixteen pages before he realized he had not taken another sip of his drink. The ice cubes had melted and he walked grimly out to the sink in the kitchen and poured the drink down the drain. He was cold sober and the sick feeling in his stomach had intensified. He walked back to his reading chair and picked up the pages and continued to read. Mrs. Kessler had taken her story through to the time when Harry had told her he was going to marry Miriam Ehrenberg. She was not against Harry marrying. It was not that. She had prayed that he would marry Fiona Lombardi. But she instinctively realized that Miriam was a neurotic, confused, spoiled, rich pseudoradical, who would make Harry's life miserable.

"Let me be wrong, dear God," she wrote. "Let the marriage be a happy one, blessed with many healthy children."

Mike thought about Harry's comments on the marriage and little Isaac. He put the manuscript down on the table beside the lamp and lay back in the chair with his eyes closed. After a while he went to his briefcase and took out his notes. Hastily he read through them once more. It was incredible! The facts were basically the same, but he had the feeling that he had read two completely different stories. Mrs. Kessler's narration of her childhood in Prosnica; of the excitement she and her mother and the entire village had felt at the arrival of the wealthy Mr. Wilensky from New York; her horror at discovering she was entrapped into a life of prostitution; her brave and hopeless rebellions and her futile, unsophisticated attempts to escape the life shed new light on the cold recital of her days on Allen Street as reported in the *Times*.

Mike read through Malka Kessler's entire manuscript again. *What courage it must have taken for her to attempt the escape; what a sacred regard for life, to fight off the urgent advice that she abort her child. Could anyone blame Malka Kessler for killing a man who stole that child and threatened his young life?*

"Harry!" he said aloud, as though Kessler were there in the room with him. "Your mama was one helluva woman!"

He realized as he reread the story that Malka had indeed spent all her years, virtually day and night after her marriage to William, in helping the people on the Lower East Side. No wonder she had come to be called the Angel of Rivington Street, as much as she was embarrassed by the hyperbolic term. She had obviously redeemed herself for whatever sins she had committed, by her dedication to the welfare of her ghetto neighbors. She had become an inseparable part of the neighborhood, in some ways its very heart. It was plain why she did not want the character of her own beloved streets changed.

It dawned on Mike that it would be criminal to force her to agree to the destruction of her building. Even as the ethical and moral certainty of this grew in his mind, he realized it was too late. The deed was done. He had already told Wertheim it was all set. He poured himself a tumblerful of Scotch, not bothering with the ice cubes. He took a long drink and flopped on the leather couch across the room from the windows. He put the drink down on the glass coffee table and slapped his palm down hard on the couch, over and over and over.

"Shit!" he said angrily.

The phone rang. He picked it up and said, irritatedly, "Yeah?"

"Mike?" asked a male voice.

"Yeah, yeah. Who's this?"

"It's Harry. What the hell did you do?"

"Oh . . . you talked to your mother—"

"Yeah. I just left her. You turned her into a zombie. How the hell did you get her to agree to tear down the building?"

"Didn't she tell you?"

"No. She just said you came and explained to her that it was the best thing to do—not just for the city, for her too."

"Yeah, I told her that—"

"But that's the same thing I told her. How come she could see it when you told her, and not when I told her? And she's acting like she doesn't give a shit."

"Harry?"

"Yeah, Mike. What the hell happened?"

"Harry, come on over. You know where I live?"

"No."

Mike told him.

"Be there in fifteen minutes," said Harry.

It was twenty-two minutes.

"You want a drink?" asked Mike. He had already broken out a bowl of ice cubes and had the Beefeater and the Chivas on the table beside the liquor cabinet.

"Yeah, please," said Harry. "The gin, on the rocks."

Mike made the drink and handed it to him.

"So what happened?" demanded Harry. "Did you drug her?"

They sat alongside each other on the leather sofa. Mike frowned, trying to determine the best way to begin. Finally he said, "How much do you know about your mother's past, Harry? Her teen years, when she first came to New York."

Harry looked puzzled. He shrugged. "She came from Prosnica in Poland. Her mother and father died. She went to work for the Borsums."

"Do you know anything about the Lexow hearings in the city on crime and police and political corruption?"

"You mean the Seabury investigation?"

"No, no. Lexow. He was a Republican state senator. This was back in 1894."

"What the hell is this, Mike? A question-and-answer game? I do a New York column, but I'm no goddam city historian!"

Mike got up and got his notes from the table beside the reading lamp and handed them to Harry.

"Run through these," he said quietly.

Harry finished off his gin, put down his tumbler, wiped his fingers on his trousers, and took the papers from Mike. He began to read. Mike had finished his own drink, so he took Harry's empty glass and refilled it and his own, and sat down on the sofa. He watched Harry, as Harry read. He felt perspiration forming on his brow and upper lip and a wetness in his armpits.

"Holy Christ!" said Harry. He read quietly again for a time, and he, too, began perspiring. Finally he said, "Mama a hooker! I can't believe it!"

He shook his head in wonder and disbelief.

"Why don't you open the goddam window, Mike?" he said. Mike walked across the room and lifted the window. A chill October wind wafted into the room.

"I showed your mother these notes, Harry," Mike said, standing over Harry, his voice quavering. "I told her unless she went along with the Rivington Village plan, we'd give them to the papers."

Harry looked at him, stunned. "You what? You sonuvabitch!"

He started to get up from the sofa. Mike said, "Hit me if you want to, Harry. Go ahead! Any prick as stupid as me deserves at least a belt in the mouth."

Harry sank back on the sofa with a deep sigh. He held his head in his hands and weaved back and forth. Mike walked back to the table by the reading lamp and brought Malka Kessler's manuscript over to Harry.

"We've got to figure some way out of this, Harry. Here— He held out Harry's mother's papers. "Read this."

Harry's blue eyes registered a mix of anger, suffering, and confusion behind the thick lenses. He took the papers.

"I don't know if your mother would want you to read it, but I think you've got to. We've got to find some way to turn this around."

Puzzled, Harry turned his attention to his mother's manuscript. He recognized her handwriting immediately. He began to read. In fifteen minutes he was weeping quietly as he read. He put the manuscript on the coffee table, took a kerchief from his pocket, removed his horn-rim glasses and wiped his eyes, then the glasses. He put the glasses back on and resumed reading. He was fighting to get his sobbing under control again, when he put the papers back on the table once more.

"I—I don't understand, Mike. You scared Mama into agreeing to the Village deal by threatening to give this thirty-year-old crap to the papers. Now you say you're sorry you did, you want to turn it around."

Mike nodded several times with a hopeless look on his face.

"So," said Harry. "What's the problem? You burn these notes. You go tell Mama you've changed your mind, she doesn't have to give up the building, and everybody's happy, right?"

Mike shook his head. He got up and fixed two more drinks, handed one to Harry, and said glumly, "You're as shook up as I am, Harry. It's not that simple. It's too late. I've already told Wertheim she agreed. He knows all about the notes on her background. He read them through before I showed them to your mother."

"Does he have a copy? Does anybody?"

"No, but that doesn't matter. He knows the story. He gave me the original scuttlebutt on it and assigned me to dig up the details. If I destroy these notes, he'll just have someone else dig out the material and do them all over again. . . . And he'll sure as hell give them to the papers if your mother doesn't go along."

Harry nodded, and began to pace up and down the room. His limp was barely noticeable.

"Yeah, I see. Close the window, Mike, will you? It's freezing in here."

Mike did, and Harry, still pacing, said viciously, "He is one filthy, ruthless, blackmailing bastard!"

"All of that," agreed Mike.

Harry stopped pacing suddenly and faced Mike. He was near the reading lamp and its light magnified the sudden gleam in his eyes behind the thick lenses.

"How much do you know about Dorothy Wertheim?" he asked.

Mike shrugged. "Some. She went to Sarah Lawrence. She works for Hallie Flanagan at the Federal Theater Project. Goes to a lot of meetings. She's a jazz buff... kind of a slob."

"No!" said Harry. "Her political affiliations?"

"I don't know, Harry. She babbles on about the Young Socialists this, and the People's Confederation for that—I never pay any attention."

Harry said, "I know Miriam is a card-carrying member of the Communist Party, and I think Dorothy may be too."

"You do?"

"I have a friend in the FBI. I can check it out."

Mike caught the fever of excitement in Harry's voice. "You mean... if she is... we'll go to Wertheim and—"

"You're fucking well right, Mike! The papers might be even more interested in a 1935 story about the young Commie daughter of the distinguished politician Commissioner Nathan Wertheim, than in a thirty-year-old rehash of the life of a little Polish hooker."

On the morning of the second day after their meeting, Mike walked into the office of Commissioner Wertheim. He did not bother to knock. The commissioner was meeting with a man from Mayor LaGuardia's office.

"I want to talk to you, Commissioner," said Mike.

Wertheim frowned, and his gray-haired visitor looked surprised and annoyed. "I'm in a meeting, Mike! Can't you see? This is Harvey Schlesinger, the mayor's—"

"Sorry, Mr. Schlesinger," said Mike. "I hate to break up your meeting, but this can't wait."

Wertheim said coldly, menacingly, "What the hell is the matter with you, Mike? Have you gone mad? I'll talk with you when we're through."

Mike smiled at him and said, "No, now!"

Mr. Schlesinger, his face pink, got up from his chair, and

went to the coat rack, got his hat and coat, and headed for the door.

"It's all right, Nathan," he said, looking fearfully at Mike. "I'll call you later."

Mike's hair looked like he had walked miles, hatless, in a strong wind. His eyes were bloodshot. In the last two anxious days he had not slept much, and had drunk more than usual. When the door closed behind Schlesinger, Wertheim stood up.

"Now explain this, you young idiot! Are you drunk? Have you—"

Mike walked to the desk and stood directly opposite the furious, red-faced commissioner.

"I've burned the notes on Mrs. Kessler. I've told her she doesn't have to go along with the Rivington Village project. I told her I was sure I could convince you it should be moved a quarter mile to the east, so it doesn't touch Rivington Street. We can call it Wertheim Village or N.W. Plaza or something like that."

Mike was speaking faster and with greater enthusiasm and emphasis than Wertheim had ever heard him.

"You *are* crazy! You're stark, raving, absolutely, totally out of your mind! How dare you—"

Mike moved to the chair beside Wertheim's desk and sat down.

"Sit down, Commissioner," he said pleasantly. "I want to tell you about Dorothy."

Wertheim flopped into his chair.

"Dorothy?"

"Yeah . . . Pumpkin," said Mike. "She's a card-carrying member of the Communist Party. One of their hottest young workers."

"Mike, have you been taking drugs? Do you know what you're saying—"

"I have a copy of her membership card and some copies of official Young Communist worker lists with specific assignments. Pumpkin has some interesting ones."

He reached into the inside pocket of his coat and withdrew two pages of paper, folded three times. He unfolded them and placed them on the desk before Wertheim. The commissioner stared first at one, then the other. In the center of one page was a photocopy of Dorothy Wertheim's membership card, and the other page contained five paragraphs describing her current assignments and activities. Wertheim looked at Mike, wide-eyed, his face turning pale. With trembling hands he crushed the two pages before him.

"That's all right, Commissioner," said Mike. "I have copies. You can keep those."

Wertheim glared at Mike, breathing hard.

"You ungrateful young bastard!" he spat.

Mike smiled at him.

"Even deal, Commissioner. We don't blackmail Mrs. Kessler into going along with Rivington Village, and I don't blackmail you by exposing Dorothy as Little Red Riding Hood."

"I—I—I thought you loved Dorothy, you bastard!"

"I like her a lot, Commissioner. A lot better than I like you, but I like Mrs. Kessler even more."

"You don't expect to continue to work for me, do you?"

"Gosh, no! I've already cleared out my desk. I'll leave today."

Wertheim said, with some hesitation, "You—you don't—you don't expect the World's Fair job, do you? I mean—you wouldn't use Dorothy's—Dorothy's activities to try to blackmail me into getting you that assignment . . . ?"

Mike shook his head.

"No. Don't worry about it, Commissioner. I don't want that job—any job—that badly."

Two weeks after Mike had resigned so unceremoniously, he and Harry Kessler took Harry's mother to lunch in the restaurant on the lower plaza in Rockefeller Center. Even through the grim years of the depression, while shacks and shanties were being slapped together in Hoovervilles on the edges of big cities all over the country, midtown New York had added to its sky-climbing glories. Along with the Empire State Building and the spectacular Chrysler Tower, Rockefeller Center was one of the three major building projects completed during those years. The thirty-one-story office building, with the grandiloquent Radio City Music Hall on its street level, had been finished in 1932. And the seventy-story RCA building, which housed the National Broadcasting Company, and the French and British buildings in the center were opened a year later. On this early November Sunday afternoon the Kesslers and Mike Morrissey had a table at the window of the restaurant, and they could look out at the brightly clad, graceful skaters, whirling about on the ice rink.

It was a celebration that, too soon, turned into something else. Malka Kessler again thanked Mike for persuading Commissioner Wertheim to change his mind. Mike had returned her manuscript to her without telling her that Harry had read it. They had both decided that it would be better to spare Mrs. Kessler the embarrassment of knowing that Harry had learned her past. The Rivington Village Plan had already been dropped, and Mike had been informed by a friend in Wertheim's office that Wertheim was working with a private corporation to create a project that would involve the tenements on Monroe, Market, Cherry, and Catherine Streets. It would be called Knickerbocker Village.

To Mrs. Kessler's repeated thanks, Mike said, "Please, Mrs. Kessler. Harry deserves more of the thanks than I. Without him I never would have been able to persuade the commissioner to change his mind."

"But was it necessary for you to leave your job, Mikey?"

Mike shrugged. "It wasn't what I hoped it would be," he said. "I'll be happier working with some big architectural firm."

Harry had been strangely uncommunicative all through the lunch. From the time he had ordered their drinks he had made spasmodic efforts to appear cheerful and celebratory, but most of the time he lapsed into moody silences. As Mike began to detail his plans, Harry stared at the untouched steak sandwich on his plate. Mrs. Kessler touched Mike's arm to interrupt him, and looked at her son.

A brooding sorrow showed behind Harry's thick lenses. He nodded wearily.

"I have to tell you sooner or later," he said. "Miriam wants a divorce."

Malka reached out and took his hand.

"She wants to marry Morris," Harry said. "A guy on *The Daily Worker* she's been seeing."

Mike said, "I'm sorry, Harry."

"Probably for the best," said Harry.

His mother said, "What will happen with Isaac?"

Harry said, "I'll have him. Miriam and Morris are going to live in Moscow. She's not fighting me for him."

Malka Kessler and Mike both expressed deep, compassionate regret over the breakup of the marriage, and the entire mood of what had started out to be a celebratory luncheon changed. All three of them felt uneasy and depressed. But

Malka, in her secret heart, could not help feeling a joyful flush over the possibility that she might somehow be involved in raising Isaac. She thought how nice it would be to have a little boy to look after once more.

PART NINE

Laura and Bill Van Gelder

David Kessler

Peter, Brian,
Frank, and Tom Morrissey

Eddie Ferraro

Leslie Kramer Hill and Robeson Hill

Eva Konyi, the Hungarian Psychic

Adventures in the Retail Drug
Capital of the World

Martin, the Meddling Leprechaun

Tulips on Rivington Street

"Since 1976 when we began to pick ourselves off the floor of the fiscal crisis, real estate developments have bolstered New York City's pre-eminence as a headquarters site for the world's leading corporations and financial institutions. . . . In 1976, only two office buildings were completed, offering only half a million square feet of space. Last year, four buildings reached completion with 2.7 million square feet. This year will see the addition of fifteen buildings with 7.5 million square feet and next year we expect seventeen buildings will be completed with 12 million square feet."

—Mayor Edward I. Koch, *New York, New York '82*, supplement to *The New York Times*, October 31, 1982

"Even a newspaper man, if you entice him into a cemetery at midnight, will believe in phantoms, for every one is a visionary, if you scratch him deep enough. But the Celt is a visionary without scratching."

—William Butler Yeats, Introduction to *Irish Folk Stories and Fairy Tales*

29

Leslie Kramer Hill shook the single dice in the deep cup vigorously and stared expectantly at Laura Van Gelder. Laura's pert oval face was puckered, eyes tightly shut in fierce concentration. She brushed vagrant silver-blond hair back from her cheek, opened her eyes, and said, "Four!"

Leslie threw the dice and it clacked and tumbled across the oak hardwood surface of the chrome-legged chess-checker table. Laura's cerulean eyes, wide, unblinking, followed the bouncing cube, willing it to make a final flop to the four-dotted surface. It did. Laura leaped to her feet and clapped her hands triumphantly. Leslie looked up at her, smiling, her narrow, long-nosed Streisand-like face expressing tolerance and encouragement in equal measure.

"Twice out of fourteen tries is not the most spectacular demonstration of psychokinesis I've ever heard about," she said, putting the dice back into the cup. Laura sat down.

"Right. Go again."

As Leslie shook the dice, they heard the sound of a key scraping in the lock of the front door. Eddie Ferraro came in. He was holding a brown paper bag as he strode through the small foyer into the expansive white brick-walled living room of the converted SoHo loft.

"You two shooting craps?" he called out, heading toward the kitchen.

"Hi, Ed," greeted Laura. "We're doing psychokinesis experiments."

Leslie kept shaking the dice. Eddie paused at the kitchen entrance, looked back, and said, "Jesus Christ, that again! How're you, Lady Bountiful?"

Sometimes he called Leslie Kramer Hill Lady Bountiful, a teasing reference to her deadly serious attitude toward her casework in the city's Welfare Department. Often he called her Susan B. because of her aggressive stance as president of the Lower East Side chapter of the National Organization for Women. Eddie Ferraro, himself a part of the municipal bureaucracy, was cynical about city services, and as an unblushing male chauvinist, barely tolerant of the organized feminist movement.

"I'm fine, asshole," said Leslie unhappily, and stopped shaking the dice. She put the cup on the table.

"You know it'll never work with this disbeliever in the room," she said to Laura. "You remember when he pissed all over the general extrasensory perception card tests."

"Oh, Eddie," complained Laura. "It was just beginning to work. . . . What have you got there?"

"I stopped at Dean and DeLuca's and got us that venison pâté. You like venison pâté, Les?"

Leslie snorted.

"Killing a deer to make a spiced mess out of his liver! How barbarian chic can you get?"

"You know Leslie's a vegetarian," said Laura.

Eddie laughed.

"I always forget. I can't believe people are vegetarians. How's Robey, Les?"

"Fine. He's meeting with the school board tonight. They want to know why he can't stop the drug dealing at the school."

"Set this stuff out while I wash up, babe, will you?" Eddie ordered Laura. She followed him into the kitchen and put the pâté and some cheeses and crackers and apples and pears out on plates. Leslie came in and helped set the repast out on the glass-topped table in the dining area. Eddie looked fresh and handsome as he joined them. He had taken off the coat and vest of his five-hundred-dollar Hart, Schaffner, and Marx suit and discarded his tie. Black, curly hair showed at the base of the V formed by the open collar of his silk shirt. He poured burgundy for the three of them.

"You can smell fall in the air," he said as he spread pâté on a cracker. He bit off half the cracker, chewed, swallowed, and drained half his glass of wine.

"When you gonna finish with the Magyar Marvel?" he asked Laura.

"We had our final meeting this morning. She checked the last of the galleys with me, and left for Raleigh. She's doing some regression demonstrations for them at the Duke University Parapsychology Lab. Then she's going home to Budapest."

"Oh! Like Les's girlhood in Barcelona!" said Eddie.

"It's true, you cynical shithead!" said Leslie. "I do have a birthmark on my inner thigh, just where it was pierced by that spiked fence."

"Three hundred years ago in Barcelona, in another lifetime, right?" scoffed Eddie. "Sure!"

Months earlier, Eva Konyi, the Hungarian psychic, who had an awesome, much-documented record as a clairvoyant, telepathist, telekinesis medium, hypnotist, and authority on reincarnation, had hypnotized Leslie Kramer Hill and regressed her to a childhood in Spain, almost three centuries earlier. The then Leslie, at age eleven, had tried to climb a spiked iron fence, and a spike had pierced her inner left thigh. The today Leslie had a birthmark on that identical spot. Eva Konyi also pointed out that the reason Leslie had learned to speak Spanish so quickly and fluently was this earlier life in Spain. Conversely Leslie had all kinds of difficulty learning French.

Leslie, and of course Laura, as editor of the Hungarian parapsychologist's new book, *All Our Lives*, subtitled: *A Psychic's Look into Your Long-ago Yesterdays and Far-away Tomorrows*, were devout believers in Eva Konyi's powers.

"She predicted Brezhnev's death," said Laura, "and she said Walesa would win the Nobel way back when he originally got in trouble over Solidarity!"

"Lucky guesses," said Eddie. "Now that she's gone, you still gonna fool with this extrasensory crap?"

"As much as I like, Eddie!" said Laura defiantly. "It's not crap. We all have extrasensory powers to some degree."

Laura had never mentioned it to her cynical roommate and lover, but she was fully convinced that she possessed some clairvoyant powers. Not developed, of course, but definitely there. On several occasions in her young life she had had premonitions of disaster. There was her first terrible experience in precognition, when she was just sixteen, in her freshman year at college. It was so devastating that years after it occurred, she still tended to wipe it out of her memory. Sometimes she was not even sure she *had* foreseen the tragic incident. But whenever she thought back on it with all the objectivity she could muster, she knew she had seen Philip kicked in the head twenty-four hours before it happened—exactly as she had envisioned it.

She had never had so precise a precognitive experience before or since, but there were other more general forebodings of disaster she would always remember. Like that day in November, twenty years ago, when she was only seven. She had awakened with an overwhelming sense that something terrible was going to happen. She cried all through breakfast, and when her mother and father asked her what was wrong all she could tell them was that she knew something bad was going to happen. They tried to reason and cajole her out of her mood, and sent her off to school. Sure enough, her brother, William, a year older than she, fell off his bike and broke his leg on the way to school that very morning. And early in the afternoon her father drove up the driveway, staggered out of the car, and into the house. He was weeping bitterly. Laura had never seen him cry before. He managed, through his sobs, to tell them that President Kennedy had been shot.

Laura knew if she ever told Eddie about that day, he would ridicule her and, in his cynical way, say her premonitions leaned heavily toward overkill. On another hot day in July, the thirteenth, in 1977 when Laura was twenty-one and had just come to New York and gone to work for the Wilson-Leigh publishing house, she had awakened with a strong feeling that something unusual was going to happen. Not necessarily bad, nor good, just extraordinary. The day passed uneventfully, until nightfall. Then a power blackout turned the city into a dark, noisy place of confusion and near-hysteria. She had bumped into a man coming out of a bar on West Fifty-first Street. It was Eddie Ferraro. They had begun to date, and a year later she was living with him.

When she mentioned this experience in precognition one night at dinner with Eddie and Leslie and Robey Hill, Eddie had said, "Ha! You knew you were going to meet a tall, dark, and handsome man, babe. But what I can't figure out is, how could you tell, in the blackout? Or maybe you just knew something great was going to happen, right?"

And Leslie had remarked, "Great, my ass! A disaster! Not the blackout! Meeting you!"

Laura and Eddie had been living together for almost five years now, and Laura felt their relationship was beginning to deteriorate. Eddie had seemed so sophisticated, so dashing, so New York at first. She had arrived in the city just a month earlier, and had started her job as an assistant editor at Wilson-Leigh the week previous to the blackout. She had never even visited New York before. Her family owned *The Courier* in Lancaster, Pennsylvania, and she had worked for eleven months as a reporter on the paper after graduating cum laude from Swarthmore College.

Swarthmore was less than ten miles from Lancaster, and only about eleven miles southwest of Philadelphia, but she only went to Philadelphia on five or six occasions. For the entire four years before her graduation Swarthmore was her entire life. Her mother, who now wrote children's books, had gone there, and so had her father, presently editor and publisher of the newspaper. In her freshman year she met and fell in love with a young premed student, Philip Cornwell. She lived in the ancient women's dorm, Parrish Hall, and Philip roomed off campus with a family in Norristown. He worked in his spare time and during the summers at the Norristown Mental Hospital.

Laura was a staff writer, and later editor of the student newspaper, and Philip was goalkeeper on the soccer team. Between the severe academic demands of the small Quaker school and their extracurricular activities, the two young people were able to spend little enough time together. In spite of, or perhaps because of, this they treasured the time they did share. On an infrequent and typical afternoon or evening date they would have a coke and hamburger at Somerville, the snack bar, then ride their bikes to Crum Wood, a forested section of the three-hundred-acre campus, and spend hours talking of their plans for their future together. Twice, in their senior year, they made love.

A week after the second time, the Swarthmore soccer team played arch rival Haverford College in the annual battle for the Hood Trophy. The day before the game, while sitting in her class in literature of the fantastic, listening to the young professor drone on about Poe, a vision appeared before her. It was so clear and sharp she might have been watching it on television. A Haverford midfielder, blond and stocky, stole the ball from a Swarthmore halfback. He dribbled past a knot of players, and ten yards from the goal the last Swarthmore defender charged to meet him. Laura could see Philip, in his flaming red T-shirt and black shorts, and the sweatband around his forehead, crouching, moving out from the net, concentrating on the contest between defender and attacker before him. Then the Haverford man feinted to his right, trickled the ball deftly to his left, and charged toward Philip. Philip hurled himself toward the ball, arms outstretched. The Haverford midfielder swung his thick, heavily muscled leg at the ball. He did not hit it squarely, and halfway through the arc of the kick, the toe of his hard soccer shoe crashed against

Philip's temple. Philip lay still on his stomach for a moment. Then his arms twitched convulsively toward his head, and he twisted over spasmodically onto his back. At his sides his fingers tore at the turf. Clutching hands full of dirt and grass, he suddenly stiffened, as though completely paralyzed. Laura felt the blood drain from her face.

The young professor looked at her anxiously.

"Miss Van Gelder! Are you all right?"

He stepped toward her, but Laura shook herself out of her reverie, and assured him that she was fine. The next day, twelve minutes into the second half, Philip was kicked into unconsciousness exactly as Laura had seen it the day before.

He was in a coma for a day and a half, and when he regained consciousness he could not remember who or where he was. He was presently still under treatment in Norristown, in the same mental hospital in which he had put so many hours helping others. The doctors said it was doubtful if he would ever fully recover. Laura visited him at least once a week for the entire year after she graduated, but he did not know her, and she finally despaired, and set about going on with her life without him.

Eddie Ferraro seemed the perfect antidote. Where Philip had been serious and introverted, Eddie was outgoing and fun-loving, if extraordinarily cynical. Cynical and sybaritic. He had gone to Penn State and had made All-American as a wide receiver on the football team. He had planned to turn pro, but in the first game of his senior year, a two-hundred-and-twenty-pound linebacker and a hundred-and-eighty-pound cornerback hurtled into his knees from opposite directions as he was attempting to catch a pass on a quick slant-in. They tore up the cartilages in his left knee beyond repair. At least as far as a career in football was concerned. He was disappointed, but quickly developed his future in new directions.

He was the pride and joy of his uncle, Gino Ferraro, a wealthy, powerful man, reputed to be high up in the Cosa Nostra or the Mafia or whatever else the organized criminal syndicate was called. He lived in a fieldstone mansion on six acres on the North Shore of Long Island. He had been arrested six times on various charges, but never convicted. He had several legitimate businesses, including a laundry service for hotels and hospitals, and an olive oil importing company. He had financed Eddie's education, and when Eddie graduated with a degree in business administration,

Uncle Gino had gotten him a job as business manager of a plasterers' and painters' union local in the city. During the administration of Mayor Abe Beame, he had arranged for Eddie to take an executive job with the city's Department of Real Estate. When Ed Koch became mayor in 1977, Eddie was moved to a key position in the Department of Housing Preservation and Development, which took over the purchase of tax-delinquent buildings from the original Department of Real Estate. Eddie was very good at the job.

Laura learned all this, piece by fragmented piece, over the years of their relationship. Eddie was not one to talk too freely about his activities. Judging from his lifestyle, Laura realized that he had money and/or income over and above what he was paid by the city. The SoHo loft in which they lived rented for eleven hundred dollars per month. Laura insisted on paying half. Eddie had furnished it in the most expensive contemporary fashion. He had two season tickets on the forty-five-yard line to the football Giants games at Meadowland and a box at Shea Stadium for the Jets games, excellent season seats to the Knickerbocker games, and a box at Shea in spring and summer for Mets baseball.

Based entirely on unintentionally overheard snatches of telephone conversation, and an occasional flip remark made by Eddie, Laura guessed that he had private, special, and very remunerative arrangements with painting contractors, who worked on one or another of the four thousand tenement buildings the city now operated as landlord. In 1978 when the Department of Housing Preservation and Development took over from the Department of Real Estate, the city owned only six hundred occupied buildings. Today in late August of 1983 New York owned not only the four thousand occupied buildings, but an additional six thousand vacant ones.

Eddie's department estimated that there were 120,000 tenants in some 40,000 apartments in the occupied buildings in the five boroughs. Almost half the tenants had incomes of less than $7,000 per year, well below the poverty level, and the rest earned not too much more. Yet the city employed thousands of people to maintain and service the buildings, including superintendents, handymen, and other more specialized mechanics. It also operated its own boiler repair shops, and purchased and warehoused thousands upon thousands of light bulbs (fluorescent and incandescent) for hallways, fuses, plumbing fittings, mop handles, plaster of Paris, and literally scores of other items.

She suspected Eddie had other sources of even more questionable income, but she blinded herself to these suspicions. At first the sheer excitement of sharing his dashing metropolitan lifestyle and the pleasure and satisfaction she got from her own job enabled her to ignore entirely the question of the source of his wealth. As the years passed and she became increasingly convinced that much of his income derived from illegal sources, she told herself it was none of her business. Yet, for her, it marred their relationship to some degree.

Leslie Kramer Hill left the SoHo apartment about ten o'clock on the evening of the psychokinesis dice-throwing experiment. Eddie went to the west wall of the room, along the central section of which were lined up an impressive array of home-entertainment devices. There was the big-screen front-projection MGA Mitsubishi VS-524 television in its polished oak hardwood cabinet, an eight-hour Mitsubishi videocassette recorder, and a Fisher 4000B1 stereo system. Eddie took a videocassette from the scores lined up along the top shelf of the bookcase, inserted it into the VCR, and pushed the play button.

"Come and share a joint and watch the fun and games with me, babe!" he called to Laura, who came out of the kitchen where she had stacked the glasses, dishes, and silverware in the dishwasher. Eddie lighted and inhaled his high-grade marijuana cigarette. The big-screen TV had a two-channel audio system and suddenly the long room was filled with the voices and laughter of two young men and two giggly females involved in a game of strip poker.

"Bet you a bra and raise you my panties," said one of the girls.

Laura glanced toward the screen and saw the large-bosomed bettor stepping out of bikini panties. She had an astonishingly small waist and a large ass. The hair on her head was blond, but her pubic hair was dark brown. The three other players were in various states of undress. The poker game was being played in the middle of a vast, circular bed. It was a porno videocassette called *Jacks Are Better*. Eddie had bought it about three weeks ago, and insisted Laura watch it with him. She had been alternately amused and disgusted by the hard-porn proceedings, but it had the effect of arousing Eddie as she had never seen him aroused before. He had been savage in his lovemaking that night. Laura did not protest, but it worried her. Normally Eddie was a passionate but skilled and even a gentle lover.

Laura frowned now as the sweet, pungent odor of the Colombian Gold joint wafted across the room.

"I can't, Eddie," she said. "I've got a new manuscript I've got to read tonight."

Eddie took his attention from the cavorting foursome on the tube and turned to Laura.

"What's this one about?"

Laura shrugged.

"It's by a man in California."

She went to the table in the foyer, where she had placed the manuscript on her arrival home. She took the title page out of the envelope as she walked back into the living room.

"It's called *The Hitchhiker's Guidebook and Pocket Companion.*"

Laura went into the small bedroom in the rear of the apartment, which she used as a study, turned on the desk lamp, and began to read the manuscript. Her boss, editor in chief Harvey Kalisher, had told her that Richard Pine, the literary agent who had submitted the manuscript, was very enthusiastic about it. Harvey had read it himself and was inclined to agree it had good commercial potential.

"It could be for this generation of young people what Jack Kerouac's *On the Road* was for his," Harvey had said. "But it needs a good deal of work. Let me know what you think."

Even though she had closed the door to the study, she found it difficult to concentrate. Eddie's interest in pornographic movies was a relatively recent development. Laura thought it had begun shortly after she introduced him to Sandy Turner and the man Sandy lived with, Hy Tower. It was just a little over a month ago in late July. Sandy had come into Laura's office about midafternoon. Excitement sparkled in her deep jade eyes as she asked Laura, "Has Konyi's book been scheduled yet, Laurie?"

"Tentatively for January. She's due back from Budapest right after the holidays."

"I think I can get her Donahue," said Sandy. "I just had lunch with one of their New York reps. He thinks Phil'll go for it."

Laura had an odd relationship with Sandy Turner. Sandy

had come to work as a secretary at Wilson-Leigh a week after Laura. Only seventeen, but an extraordinarily sophisticated, smart-looking seventeen, she was tall, five ten, with the slender, graceful body of a fashion model. She was intelligent, ambitious, and worked hard. Her father and mother were both in the film business in California, he a producer, she a production designer. Laura helped her move up quickly from secretary to assistant in the publicity department, and now, at twenty-three, she was head of the department.

There were nasty rumors in the office, and to some extent around the trade, that Sandy had won her way on her back. Laura despised the gossips and their tales. She found herself the staunchest defender in the publishing house of Sandy's morals, integrity, and public relations skills. In spite of this she and Sandy developed no intimate personal or social relationship. Every time a new book of Laura's was released, Sandy worked hard to publicize it. At such times, she and Laura would inevitably have a series of luncheons, but they talked strictly business at these sessions. Laura did not understand why this was. She thought it might be their age difference. Although she was only four years older than Sandy, she felt a larger gap than that between them.

But on this Friday afternoon, on the twenty-second of July, Sandy asked, "You and Eddie doing anything tonight?"

Sandy knew that Laura was living with Eddie Ferraro, just as Laura understood that Sandy was living with a man named Hy Tower, but the couples had never met or gone out together before.

"We're going to the Diana Ross concert in the park," said Laura now. "Why?"

"You are? So are we, Hy and I! Come with us, and we'll have supper after at the Tavern on the Green."

"We're going with some friends of ours, Leslie and Robey Hill," said Laura. "I'll call them and we'll all go together."

They were all Diana Ross fans, though Leslie constantly argued with her husband that Ms. Ross could not carry Barbra Streisand's Tampax.

"Streisand's all right," acknowledged Robey, "but that's purely pseudo soul she sells. With Miss Diana it's the genuine article."

The concert was a smashing success, one of the Parks Department's super events. The police estimated that close to three hundred and fifty thousand people crowded into

Central Park and cheered the talented black woman through her repertoire. It seemed like all of Harlem and most of the city's Latinos had turned out along with hordes of Caucasians of all origins and ages. The concert started at six o'clock, when the hot, humid day was just beginning to cool, and the eight hundred and fifty policemen assigned to the event had no problems at all. Then just before eight o'clock when darkness had fallen and the show was almost over, Hy Tower yelled over the hubbub of the mob to his companions, "Let's split. I got a reservation at the Tavern for eight on the button."

They squirmed and pushed their way out of the good-natured crowd and made their way to the Tavern on the Green at Sixty-seventh Street and Central Park West. Hy knew the maître d' and they were given an excellent table on the patio. At Tower's urging, Robey and Leslie were telling stories about how they had met during the civil rights march from Selma, Alabama, to the state capital, Montgomery, in March of 1965.

"Robey was something else," said Leslie. "It was all madness and mayhem. When we left Selma the fucking state police charged us. They blasted us with tear gas, slashed us with whips, and busted heads with their nightsticks. Through it all this little nigger"—she placed a hand on Robey's arm—"led our group. Stood off those redneck cops quietly, without raising his voice. It was unbelievable. Talk about inspiration! You never saw anything like it!"

Robeson Hill had received his masters' degree in philosophy from Howard University (the eighty-percent black school in Washington, D.C.) the December before the march. He had been active with the Reverend Dr. Martin Luther King from the beginning. He was also a recognized authority on black history in New York City. Indeed he had written his thesis on the 1741–1742 so-called New York Negro Conspiracy and the trials that followed. A hundred and fifty slaves had been accused of a plot to burn down the city, kill all its white male inhabitants, and ravage their women. At the end of the trials thirteen slaves were burned at the stake, eighteen (along with four whites) were hanged. Seventy more people (mainly black slaves, along with a few Spanish blacks and a handful of whites) were banished from the city.

Now Robey smiled tolerantly as his militant Jewish wife raved on. Finally, he interrupted in his deep, rich voice,

"This insane child should never have made the march. It's a wonder she wasn't killed. She was fanatical and fearless." He smiled at Leslie. "Fanatical, *stupid,* and fearless."

"Bullshit, Robey," said Leslie.

"How old were you?" asked Hy.

Robey answered. "Sixteen, I think. Right, my dear?"

"Almost seventeen," said Leslie.

"Wasn't that when they killed that white lady from Detroit?" asked Laura.

"Yeah, just outside Montgomery on the day we got there. Fucking KuKluxers shot her dead—" cursed Leslie.

Then the commotion erupted outside the Tavern patio. It came from the direction of the parking lot. The diners stared in worried concern toward the sound of the disturbance. Robey stood up at the table and pointed.

"They're up on the roof!"

Even as the patrons looked toward the clumping clatter on the Tavern's roof a half dozen young men dropped into the dining area. They were dirty and sweating, dressed in a random assortment of colorful shirts and chinos, all wearing sneakers. Some of them brandished knives, others lead pipes. They dashed around among the terrified customers, shouting obscene threats and war cries, snatching a purse here, tearing a chain from a neck there. Two of them, olive skinned, acne dotted, and glistening with sweat, advanced on the table occupied by Laura and her friends. The taller of the two slashed back and forth before him with a switchblade knife, the other brandished a twelve-inch lead pipe.

Hy Tower, at the edge of the table closest to the advancing young hoodlums, grabbed the half-empty bottle of burgundy by the neck and held it shoulder high. Eddie turned his chair so he faced the hoodlums, and leaned back, relaxed but ready to spring. Robey watched quietly. Leslie rose and hurled a bowl of sugar cubes at the one with the knife. He laughed and kept advancing slowly. Laura and Sandy looked frightened. Hy Tower bellowed, "You motherfuckers come near this table, you'll be picking glass outta your head for a month!"

Hy was not really Tower's name. It was Francis, and he was called Hy for the simple reason that he stood six nine. He also weighed two fifty-five, and for the past two seasons had been among the top five rebounders in the National Basketball Association. The marauders changed course and headed for tables at the opposite side of the patio. Eddie Ferraro chuckled.

"A quiet summer evening in our fair city." Hy sat down again, swearing.

"I'm glad none of those youngsters are black," said Robeson Hill. A half dozen uniformed policemen burst into the patio area, nightsticks held high. The young hoodlums scampered out on the opposite side and in moments peace was restored. The police moved among the customers, disgustedly making notes of names, addresses, items stolen, confused descriptions.

"The Knicks would be proud of you, Hy, old boy," said Eddie. Sandy Turner did not notice the slight edge of mockery in his voice.

"I'm proud of you, too, baby," she said and touched Tower's hand affectionately.

It was then that Laura, sitting across the table from them, noticed the way Eddie Ferraro was looking at Sandy Turner. Sandy was wearing a loose green silk blouse which matched her jade eyes. Though she had small breasts the nipples pushed provocatively against the smooth silk. It was plain she wore no bra. Her eyes sparkled and her long, oval face, with its high cheekbones and hollow cheeks, was flushed. Laura had seen the gleam of lust in Eddie's dark Italian eyes before. It was unmistakable, and rarely displayed in public. He made no effort to conceal it now as he leaned toward Sandy.

Things settled down rapidly in the restaurant, and they proceeded with supper. They talked about growing crime in the city, particularly juvenile crime. Eddie and Sandy Turner did not participate in the general conversation. While Hy Tower was making the point that the same conditions existed in every major city in the country (he saw it everywhere when the Knicks played their away games), Eddie launched a private conversation with Sandy. He tapped her forearm, and she turned from Hy to him.

"Excuse me," he said, leaning closer to her, speaking directly into her ear. "You and Hy live together, right?"

She nodded.

"How long?" he asked, smiling.

"Almost a year now."

"You partial to basketball players?"

"Hy's nice."

"I can see that. Is it strictly Hy?"

Sandy glanced nervously across the table at Laura, seated

between Leslie and Robey Hill. She answered Eddie's question with another smile and an almost imperceptible negative shake of her head. She leaned closer to Eddie, and he positioned his head so that she could almost whisper in his ear.

"Hy and I both like groups, threes, fours, sometimes even more."

Eddie grinned and nodded.

"Yeahhhh," he said, and Sandy whispered, "I don't think Laura would approve."

Eddie straightened up, leaning away from her, and shrugged. "I don't know. Never asked her."

The waiter brought a baked Alaska for Hy and coffee for all of them. When they finished Hy insisted on taking the check. Eddie realized that the average salary of players in the NBA was more than two hundred thousand dollars per year, and Hy was in the middle range. He didn't argue for the check. Nor did Robey.

"Let's all go to our place. We got a fine pad across town on Sutton Place," said Hy. "I've got some goodies and we can fly into the weekend!"

Robey had an early morning meeting with two young narco officers from the New York Police Department, who were posing as students at the Harlem high school where Robey had been the principal for the past five years. Leslie had had a bad day so she and Robey declined to party with Hy and Sandy. And Laura had been developing a headache, and said she, too, had work to do in the morning. For a moment, Eddie thought he would insist that he and Laura go along, but when he saw the frown on Laura's face, decided against it.

Eddie and Laura made love that night in spite of her headache, but Eddie's usual enthusiasm and passion were lacking. To Laura it seemed their relationship had headed steadily downhill from that evening on. A week later he had brought home the porno cassette, which was now distracting her from the manuscript before her. Then she heard Eddie walking toward the study. He came in, and as she turned to look at him, he advanced upon her. She could see the bulge to the left of the fly of his trousers.

He came up behind her and reached down and cupped his hands over her bosom. He caressed her breasts for a moment, then unzippered the shirt of her cotton jumpsuit, and reached in under her bra and lifted her breasts out of the bra. As he bent over to kiss the top of her silver-blond head, he saw the top page of the manuscript.

THE HITCHHIKERS' GUIDEBOOK
AND POCKET COMPANION
by David Kessler

"Forget Kessler, the hitchhiker," he said hoarsely, swiveling her chair around, and kissed her fiercely on the mouth, holding her head in both hands. "Eddie wants to play!" he panted, almost breathless.

Laura felt the same passionate animal response she had always experienced with him. He had always held an enormous sexual attraction for her. She got up from the chair and he took her in his arms. He hugged her to him so tightly that she could feel his stiff burning member through his trousers and her jumpsuit. He pulled the zipper of the suit farther down and helped her wriggle and step out of it. He tore the bra from her shoulders and tossed it aside. He lifted her in his arms and carried her toward the bedroom sucking her breasts hungrily, first one, then the other. She held his head against her. Before setting her down on the bed, he bit her nipple.

"Not too rough, Eddie. Not too rough tonight, please!" she whispered.

He was not too rough. Indeed her plea seemed to have moved him in the opposite direction. His ardor seemed to diminish as he undressed. His lovemaking, inexplicably, became cursory. When they finished he lay with his hands beneath his head, staring at the ceiling.

"You know what would be nice, Laura?" he asked dreamily.

She waited.

"If we had Sandy Turner come to bed with us one night," he said, "the three of us. You think you'd like that?"

Laura sat up in the bed.

"You're not serious, Eddie!"

He turned toward her.

"Dead serious," he said.

"Forget it," she said emphatically, and climbed out of the bed. She walked to the closet and got a robe. She slipped into it and went back to her study. Try as she might she could not get back into the hitchhiker manuscript. It was almost three o'clock in the morning before she gave up and returned to bed. Eddie was fast asleep, lying on his side, snoring lightly.

30

Laura felt a little foolish and out of place, but she was enjoying herself. She and Eddie Ferraro were gastronomic adventurers. During their five-year relationship they had dined in almost every conceivable kind of ethnic restaurant. But it remained for David Kessler, a brash and pushy young author from California, to take Laura to her first kosher Chinese eating place.

She sat in the brightly lit, aromatic dining room of Bernstein-on-Essex Street surrounded almost entirely by obviously Orthodox Jewish people. Fully three-quarters of the men in the room wore yarmulkes, many had long black beards, all were dressed in gray or black suits, mostly polyester, and had highly polished black leather shoes.

A dignified gray-haired Chinese maître d' had greeted Laura and David and escorted them to the dining room. A chubby, obviously Jewish, pink-faced waiter, wearing a yarmulke with red tassels lending an Oriental touch, handed them menus and tied plastic bibs around their necks.

She asked David what *Kashruth* meant.

"It just means keeping kosher," he said. "You'll love this food, Miss Van Gelder. I know you will!"

"Are you Orthodox?" asked Laura.

"Gosh, no! Not at all! Neither I, nor any of my family. Even my grandfather, Harry, was a very secular Jew. I just love Bernstein's food. When I was here in seventy-six I ate here all the time."

Laura looked at the menu. "You'd better order for me, David, please," she said. He did. They shared an appetizer of fried rice with salami, and then he ordered for her the Hung Shu Bolo Gai, which was breaded boneless chicken with Chinese vegetables and pineapple. For himself he ordered the Fong Wan Gai, twin boned breasts of chicken stuffed with hickory-smoked pastrami, dipped in gently fried egg batter and topped with Chinese vegetables. David insisted they eat with the wooden chopsticks. From previous experience in

Chinese restaurants Laura had become fairly proficient in using the sticks. David was less skillful, but he persevered. Laura admitted the food was unusual and unusually delicious. And they talked. His boyish enthusiasm charmed her. He talked about his family, but mostly about his book.

"I'm anxious to read your rewrite on the New York section," said Laura, sipping the oolong tea, which came with the dinners.

Laura had found that David wrote well, in a highly literate yet informal style, but he had an exasperating tendency to begin on a subject, then go off on a tangent for a half dozen or more pages before coming back to his original theme. The problem was that some of these excursions were in themselves fascinating, but they needed severe pruning and tightening. His hitchhiking covered the summers of 1976 through 1982. Each year he flew to a starting point in a specific region of the country, and from there, wandered as his fancy took him, within the region, from one place to another. Then, each year before his classes were to resume, he flew back to Berkeley with his notes, and wrote as he had time between his studies.

In that first summer of 1976, he had decided to begin his travels in New York City. His grandfather, Harry Kessler, had written a column called My New York for the *Herald Tribune* in the twenties and thirties. David had thought it would be interesting to see what changes had taken place in certain places and sections of the city about which his grandfather had written. This turned out to be the first of the twelve parts into which the book was divided. It was called *What They Did to Grandpa's New York*. On arriving in the city David had made his way directly to the old tenement on Rivington Street where his grandfather had lived with his mother and father, David's great-grandparents. David's own father, Isaac, had also spent part of his youth there. He wrote of the changes on the Lower East Side. Discovering that many tenements in the area had been burned out, he sidetracked into a discourse on arson for profit which went on and on.

This chapter also included changes in the Bronx Zoo, to which his grandfather had been taken as a boy and about which he'd done a column years later. Here again David wound up with an overwritten sketch of a deranged but harmless bag lady, with whom he had had a long conversation on the subway ride to the zoo. He did three pages on the horrendous condition of the subway cars with their filthy floors, shattered windows, and graffiti-covered walls and cars, and the strange riders, some zombielike, some menacing. Finally he returned to the zoo and wrote an amusing report of his imagined conversation with an old chimp.

But where he wrote endlessly was in the section on the waterfront as it had been when Harry Kessler did a July 4, 1936, column, and how it was during the 1976 bicentennial celebration, when David watched an imposing flotilla of clipper ships sail majestically down the bay. He veered into a condensed history of clipper ships.

"Did you cut the clipper-ship stuff?" asked Laura. He nodded, chewing his Fong Wan Gai. He swallowed and said, "Every word is like cutting out a piece of my heart."

Laura smiled at him. Most authors, especially younger ones, tended to consider every word they wrote a precious gem. David Kessler was twenty-three, not quite four years younger than Laura, but to her he seemed much younger than that. His curly black hair, thick black beard, and mustache did little to make him appear older. He had a large nose and bright, intelligent amber eyes.

"Someday," said Laura now, "you can write a whole book about clipper ships. This one has to be tightened to a respectable and publishable length."

"I know," he agreed sadly. "After dinner can you stop by my place with me? The books came."

He had burst in on Laura at the Wilson-Leigh offices three weeks earlier, looking like a tall, slender lumberjack in plaid cotton shirt, denim jeans, and heavy hiking shoes. Always eager to learn as much as possible about her authors before she began to work with them, Laura invited him to a small restaurant on Madison Avenue, just a few blocks from the office.

He'd grown up in Northridge, California, in the San Fernando Valley, and gone to elementary and high school there. He was a brilliant student, well ahead of young people his own age, and at sixteen, he entered the University of California at Berkeley, majoring in English. Fresh out of graduate school he had taken a job as associate professor of English at a small college in Oregon. He had finished *The Hitchhiker's Guide and Pocket Companion* at the end of his first full semester of teaching. When his agents sent word that Wilson-Leigh was going to publish his book and pay him a modest advance, he decided to quit teaching and devote his full time to writing. Eight days before he showed up at Laura's office he had come to New York at the Pines' request to work with a Wilson-Leigh editor on cutting and doing some rewrite on the book. He was more excited than he ever had been in his life. He was certain he was going to have a best-seller and become famous.

He had spent days searching for an apartment in the city, and was horrified at the rents demanded. He found nothing he could afford. Then an inspiration hit him. As he had in 1976, seven years earlier, he went again to the old tenement on Rivington Street. The building, and particularly the first floor, was even more dilapidated than he had found it during his 1976 visit. He made a deal with the Puerto Rican landlord, Al Mejias, for a ridiculously low rent. He agreed to remodel (reconstruct would be more accurate) the entire first floor, in view of the insignificant rent he would be paying.

He had spent endless hours in the past week at Goodwill Industries, shopping in second-hand furniture stores and five-and-tens, securing some chairs, a table, a desk, and dishes, cookware, and other necessities for housekeeping. He had also taken from the library books on electrical work, painting, plumbing, woodworking, plastering, and studied them and applied his newfound knowledge to making the apartment livable. And at the end of each day, when he was physically exhausted, but not mentally tired, he sat down at the improvised desk he had constructed and reviewed his eleven-hundred-page manuscript.

During that first meeting with Laura in the Madison Avenue restaurant, she had asked him if he'd had any trouble finding an apartment.

"I sure did!" he said. He told her about settling in on Rivington Street. "It was about the only place I could afford, and there's something special about living there . . . in spite of the condition of the place. It's the same building I wrote about in the book—where my great-grandparents, my grandfather, and father lived."

"That *is* something special," said Laura.

"Have you been over there recently, to the East Side, I mean?"

"No. We never get over that way. We live on Greene Street across town on the West Side. You know the SoHo section?"

David shook his head. "It's unbelievable. I thought we had a bad drug scene at Berkeley, but I've never seen anything like the East Side. They deal right out in the open in the streets. They've taken over some of the abandoned buildings and set up shop just like regular legitimate retail businesses. They've got kids in the streets hustling all kinds of horse and coke. They even have brand names. A kid no more than fourteen stopped me the other day and asked did I want some Eagle, best horse in the city, lowest price in town. I can't figure out how the city stands for it."

Laura said, "The city's trying to do something about it, but it's a terrible problem. My friend Eddie Ferraro works for the city, the housing department. They own a lot of those abandoned buildings and he tells me that the cops arrest some of the runners and dealers all the time. But few of them ever go to jail. They apparently work for well-organized and -financed operators."

David nodded. "I know."

"Aren't you a little frightened living there . . . even though your grandfather—"

David smiled and interrupted. "A little, to be frank," he said. "But on the other hand it's pretty exciting too."

"Well, said Laura, "tell me about your family. What do your mom and dad do?"

"My father's an accountant and my mom helps him in the office. They've got a nice practice. I did an article for *Los Angeles* magazine on one of their clients, U.S. Entertainment Corp."

Laura realized that in his conversation, David had the same tendency to go off on tangents as he did in his writing. With boyish enthusiasm he told her about the magazine article, which dealt with bingo games operated by U.S. Entertainment for the Morongo Indians in Riverside County.

"Did your grandfather do any writing other than his column?" Laura interrupted as David was detailing the Bureau of Indian Affairs' attitude toward the growing trend to big-time bingo on the reservations.

"Oh!" said David, "I have wandered, haven't I! I seem to do that. Yeah, he wrote three nonfiction books."

He immediately plunged into a description of the works of Harry Kessler.

"First one he did was about my great-grandmother, a lady named Malka Kessler. She's the one lived in the apartment on Rivington Street. The book was called *Mama Was No Angel*. It was an excellent book. My great-grandma was a hooker, and—"

"Oh, David! Really?"

He nodded, smiling. "It's a great story. She killed a man who kidnapped my grandfather, Harry."

"Do you have the book? I'd love to read it."

"I don't have it here with me, but I can write my father and ask him to send me a copy. He has a number of copies. Poor old Malka emigrated from Poland when she was eighteen, I think. She was a white-slave victim. My grandfather's title was a little tricky. His mother escaped her degrading life as a prostitute by sheer guts, and spent most of her years helping her neighbors on the Lower East Side. They did call her the Angel of Rivington Street, but my grandfather's theme was that she wasn't an angel—just a flesh-and-blood woman, who whored and killed, but overcame terrible odds to live a life of good works. I always remember the last lines in the book."

In the dim light of the bar his eyes were moist. He cleared his throat, and said, " 'Mama wasn't an angel. But you might make a case for her sainthood.' "

A sad look came over his face.

"She died of cancer two days after Hitler invaded Poland in 1939."

He finished his gin and tonic, noted that Laura had finished hers, and ordered another round.

"He wrote two other books," he said. "One was about a good friend and benefactor of his named Kevin Morrissey. Morrissey was a crooked cop who became a theatrical producer and a nightclub operator during Prohibition. The book is really about his wife, an actress named Lilly Welcome . . . well, about both of them, their love story. It was called *The Lilly and the Cop*. Would you like to read that too?"

"Yes, I would, David."

"Then his last book was about his experiences in World War Two in the OSS."

"I'd like to read all three if you can get copies," said Laura. "I had an ancestor who did a book about his experiences in the Civil War. *Antietam Journal* it was called. He was my great-great-grandfather, Fred Van Gelder, Jr. The last remaining copy of the book is my father's proudest possession. . . . What about your grandmother?"

He shrugged.

"I don't know much about her. It seems she and my grandfather had an unfriendly divorce. She left my father and married some man and went to live in Russia. Once I heard my grandfather telling my father about an episode with her. He was pretty bitter about her. He called her Mrs. Commissar. He sometimes talked about her family too. I think they were wealthy. He called her father the Toilet Paper King."

Another ten days had passed since their lengthy meeting in the restaurant. David was making good progress. With Laura's guidance and warm encouragement he had reworked the New York section and tightened up and rewritten more than half the book. Not only did he drop in on Laura at the office every day during this period, but he had taken to calling her every night at home. He insisted on reading to her sections he had rewritten, and asked her help when he reached a portion of the narrative where he was stymied. Eddie Ferraro answered the phone several times when David called, and the third time, before David identified himself, Eddie said irritably, "Yeah, I know, the hitchhiking author from Berkeley. Hold a minute."

Laura was in her study, and he yelled, "Laura! Guess who?"

Laura and Eddie's relationship had not improved at all. Since the night of the Diana Ross concert he had stayed away from the apartment overnight a half dozen times. Laura said nothing about it. They had made love just twice, both times without passion or any sense of fulfillment.

Now on an Indian summer evening, David paid the check at Bernstein's-on-Essex Street.

"I don't know how I can ever repay you for the work you're doing with me on this book, Miss Van Gelder," he said as they walked over to Rivington Street. "I know it's way above and beyond the usual contributions of an editor."

"Not really, David," said Laura, "but there is one thing you can do for me. Call me Laura. I want to stop feeling like your spinster schoolteacher."

"Hey! Sure! Thanks!" said David.

Despite having been alerted by David's description of the Lower East Side, Laura was shocked as they turned into Rivington Street. The streets were strewn with rubble and litter. Graffiti, in spray paint and chalk, defaced many areas of the old, abandoned buildings, and some of those still occupied. There was an unpleasant odor of urine, excrement, and garbage as they passed a line of five battered, overstuffed trash cans. They neared the relatively undamaged tenement in which David lived and a sickly, malaria-skinned youth with a runny nose galloped across the street to them. He could not have been more than fifteen.

"Folluh me," he whispered hoarsely to David. "Right downna block. Best coke inna city. Dime-a-bag."

David took Laura's arm and pushed ahead of the youth. On the battered, black-painted doors of a burned-out building two doors from David's house, there was scrawled, in large letters in chalk, the advertisement, Works for Rent! $2.00!

"See that," said David, indicating the message with a nod of his head. "You get a hypodermic needle, a string of some kind to tie around your arm, a bottle cap, and a dirty spoon. You might also get hepatitis, syphilis or AIDS, but there's no extra charge for that."

Eddie, as well as David, had told Laura about the scene here on the Lower East Side, but she suddenly realized that one had to see it to really feel the impact. The Hung Shu Bolo Gai turned sour in her stomach and she felt faint. As they were about to enter David's building she halted suddenly, touched his arm, and took a deep breath.

"Are you all right?" asked David.

"In a minute . . ." Laura nodded.

They walked up the stoop and into the building. David's apartment ran the length of the left side of the entire first floor. He had three dead-bolt locks on the door and each had to be opened with a different key. When he opened the door and they stepped over the threshold into the long, narrow parlor, Laura experienced a remarkable and sudden change. The nausea vanished instantly and completely. Two steps into the room she had the strong sense that she had been here before, many, many times. Not just *been* here, but *lived* here.

She stopped and stared, wide-eyed, around the room. It looked like a college boy's room in a dormitory. David had done an extraordinary job on the place in the short time he'd lived here. He had put fresh wallboard on all four walls and painted the board bright yellow. The room had a sunny look in spite of the fact that little light came in from the windows in the front and on the left side, only yards away from the neighboring tenement. On the yellow walls, well-positioned, were colorful posters.

On the right of the room, two feet from the wall, was a sofa, its age and tattered condition camouflaged by a bright orange and beige slipcover of inexpensive material. The cover fit too snugly, like a dress a size to small on a plump woman. Behind the sofa was a bookcase made of plain pine planks separated at each end and in the center by concrete blocks. There were not yet many books on the shelves. A small radio and a nineteen-inch black and white TV sat on the top plank.

Laura stood quietly and continued to stare around the room. Surely it did not remind her of her room in the Swarthmore dorm at Parrish Hall, although she, too, had adorned her walls with posters. It flashed through her mind that there was a connection with Philip, but he had lived with the family in Norristown and Laura had only been to his room there once. And it did not look like a college boy's room.

She had never set foot on the Lower East Side of the city in all the time she had lived here. She obviously could never have been in this building on Rivington Street before. Yet the feeling persisted. She not only had been in the building, but it had been her home. She thought of the night Eva Konyi had regressed Leslie Kramer Hill into a childhood three hundred years earlier in Spain. All this went through her mind in less than a minute. David grasped her upper arm and shook her.

"Laura! Laura! Are you all right?"

Laura looked at him as though surprised to see him there beside her. She shook her head, then nodded. David led her to the sofa.

"You look so pale! Can I get you something? Water? A little wine?"

"No, no. Thanks, David. I'll be fine. I was just a little dizzy . . . or . . . or . . ." She grinned. "Maybe that kosher Chinese food does funny things to me."

He went into the bedroom he had converted into a study and brought out three books and another fifty pages of manuscript. The strange feeling of déjà vu persisted as she continued to look around in David's momentary absence. As he set the books and manuscript on the old, scarred coffee table in front of the sofa, she said, "David, would you show me the rest of the apartment?" She felt she had to find a clue to her mysterious sensation.

"Of course," he said. "I've still got a lot of work to do on it, but sure."

The apartment was what used to be called a railroad flat, with one room leading into another. One of the four bedrooms David hadn't touched at all. The two others had freshly painted white walls, decorated with inexpensive framed reproductions of paintings, by Monet, Degas, Gauguin. One had an army cot with blanket and pillow and a battered maple dresser. The other, larger bedroom had a thick, brand-new king-size mattress with pillows, sheets, and blanket, lying flat on the newly painted wood floor, over disassembled tops, bottoms, and sides of thick cardboard boxes. On the left side of the mattress, resting on an orange crate, was an alarm clock. In this room, too, there was a battered dresser, this one of oak veneer. The bedroom David had converted into his study had a large wooden door, lying flat on double tiers of red brick on each of its four corners. A nicked and scarred wooden chair, painted the same green as the improvised desktop, stood before it. On the desk was a portable typewriter, a loose pile of manuscript, and a ream of blank white paper. At the right-hand corner of the desk stood three framed photographs. David reached up and tugged the string on the overhead lamp he had wired to run along the wall behind the desk and across the ceiling. In the sudden bright light Laura picked up one of the photographs.

It showed a man, a woman, and a small boy. It was sepia-toned, obviously taken at the turn of the century. The man, about forty, wore a high starched white collar, a dark tie and suit. He had a rather large nose and a sad, uncertain look in his dark eyes. Despite the raised chin, the heroic stiffness of his posture, seated in a thronelike chair, there was an aura of weakness about him. Beside him stood a young boy, perhaps six, with a serious look on his face. He resembled the woman, standing behind them, as much as the man. The woman, in her early or midthirties, rested one hand lightly on the shoulder of the man, the other on the boy's. Her raven hair was piled softly on her head and there was a look of fierce pride on her strong oval face.

"That's my great-grandmother Malka and my great-grandfather William. The little boy is my grandfather Harry," said David.

Laura replaced the picture and David handed her the

second group photograph. This, too, showed a man, a woman, and a young boy, but it was in full color. The man, about forty, resembled William Kessler in the first photograph. He had the same large nose, but his expression was gentle rather than meek. He looked rather sickly, with hollow cheeks and sunken dark eyes. The woman seemed ten years younger and was blond and slender. The boy looked like his father, again the largish nose, and the dark eyes and hair. David chuckled.

"That's me and my mother and father. It was taken in the late sixties, sixty-nine I guess. I was about nine. My father was just recovering from his second mild heart attack. He had his first one right after he came back from the Korean War. They seem to run in our family. My grandfather died of a massive coronary in fifty-seven. He'd had an earlier attack right after he came back from World War Two in forty-six. That was the year he sold the tenement on Rivington Street and moved out to California to live with my father, who was in his second year at Cal State Northridge. My great-grandfather William also died of a myocardial infarction."

He gave a weak, helpless smile.

"I guess that's the way I'll go too," he said.

"Not if you exercise and watch your diet," said Laura.

"Anyway," continued David, "my mother and father were very active in Vietnam antiwar demonstrations. They even took me along on protest rallies several times. You remember, sixty-eight was the year Bobby Kennedy and Martin Luther King were killed, and around that time the facts about My Lai came out. My mother and father took it all very personally and seriously."

He shook his head as Laura replaced the picture.

"Jeez," he said, "those were terrible days. Even at nine or ten, or whatever, I felt the tension, the general air of desperation, the confusion."

"I know," said Laura. "I was in high school, and we all felt the same way. My father ran all kinds of editorials in the paper denouncing the war, and even in school we were doing all kinds of antiwar things. . . . My father was in the Korean war too."

She looked inquiringly toward the third framed picture on the desk. It was an excellent bit of color photography. It showed a young girl, who appeared to be a stocky, well-developed seventeen or eighteen, dressed all in red, red wool cap, bulky crew-neck sweater, and stretch pants of the same shade of crimson. Silver-blond hair showed beneath the red wool cap and the girl's cheeks were almost as scarlet as her clothing. She had a small pug nose and her broad vivacious smile exposed even, gleaming teeth, whiter than the snow. Laura thought she resembled David's mother somewhat.

"Such a striking photograph, David," she said. "Who's the girl?"

"That's my sister, Debbie. I took it last winter when she visited me at school. We took a ride and came upon this pear orchard in the Tualatin River Valley."

"She's very pretty," said Laura.

Just as they returned to the long parlor and Laura, at David's urging, began to read the newly rewritten pages of the manuscript, there was a timid knock at the door. David opened it and a tiny, frail middle-aged woman came into the parlor with him. She held a covered casserole dish in both hands.

"I thought, maybe, Davey, you like some *arroz con pollo*. I make too much, an' Fernando, he stop eating."

She stopped abruptly as she saw Laura.

"Oh—I am sorry, Davey. I do not know you have company."

"That's all right, Mrs. Torres," said David, but she hurried by Laura into the kitchen and came out, bowing apologetically to Laura.

"This is Miss Van Gelder, my editor," said David. The thin, sallow-complected woman bowed to Laura again and hurried to the door.

"I come back later, Davey," she said. "About Fernando . . . later . . ." She turned to Laura. "It is pleasure to meet you, miz . . . Excuse."

"I'm happy to meet you, Mrs. Torres," said Laura, but Mrs. Torres was already gone. David sat down beside Laura.

"Wonderful people," he said. "They live across the hall. The father is a sickly man. I don't know what he has, maybe TB or something, a bad chronic cough. He's the janitor for the building, but Felipa, that's Mrs. Torres, she does most of the work. It's funny. Ramon, Mr. Torres, and the landlord, Mejias, grew up together as boys in San Juan, and they served together in Nam. Ramon came back broke and sick. Mejias pushed drugs in Nam and came back fat and rich. Now he owns some of these buildings, and Ramon thinks he runs one of the neighborhood drug operations. He lives in an apartment in Riverdale with a flashy girl, who models and mud wrestles. And poor Ramon barely gets by."

"It's always so touching," said Laura, "the way people who have so little are willing to share. I gather Mrs. Torres brought you some chicken and rice."

"Yeah, it's embarrassing sometimes. They've kind of adopted me."

Laura smiled.

"How do you know all that—about the family, and Mejias? You've only been living here a month or so."

"Mrs. Torres and Ramon, they both like to talk. He comes in to spend a couple of hours with me about every other day. He likes to play checkers, but most of all he likes to talk. And Mrs. Torres, she treats me like a son. Like I'm a big brother to Fernando, her youngest boy. She's worried right now. We suspect the kid may be working as a lookout for the drug people. Last week he came home and gave her twenty-five dollars. He said he got a job in one of those new markets in the South Street Seaport, but I talked to him, and I knew he was lying. I grabbed his arm and pulled up his sleeve and sure enough there were three needle marks. He said a buddy had just talked him into shooting a couple of times, but he was quitting."

"My God," said Laura. "How old is he?"

"Twelve, I think. Maybe thirteen. When Miguel, his older brother, was around, he kept the kid straight. Miguel was one of the original Guardian Angels here in New York. You know about them?"

"Oh, yes. Whatever did happen to them?"

"I think the police broke them up. The feeling seemed to be that they were too much like vigilantes and were bound to make more trouble than do good."

"So what happened to Miguel?"

"Well, about two years ago, when he was seventeen, he went out to L.A. to set up a Guardian Angel organization out there. But I guess they ran into the same trouble they did here. Meantime he met a nice young girl, who was a checker in a supermarket, and he got a job driving a bakery truck, and they're married and have a baby. They live in Boyle Heights. He writes all the time. He worries a lot about Fernando. . . . You want anything, Laura? Some wine?"

"No, thanks, David, I'm fine. Do the Torreses have any other children?"

"Yeah, a daughter, Maria. Fine girl. She's eighteen. Goes to a secretarial school in the daytime and works as a waitress evenings. Mrs. Torres had three other kids between Maria and Fernando, but they all died. She almost lost Fernando at birth too. I guess that's why she worries so much about him. And I'm afraid she has good reason."

David picked up the manuscript on the scarred table.

"Can you stay and read this while you're here, Laura?"

Laura looked at her watch. It was twenty minutes to two, and there was no need for her to rush back to the office. She took a pencil from her purse and began to read the manuscript, making marginal notes and comments as she read. David paced restlessly, went into the kitchen, returned with a glass of wine, paced again. Finally Laura finished.

"This is much better, David. But I think you can still tighten it. I've marked the places. And I think the section on the Cubanization of Miami is a little overwritten, too flamboyant. Maybe you can tone it down a bit."

"You're a tough editor, Laura. But I'm really grateful."

He walked her over to Broadway to find a taxi to take her back uptown to her office. She accomplished little in the hour and a half she spent at her desk. Her mind darted back and forth between wondering about the strange feeling she had experienced in David's apartment in Rivington Street, and brooding over the grim drug situation on the East Side and the travail of the struggling Torres family.

On her way to meet Leslie for dinner at a midtown Italian restaurant near the NOW headquarters, she thought how nice it would be to be in a position to help people like the Torreses. No wonder Leslie got such satisfaction out of her work. Even at the NOW meeting, where they were discussing plans for funding a new center for abused wives, she could not get her Rivington Street experience out of her mind. She had told Leslie about it over dinner, and Leslie thought it entirely possible that she or someone very close to her had lived in a house there many years ago.

Laura was thinking again about frail, haggard Mrs. Torres when she turned the key in the door of the apartment on Greene Street. It was almost midnight. As she stepped into the dark foyer and switched on the light, she thought, *It's ridiculous, but I swear I felt more like David's apartment was home than I do here. Maybe I'm going a little crazy.* And then she heard the giggling sound from the bedroom. She saw, walking through the modern living room, that light was coming from the half-open bedroom door. She strode quickly to the door. Eddie was sitting up in bed, two pillows crushed behind his broad back. The thin wool blanket was pulled up to just below his navel. The curly black hair on his shoulders, chest, and upper abdomen shone moistly in the glow from the bedside lamp. Scrunched down beside him, the blanket clutched at her neck, was Sandy Turner. Her jade-green eyes were wide, expectant, not certain of Laura's reaction.

"Hi, babe," greeted Eddie. "Get out of your clothes and jump in."

Laura's face turned deep rose, a mix of embarrassment and fury. The anger blazed in her eyes and showed in the grim set of her mouth. She stood there, glaring and trembling.

Now Laura's reaction was clear. Sandy slithered into a sitting position, still holding the blanket at her throat. Eddie was now exposed to just above his knees, but he sat back unselfconsciously and grinned.

"Eddie—ss—ss—said you wanted it . . . uh—uh—us three to—together," Sandy stammered.

"Get out of that bed, Sandy!" ordered Laura grimly.

Sandy flipped the blanket away from her and ran, naked, across the room to the bathroom. She was long-legged, almost flat-chested, an androgynous figure. Eddie said, "For crise sake, Laura, don't be so fucking puritan. It's nineteen eighty-three."

"Five years, Eddie," said Laura wearily, "and you don't know me at all. I'm glad we never married."

Sandy came out of the bathroom. Her silken honey hair was a mess. Lipstick was smeared on her mouth. Her tan velour blouse and brown wool skirt were wrinkled.

"I—I—I can't find my pants," she said timidly.

Eddie reached down under the blanket, searched around with his hand. He tossed the black silk bikini toward Sandy. It fell at her feet and she picked it up. Laura looked at her contemptuously.

"I—I'm sorry, Laura. If Eddie—"

"Get out, Sandy," said Laura quietly. "Get the hell out of here. I don't want to hear any of your bullshit apologies or excuses."

Sandy almost fell over twice before she succeeded in stepping into her panties. She hurried to the closet and got her heavy wool plaid coat and knitted cap. At the door to the apartment she called back, "I am—I truly am sorry, Laurie."

The door closed and Laura turned to Eddie.

"Now you can get out, too, Eddie!" she said firmly. He sat back and laughed uproariously.

"I don't *believe* you!" he said. "Me? Me get out? Who the fuck's apartment you think this is? I was here when you moved in. If anybody's getting out, it's gonna be you, baby."

Laura realized he was right. Of course it was Eddie's apartment. Since she had been paying half the rent for five years, she had merely come to think of it as her own. She turned now and walked to the door.

"I'll pick up my things tomorrow or sometime," she said. She walked five blocks in the cold, black night before she found a taxi. She gave the driver the Hills' address on Bank Street in Greenwich Village. As he flopped the flag, she rested her head on the back of the seat and cried quietly.

31

Laura lay beside David Kessler on the mattress on the bedroom floor. He held her hand. He was still breathing heavily. The small room was warm from the heat of their bodies and the electric heater in the corner. The heater's glow shimmered in the darkness. Laura's eyes were closed, but she was not asleep. It had never been like this with Eddie, never! David's lovemaking reminded her a little of the second time with Philip. There was that same tender, almost reverent quality to his touch, his kisses, his every movement, even after he entered her. But he seemed more experienced, less awkward than Philip and he brought her to a splendid orgasm.

On this brisk October night, three weeks after she had found Sandy Turner in her bed with Eddie, the pragmatic side of her psyche now began to diminish the euphoric feeling of fulfillment. Did she really love David or was she just on the rebound from the unpleasant end of her relationship with Ferraro? Had she made love with him tonight because she was a healthy young animal, who hadn't been with a man in more than a month? Or because she'd had too much Chianti and brandy? Wasn't he too young for her? Had she simply succumbed to his unrelenting flattery, his attitude of admiration, respect, almost adoration?

Harvey Kalisher, her editor in chief, had become increasingly enthusiastic about David's book as Laura turned in section after section of the cut and rewritten work. He had told her that if they could finish by mid-October he might be able to convince sales and marketing that they should rush it into distribution as a special February release. Laura had worked with David at the Rivington Street apartment for hours every day, including weekends. He could not find enough words to praise and thank her for the help she was giving him. When she had told him she was living with the Hills and gave him their phone number, he'd inquired, "What happened with you and Ferraro, Laura . . . if you don't mind my asking?"

"I don't know. We just weren't seeing eye to eye on some important things."

"The guy must be an idiot," said David, "to give up the smartest, most beautiful woman in New York City."

"Flattery will only get you orders to cut another twenty pages out of the Texas section," said Laura and smiled. "Let's get back to work."

She had long since discovered that he was given to hyperbole. He was the same way about the book. He was certain it was going to be a best-seller. Thanks to Laura! He just knew it! He almost had Laura believing it. She did enjoy working with him. And she found working in the Rivington Street apartment pleasurable. Incredibly, the feeling that she belonged here persisted. She also found it desirable to work away from her office as much as she legitimately could, since it helped her avoid Sandy Turner. Yes, she enjoyed working with David more than she had ever enjoyed working with any author. His boyish enthusiasm was infectious. And God knew that after the demoralizing, image-destroying experience with Eddie and Sandy she could use generous doses of stroking. She grew fonder of him each day. She loved to listen to his big-brother meetings with young Fernando Torres. From the sessions she inadvertently overheard she got the impression that the boy was simply telling David what David wanted to hear, and would continue to live as he pleased. But David thought otherwise. He was convinced Fernando had given up shooting cocaine. There were no more needle punctures on the child's arm. He continued to give his mother and father modest amounts of money and had taken David over to the South Street market where he claimed he worked.

David even made her ordeal of looking for a new apartment (while she lived with the Hills) bearable. Barely bearable. It was a depressing and frustrating hunt. Laura was aware that rents had skyrocketed in the city, but she had no idea how drastically. On the first of October, the Hills' landlord had told them that when their lease expired in January he was raising their rent fifty percent. Welfare workers' and high school principals' salaries being what they were, they could not afford such an increase. So Laura and Leslie went apartment hunting together. With no success. And Laura felt, more and more, that she was imposing on the Hills.

Now, as she and David lay side by side, he raised her hand to his lips and kissed her fingertips.

"You asleep, Laura?" he whispered.

"Uh-uh." She turned and looked at him. The heater cast an orange-tan glow on his face. He looked like a young satyr in an illustration from Dante's Inferno. He released her hand and cupped her chin and leaned over and kissed her on the mouth. As he turned toward her she felt that he was rigid again. The area around the hard nipples of her full breasts tingled. He said hoarsely, "Could we—could we one more time?"

Laura turned to him and put her arms around his shoulders.

"Nice," she whispered, "but if we're going to keep doing this, we'll have to get a bed."

What they were celebrating was word from Harvey Kalisher that the book was indeed scheduled for February publication with a substantial initial print order and a respectable promotion budget. When Laura had come to the apartment on Rivington Street that afternoon with the news, David hugged her and danced her around the room. He insisted on taking her to dinner at a new Italian restaurant. A new art gallery and a boutique flanked the restaurant, and five doors down the street an old tenement was in the process of being drastically remodeled.

"Amazing that people are willing to invest in an area like this," David remarked.

"It's one of the things I love about New York," said Laura. "The city is always rebuilding itself. No matter how bad a neighborhood gets, a gentrification movement always seems to develop. The same thing happened in SoHo and seems to be happening right now north of Houston between Broadway and the Bowery. They're calling it NoHo."

At dinner they finished two bottles of Chianti. They walked back to the apartment holding hands. As soon as they stepped through the door, even before they removed their coats, David took her in his arms. He looked into her eyes and said passionately, "You know this, don't you, Laura? I've been in love with you from the first day we met!"

Laura had sensed it, of course. And she was increasingly certain that she felt the same way about him. They sat on the sofa a while, Laura snuggling in David's arms. They finished half a bottle of brandy and soon found themselves on the mattress in the bedroom. Despite the lack of a bed, their second coupling was as thrilling and fulfilling as their first. Again they lay back, with David holding her hand, sighing, and breathing hard. This time Laura's contentment was such that she refused to entertain her mind's questions as to why she and David had, at last, become lovers. *I love him,* she told herself, *and that is that!*

She was almost asleep when she sensed that he was facing her again, leaning on an elbow, looking down at her.

"Laura?" he whispered. "Laura?"

"Uhm?"

"I'm going to start a novel," he said. "About a boy and a girl during my great-grandma's time here on the East Side, the Jewish period."

"That'll be nice," murmured Laura sleepily.

"Laura?"

"Uhm?"

"Will you move in with me? Please move in with me! I need you!"

"We'll see, David. Go to sleep."

She woke about seven, her usual time, even though it was Saturday. She looked down at David. He was fast asleep. It was funny how, beard, mustache, and all, he still looked like a little boy. She kissed his cheek lightly, and went out into the kitchen and made coffee. Drinking it and nibbling a piece of dry toast, she thought what a wonderful night it had been. She had an appointment to meet Leslie at noon. They were going to continue their search for apartments, then see Barbra Streisand's new film, *Yentl*, and have dinner together.

She wondered if David had really asked her to move in with him last night or if she had dreamed it. If he had asked her, and if he asked her again this morning in the cold light of day, she wondered what she should say. She was quite sure she loved him, even though he seemed a little young for her. Before, during, and after their lovemaking, he had told her eloquently and with shameless hyperbolic imagery how much he adored her. After her experience with Eddie, she wasn't sure it was a good idea. But it was tempting. Maybe she would talk to Leslie about it. Leslie and Robey had both met David and they liked him. Leslie liked him a great deal more than she had ever liked Eddie.

Before Laura finished her second cup of coffee, David came out of the bedroom in a dark wool robe. He was rubbing his eyes. He stood over her at the kitchen table.

"I love you, Laura," he said quietly. "Will you?"

"Will I what?"

"Move in with me. I adore you. I need you the way flowers need the sunshine and the rain, the way birds need—"

"My God, David! So early in the morning?" She smiled at him. "Maybe. I'll have to think about it."

"Take all the time you need," he said. "When I get through showering you can tell me you will."

He kissed the top of her head and went into the bathroom.

Three weeks later, once again at the breakfast table, David said, "Laura, I'm the happiest and the luckiest man in the world"—he chuckled—"and maybe even the most talented."

Laura had moved into the apartment on Rivington Street. She had asked Leslie's advice and her old friend had said, "He's a nice enough guy, but sometimes I think we make it too easy for these fucking—and I use the word advisedly—these fucking men. They get what they want and then—" She shrugged. "Who knows? Maybe you should hold out for a wedding ring."

"You didn't . . . with Robey."

"I know, but Robey's one in a million."

"Then you think I shouldn't move in?"

"You know you'll probably have to mother him," said Leslie.

"What do you mean?"

"He's the little-boy type, probably'll never grow up."

"Is that all bad?"

"Not necessarily. You're the good old deluxe model earth mother."

"He's nice."

"You love him?"

"I think so."

"Well, then, give it a shot. What the hell've you got to lose except maybe another nick in your heart."

It had been an exceptionally good three weeks. Laura had become acquainted with all the Torreses and a number of the other remaining tenants in the building. There were six elderly Jewish couples. Of the six only two had grown children still with them. Her favorite couple was the Sapersteins, who had four children and eleven grandchildren. Sarah and Abraham ran their small bagel shop on Essex Street and were willing workers in the neighborhood association.

There were three other Puerto Rican families and two elderly Italian couples. Laura got along well with all of them. She and the Torreses' eighteen-year-old daughter, Maria, had already become especially good friends. Maria wrote poems, and though they were awkwardly constructed, the sentiments and philosophies they tried to express were touching and often wise.

During the same three weeks Laura had read all three of Harry Kessler's books. He was a perceptive writer with an offbeat sense of humor and keen insight into human behavior. Of the three she found *Mama Was No Angel* the most interesting, although she also enjoyed the other two. In the book about his mother, Harry Kessler had interspersed his own narrative with large sections of a memoir his mother had written over a period of years. Malka Kessler's own words had a simple eloquence that gave great power to the story. The Sapersteins had invited David and Laura to a Sabbath supper the day after Laura finished reading the book. That night Laura had told David, "You know, Mrs. Saperstein reminds me quite a bit of your great-grandmother Malka. I wonder about her young girlhood."

"I think Mr. and Mrs. Saperstein were both in concentration camps," said David, "but you'll never get either of them to talk about it."

The day after Laura agreed to move in, she and David went to Bloomingdale's and bought a king-size bed, upon which David's excellent mattress could be placed. Their lovemaking could not be improved upon, but it and sleeping became somewhat more comfortable than during the mattress-only days.

Laura was happier than she had been in a long time.

David was ecstatic. Every day he asked her if there was anything new about his book. When would the jacket art be ready? What would it be like? Which of his photos were they going to use on the back of the jacket? Were there any new promotion plans? Were they planning to have him do a tour of major book markets and arrange his appearance on the television talk shows? Laura was amused by his restless enthusiasm. She also worried a little over the fact that he was raising his hopes for the book's success so stratospherically. She knew the odds against a book by a new writer becoming a best-seller. But she did not have the heart to suggest there was even the remotest chance the book would not make David famous.

When he was not dreaming out loud about *The Hitchhiker's Guidebook*, he was hard at work on the outline of his novel. Here again Laura tried to talk him into choosing another milieu and theme. They discussed it often. In the very beginning she had said, "I'm not too sure it will work, David. Stories about the Lower East Side in the first quarter of the century, during the Eastern European immigration, have been done over and over. A year, year and a half ago Howard Fast had a best-seller called *Max*, about an East Side Jewish boy, who became a movie mogul in the earliest days of the silent films. And a woman named Meredith Tax did a good book—it was a Literary Guild selection—actually called *Rivington Street*—"

"I know, Laurie love, I know," said David, with all the confidence of a young author whose first best-seller was due out in a couple of months. "I read them both. In *Rivington Street*, too, the daughters become big successes. My book will not be in that same old vein. My Jewish family, the Levinskys, father, mother, children, will never get out of the ghetto, yet they'll live happier, more fulfilling lives than others who become superstars, millionaires, bankers. . . ."

It was impossible to deter him from his vision. While he acknowledged over and over again the invaluable contributions Laura had made to the hitchhiker work, he seemed to have convinced himself as he began the outline of his novel that he knew a good deal more about writing than did she. Yet Laura had to admit, as he developed the outline—with substantial guidance from her—that he might have something in his approach.

The last week in November, Laura got an overseas phone

call from Eva Konyi in Budapest. The psychic told her she would be unable to come to the United States until spring. She had been summoned to the Soviet parapsychology unit in Moscow, the Popov Institute, and would be there in the offices of the Moscow Radio Engineering Institute for months.

"Oh, I'm so sorry, Eva—" Laura began.

"It's not too bad, dear Laura," interrupted Eva, in her deep, husky voice. "Already we have excellent comment in magazine *Publishers Weekly* and more will come when book comes out. Will sell well. In California will become best-seller, but not in rest of country. But will sell long time."

Laura was taken aback. The favorable *Publishers Weekly* review had appeared in the issue of the book-trade publication that had arrived at Rivington Street two days earlier. There was no way it could have reached Budapest in that time. Laura realized someone could have cabled or phoned the review to Eva, but she doubted it. And as they continued their conversation Eva surprised Laura yet again. Laura had not mentioned her newfound contentment, but Eva suddenly dropped talk of the book to say, "I am so happy, dear Laura, to feel how happy you are, more happy than for long time. Is new young man, no? Tall, with big beard and talks much."

Laura joyously admitted her relationship with David, and she could not resist telling Eva Konyi about her mystic feelings about the apartment on Rivington Street. Ms. Konyi gave a deep-throated chuckle.

"You remember long discussion we have on regression chapter, dear Laura? All peoples' past lifetimes not separate experiences, all connected together. Like squirrels with nuts people hide impressions in subconscious. When I come back perhaps you will permit I regress you."

"Yes, yes, Eva."

There was a long silence on the phone and then a crackling sound of interference of some kind, and then Laura heard deep, labored breathing.

"Eva? Eva! Are you there?"

"Yes, dear Laura. I must go now, but—"

Again a pause and the labored breathing. Then Eva Konyi said, in a subdued, spiritless voice, "Proceed with care, dear Laura. . . . Talk more with young man. . . ."

"What do you mean, Eva? What—"

"Far away, across all America, young man has trouble. . . . Be strong. In spring I will see you."

The crackle of interference sounded again, and then a popping sound, the hum of the disconnected line and finally silence. Irritated and disturbed, Laura went back to her work. She found it difficult to concentrate. What could Eva Konyi have meant about David having trouble? Across America could well mean California. She was fretting over the question when Sandy Turner came in to her office.

"Could I talk with you, Laurie? Just a minute?"

Laura did not invite her to take the chair at the side of her desk. Sandy stood before it as Laura looked up at her with a hostile expression on her face.

"I've just resigned, Laurie. I want to say good-bye. I'm going back to California."

A sudden feeling of guilt swept over Laura. She thought she may have caused Sandy to quit a job she knew the slender girl liked very much.

"Sit down, Sandy. Why are you leaving?"

Sandy sat and tugged her skirt down over her boney knees. She shrugged.

"My dad's doing a new picture and he wants me to handle publicity on it. I'd rather stay here, but nothing's worked out very well." She looked sadly and apologetically at Laura. "I didn't mean to break up you and Eddie."

"You didn't. We weren't getting along; hadn't been for quite a while."

Sandy ventured a feeble smile.

"Well, I'm glad about that. I mean, that it wasn't my fault. Hy and I split up, too, and I moved in with Eddie after I was sure you weren't coming back... but we decided to call it off too."

"I'm sorry, Sandy."

Sandy stood and held out her hand to Laura.

"You've always been very good to me, Laurie. If you get out to the coast, I hope you'll look me up. I'll write and give you my address when I get settled."

Laura shook her hand.

"Thanks, Sandy, and good luck."

"I—I—hope you and David Kessler work out, Laurie. I hear he's very nice."

Laura blushed. There were no secrets in the Leigh-Wilson offices. And she had been proclaiming David's charm and brilliance to all her co-workers who would listen. Lately she had been laying the groundwork with Harvey Kalisher and the key people in sales and marketing for what she hoped would be enthusiastic acceptance and a big advance on *The Levinskys*.

She heard the clattering of the typewriter as she came into the Rivington Street apartment that evening. From the busy sound there certainly seemed nothing wrong with David. She stood at the door of his study before he was aware she had come in. Then he stopped typing, popped up from his chair, rushed to her, and took her in his arms.

"Hi, Laurie love!" He kissed her cheek, then her lips. "I'm really rolling! The outline's shaping up beautifully!"

She smiled, relieved.

"You're all right?" she asked.

"Not all right! Spectacular! What's the matter?"

She told him about the phone conversation with Eva Konyi, and when she mentioned that Eva had indicated there was trouble across America, involving him, a worried frown came over his face.

"I'll call home right after dinner," he said. He did and his father and mother assured him everything was fine. He told them about the great novel he was outlining, and about the plans at Wilson-Leigh for the hitchhiker book. Laura was a little surprised that he did not mention her. He had told her that he had written his father and mother about her. But then she realized he had not asked about his sister, either, and she was so relieved to learn there was nothing wrong in California that she dismissed her fleeting puzzlement. David hung up and said, "Chalk up a miss for the great Konyi!"

The first week in December Eddie Ferraro called Laura at her office and asked her to have lunch with him. When she had gone back to the SoHo apartment with Leslie to get all her possessions three days after coming upon Eddie and Sandy in bed, Eddie had been abjectly apologetic.

"I'm sorry it's ending this way," he'd said. "I was a real shit to talk to you the way I did the other night."

"You can say that again," said Leslie, piling Laura's books in a cardboard carton. Eddie ignored her.

"You're the best woman I've ever known," he said to Laura. "I hope we can still be friends, good friends like we always were."

Laura said, "Sure, Eddie. Friends," and folded her best suit carefully and placed it in her suitcase.

She still felt kindly toward him. They had had some good

years together. On this chill December day she met him in a small French restaurant on Madison Avenue where they had often lunched and dined. He ordered dry martinis for both of them and looked admiringly at her.

"You sure look great," he said.

Laura had worn her best suit, soft gray-white wool, and a high-collared blue silk blouse, which brought out the azure of her sparkling eyes. It pleased her that Eddie noticed.

"Thank you, Eddie," she said, and added with a regretful note in her voice, "You look a little tired."

He nodded. "It was a mistake, Laura. A big mistake."

"What was?"

"My forcing you to leave. The whole dumb business of thinking I wanted parties...orgies. Ridiculous. Boring. Fucking people are crazy!"

Laura looked sympathetic.

"I really never did think you were the type, Eddie. I was surprised when you began to play those porno movies. I remember you never even wanted to see *Deep Throat.*"

Eddie grimaced and backed away from the table as the waiter put the martinis before them. When he left, Eddie said, "Only thing I can think is it must've been some kind of stupid midlife crisis."

Laura lifted her martini.

"Well, you're past it, Eddie. Here's to health and happiness the rest of your life."

He lifted his glass.

"To yours." He paused, then added, "To ours."

They drank.

"I'm sorry it didn't work out with Sandy," said Laura.

"No way," said Eddie. "Never could. I knew the third day after she moved in. You probably know she's a user."

"Grass? Of course. So... ?"

"Not just grass. Coke. Didn't you ever notice?"

"No. She was always a little uptight, but no more so than lots of other people. Are you sure?"

"She snorted the night you came in. And a couple of lines every night before bedtime."

"That's terrible," said Laura. "She's a nice girl."

"Nice, but mixed up. Bad news—for herself and whoever gets too close."

Laura was halfway through her seafood salad when Eddie

pushed aside his sole filet and asked, "You still with the hitchhiker?"

"David! David Kessler. Yes. We're very happy, Eddie."

He shook his head. "He's not for you, honey."

"Don't be silly, Eddie. You don't even know him."

"I know enough. I know he practically had you do his goddam book all over for him, from scratch. He leans on you too much, uses you!"

"I'm an editor. It's my job."

He reached across the table and took her hand.

"I want you to move back, honey. We belong together. I swear I'll never—"

Laura looked startled. She withdrew her hand and interrupted more emphatically than she intended.

"I *couldn't*, Eddie! It's *impossible*! I—I—love David."

He looked hurt and angry.

Laura said, "Please, Eddie, let's be friends." She gripped his hand, still resting on the table. "Good friends!" she pleaded.

He looked at her earnestly.

"Marry me, Laura. I want you to marry me."

She was touched. It took the rest of the luncheon and two brandies that followed before she could convince him that she could not marry him. He was silent and grumpy as he walked her back to her office. At the Fifth Avenue entrance to the marble-and-glass skyscraper, she held out her hand.

"Friends, Eddie? Best of friends?"

He didn't take her hand, but he looked into her eyes, misty with cold, and nodded and said, "Best—of friends."

The cold had brought tears to his eyes too. He turned and whistled for a cab as she went into the building.

David was pecking away at the typewriter again when she got home that evening. He kept working while she got into a housecoat and put two packages of Stouffer's Shrimp Newburg into a pot of boiling water. When he came out into the dining area they had set up at the end of the parlor nearest the kitchen, he said, "I'm stuck, Laurie love. I've been struggling all afternoon with what happens to Hymie Levinsky right after the war. After dinner maybe you can read what I've done and we can work it out."

"Okay. I had lunch with Eddie Ferraro today," Laura said.

"That jerk! I had an interesting lunch with Bernie Teitlebaum, a friend from Bennington. Turns out he's a writer too."

"Oh?"

"Yeah. He was editor of the school paper last semester. He left me a short story he wrote. I think it's pretty good. He knows the drug scene down here and at school cold. I told him I'd ask you to read it. I gave him your office phone number."

He poured white wine into their glasses.

"You don't mind, do you, Laura?"

Laura had a compulsion to tell David about her lunch with Eddie. She held out until they had finished dinner. Then she could resist no longer.

"Eddie asked me to marry him, David," she said. David picked up both their plates. Before he headed toward the kitchen with them, he laughed.

"He's got to be kidding!" he said. He put the plates in the sink and returned to the parlor. He refilled both his and her glass with the chenin blanc, picked up the glasses, and headed toward his study.

"Let's go to work!" he said in his hearty, boyishly enthusiastic way.

It was eleven days later on a Friday night less than two weeks before Christmas that a man rang the buzzer of the Rivington Street apartment. David was in his study working on a sample chapter to go with the outline of *The Levinskys*. Laura was stretched out on the sofa reading the last ten pages of the outline. She answered the door. The man was tall and slim, almost gaunt. He was in his late thirties, possibly early forties. He had large ears and a tired, sad face.

"Evenin', miss," he said, holding out an open wallet showing a badge and a photo on a card identifying him as a member of the New York City Police Department.

"My name is Morrissey. Are you Laura Van Gelder?"

"Yes. What's wrong?"

"Don't be alarmed, miss. May I come in?" asked the plainclothes officer.

"Of course. Please do."

Laura led him to the sofa. He took off his narrow-brimmed felt hat.

"Take off your coat. Sit down," she invited.

"Who is it, Laur?" yelled David from the study. Laura went to the study entrance.

"It's—it's a man from the police."

David returned with her. The detective dropped his heavy

coat over the arm of the sofa and said, "Do you know a Bernard Teitlebaum, Miss Van Gelder?"

"Yes!" said David excitedly. "We both know him. What's happened? Has he been busted?"

Laura had never yet met the Bennington student. She had read the short story he had left with David and found it quite hopeless. It was apparent he knew the drug scene well, but he had absolutely no sense of construction, drama, character development, suspense, or any of the other elements of acceptable fiction. Laura had expressed her opinion to David and he had said, "Well, maybe you can help him with it, Laur. He's a nice guy."

The detective said, "His body was found yesterday afternoon in an alley on Avenue C. He'd been strangled and stuffed in a plastic trash bag. He had your phone number in his address book, Miss Van Gelder. We thought maybe you could help. . . ."

32

They sat on the unevenly overstuffed sofa, Laura flanked by David and the detective. Morrissey's announcement had shocked them both. She listened tensely now as David explained why and how Bernie Teitlebaum happened to have Laura's office phone number in his book.

"So *you* were his friend," said the detective quietly. He took a dog-eared pad out of his inside coat pocket, flipped a few spiral-bound pages, read his notes for a moment, and said, "Did you by any chance have lunch with him at Bernstein's two weeks ago?"

David smiled nervously. "You guys certainly work fast," he said. "How did you know?"

"A waiter there gave me a pretty good description. Did you know Teitlebaum was dealing?"

"Yes, he told me he was. On a real small scale, of course. Just with some of the kids at school."

Laura sensed a sudden tension in the detective sitting beside her. She turned away from David toward him. He seemed to have stiffened. His short-cut gray-streaked hair, even his thick black eyebrows, appeared to bristle. He had a broad, generous mouth, but now the corners were downturned in anger. She saw his jaw muscles tighten.

"*Just* the kids at school!" He repeated David's words angrily. "*Just* the kids!"

"Well—I—I—mean—" said David. "He wasn't—"

"You live here, Mr. Kessler?" asked the detective coldly, fighting to regain control of himself.

"Yes. Miss Van Gelder and I—we—"

"You two married?"

Laura said icily, "I don't see that that's any of your business."

The detective held a stub of pencil over his notebook. He smiled a cold smile at Laura and said, "I take it that means no. Just like to be thorough, *Miss* Van Gelder."

He asked Laura and David their occupations and then whether they were into drugs at all. They said no.

"Not even pot?" He seemed skeptical. Laura had smoked occasionally while living with Ferraro, but neither she nor David smoked at all now.

"Not even filter-tip lights, sir," she said sarcastically.

He made no direct accusations, nor even any strong insinuations, but Laura got the impression from his questions that he suspected David of being involved somehow with the Bennington student's drug dealing. Finally he closed his notebook and returned it to his pocket. He got up and struggled into his heavy overcoat.

"By the way," he said, "could I have the story Teitlebaum gave you? I'll make a copy and get it back to you tomorrow."

"Well . . . ?" said David, who had grown increasingly uneasy during the detective's interrogation, "I don't know—it's—"

"Of course you may have it," said Laura, looking mildly irritated at David. She went into her study and brought out the manuscript in a fresh buff Wilson-Leigh envelope.

When the detective left, David said angrily, "What the hell'd you want to give him Bernie's story for?"

Laura looked at him in astonishment.

"Why on earth not, David?" she asked, surprised and irritated at his attitude.

"Well, it's about dealing drugs. It could blemish his reputation, hurt his family. We could have said we gave it back to him."

"I can't believe this is you speaking, David! The poor man is dead! They know he was dealing!" She paused, and then asked quietly, "*Do* you know anything about who killed him,

David? Did he say anything to you when you last saw him? Was he frightened?"

"No. You heard what I told Morrissey. The only thing I didn't tell him was that Bernie asked me whether you and I might like to deal a little. You know . . . around the office, with friends . . . stuff like that. I told him no way would we be interested!"

"You never told me that, David."

"There was no reason I should. The whole idea was ridiculous. Why would I even mention it?"

At three the next afternoon the receptionist phoned in to Laura that a Mr. Morrissey was here to see her. Annoyed that he had not bothered to call for an appointment, Laura nevertheless had him come in.

"Sorry to bother you, Miss Van Gelder," he said, holding his hat in one hand and the manila envelope in the other. "I was in the neighborhood and I thought I'd return Teitlebaum's story."

He dropped the envelope on the desk.

"Got a minute?" he asked, moving toward the chair at the side of her desk.

"I suppose so. It would be better if you'd call—"

"I know. I'm sorry. I will in the future."

He kept his coat on, but placed his hat on the corner of her desk and took the chair.

"You read the story?" he asked.

"Yes. I didn't think it was very good."

He smiled. When he wanted to, for a man with such a rugged face, he could smile nicely.

"I wouldn't know about that," he said. "But it's right on the button."

"The button?" said Laura, puzzled.

"He's changed all the names, but he tells about the drug operation exactly like it is. He describes it all, from the kid lookouts to the steerers to the dealer. He tells how he hooks the kids at school with the parties, the free samples. He even has a character who heads up the organization his dealer buys from, who's a lot like a man you might know."

It flashed through Laura's mind that he might mean Eddie Ferraro. He paused and stared directly into her eyes. His jade-green eyes had the penetrating quality of laser beams.

"That filthy bastard who owns your building," he said with

soft vehemence. Laura was flustered. Morrissey watched her cheeks redden in confusion.

"Excuse the expression," he said.

"You—you mean Mr. Mejias?"

"He used to have his tenements torched till a few years ago when he got a piece of the heroin and cocaine action," said Morrissey. "You mean you live there and you've never even met him?"

"He doesn't come around. David rented the apartment from him. I moved in later. Mr. Torres collects the rents for him."

"Then David knows him," said Morrissey. "How well, you think?"

Laura said angrily, "Mr. Morrissey—detective—sergeant—whatever you are. David has nothing to do with any of this. I know him. I can assure you—"

Morrissey raised his hands, palms facing Laura as if to ward off the force of her words.

"All right, all right, Miss Van Gelder. I haven't accused Mr. Kessler of anything. I'm just doing my job."

Laura told David about Morrissey's visit when she got home that evening. David seemed uncharacteristically uneasy and nervous. Contemptuously he dismissed Morrissey and his suspicions, but at dinner he said, "Laura, I may have to go home for a few days. My mother called this afternoon. My father's not feeling too well. He may have to have a pacemaker put in."

But he did not leave. In the morning he finished the last of the three chapters he had written to go along with the outline for *The Levinskys*, and brought them up to Laura's office. He seemed to have completely forgotten Morrissey's suspicions and his father's condition. He was his usual aggressive, enthusiastic self.

"How soon do you think you can get a decision, Laura?" he asked as he placed the tightly packed envelope on her desk. She smiled and shrugged.

"I don't know, David. Don't be impatient. I'll get an answer as soon as I can. Did you get a copy to the Pines?" Laura always respected her relationship with literary agents.

"I didn't make a copy, but I'll tell them about it next week."

"I'll make a copy for them," said Laura.

"Did the copies of the *Hitchhiker* come in yet?" David

asked eagerly. Laura reached across the desk and touched his hand.

"Any day now, David," she said.

He kissed her on the cheek and said, "I'm going over to the library to pick up some of Jacob Riis's books. See you tonight."

An hour and a half after he left, Harvey Kalisher brought in one of the first copies of David's book, a small supply of which had just arrived from the bindery.

"Here it is, Laurie! The maiden work of your good friend!"

"Oh, thank you, Harvey."

She held it up and stared admiringly at the colorful jacket. It showed a tall young man walking away from the viewer, along a dirt road flanked on either side by an intriguing mix of farmhouses and skyscrapers, palm trees and pines. On the horizon the arch of a rainbow was fragmented by ugly smoke-colored clouds, an A-bomb mushroom ripping into the multitinted demicircle. Across the top of the jacket was the title and at the bottom, A Now Generation Journey by David Kessler.

"David loves this jacket," she said to Harvey. She herself thought it somewhat gaudy, but she had never said so to David or the Wilson-Leigh art director.

"Keep your fingers crossed, Laurie," said Kalisher. "We're getting out copies for prepublication reviews today."

Laura beamed, raised her right hand and crossed the index and third fingers. Then she picked up the envelope with the outline and chapters of *The Levinskys*.

"David just brought in the material on the novel. What would you like me to do with it?"

"Good, good," he said. He took the envelope. "I'll have Sally read it over the weekend."

Sally Harbach was an associate editor and very conscientious. Laura felt certain she would have a report by the beginning of the week. She left the office early with the copy of *The Hitchhiker's Guidebook*. She had considered holding the book until Christmas Eve and giving it to David for a present. But she felt it would be cruel to make him wait a day longer than necessary. She herself couldn't wait to witness his reaction. She knew it would be like watching a child open the Christmas present he wanted more than anything else in the world.

When she hurried up the stoop and into the first-floor

hallway, she saw that the door to the apartment was wide open. She heard the sounds of people walking about and talking. She recognized David's voice, although it was unusually high-pitched and excited. He stood in the middle of the parlor with two uniformed policemen. The shorter of the cops was making notes in a small pad as David talked. He saw Laura and moved away from the policeman toward her.

"They robbed us, Laurie!" he said. "Broke the goddam bedroom window and—"

The cop who had been taking notes yawned and said, "Could we finish up here, buddy? The radio, a Panasonic you said, the TV—was it sixteen-inch, nineteen, black and white, color, what?"

"This is Miss Van Gelder." David introduced Laura. "She'll have to tell you about the jewelry . . . whatever."

"Sorry about this, ma'am," said the younger of the two policemen, who was not taking notes. "Happens all the time as you prob'ly know. Junkies gotta get money for their habit."

"The TV," said the shorter cop impatiently.

"Nineteen, I think," said David. "Color. A Sony. And the typewriter was a Coronamatic 2100 portable—"

"Hold it, hold it, mister. Not so fast. How you spelling Coronamat?"

Laura went into the bedroom. All the drawers in the dresser had been pulled out and her underwear, blouses, sweaters, and handkerchiefs lay strewn about the room. Her empty jewel box, lid open, was on the end table. In her study she discovered that her IBM Selectric was gone too. When the policemen had made their tallies and left, cautioning David and Laura not to build their hopes for recovery of their property too high, David sat dejectedly on the sofa, head in his hands. Laura was especially saddened by the loss of a small copper bracelet with the tiny figure of a horse soldered on it. Her father had given it to her mother on their wedding day, and her mother had given it to her when she graduated from Swarthmore. It had been passed down through many generations of Van Gelders. The rest of her few items of valuable jewelry had been insured.

"We ought to get out of this fucking place!" said David bitterly. Laura looked at him pityingly. The burglary did not have the same devastating effect on her. Her feeling of belonging here in this place on Rivington Street was not diminished by the incident at all. Indeed she felt her resigned, pragmatic attitude most natural until David began to curse the situation. Then she marveled again over the affinity she felt to the building and the street, and she continued to accept it without question.

But she urgently wanted to cheer David up. She took the fresh copy of *The Hitchhiker's Guidebook* from the envelope she had placed on top of a bookshelf and walked to him. He was still sitting, elbows on knees, hands against cheeks, staring at the floor.

"I've got something for you, David," she said, holding out the book, jacket front turned toward him, at face level. He looked at it. It might have been a magic wand. It transformed his bearded face from a mask of sorrow to one of joy. He jubilantly yelled, "Hey!" and took the book from her hand and leaped to his feet. He held it out at arm's length and stared admiringly, a long minute, at the jacket. Then he skipped to Laura and threw his arms around her, and began to dance her around the room.

"David Kessler's first best-seller!" he sang. "David Kessler is on his way!"

It was on Thursday, December 15, that the apartment was robbed and Laura brought home the copy of David's book. From the moment he held it in his hands he seemed to become totally obsessed with it. He insisted Laura set up appointments for him with all the key people at Wilson-Leigh, Toni Whittaker, the new director of publicity; the promotion manager; the advertising and marketing heads.

"Now, David," Laura warned. "You mustn't make a pest of yourself. It would only be counterproductive. These people are all professionals and they really don't welcome authors telling them how to do their jobs."

"I'm not going to tell them, Laurie love! I'm just going to give them some ideas. Like—listen to this—I go to every major book market that I covered on my travels, dress in my hiking clothes, and make appearances in all the top bookstores, especially the chains, Waldenbooks, Dalton, Crown, to autograph copies. Then—"

Laura smiled at his breathless enthusiasm.

"Okay, okay. I'll do what I can."

"When can you get some more copies, Laur? I want to send them to my mom and dad and a bunch of other people. . . ."

"As soon as a decent supply comes in," said Laura.

The next morning Ramon and Felipa Torres came in just as Laura was getting ready to leave for the office.

"Jeez, kids," said Ramon, punctuating every few words with his chronic cough, "terrible what happen to your place. Did they get much? We was uptown at Al Mejias's office yesterday and then went to see Felipa's mother in the Bronx. Jus' heard about it this morning."

"It was bad enough," said David, "but I got something to show you."

He rushed into his study and came out with the book. They oohed and ahhed and congratulated him.

"You're sure a smart boy, Davey," said Ramon.

Then Felipa turned serious. "We have trouble too. Fernando, he don't come home again last night. T'ree times last two weeks he don't come home."

David patted her shoulder.

"Don't worry, Mrs. Torres. I've been keeping an eye on him. He has a friend, Javier Gonzales, who works in one of those South Street stores, too, and Ferdy stays at his house now and then. They're both good kids."

"Tha's what Ferdy tells us, too," said Ramon, "but we're not so sure."

David said, "I'll talk to him again. But I wouldn't worry if I were you. When Laurie gets me some extra copies I'll autograph a book for you."

Ramon looked pleased. Neither he nor Felipa read very much, but he was flattered nevertheless. Laura finally asked Ramon if he knew of someone who could install bars on their windows, and he said he did and would arrange to have it done.

"You people been warm enough?" he asked.

"Most of the time," said David. "When it's too cold, we just wear sweaters."

"I talked to Mejias. I tol' him we need new boiler. Old one's about to go. I don't want it should break down in middle of winter. Would be very bad! He say he'll think about it. Sonabitch"—he stopped to bring a prolonged coughing attack under control, then looked apologetically at his wife and Laura—"he can afford ten new boilers with money he makes on the drugs, but I don' know if he gonna do it."

Fernando did indeed come home about noon on Friday, tired but none the worse for wear. He said he had stayed with Javier on Second Street. He told his mother and father that he had a day off from his job, and slept most of the afternoon. That afternoon Laura arranged an appointment for David for the following week with Horace Kingsley, the head of her company's marketing department. She also invited Toni Whittaker over to the apartment for brunch on Sunday, along with Eddie Ferraro and Robey and Leslie Hill.

The brunch turned out to be a rather awkward occasion. It seemed that no matter the conversational subject, David always brought the talk back to his book. Robey and Leslie described the terrible time they were having finding an apartment they could afford. They invited everyone present to a party they were going to have Christmas afternoon.

"I hope you'll all come, 'cause a week later we'll have to have all our parties out on the street," said Leslie.

David asked Toni Whittaker where she lived, and said it was a shame that his book wasn't going to be released in time for the Christmas market.

"It would make a great gift," he said.

Laura, slightly embarrassed for him, changed the subject. "We've had quite a week," she said. She told briefly about the death of Bernie Teitlebaum, Detective Morrissey's investigation, and the Thursday burglary.

"I know Morrissey," said Eddie, spreading cream cheese on a toasted bagel and laying a strip of smoked salmon over it. "Both he and his brother, Tom, are good friends of mine. When Koch brought together the police, the transportation, and the housing departments—and even brought in the Feds—to make a coordinated effort to slow up the drug business here on the East Side last year, Frank and I worked with some of the transportation people for a couple of months. He operates out of the Ninth Precinct under Lieutenant Nasta, the head of the Manhattan South narc unit. He's one dedicated cop!"

Laura nodded agreement. She sipped coffee and said, "He seems fanatic at times."

Eddie said, "About a year ago his wife and four-year-old boy were killed by a young college kid who slammed into their car head on, driving while stoned to the eyeballs. Ever since, Frank Morrissey's been trying to wipe out the drug operations on the East Side single-handed. You should've seen him in a raid the cops did right here on Rivington Street, summer before last. They arrested over a hundred guys. Most of them were charged with felonies, some with misdemeanors. They picked up about a half pound of horse, and I don't know how much cocaine."

He sighed and took a swallow of his black coffee.

"More than half those bastards were immediately released. Most of the others got out right away on bail, low bail, put up by their organizations. Maybe a dozen went to jail, and those maybe for ninety days. But in the raid Frank himself brought in six dealers, one of whom he almost beat to death. The guy was working the school yards. Frank was called up before Internal Affairs, but he had witnesses that the guy pulled a knife on him."

Robey Hill said, "The city's been concentrating the war against drugs here on the Lower East Side. They got a quarter-million-dollar Federal grant to hire some extra narc prosecutors, and I don't know what else. We could surely use some of that attention up in Harlem."

David began to whisper to Toni Whittaker, seated beside him. Laura, on David's left, could make out some of what he was saying. It was to the effect that he was doing an East Side novel for Wilson-Leigh. Laura could see that the pert young publicity director was annoyed at David's whispering. She was evidently interested in the narcotics discussion.

Eddie Ferraro said comfortingly to Robey, "Well, now that you've got a nigger police commissioner, Robey, maybe you will get a little more action up there in Harlem."

Robey nodded tolerantly.

"I don't know how much difference it will really make. But Ben Ward's been a first-rate corrections commissioner. I'm sure he'll make an excellent police commissioner. And it's nice to know that come the new year, the city will have the first black police commissioner in its history."

Leslie said, "It's only happening because our shrewd Jewish mayor knows what he's doing. When the Black United Front and the Guardians finally got him and the cops up before a hearing of the House Committee on Criminal Justice on charges white cops were killing too many poor niggers, good old Koch just said, 'Okay, fellers, we'll put our best nigger in charge of the whole department, and see if he can stop it.' The simple fucking truth is McGuire was a perfectly able and honest commissioner and in any big-city police department there'll always be some ignorant, bigoted redneck pricks who get their nuts off killing minority kids."

The Black United Front was a national organization of

Negro religious and other leaders, which had been checking out allegations of police brutality for years. Its president, the Reverend Herbert Daughtry of the House of Lord Pentecostal Church in Brooklyn, was a friend of the Hills. The Guardians were a fraternal group of black policemen who were constantly campaigning for having more black officers promoted to the top ranks of the department.

"Whatever the reason, Leslie dear," said Robey quietly. "It's welcome progress."

"Sure," said Eddie. "You got Jesse Jackson giving the Democratic Presidential candidates fits."

Leslie glared at him.

David said, "I was just telling Toni about my novel. I'm doing a book on the Lower East Side at the turn of the century. There wasn't any big drug problem in those days, except for the opium dens over on Mott and Pell streets."

Leslie looked at David with some irritation. For a second Laura feared she was about to say something scatologically scathing to him. But Leslie just shook her head and bit angrily into a prune danish.

Eddie Ferraro called Laura at the office the following morning and asked her if she was free for lunch. She was and they ate at their favorite French restaurant.

"You know, honey," said Eddie, "that hitchhiker of yours is a royal pain in the ass."

"He's just young, Eddie. Young and a little self-centered. Many writers are."

"How can you prefer him to me?"

"We're friends, Eddie. Remember? There's no question of preference."

He smiled.

"Friends," he acknowledged. "That's what I wanted to talk to you about. You're the friend I trust more than anybody in the world."

Laura looked pleased and curious.

"I want to buy that building you live in, but I can't do it in my own name. I want you to buy it for me."

"I don't understand."

"Right now, with the drug situation what it is in the neighborhood, good, basically solid buildings like that one can be picked up for spit. The guy that owns it—maybe you know him—is Al Mejias."

Laura said, "I know of him."

"He's a no-good bastard—"

"That's what Detective Morrissey said about him."

"Yeah, it's the last building in the area he still owns. Three, four years ago he owned about eight of them and he had a deal with an arson ring. They burned them out and he collected big on the insurance. He's lucky he never got caught. Now he heads up one of the smaller of the forty or so narc organizations operating in the neighborhood, and he's doing very well. He needs the building like he needs a hole in the head. He's let the first three quarterly property-tax payments on the building slide this past year."

The waiter came and took their order, dry martinis, then the halibut special of the day. Eddie continued, "Used to be that the city would let a landlord get behind three whole years, twelve quarters, on property taxes before we would take over. The result was the buildings would go completely to hell by that time. Now the law is we take over after they miss just four quarterly payments. That building's in pretty good shape. Needs a new boiler, a face-lift, some redesign and reconstruction—comparatively simple—and in a couple of years, maybe five, the gentrification program will take hold, the area will be another SoHo, and the building'll be worth a fortune."

"So why can't you buy it yourself?" asked Laura.

"Conflict of interest," said Eddie. "Maybe I could get away with it, but I don't want to take the chance."

"What about Uncle Gino?"

Eddie laughed. "He loves me, but he'd want too big a piece."

Laura said she would probably do it, she certainly didn't see what she had to lose, but she would like to think about it. When she got home that night, she told David about Eddie's proposal.

"I don't think you ought to get mixed up with Ferraro," he said curtly. "Did you set up the appointment with Henshaw? I worked out this great idea where we could give away backpacks with the jacket of the book stamped on them in a drawing they could hold in the bookstores."

Henry Henshaw was the promotion manager of Wilson-Leigh.

"Henry's going on vacation through the holidays. He won't be back until after the first of the year."

They were holding this discussion in David's study, where he was sitting at the rented portable at his desk, typing out publicity and promotion suggestions. Laura noticed something odd about the framed photographs on the desk. It took her a couple of minutes before she realized that the one of David's sister in the Oregon pear orchard was missing.

"What happened to Debbie's picture?" she asked.

David appeared flustered.

"What? Oh, didn't you notice? Those bastards who robbed us took it."

Laura wondered why they didn't take the other two. The frames were at least as expensive as the frame holding the picture of Debbie.

33

Laura thought what strange Santa Clauses Leslie and Robey Hill made. And all day long she had been calling Eddie Ferraro Rudolph (as in the red-nosed reindeer). She and her three friends had started the custom in the Christmas of seventy-nine. It had been Leslie's idea. They pooled some money and Laura shopped for a bunch of toys and made up baskets filled with candies and other goodies, for a list with names and descriptions that Leslie prepared. The list consisted of Leslie's present welfare clients in Harlem plus a half dozen families on the Lower East Side, whom she had serviced during an earlier assignment in that area.

Early in the morning on Saturday, the twenty-fourth, Eddie picked up Laura on Rivington Street and then drove over to Bank Street to collect the Hills. It was snug in the heated car on this blustery, bitterly cold Christmas Eve day in 1983. There had been a modest snowfall and the streets were sloppy and gray, and Eddie drove carefully. Leslie directed him into the deserted, shabby Harlem streets and they stopped at one blighted, graffiti-decorated tenement, then another. Leslie selected the appropriate gifts and she and Robey went into the buildings to distribute them to the welfare families (usually a haggard mother and three or four small children). Eddie and Laura stayed in the car during the Harlem phase of the trip, with Eddie grumbling that he did not know why he had let Laura and Leslie talk him into this annual expedition.

"Shut up and check your sheet for the next stop, Rudolph," said Laura gaily.

"How about buying the building for me, Laurie?" he asked during one stop. "You made up your mind? Okay?"

"Sure, Eddie. Right after the holidays."

When Leslie and Robey dashed out of the decrepit buildings and across the slushy street back to the car, Robey would hold the door open and Leslie would plunge into the cozy interior, muttering something like, "Coldest fucking Christmas we ever had; goddam, it's freezing!"

But Laura could see the happy gleam in her dark eyes and the repressed smile on her face. Robey said, "Well, you did it again, Mrs. Santa. I've never seen kids look so happy."

"Next year you're gonna wear a Santa suit, Robey," insisted Leslie. "These kids gotta believe there's a black Santa."

By three-thirty in the afternoon they had made all the Harlem stops on the list, even though they took a quick lunch break in a coffee shop on 125th Street. Eddie was relaxed, steering the big car down the East River Drive. On their left the water looked cold and ugly and across the narrow river the Long Island shore seemed stark and melancholy. On the right, as they rolled by Stuyvesant Town, past Fourteenth Street, there loomed the succession of housing projects. Leslie, seated alongside Robey on the right side of the wide plush rear seat, stared out the window at the buildings.

"They must be spinning in their graves," she said, shaking her head. Laura, seated beside Eddie up front, turned to Leslie and said, "Who?"

Leslie nodded toward the rectangular hulks of the buildings and pointed as they rode slowly by.

"There're the Jacob Riis houses..." she said, "the Lillian Wald project..."

And as they glided smoothly past East Houston, "... the Bernie Baruch houses."

She shook her head sadly.

"They were all built with such high hopes for making things better. You think it'll ever get any better, Robey?"

"It's gotten better, some," said Robey, hugging her to him. "And we must keep trying at any rate, mustn't we?"

Eddie drove into Delancey Street where they made their first stop. On the East Side distribution, Laura went into the dismal, cockroach-infested homes with Leslie, since some of these Caucasian poor hated and feared Negroes. They had made four stops when they turned into Second Street. Suddenly Eddie braked the car.

"I don't believe it!" he said, startled.

Laura, Leslie, and Robey looked in the direction Eddie was staring as he pressed the switch to lower the window at his left. Coming out of the battered door of an abandoned, six-story, boarded-up tenement was Detective Morrissey. He held a scrawny, frightened man in a filthy sweatshirt and heavy gloves by the collar and was shoving him angrily across the sidewalk. Behind the detective and his captive, five poorly dressed, shivering youths watched dazedly. Their muttered obscenities popped from their frozen mouths in bursts of vapor.

"Hey, Frank!" yelled Eddie.

Morrissey stopped and looked toward him.

"Hi, Ed," he shouted back, maintaining his tight grip on the scruffy thin man. Pushing the prisoner ahead of him, he came to the car. His cheeks and jaw were dark with a day's growth of stubble. He peered in and saw Laura.

"You gonna be home later, Miss Van Gelder?" he asked, breath cloudlets exploding from his stiff, chilled lips, his nose a brilliant scarlet. Laura nodded, looking anxiously at Morrissey's captive.

"All evening," she said. "Why?"

"I think we got the guy did Teitlebaum, and I've got something for you."

"Want a lift, Frank?" asked Eddie.

"No, thanks. I'm parked right around the corner."

"Don't you cops ever take a day off?" demanded Leslie irately.

Morrissey jerked at the collar of his prisoner, who was muttering incoherently something about his rights, through chattering teeth.

"These animals never do. This shit was selling right in that building. . . . See you," he said and started up the slushy, litter-strewn street, dragging the unhappy drug dealer beside him. Laura stared at the building from which Morrissey had come. Across a fire escape on the second floor was draped a large, soiled red banner on which was printed in large letters:

DRUGS ARE SUICIDE

But what held Laura's attention was a huge wood mural,

about twelve feet high and eighteen feet wide, that had been erected against the face of the abandoned tenement on the ground level. In large, expertly printed letters was painted the dedication:

En Memoria De
Carmen Iris Rivera
11/20/67— 7/25/83

Beneath the dates of the girl's birth and death someone had scrawled a few Spanish phrases of undecipherable graffiti.

"What's that?" asked Laura, as they began to pull away.

"A homemade neighborhood memorial to a kid caught in the cross fire during a shoot-out between a couple of drug dealers last July," explained Eddie.

The encounter with Morrissey dampened the spirits of the Santa Clauses, but only temporarily. When Laura and Leslie distributed the gifts in the last two homes on their list, Laura felt a renewed glow. The joy on the faces of the children in the two families would stay with her a long time. She felt a deep sense of contentment as Eddie dropped her off at the Rivington Street apartment.

"See you tomorrow," said Leslie. "Come early." She and Robey waved as Eddie headed across town to Bank Street.

As Laura turned the key in the door, she hoped David would be feeling better. She had tried to persuade him to come along on the gift-distribution expedition, but he said he was too upset, he was not feeling well. Laura was glad she had gone. She needed the lift the expedition had given her.

The entire previous week had been difficult. On Monday Sally Harbach had come into her office and nervously handed Laura her report on David's outline and chapters of *The Levinskys*.

"I'm sorry, Laurie," she said, "if I'm being too harsh. But I didn't like it too well. Would you read my report, please? If you think it's way off base, I'll be glad to do it over, tone it down . . . but I—I really don't think it would make a solid book."

Laura said, "Don't feel bad, Sally. If you didn't like it, you didn't like it." She handed the report back to Sally.

"I appreciate your offering to let me read it, but I can't. It wouldn't be right. Just turn it in to Harvey."

She *was* irritated that Sally hadn't liked it, but she was a professional and she knew that Sally was giving her honest opinion, and that she could well be right. Laura herself had had continuing doubts about whether the story would work, or whether David was an accomplished enough writer to bring off the character delineations essential to the story's success. As soon as she got home that night David asked whether Sally had turned in her report, and Laura lied to him.

"She won't be able to get to it for a while, David," she said. "Harvey gave her another manuscript—a rush assignment."

David grumbled and asked whether it might be a good idea for him to call Kalisher and see if he could speed a decision. Laura vehemently insisted he do no such thing.

Later in the week David had his meeting with Harold Kingsley, the marketing vice-president. Kingsley came into Laura's office at the end of that day and said, "Your friend comes on pretty strong, Laurie. Maybe it'd be a good idea if you cooled him off a little."

Again when David asked her that night whether Kingsley had said anything about the meeting, she lied. She said, no, he hadn't. Toni Whittaker had complained to her yesterday, Friday, that David was nagging her to death and asked if Laura could persuade him to lay off. But again Laura said nothing to him.

She was worried and unhappy. Her relationship with Eddie Ferraro had taken five years to deteriorate, but now her romance with David seemed to be threatening to dissolve in less than six months. He had become utterly self-centered and concerned only with his book and the prospects for the unwritten novel. He was irritable and edgy a good part of the time and their sex life was going bad. Laura began to wonder if she hadn't made a big mistake in becoming involved with him so soon after her breakup with Eddie.

And then, last night, there had been the telephone call. She and David had finished dinner and Laura was wrapping the toys she, Eddie, and the Hills would be distributing Saturday.

"You sure you won't come along, David?" she had asked. "It's really fun. And you've got such a great beard. We could pass you off as Santa's son."

"No," he said. "I'm not feeling all that well. I feel a cold coming on, and the weather's so lousy."

The telephone rang and since Laura was closest to it, she

picked it up. It was a person-to-person call from California for David. She handed him the phone and went back to wrapping.

"Hi, Dad," she heard him say, "same to you. My book's out." He suddenly sounded animated. "I'll have some copies for you sometime next week, I think. It's great—"

Laura looked up from her wrapping as he stopped talking. After several minutes of silence, during which his face clouded, he said angrily, "It's ridiculous. No! The hell with it. No! I can't come home. I've got work to do on plans for promoting the book . . . and I'm doing a novel . . . and—"

Laura was startled to see the color vanish from his face as he listened again, this time for less than a half minute. Then he said furiously, "Well, I don't give a shit! I won't, Dad. I won't come home!" And he slammed the phone down in its cradle.

He looked at Laura, who was watching him now, with deep concern in her blue eyes.

"What's wrong, David? Is your dad all right?"

He stared at her, an unhappy, angry look on his face.

"What? My dad? Oh, yeah, sure. He's fine. It's—it's—my aunt and uncle are coming out from Chicago to stay through the New Year and—and he wants me to come home."

Laura saw an opportunity to get David away from New York and out of Wilson-Leigh's hair for a while; a chance to reevaluate her relationship with him. She said sympathetically, "Why don't you go, David? There's nothing much you can do here through the holidays. Matter of fact very little happens around the publishing business at all now through the beginning of the year. It would be nice for you to spend a little time with your family again."

"I don't *want* to go," he said sullenly, and went into his study. In a moment she heard him pecking away at his typewriter.

When she came in Saturday evening just as a frigid darkness fell on the city, she saw that David had not finished decorating the small artificial Christmas tree they had bought. He was lying on the sofa, reading one of Jacob Riis's books.

"Oh," she said, "you haven't been able to finish the tree."

"I don't feel like Christmas," he said moodily. She went to the sofa, sat down beside him, and leaned over and kissed him. He edged away from her.

"Jeeez, you're cold!" he said, and struggled up from the sofa and went into the bedroom and got a heavy sweater. He struggled into it. Laura planned to call her family in Lancaster as she did every Christmas Eve, but thought she would try to cheer David up a bit first.

"Would you like a hot rum toddy?"

"Yeah, fine," he said, and stretched out on the sofa again. She was making the rum drink and telling him about the happy reactions of the various families they had visited. He reluctantly went back to decorating the tree as she talked.

"But the most amazing thing of all," she said finally, "over on Second Street we came upon Detective Morrissey. He said they got the person who killed Bernie Teitlebaum. He's going to come by later. You won't believe this, David. He was busting a drug dealer—on Christmas Eve. Can you imagine?"

"Who killed Bernie?" asked David.

"He didn't say."

Laura brought in the steaming pitcher of buttered rum toddies and Swarthmore mugs. The buzzer sounded and when David opened the door, there stood the detective himself. "Season's greetings to both of you," he said. "Am I interrupting anything?"

"No," said David. "Laura was just telling me the news."

"Merry Christmas, Sergeant," greeted Laura. "Please sit down and have a toddy with us."

Morrissey looked at his watch.

"I've got a few minutes," he said. "I'm on my way to Scarsdale to spend Christmas Eve with my brother and his family."

He placed his hat and coat on the sofa beside him and accepted the steaming mug of buttered rum Laura handed him.

"To your health," he toasted.

David cupped his mug in both hands, warming them. "Did you really find the guy who killed Bernie Teitlebaum?"

Laura returned the toast, and David did, too, absently. Morrissey sipped and put his mug on the table.

"We did," he said. "Guy named Nunzio Fabrizzi. He and a bunch of other kids from Bedford-Stuyvesant got involved with some minor mob members when they were in their teens. He's been freelancing as a hired killer and general all-around no-good. He'll work for anybody stupid enough to give him a gig—or often as not he'll knock off somebody because he doesn't like them, or because he thinks they crossed him, or just for laughs."

He stirred the toddy with the cinnamon stick and took a long drink.

"We kept him away from his free-base pipe for a couple of days and he sang like a glee club. He told us everything except who hired him. He said the Teitlebaum kid cheated him in a drug deal."

He reached over and took a long, heavy paper envelope out of the inside pocket of the overcoat on the sofa beside him. He spilled its contents onto the table. There were a string of pearls, two rings, a digital gold wristwatch, a brooch with Laura's birthstone, a sapphire, and the copper bracelet with the tiny figure of the horse.

"You might check to see if anything's still missing," he said to Laura. She sorted the items and said, "No, nothing. I think everything's here. What a wonderful Christmas gift. Thank you, thanks, Sergeant!" She put the copper bracelet on her wrist.

"How did you ever find these?" she asked.

Frank Morrissey beamed and took another swallow of his toddy.

"Sometimes it's a small world in police work," he said. "Young Andy Kerrigan, one of the Ninth Precinct cops who responded when you were robbed, is a friend of mine. He and his father and I often go to the hockey games together. Last Wednesday at the game he told me he'd been over here on a breaking and entering. I had taken in Nunzio three days before. When Andy told me about the missing jewelry I remembered that Nunzio's closest pal, when they were growing up, was a ratty kid named Moishe Kalbfleisch. When Nunzio became a hit man, Moishe began fencing, but he fenced jewelry exclusively. He opened a couple of legit jewelry shops, one on Seventh Avenue near Twenty-sixth and another over in Brooklyn, but he continued to fence. I just thought there might be a chance whoever robbed your place might have taken the jewelry to Moishe. Kerrigan paid Moishe a visit, and sure enough there it was."

"Did you get any of my stuff?" asked David. "I sure miss that typewriter. I can't get used to this damned rental."

"Sorry, Mr. Kessler. These junkies generally sell off stuff like typewriters, TVs, and radios to individuals. They get a better price that way."

Morrissey finished his toddy.

"Ready for another?" asked Laura, heading for the bookshelf where the pitcher sat on a hot plate. The detective looked at his watch again.

"No thanks. I'd like to, but I'd better not. My sister-in-law'll murder me if I'm late for the festive goose."

"How did you find out about Nunzio?" asked David. Morrissey smiled as he got into his overcoat. He shrugged.

"Usual way," he said. "Through a snitch."

He chuckled. "But if I told you about this snitch, you wouldn't believe me anyway. He's a leprechaun."

He bade them the season's greetings again and left.

"I didn't think Sergeant Morrissey could ever be in such a good mood," remarked Laura.

David said, "I suspect he had a few drinks before he got here."

Laura poured another toddy for David and herself and sat beside him on the sofa. She lifted her mug to him.

"To us, David."

He raised his mug and said, "To *The Hitchhiker's Guidebook and Pocket Companion*. May it go all the way to number one!"

Laura did not drink. She put her mug down abruptly and said, "I've got to call my folks."

As she sat in the new wing chair she had bought and punched the buttons on the phone on the table beside it, she felt a sudden premonition of disaster. Then her brother's voice said hello. She forced herself to sound appropriately cheerful.

"Hi, Billy. Merry Christmas."

"Same to you, Laurie."

His voice sounded flat and sorrowful.

"What's the matter, Billy?"

"Mom and Dad are at the hospital. They took Gramps this afternoon."

Grandfather Lawrence Van Gelder was eighty-four years old. He had been a heavy smoker all his life, despite the warnings of the United States Surgeon General. He had suffered intermittent attacks of emphysema, so William's announcement did not really come as a surprise to Laura. Nevertheless she was shocked. Christmas Eve seemed the wrong time for him to be hospitalized again.

"Emphysema?" asked Laura.

"No. Empyema. About a week ago he developed pneumonia. The weather's been so bad. The doctors loaded him up with antibiotics and they thought they had it under control, but then it got worse and he came down with this empyema."

"What the hell is it—empyema?"

"It's pretty rare these days. Usually the antibiotics will prevent it, but in Gramps's case they didn't. Pus forms in the space between the chest wall, the pleural cavity, and the lungs, as I understand it. Dad called a while ago. He said they were going to have to operate."

"I'll catch a train first thing in the morning," said Laura.

"No, no, Sis. Mom and Dad don't want you to ruin your holiday. There's really nothing you can do—"

"See you in the morning, Billy," said Laura and hung up. She was extremely fond of her grandfather. He had lavished love, money, and gifts on her ever since she was a small child, but more importantly, he had urged her to pursue a career and become an independent woman. During his reign the family newspaper had reached new pinnacles of prestige in the community, even to some degree in the state, and had achieved enormous financial success.

"What's wrong, Laur?" asked David when she went into the bedroom to begin packing. She told him.

"How old is he?" asked David, standing in the doorway, watching her toss apparel into the suitcase.

"Eighty-four," she said. "Obviously, it could be bad."

"I don't mean to sound callous, Laur, but why don't you go Monday, after Leslie's party?"

Laura looked at him with a mixture of disbelief and disgust. She shook her head.

"I'm leaving in the morning."

"You think Toni Whittaker will be at the party?"

She had an impulse to turn on him and scream, *If she is, don't keep hitting on her about the goddam book!* but she just shook her head again and said wearily, "I don't know, David. I don't know."

At seven o'clock Christmas morning she was at Pennsylvania Station, bustling even at that hour. Less than three hours later, as she opened the door to the attractive, colonial frame and stone house on Tulip Lane in Lancaster where she had grown up, she sensed the deep air of gloom. When she saw her mother, sitting on the sofa, weeping quietly into a handkerchief, with her brother holding her hand, she, too, felt like weeping. Her father was on the telephone, and he nodded somberly to her as he spoke. She dropped her suitcase and rushed to her mother. She put her arms around her and hugged her tightly. She looked across her mother's bent back at William. He whispered sadly, "Three o'clock this morning." His eyes were wet too.

Laura phoned Harvey Kalisher Monday morning and got his permission to stay with her family until the week after New Year. That afternoon Leslie called her to ask if there was anything she or Robey could do. In the evening Eddie Ferraro phoned. Of course there was nothing any of them could do, but Laura found some comfort in their sympathy and concern. The church ceremony and funeral were attended by close to a hundred people, family, friends, and dignitaries from Lancaster, Philadelphia, and other parts of the state. Both congressmen and the senator from Pennsylvania paid their respects.

On the fourth day of the new year Laura, her brother, and her parents held a meeting with the family lawyer, Ezra Hutchins. Lawrence Van Gelder had left his majority stock in the family newspaper and all his property to his son and daughter-in-law. He bequeathed one hundred thousand dollars each, with no strings attached, no conditions as to usage, to Laura and to William. In the days that followed, grieving notwithstanding, the family, Hutchins, the president of the Van Gelders' bank, and the newspaper's financial vice-president met several times to discuss investment possibilities for Laura and William. The general consensus of the financial experts was that the bulk of the money, if not all of it, should be invested in real estate. All believed that the inflation would continue despite the decrease in the rate during the Reagan Administration. The near two-hundred-billion deficit had them all greatly concerned.

Laura mentioned Eddie Ferraro's intention to buy the Rivington Street building, and his reasons for it. Her father, his lawyer, and his banker were all aware of the way real estate values had appreciated in other depressed areas of metropolitan cities where gentrification programs had been effectively carried out. It was finally decided that William would take a leave from the history classes he taught at the Lancaster high school and go back to New York with Laura to explore the desirability of buying properties similar to the building on Rivington Street. They were aware that Eddie Ferraro was familiar with conditions throughout the city, and Laura assured them Ferraro would help in every way possible.

On the train on the way to New York on a frigid Monday morning in the second week in January, Laura told her brother about the strange feeling she had had about the house on Rivington Street the very first day she entered the building.

"I don't know what it is, Billy, but I just feel as if I belong there . . . like I've lived there a long time . . . sometime. Does that sound idiotic?"

"A little," said Bill Van Gelder, "but I've heard of stranger things."

Laura told him about having worked with Eva Konyi on her book, and about the astonishing stories of regression and other psychic experiences the Hungarian woman related.

"She regressed my best friend three hundred years, back to Spain," said Laura. "I swear, Bill. It's true."

"When are you and Eddie going to get married?" asked Bill as the train racketed across the barren, snow-covered countryside. On numerous visits to New York during his summer hiatuses, Bill Van Gelder had met Eddie Ferraro and spent quite a bit of time with him. He was fond of Eddie, and had been the major force in persuading his mother and father that there was nothing so terrible about Laura and Eddie living together; young people these days liked to be sure of their compatibility before making the total commitment.

Laura blushed and stammeringly told him about her breakup with Eddie and her relationship with David.

"And now I'm not so sure that David and I are right for each other, either. I—I'm kind of ashamed of myself, Billy. I don't seem to be able to—"

"Nonsense!" said Bill. "It will work out. You're too fine a woman not to wind up with a good man one of these days—and I mean a good man you'll marry."

Laura patted his hand and smiled.

"Never mind me. What about you? Have you found a good woman yet?"

Bill shook his blond head.

"No. I'm still playing the field, that is, to the extent that I play at all. I haven't told you. I'm working on a biography of William Penn. Between that and the work at school, where I'm also assisting the football coach, I don't have too much time for romantic alliances."

"Oh, how wonderful, Billy. How far along are you?"

"I'm still working on the structure from my research, and

I've roughed out a couple of outlines and done four rough drafts so far of what might be a first chapter, none of which I particularly like. It's tough." He paused.

"You're the one in the family who should be writing, Laurie. Editing's fine, but you've got the talent to do some fine writing. You always did have."

"Let me see what you've done when you're ready, Billy. Maybe I can help."

At Rivington Street David greeted her exuberantly, hugging and kissing her warmly.

"I've sure missed you, Laur!" he said. She introduced him to Bill, and David told him how glad he was to meet him.

"I told the Torreses you were coming in today," said David, "and they insist we join them for dinner. They want to celebrate a belated Christmas with us."

Laura had bought gifts for all the Torreses as well as for David, but her sudden departure for Lancaster had, of course, prevented her from distributing them. Mrs. Torres had prepared an excellent dinner and Maria and young Fernando had pooled the money to buy a bottle of wine. Before they began eating Ramon said a prayer, punctuated with the inevitable coughing, and then lifted his glass.

"An' God bless our good friends, David and Laura," he said, and coughed again. "Because David has been fine big brother to him, our Fernando has not missed day of school for more than a whole month. In his job he is promoted to stock boy, not just errand boy. An' Laura helps our Maria so much, Maria wishes one day she's gonna be just like Laura. We love you an' we thank you. An' God bless you."

It was a warm and festive evening. Mrs. Torres had embroidered a lovely cotton handkerchief for Laura and knitted a wool scarf for David. David and Laura had purchased simple gifts for each of the Torreses: a book of poetry for Maria; a transistor radio for Fernando; a heavy wool sweater for Ramon, and a colorful, warm shawl for Felipa. Laura gave David a cashmere sport coat and David gave her a leather-covered engagement book with her name embossed on it in gold.

Bill Van Gelder watched the proceedings with a broad smile on his face. He didn't know people like the Torreses. Maybe, he thought, Laura has something in the way she feels about this place. Maybe she does belong here. Laura was pleased about the evening, especially about the fact that

David did not once mention *The Hitchhiker's Guidebook* or his East Side novel. Three days later the prepublication review of the *Guidebook* appeared in the new issue of *Publishers Weekly*.

34

David paced back and forth in the parlor like an agitated zoo lion, reading angrily and breathlessly as he stalked the room.

> "'There has been frequent commentary of one kind and another,'" he orated bitterly, "'on the so-called me generation. But in this first work, Kessler, a self-appointed spokesman for that generation (unintentionally it is assumed), exposes the egocentric mind, the shallow heart, and the bankrupt philosophy of so many of today's young people.'"

He interrupted himself.

"Christ on a mountaintop! What a prejudiced, ignorant misreading!" Then, still pacing, he read on:

> "'No matter where Kessler traveled, no matter whom he encountered or the events he witnessed, his sophomoric observations and didactic judgments reveal a callow self-centeredness—'"

He hurled the magazine against the wall above the bookcase, where it fluttered to the top shelf, pages torn and askew.

"Can you believe such shit?" he yelled.

Laura had just arrived from the office that evening and had hardly removed her coat and wool cap when David had waved the magazine at her and insisted on reading her the review. Now as he flopped to the sofa and slapped a hand furiously against his thigh, she said soothingly, "Don't take it too seriously, David. *Publishers Weekly* has been wrong before. Being savaged by critics is an occupational hazard in the life of an author."

"I'm going to write them and demand to know who wrote that stupid crap! I'm going to—"

"It's just a trade journal, David," interrupted Laura. "It doesn't have a very large circulation. It—it—" She knew full well that while the magazine was not read by the general public, it was consulted by thousands of booksellers and influenced many of them in deciding whether or not to stock a given work. She could not honestly minimize further the potential effect of the negative review. Bill Van Gelder, who was staying with David and Laura, arrived a few minutes after another stuttering, futile effort on Laura's part to console the bruised author. David retrieved the damaged magazine from the bookshelf, found the page with the review, and handed it to Bill.

"You've got to read this, Bill. Imagine a critic being this stupid. It must be someone a hundred years old, who hates anyone under sixty!"

All the while Laura was preparing dinner and while they ate, David ranted. Finally Bill excused himself, saying he had a date to meet a fraternity brother whom he hadn't seen in a couple of years.

"Don't make any arrangements for tomorrow night, Billy," said Laura. "Remember, we're having dinner with Eddie."

The following evening the nonstop elevator zoomed Laura and Bill up to the Windows on the World on the 107th floor of the World Trade Center Building near the tip of the island. Despite the wind and the cold Bill insisted on going out on the observation platform atop the building to view the city and the surrounding countryside through the twin-lensed coin-operated telescope.

"Your brother's crazy!" said Eddie as he and Laura waited for Bill to come back inside. In a moment he did, his face already scarlet and stiff, his eyes moist from the frigid breeze.

"God! What an incredible sight!" he exclaimed. "This truly is a magic city."

He insisted on standing inside and staring through the thick double windows at the spectacular vista of illuminated skyscrapers, the stringed jewels flung across the city's bridges, the glistening ebony rivers, and the scattered firefly lights in buildings over in Brooklyn and across on the Long Island and New Jersey shores.

Finally they persuaded him to come into the elegant Hors

d'Oeuvrerie, where they had drinks and, at Eddie's urging, the spicy Kyoto beef rolls.

Bill neglected both his beer and the pungent beef delicacy. "You look uptown and east and west for miles and miles at all these buildings," he said in awestruck tones, "and it's hard to believe that three hundred years ago it was all forest and marshland, full of wild beasts and—"

Eddie sipped his martini and interrupted. "Still plenty of wild beasts down there."

Bill ignored the comment. He rambled on, "Did you know that when the Dutch settled New Amsterdam"—he grinned at Laura—"maybe including some scruffy ancestors of ours, Laurie, the village extended only from the tip of the island to Wall Street. The burghers built a wall there to keep out Indians and wolves. That's how it got its name. Everything beyond that was wilderness."

"Like I say," said Eddie, laughing, "a lot of it still is."

William Van Gelder rushed on.

"I've been a busy tourist the last couple of days while Laura's been at work. Day before yesterday I took the boat out to the Statue of Liberty and went through the American Immigration Museum. Did you two ever go?"

"I'm ashamed to admit I've never been to the Statue of Liberty," said Laura.

"I've lived here all my life and I've never been," said Eddie.

"The museum is a course in the history of New York all by itself," said Bill. "Did you know that from 1892 through 1954 alone seventeen million immigrants came through Ellis Island? Your forebears, Eddie, and ours. They estimate that those seventeen million are the ancestors of about forty percent of the nation's entire population, well over a hundred million Americans."

"You are a history teacher all right," said Eddie.

"The statue itself is in pretty bad shape," said Bill.

"I know," said Eddie. "The guy I'm planning to use on rehabilitating and fancying up the Rivington Street building is on a committee of American and French architects who are going to do a thirty-million-dollar face-lift job on the old girl. They want to have her looking like sweet sixteen in time for the centennial of her dedication in 1986. Tom just got back from a meeting in Washington with the National Park Service people. Morrissey's the perfect man for the Rivington Street job. His firm, Morrissey, Hellman, Kleindienst, and Morrissey, has done some great work in the city, and Tom's especially good at restorations."

"Is that the one who's related to the detective?" asked Laura.

"Right," said Eddie. "Frank's brother. Now let's talk about your buying the building for me, honey. I think Mejias is ready."

"Eddie, are there any other buildings in the area for sale?" asked Bill.

"Not in as good shape as the Rivington Street place. Why?"

Bill explained about the legacy their grandfather had left them, and their decision to invest in real estate.

"Great," said Eddie. "You can come in on the Rivington Street deal with me. We'll form a corporation or a partnership or whatever the accountants say, and really build us something." He grinned at Laura. "I've been trying to form a legitimate partnership with this gal for months now." Eddie took a sheet of paper from the inside pocket of his jacket. "Here's a list of the things that are wrong with the building and some rough estimates—exaggerated a little—of what it's going to cost to fix 'em up. Boiler's about to go; roof in terrible condition; walls and ceilings in most of the apartments cracked; termites in sections of the foundation; stuff like that. If you bone up on this stuff, Laurie, and come on like a real expert, you'll be able to knock Mejias down to almost nothing for the place."

"Should I go along with Laura to see this Mejias?" asked Bill. "I've only got a couple more days. I've got to get back to school."

"No, no," said Eddie. "Mejias is a pushover for pretty girls. He'll want to show Laura what a generous big shot he is, especially when she throws in her expertise along with her big blue eyes, her million-dollar smile, and that figure."

"You can be pretty silly, Eddie," said Laura.

Bill Van Gelder was shocked at the check. It came to more than sixty-five dollars each, but Eddie gave the Italian waiter two one-hundred bills and one fifty and told him to keep the change.

"Eddie does pretty well, doesn't he?" commented Bill, as he and Laura sat back in a taxi on the way to Rivington Street.

"Yes, he always did."

"What did he mean by saying he's been trying to create a partnership with you for months? Does he want you to move back in with him?"

Laura smiled, a bit self-satisfiedly.

"He wants to marry me."

"Great! You going to?"

Laura shook her head.

"I don't think so. We get along much better as good friends."

"It's none of my business, Laurie," said Bill tentatively, "and . . . it's just my opinion, but I like Eddie a lot better than David."

Laura shrugged.

"Sometimes I think I do too."

"You going to tell David about buying the building?"

"I don't think so. I don't know how he would react to discovering I was going to be his landlord, or landlady, I guess. Maybe after we make the deal with Mejias."

When they got home David queried Laura again about whether she had any word on *The Levinskys*. Harvey Kalisher had given the outline and chapters to another editorial associate for a reading, but she just told David that there was no decision yet. He then complained that he had called Toni Whittaker three times and left a message each time and she had not called him back.

"Sometimes I wonder if that secretary of hers gives her the messages," he said.

"She's a very efficient woman," said Laura. "Toni's been pretty busy. They're working on the program for Eva Konyi's book."

Eddie Ferraro had told Laura it would be advisable to see Mejias as soon as convenient. He had heard from several sources that Mejias was eager to dump the building. He also suggested to Laura that she not phone ahead for an appointment.

"If you just bust in on him by surprise some afternoon, it'll give you a little advantage," he said. "He's in his office from two to four every day, then he goes over to that crappy nightclub where they stage the mud wrestling three times a week."

On an impulse the Wednesday of that week, right after lunch, Laura decided to visit Mejias. His office was in one of the older business buildings on Forty-second Street.

* * *

A black-haired, buxom woman in her early thirties, wearing a tight purple sleeveless sweater, sat a small desk in the tiny reception area.

"Kin I help ya?" she asked Laura pleasantly.

"I'd like to see Mr. Mejias, please."

An oak veneer door with "Alexander A. Mejias, Pres. –Chm. Bd." painted in gold leaf in one corner, stood halfway open behind and to the left of the receptionist. A potbellied man in a blue polyester suit with white stripes appeared in the doorway.

"Come in, come in," he invited in a husky bass voice. He held the door wide open and waved Laura in with a flourish and a small bow. He closed the door and lumbered around and sat in a thronelike leather chair behind his enormous leather-topped desk.

"Have a seat, kid," he urged. As Laura sat in the chair beside the desk, he said, "Ya come about the ad, right?"

Laura assumed he had placed an ad offering the Rivington Street building for sale. She was glad she had decided to call on him today, before too many other prospective purchasers answered the ad.

"About the—" she started to say, but he grinned a broad, beefy grin and interrupted.

"Take off ya coat."

She rose and did so and he hurried to her and took it and hung it on a coat rack in the corner of the office. Laura watched him as he waddled back to the big chair behind the desk. He looked at her appraisingly and leered.

"Well," he said, "ya got the body for it."

Laura had the uncomfortable feeling that he was undressing her with his dark eyes. There was no mistaking that he was staring at her bosom. He wet his thick lips. Laura felt a flash of anger at herself for instinctively raising her hand to her chest as though to obstruct his view.

"Stan' up and turn aroun'," he ordered. "If ya ass is as good as ya tits ya got it."

Laura flushed and said furiously, "What the hell are you talking about, Mr. Mejias?"

A startled look came over his round, swarthy face. He spread his pudgy hands.

"Da job," he said. "What da hell ya t'ink I'm talkin' about. The mud-rasslin' job."

Laura could not help laughing.

"It pays good and da tips're outta dis world. Ya kin take down four, five hun'red bills a week."

Laura said, "I'm sorry to disappoint you, Mr. Mejias, but I'm not a mud wrestler. I'm in the real estate investment business. I want to buy your Rivington Street property . . ."

"I'll be a sumbitch!" exclaimed Mejias. "I ought've known. Ya too classy lookin' a broad t'be rasslin'."

". . . if the price is right," said Laura, ignoring the compliment. "I know you're behind on your city property tax and the building's falling apart and the police say the neighborhood's the retail drug capital of the world, and—"

"Whoa! Whoa, lady! Dat buildin's da best on da block." He grinned at her. "But I like ya. I t'ink we kin do business."

Laura spent the next hour detailing the shortcomings of the building as listed on Eddie's sheet. She mixed her analysis of the building's worth with frequent flattering remarks about Mejias's business acumen and expressed awe at his broad range of interests. By four-thirty they had agreed on a deal, which was one-quarter of what Mejias originally asked for the property and about ten percent less than Eddie Ferraro thought they would have to pay. Laura and Mejias arranged to have their attorneys draw up the papers before the week was out. Laura phoned her office to say she would not be back that afternoon. Then she phoned Eddie to tell him about the deal she had made.

"Just like I figured," he said. "You're not only sexy but you're smart, honey."

"Maybe you're right," she said. "He offered me a job mud wrestling at Dreamland."

"If you took it," said Eddie, "it would probably become my favorite sport."

In the cab downtown she decided she would tell David she was going to be his landlady after all. But when she came into the apartment she found he was not there. When she went into the bedroom to hang her coat, she discovered that all of David's clothes were gone. She went to his dresser and the drawers were empty. Puzzled, she rushed into his study. The framed photographs of his family and everything else except the telephone had been cleared from the desktop. The wastebasket beside the desk was crammed with crushed papers and file folders. She went through some of the crumpled pages and discovered that they were his notes on *The Hitchhiker's Guidebook*, copies of his promotion plans for the book, and some material on *The Levinskys*. Then a glitter in the basket caught her eye. She removed some more of the paper and torn cardboard and saw the framed photograph of Debbie in the Oregon pear orchard. *Why on earth had David told her the thieves had stolen it? Or had they, and returned it?* Shards of broken glass lay around the picture and frame. The silver-plated frame was badly bent. The photograph was crushed and cracked. She looked through the drawers in the desk, then went back into the bedroom, and through every room in the apartment looking for a note of some kind. She found nothing. She was back in the parlor, looking along the bookshelves, when the door buzzer sounded. She looked through the peephole and saw that it was Ramon Torres. She let him in.

"What happened with Davey?" he asked, deep concern showing on his gaunt olive face.

"I—I—I don't know, Ramon. What do you mean?"

"This morning, little while after you left for work, I see him come runnin' outta the building with a big suitcase. I holler, 'Hey, Davey, where you goin'?' He don't even turn aroun'. Jus' keeps runnin' up toward Ludlow, lookin' around', like maybe he's lookin' for a cab."

Laura shook her head.

"I don't know where he's gone. He took all his things."

She could not believe that the *Publishers Weekly* review could have upset him so enormously that he would run out on her. She did not know what to do. Bill was not going to be home until late. He and his fraternity brother were having dinner and going to a Woody Allen movie. She phoned Leslie, on the remote chance David might have said something to her. Leslie hadn't heard a word, she was as surprised as Laura.

She phoned Toni Whittaker, who was still in the office. Toni had not had a call from David that day. She said, "I'm sorry I didn't get back to him the other day, Laurie, but I've been real busy. I've got some great breaks lined up on the Konyi book."

Laura went into the kitchen and made herself a pot of coffee. She sat at the table trying to figure out why David had left so abruptly. She wondered about the smashed frame and crushed photograph of the girl in the pear orchard. Maybe it wasn't his sister. She tried to analyze her feelings. She was worried about David, true. But underlying her concern, there was a sneaking sense of relief. She just hoped nothing terrible had happened. Then she remembered Eva Konyi's strange remark about something happening across the country. She decided to call David's parents' home in Northridge, California.

A man answered. The voice sounded strained, as though the man was under great tension.

"Mr. Kessler?" asked Laura.

"Yes, this is Isaac Kessler."

"Is David there?"

"Who is this?"

"It's Laura Van Gelder. I'm calling from New York. David and I, we're—we're friends."

A note of hostility crept into the man's tone.

"I know. The woman he was living with."

"Yes," said Laura. "Is he there? He left here early this morning and—"

"He came home, Miss Van Gelder, but he is not here now."

"Is he all right? Is there anywhere I can reach him?"

"He will *be* all right," said David's father, with a distinct edge of bitterness in the voice now. "But you can't reach him. I'll tell him you called."

"Are you expecting him? Is he staying with you?"

"Yes. For now he is staying here. I'll tell him you called."

There was a sharp click and Isaac Kessler was gone.

35

Harvey Kalisher pushed the envelope across the desk and, with a note of regret in his voice, said, "Sorry, Laurie. I think we're going to pass on *The Levinskys*. I've had three readings, and all of them consider it doubtful."

Laura smiled at the balding, scholarly editor in chief.

"Sure, Harvey, I understand."

He patted a cardboard box on the desk before him.

"I'm buying this," he said. "*The Beneficent Bomb*. I think it's right down your alley."

"Is it fiction?"

"Uh-uh. It's by two professors at the University of Toronto. One of 'em has a Ph.D. in sociology and literature, and the other's a neuroscientist. They're both disciples of the late

Marshall McLuhan. Their thesis is that the nuclear bomb is the ultimate information medium. They say the bomb binds people together like nothing since the Middle Ages and that the shared myth of total and imminent destruction has physically changed the way billions of synapses connect in people's brains."

"It sounds pretty far out," said Laura.

"Not any farther out than Konyi's experiences and work, and a lot more scientific," countered Kalisher. "By the way, the Konyi is taking off nicely. I think we'll hit the Southern California best-seller lists next week. Largely thanks to your fine work in shaping it up."

"Good."

Four days had passed since she had spoken to Isaac Kessler and David had not called back. She was still consumed with curiosity over his sudden and obviously distraught departure. She had discussed it with her brother, but his only comment was that David had always seemed uptight to him. He could not even make a guess as to why David would have destroyed the girl's photograph, after having lied to Laura about it in the first place. Laura did not know whether to tell David about Wilson-Leigh's decision to pass on his novel, but she thought it would be a good idea to call California again. She could gauge his mood, and based on that, decide whether to break the bad news to him. As soon as she got home that afternoon she placed the call.

Isaac Kessler answered again. Even in his brief "hello," Laura detected the tension. Again he informed Laura that David was not there. Again he sounded hostile.

"Did you tell him I called?" asked Laura.

"Yes, Miss Van Gelder. Of course I told him."

"Sorry, Mr. Kessler. I just thought maybe you might have been busy—and forgot—"

"No. I did not forget. I told him. And I will tell him that you called again."

"When do you expect to see or hear from him?"

"Later tonight he'll be home. Good-bye."

"Mr. Kessler! Please! Just a minute!" Laura's voice took on an urgency. "Is your daughter home?"

"My daughter? What are you talking about? I don't have a daughter!"

"Oh, sorry. I—I guess I'm—mixed up. Forgive me. I *will* appreciate it if you'll ask David to call me."

"I will. I will. I said I would and I will, Miss Van Gelder."

This time he cut off the connection without saying good-bye.

The following afternoon Laura, her brother, and Eddie Ferraro had their first meeting with Thomas Morrissey. The firm's offices were on the thirty-seventh floor of the Citicorp Building. On the handsome mahogany paneled double doors, in small, dignified polished brass letters was the legend, *MORRISSEY, HELLMAN, KLEINDIEST & MORRISSEY, INC*. A cold early afternoon winter sun flooded Tom Morrissey's handsome office. Stockier and heavier than his brother, he had the same large ears. His hair was grayer, even though he was a year younger than the detective. His brown eyes were clear and not nearly as tired and sad-looking as Frank's.

On a wall was a dramatic photograph of the AT & T Building, which *The New York Times* architecture critic had called "the first Chippendale skyscraper." And alongside this was a handsome photograph of Philip Johnson, its modernist architect. The photograph was affectionately autographed "To my talented young friend, Tom Morrissey."

Laura and Bill took an immediate liking to Morrissey. He and Eddie Ferraro had obviously worked together before and seemed like warm friends. Morrissey told them he would gladly take on the assignment of redesigning and supervising the reconstruction and modernization of the Rivington Street building.

"I agree with you, by the way," he told them, "that the gentrification program in that area will be every bit as successful as the SoHo development."

On a maple table behind his desk were stacked several large books on architecture and a small pile of magazines. Prominent on the table were three photographs. The one in the center was obviously a family portrait. Tom Morrissey sat on an attractive flowered sofa with one arm around the shoulder of a young blond woman who looked like Princess Di. His other hand reached down and rested on the shoulder of a little girl with long blond curly hair. Two other girls, with hair as long, blond, and curly, snuggled closely on either side of the pretty child Tom was touching. They seemed younger than their sister, and both were reaching over and resting pudgy hands on the folded hands of the older girl. All three children wore shy, beatific smiles and Tom's wife had the contented smile of a proud mother. Only Tom himself looked serious. His wife held a sleeping baby in her arms.

"What a lovely family," commented Laura. "How old are the children?"

Tom beamed. "Marianne, the one in the middle, is five. Jackie, on her left, is four, little Phyll is three, and the one in Phyllis's arms is just a year old. He's a boy. We named him Frank after my brother."

Bill was looking questioningly at the other two photographs. To the left of the family group was a sepia-toned photo with several cracks running across its surface. It was obviously a carefully retouched reproduction of a very old photograph. It showed two young men in what appeared to be police uniforms of the nineteenth century. Each had an arm around the shoulder of the other and they were grinning broadly.

"That's my great-great-granduncle Ned," said Morrissey, "the one on the left. The man with the mustache is his partner, Gustave Winckler, whom they called Dutch. The original picture was taken by Mathew Brady, the famous Civil War photographer. I don't know if it's true or not, but family legend has it that Ned Morrissey and Dutch Winckler were part of Abraham Lincoln's bodyguard when Lincoln made his first New York City appearance at Cooper Union Hall. My grandfather had copies made of the original for everybody in the family before he died."

He pointed to the photograph flanking the family picture on the right. It was of a young man in a white naval uniform and cap, who looked a good deal like Tom Morrissey, being decorated aboard a warship by a distinguished white-haired naval officer.

"That's him. My grandfather Michael. He was a Seabee in World War Two. He's the first Morrissey in the corporate name. He founded the company right after the war. I just became a partner six months ago."

Bill Van Gelder said, "I understand you're working on the French-American team of architects and engineers who are supervising the restoration of the Statue of Liberty."

"Yes. After standing out there in the harbor for over ninety-seven years the great lady really needs some attention. When she was originally reassembled by our workmen when the French shipped her over in 1884, they put her head about two feet off center. That's caused one of the spikes in the crown to poke a hole in the torch-bearing arm, and the hole's full of growing plants. There're some bad leaks in the torch and some of the copper sheeting will have to be replaced."

He waved a hand.

"Don't get me started on that," he said, "or I'll hold you up all afternoon talking about it."

"Is it really going to cost thirty million?" asked Eddie.

"Just about, but the money'll come from public donations that'll be solicited by the Statue of Liberty–Ellis Island Commission of the Interior Department. They won't have any trouble raising it. We've still got a lot of people in this country who believe in what she stands for."

Laura mentioned that she had met his brother, Frank, and briefly described the circumstances and his successful solution of the murder of Bernie Teitlebaum. Tom Morrissey nodded approvingly.

"Frank's quite a man," he said, chuckling. "Between his dedication and his leprechaun, the bad guys don't have too much of a chance."

Leslie and Robey Hill came over to Rivington Street that evening. Laura was preparing a farewell dinner for Bill, who was to return to Lancaster in the morning. Eddie Ferraro rounded out the party. He had brought four bottles of a vintage Bordeaux and Laura broiled thick Spencer steaks for all except Leslie, for whom she broiled a fresh trout. She also served baked Idaho potatoes with sour cream and chives and a green salad, for which Eddie prepared his specialty, a garlicky Italian dressing. For dessert they had a chocolate mousse, which Leslie had bought in a fancy bakery in the Village.

During dinner Laura told the Hills about the gratifying meeting with Tom Morrissey, and the exciting plans they had discussed for the building. The Hills had not yet found an apartment, but their landlord had agreed to give them an extension until February 1.

"I don't know why this hasn't occurred to any of us before," said Laura. "Why don't you move into one of the vacant apartments on the third floor front?"

Leslie said, "I think we'd like nothing better than to live here in your building—right, Robey?—but are the apartments in livable condition?"

"They need work, but I'm sure Eddie can line up the necessary plasterers and painters and whoever to get one ready by the first."

She looked at Ferraro, defying him to say no. He laughed.

"I think so," he said. "It would be good having you in the building. But you know it's not rent-controlled."

He turned back to Laura.

"After we get them in on a short-term lease at a reasonable rent, we'll soak them with a hefty increase."

"I think you would, you bastard," said Leslie.

"He wouldn't dare," said Laura. They agreed on a monthly rent that was less than the Hills were now paying on their Bank Street place.

"You know, Ferraro, you're not such a bad guy after all," said Leslie.

"Don't go soft on me, Lady Bountiful," retorted Eddie. "It doesn't become you."

"Aah, fuck you," said Leslie, giving Eddie a warm smile and emptying her wineglass. Eddie refilled it.

"We appreciate it," said Robey. "I was beginning to think we were going to have to move into one of Eddie's below-the-poverty-line buildings."

When they were drinking coffee, Leslie asked Laura, "Have you heard from David yet?"

Laura said no. She had still not told anyone but Bill about David's odd behavior in connection with the picture of the girl in the pear orchard. She said nothing now about the two calls she had made to California.

Eddie said, "Just keep your fingers crossed the hitchhiker doesn't come back."

"I'm sure I'll hear from him," said Laura, feigning little concern. "Some kind of problem must have come up at home for him to leave in such a hurry. If I don't hear from him by the end of the week, I'll call his parents' home in Northridge."

The next morning, after Bill left, Laura found a letter in her mailbox along with the junk mail. The postmark on the envelope was Northridge, California, and she hastened back into the apartment, tearing open the envelope as she went. She did not even bother to remove her coat. It was a long letter, fourteen pages of single-spaced typing on buff six-by-nine paper. The many words and sentences that had been crossed out indicated the difficulty David had had in writing the letter. Laura sat in the new wing chair and read:

Dear Laura,

I'm sorry I missed your phone calls. I'm sorry I didn't

return the calls. I'm sorry about everything. But I didn't know what I could say to you. And I still, right now, don't know what to say. I just did, ultimately, what I had to do. That girl in that photograph I kept on my desk, the one I told you the hoodlums had stolen, that wasn't my sister at all. I have no sister. The girl was—I mean, is—Debbie Grossman. She was a freshman in high school in Northridge when I was a senior. We had a very torrid romance and vowed, as they say, eternal love.

We were inseparable and had frequent intimate relations, and we continued the relationship all the while I was at Berkeley and after I started teaching. She would come up to Berkeley or I would come home every weekend. The only time I didn't see her was during my hitchhiking excursions, except for the summer I did the western region. She made that trip with me. When I got the job teaching in Oregon, she was a junior at Cal State at Northridge. I began dating other women, and had a couple of semiserious affairs, but then Debbie transferred to my school in Oregon and our relationship became more intense than ever. Some of the professors at Oregon began to warn me that I was jeopardizing my job and my career by consorting with a student, and I told Debbie I thought we should see each other less, and be more circumspect about seeing each other when we did.

She didn't like that. To teach me a lesson, I guess, she started going out with some of the seniors at the school. Particularly with a jock who was the leader of a pretty wild bunch. I didn't like her seeing other guys and told her so. But she was stubborn and willful. Finally we had a heavy argument and stopped seeing each other. That was just a couple of weeks before I got word about Wilson-Leigh taking my book. I was glad to get out of Oregon and come to New York.

Now this is the hardest part of all, Laur. I did, truly I believe, fall in love with you. I was not just using you, as I'm sure you suspect now. But pretty soon after we began to live together, I got a call from my father. He told me Debbie was pregnant and that he and my mother felt I should come home and marry her. Her parents and mine, I should mention, are old, old friends. Her father, as a matter of fact, was in Korea with my father. I flatly refused. First, I was sure I was madly in love with you. Second, I did not want to leave New York in any event. Third, I told myself that the baby wasn't mine, that Debbie had been screwing around with the jock and I don't know who else. But I must admit I never really believed that last. Debbie loved me far too much to sleep with anyone else. She just wasn't—I mean isn't—that kind of girl.

Anyway, my father kept bugging me to come home and marry her and I kept refusing. I was very upset over the situation. I was furious with Debbie. I felt she was trying to trap me. I'm sure you noticed the change in me over the months. I became nervous and crazy. I didn't know what to do. My father was getting more and more insistent that I come home and marry Debbie. She was in her fifth month and showing plainly. I still refused to go home. I was so involved with the book and with my career as a writer, I couldn't stand the idea of leaving it all. I kept telling myself it wasn't my baby.

Then right after *Publishers Weekly* ran that dumb review my father called me again. It was right after you left for work that day. He said Debbie had swallowed practically a whole bottle of some kind of sleeping pills and was in the hospital. They didn't know if they could save her. I can't tell you the guilt I felt, Laurie. I realized—anyway, I think I did—that I loved Debbie. I knew the baby was mine. I got out to Kennedy and on the first flight for L.A.

Debbie lost the baby, but she is all right now. That is, she will live, though she is still pretty sick. As soon as she's better, we're going to get married. I know you must think the lousy review of the book had something to do with my actions. And you may be right. I don't really know. I don't think so. I do know, though, that I want to go back to teaching, and settle down out here with Debbie. If Wilson-Leigh decides they want me to do *The Levinskys* I will work on it in my spare time and I will do the best job I can on it.

I don't know what to say to you about all this, except that I am sorry if I hurt you. I did love you and I still do, but not in the same way I love Debbie. I am truly grateful for all you did for me. I don't think I ever would have been able to get *The Hitchhiker* in shape without your expert help. I doubt that I'll be able to do a novel without your help. I wouldn't blame you, of course, if you decided not to work with me, but I would be eternally grateful if you would.

I hope I haven't hurt you too much, Laurie. You're a wonderful woman and you don't deserve to be hurt. I think I am doing the right thing. I pray to God I am. I hope I am not as mixed up as I sometimes think I am.

Again my deepest thanks for everything you have done for me.

Love,
David

The pen-written signature was shaky.

Laura read the last page of the letter and placed the stack of pages on the table beside the chair. Her eyes were moist, but she did not cry. There was a heavy feeling in her chest. She felt something between sorrow and anger. She didn't know whether she was sorry for herself, David, or Debbie. Or all three. She didn't know whether she was angry at herself or at David. She decided she was angry at David. She took off her coat and went into the kitchen and made a pot of coffee. When she poured herself a cup, she read the letter over again. She considered the idea of phoning the office and saying she wouldn't be in, that she wasn't feeling well. Just when she decided that was nonsense, and she would go in after all, the door buzzer sounded.

She saw Frank Morrissey's rugged face through the peephole. She opened the door. He came in.

"Hi," he said, removing his wool cap. "I was hoping I'd catch you before you went to work."

"Hello, Sergeant. Please sit down."

"Thanks." He sat on the overstuffed sofa.

"Would you like a cup of coffee? I just made some."

"Yeah, that'd be nice. It's cold out."

All the while he spoke, he kept looking around the parlor, and craning his neck toward the open doorway leading into the other rooms. Laura came out of the kitchen with the coffeepot and two clean cups on a tray. He had risen and was looking into David's study.

"Mr. Kessler's gone, right?" he said, taking his seat on the sofa.

"Yes," she said quietly. "Did Eddie tell you?"

"No, no. I haven't seen Eddie in a while, not since that day before Christmas."

"How did you know?"

"It's crazy. There's this leprechaun," he said. "Martin's his name. Been visiting me off and on ever since I went to Ireland. He came last night and told me Mr. Kessler went to California."

Laura looked at him intently, trying to determine whether he was pulling her leg. She leaned a bit closer to him as she poured his coffee, half-expecting to smell whiskey on his breath. No whiskey. Then it occurred to her that what he was saying was no stranger than some experiences she herself had had, and the many she had learned about in working with Eva Konyi.

"Funny," he said, "Irish legend has it that leprechauns are supposed to be nasty little buggers, practical jokers, trouble-makers. But Martin's been a big help to me many a time through the years."

He looked at her intently over the lip of his cup as he drank. There was a twinkle in his tired brown eyes.

"Do you believe in leprechauns and such, Miss Van Gelder?"

"Well . . ." said Laura hesitantly. "I never thought about them very much, but I do believe in all kinds of psychic phenomena and extrasensory perception; precognition, photokinesis, regression . . . I suppose if I had to say yes or no, I'd probably say yes."

Morrissey smiled his warm smile.

"I thought you would. Anyway, I came this morning for several other reasons than to see if Martin's tip on your friend Mr. Kessler was correct. I saw my brother, Tom, day before yesterday. He told me you and Eddie bought this building, and he's going to work with you."

"That's right. I was quite impressed with your brother. He's nice."

"Oh, yes. He's all of that and more. I know you've got some empty apartments in the building, right?"

"Yes, we do."

"I've been living in a hotel uptown on the West Side for over a year now, and I'm mighty tired of it. Could I take one of the apartments?"

"Of course. We're about to start work on one of the two on the third floor. Maybe we could do the other one at the same time. I'll check with Eddie and Mr. Torres, and see what they say. Would you like to look at the apartment?"

"Some other time. It's not necessary. I'll take it, sight unseen."

He took another swallow of coffee and the twinkle returned to his eyes.

"At the risk of having you think I'm even stranger than you no doubt already do, I've got to tell you one other thing."

Laura smiled at him and said, "Oh?"

"When I came to bring back your jewelry on Christmas Eve and you gave me the glorious rum toddy, I had a strong feeling that I should be living in this building, that there was something special about it."

He looked at her thoughtfully.

"It *is* in the best condition of any of the buildings in the area, and it *is* just a few blocks from the Ninth Precinct, where I work, so maybe that's all there is to it . . . but I still have the feeling there's something more. And . . ."

He hesitated and took another sip of his coffee before he said, ". . . and last night when Martin told me Mr. Kessler had gone to California, he also scolded me. *'Have ye not given a thought t' movin' into that house, ye foolitch lad?'* "

His imitation of the leprechaun's accent and high-pitched voice amused Laura. He concluded, "So here I am."

They agreed on terms and Morrissey said, "There's still another reason I've come by this morning, Miss Van Gelder. Tomorrow we start what the department, in its best *Hill Street Blues* style, is calling Operation Pressure Point. We'll have well over a hundred cops, uniforms, undercover squads, and dogs, police cars, and vans, and even a helicopter. There'll be a coordinated action to close down the shooting galleries and bust every dealer and junky we can grab. It'll be concentrated mainly over in Alphabet Town between Second and Sixth streets and Avenues A and C, but there's no doubt there'll be a spillover into the adjoining streets, Stanton and here and Delancey and all the cross streets. I think it would be a good idea if you didn't go out again after you get home from work. Or maybe you could get Eddie to come over and stay with you. I'll look in now and then, if it's okay, and I get a chance."

"How long will the action last?"

"Probably through day after tomorrow, Friday. You might want to let everybody in the building know about it. But please, if you think any of 'em might be connected to the drug scene, don't tell them."

When Morrissey left, Laura went up to the Torreses' apartment. She told Ramon about their second new tenant in as many days, and about the upcoming Operation Pressure Point. She asked him to pass the word on to the tenants.

"You might suggest to the Sapersteins that they keep the bagel store closed till Monday. They always close on Friday at sundown anyway." She started out of the apartment, but turned back.

"And, oh yes, maybe it would be better if you don't mention it to Fernando. Just in case he still feels close to some of his old drug friends."

Morrissey's visit had temporarily driven David's revelations from her mind, but on the way to the office she thought about him and Debbie Grossman again. She was surprised to discover that apart from a deep sympathy she felt for the girl, whom she'd never met, she now felt much more pity than anger for David Kessler. When she got to the office she phoned his agent, telling him Wilson-Leigh had decided to pass on the novel.

"I would appreciate it," she said, "if you would notify David. I haven't told him yet, and I don't expect to be talking to him. And, of course, you may pick up the outline and the chapters anytime—and good luck with it."

The young agent thanked her and said he would come by during the afternoon, and would get in touch with David right away.

Operation Pressure Point proved an exciting two days. The NYPD helicopter, like a surrealistic avenging angel, flying low over the dilapidated tenements, thundered through the frigid January days. And after a short break, when night came, its battering blades sounded even more terrifying as its brilliant superpowered searchlight illuminated the dark snow- and slush-covered streets like a monster cops-and-robbers movie set. The air cops communicated with their colleagues in the streets, directing them to locations where dealers and junkies and some hapless innocents scrambled in frantic confusion.

For thirty-six hours it was bedlam as special narc officers, leading trained German shepherds, crashed into abandoned buildings where the dogs sniffed out the shooting galleries.

The cops herded dazed junkies out of their dreary, arctic hells and into the police vans. In the earliest stages of the action, undercover detectives, including Frank Morrissey, bought cocaine and heroin from scores of dealers and arrested them on the spot.

Incredibly, no one—except a few bruised dealers and addicts—was injured, even though the police made a hundred and seventy-five arrests. Close to a thousand glassine envelopes of Black Sunday, Natural D, Executive, Eagle, Toilet and other high-purity heroine, and Green Tin, Mr. C, Jupiter, and many other potent cocaine brands were confiscated.

"Very good, very flashy," said a cynical friend of Eddie Ferraro's who owned a pizza shop on the corner of Rivington and Ridge, "but we've had wholesale busts before. Election time is coming up. When the election's over, all the dealers'll be back and we'll have a handful of grumbling cops yawning as they watch the action."

But Laura did not think so. She considered the successful crackdown another step in the gentrification of the area.

36

Laura sat at her brand-new IBM word processor at her brand-new desk in the newly decorated study in her Rivington Street building. Indeed the building itself, inside and out, looked brighter and fresher than it had looked the day it had actually been completed. It was spring—well, in six days it would be spring officially—and everything seemed sparkling and pristine. Laura was a new Laura Van Gelder!

She glanced at her notes and began to type.

"Stuyvesant obviously was a very strict disciplinarian. There is mention in one of the City History Club monographs of a young Dutch boy named Willem Van Gelder, who was given forty lashes in the public square because he stole a few tulip bulbs from the director general's garden."

She smiled to herself.

"Another omen, woman," she said out loud. Her favorite flower had always been the tulip. Ever since she was a small child. The phone rang and she picked it up and said, cheerily, "Hello."

"Dear Laura," said the familiar, husky, accented voice of

Eva Konyi. "I am back in America. I am in Washington, the Columbia district, not the state. A week I will be here. Then I will come to New York. Well, say me hello, my dear Laura!"

Laura recovered from her happy surprise.

"Hello, hello, hello!" she said. "How wonderful you're back, Eva. You must stay with me. When are you arriving? And how? I will come and meet you. I can't wait."

"How excellent!" said Eva. "You are more happy even than the last time I talk with you. You have new house, yes?"

Eva Konyi had demonstrated this uncanny power so many times, it hardly surprised Laura anymore.

"Yes. And I have a wonderful guest room for you. When are you coming—exactly?"

"Day after Easter, on Monday, I will come by airplane to your Kennedy port. Eastern number sixteen, arrival ten-twenty in morning."

Laura scrawled the information on a pad.

"Good. I'll be there to meet you. What—"

A guttural, impatient bass voice, speaking what Laura thought was Russian, sounded in the background.

"I must go now, dear Laura," said Eva. "I will see you soon."

Right after David's departure and Bill Van Gelder's return to Lancaster Laura had lived alone for the first time in six years. For ten days or so it seemed strange. But one night as she lay awake she thought about David, and how poorly his *Hitchhiker* book had done, and the rejection of his novel *The Levinskys*. (Four other publishers had passed on it.) She had felt, and as she remembered, she had tried to caution him, that a story about the Jewish period on the Lower East Side had been done too many times. Then an inspiration came to her out of nowhere. Later she thought, possibly out of the very walls of the bedroom in which she lay.

The building! This building on the small piece of Manhattan Island it occupied! This building in which she felt she belonged the first day she had come here! Who had lived here in the years gone by? More fascinating yet, what kind of building had existed here before this tenement had been constructed? Who lived there then?

She pondered, trying to place the streets in relationship to one another. Rivington Street, of course, was north of Wall Street. As Billy had pointed out, it had been part of the wilderness beyond the wall. But as the city grew, someone had built a house here. No doubt a house with a thatched roof, maybe made of mud or clay or stone or wood . . . or what? Who was it that lived in that first primitive house? She leaped out of bed and rushed into the parlor and switched on the lights. She was wide awake. David had not taken any of his books with him. She found Harry Kessler's book *Mama Was No Angel*. She flipped through the pages, refreshing her memory by stopping and checking a passage or a page or two here and there.

Yes, Harry Kessler, David's grandfather, had lived in the building with his son, Isaac, but sold it soon after his mother, Malka, died. Malka Kessler and her husband, William, had owned the building. She thought there might be some reference to who owned it before Malka and William, but she could not find any reference to inform her. She remembered that William and Malka Kessler had been good friends with a couple named Martin and Hannah Morrissey. She found the place in the book where they were involved. Martin the *third*, yet!

She put the book back on the shelf and took out the one beside it, *The Lilly and the Cop*. The main character in this was a Kevin Morrissey. She searched until she discovered that Kevin was the brother of Martin the third. She remembered that Tom Morrissey had said the policeman who had been a Lincoln bodyguard was his great-great-granduncle Ned Morrissey. She wondered if Ned had lived in this house, or its forerunner. Or if he knew a Kessler who did. A vague recollection fluttered in her mind about a Kessler—or at least she thought it was a name something like that—whom her own great-great-grandfather had written about in his Civil War book. It was a long time ago that she'd read the book. She looked at the cuckoo clock on the wall alongside the window, which Eddie had given her. It was a little after one o'clock. But she could not resist. She phoned her home in Lancaster. Her father's voice, raspy with sleep, and grumbly, answered.

"Pop," said Laura excitedly. "Excuse me for waking you, but I've got to know. Did your great-grandpa Fred Van Gelder write about a New York man named Kessler?"

"What? Are you drunk, Laurie? Have you been drinking?"

"No. I'm sorry to wake you. I know it's late, but I must know."

"Kessler?" he said, "I think so . . . or Essler . . . something like that. If I remember correctly, he was the soldier who got stung by the bees."

"Yes! Yes!" said Laura. "That's the one. Can you send me the book? I'm going to do a novel!"

"That's fine, Laurie. I'm glad to hear it. You'll do a good one. I'll get the book to you first thing in the morning. Take good care of it. It's the only copy I've got."

"I will, Pop. I will. Oh, I love you. Give my love to Mom and Billy and all. Go back to sleep. I love you."

Her father was not sleepy anymore. He laughed.

"I love you, too, baby. Good night."

She went to her rented typewriter and began to sketch out ideas for the book.

"There is a place on Manhattan Island called New Amsterdam. Over the years from the date of its settlement in the seventeenth century to the present time, a number of structures have risen on that place and a number of people have lived out their lives there. Their births, their deaths, their joys, their sorrows, their struggles, their triumphs were played out there. There were three families..."

She paused, rested her elbow on the desk, leaned her chin on her cupped hand, and stared out the window at the black night. Then she typed again.

"There was first a Dutch family. Then an Irish family. And then a German-Irish family..."

Dawn was breaking, cold and gray, when she had completed a twenty-two-page outline of the story of the house on Rivington Street. She went back to bed, but could not sleep. For an hour or more she tossed and turned, and then got up and took a shower and went into the kitchen and put on coffee. She had three cups of coffee, writing all the time, and then she typed out the notes.

She got into the office an hour before Harvey Kalisher arrived. Impatiently, having trouble keeping her mind on the manuscript, she worked on *The Beneficent Bomb*.

"Lord, you're high!" said Harvey as she took the chair at the side of his desk.

"I'm going to do a novel, Harvey. Do you think you could swing a leave of absence for me?"

"For how long?"

She shrugged.

"I don't know. Say a year?"

She began to tell him about the novel, but then she

handed him the manila folder in which she had inserted her outline, and interrupted herself.

"Here's a short outline. Please read it and let me know what you think."

She left his office and in a half hour he called her back in.

"I love it, Laurie," he said. "It's a big job. You sure you want to sweat out the research involved, the grind—"

"Oh, yes, Harvey." She smiled ruefully. "I know it sounds crazy, but I really don't have a choice. I feel like I've got to do it."

He nodded approvingly.

"Fine. Go on up to Toronto for a few days or a week and work out those changes we decided we need on *The Bomb*. Come back and finish up the book and I'll arrange the leave."

Impulsively, she dashed to him and kissed him on the cheek.

"Thanks, Harvey. Thank you!"

The two Toronto professors were friendly, but worked at a maddeningly deliberate pace, and were given to long debates over every change Laura suggested. It took her a full week to get the manuscript altered as she and Harvey felt necessary. Then she spent another week doing the final edit on it. In between she began her research. She haunted the librarians at the City History Club and read scores of monographs on New York's earliest days. She finally located two volumes of their selected monographs, published in book form in 1899 by G. P. Putnam's Sons. A charming and most helpful lady at the New York Historical Society on Central Park West gave her a great amount of interesting information on James Rivington, the London bookseller, printer, and newspaper publisher after whom the street had been named. She thought she would probably use Rivington as one of the characters in her novel.

When she finally completed *The Beneficent Bomb* she plunged into her research and began making notes and plotting the story full-time. She became obsessed with the project to the degree that her friends teased her about it. But they also helped. She was discussing the early eighteenth-century phase of the city's history with Leslie and Robey in their apartment one evening, when Robey said, "I've got a little present for you, Laurie."

He went to his bookcase and withdrew a yellowed paperback book. He handled it very carefully.

"This is an original copy of a book published in 1741." He handed it to Laura. She held it gently in both hands.

"Wow!" she said. "What a title!"

It was:

A JOURNAL IN THE PROCEEDINGS IN THE DETECTION OF A CONSPIRACY FORMED
By Some White People in Conjunction
With Negro and Other Slaves
For Burning the City of New York in America
and Murdering Its Inhabitants
By the RECORDER OF THE CITY OF NEW YORK

"Turn to page sixty-six," said Robey. "Carefully."

Laura did, and as soon as she glanced down at the small printed lines, her own name caught her eye. The page recounted the formation of the Grand Jury of the Supreme Court of Judicature in April of 1741. Listed among the jurors' names was one Harman Van Gelder.

Even Eddie Ferraro, who complained when Laura refused every other date with him, even to such outstanding entertainments as *Cats*, *La Cage aux Folles*, *Terms of Endearment*, a Knicks-Lakers game, and dinner at the Four Seasons—even Eddie helped. She was going to have to move in with him for a couple of weeks while workers were remodeling and renovating her own apartment in the Rivington Street building. The week before he dropped in and handed her a gift-wrapped oblong package. It was a copy of a large paperback book called *The Columbia Historical Portrait of New York*.

Laura began to flip through it, fascinated. She came upon a map based on a survey of the city of New Amsterdam in 1656, made by "setting off and laying out stakes." The map gave all the Dutch street names and showed the numbered locations of the houses of all the burghers and the businesses, the taverns (of which there were many), the churches, warehouses, et al. There were one hundred and twenty houses in the village at the time, and the book contained sketches and paintings of many of them. Laura glanced through the book, then put it down on the sofa and leaped up and kissed Eddie on the cheek.

"Thanks, Eddie. It's a wonderful book."

"I'm only giving it to you in the hope that when you move

in with me next week, you'll let me seduce you, out of sheer gratitude, if nothing else."

"Now, Eddie!" she said. She would have moved in with Leslie and Robey instead of with Eddie, but the carpenters, painters, and plasterers were working on their apartment too. The Hills were staying in Harlem with a Baptist minister friend of theirs. As it turned out, Eddie behaved during Laura's stay, restricting all his passes to verbal romantic and marital suggestions, some jocular and mildly bawdy, some serious.

A good deal of Laura's research material on the Irish family in her story came from her ever-closer relationship with the Morrisseys. Phyllis Morrissey, especially, provided her with what she found to be fascinating background on the family. Phyllis was twenty-seven, the same age as Laura. She was an Englishwoman, born in Shropshire, whose maiden name was Willet. She was happily intrigued when Laura told her that a man named Thomas Willet, an Englishman, had become the first mayor of New York, when it became New York City. In many visits, some in the company of Frank Morrissey and some by herself, to the home of Tom and Phyllis Morrissey in Scarsdale in Westchester County, Laura had discovered that Phyllis was an inveterate reader. She was particularly fond of historical and generational novels as well as true stories of famous families.

Laura became Aunt Laurie to the three little girls and frequently took them to the Bronx Zoo, played with them on the swings in the expansive dogwood-fringed backyard, and otherwise entertained them, and brought them small gifts. Phyllis freely discussed the Morrissey family with Laura as they sat together watching the children play nearby. Most of Phyllis's information was firsthand, since it came from Tom himself. She and Tom were extremely close and held no secrets, personal or family, from one another.

Tom and Frank were as different as siblings could be, although both had survived identical tragic experiences. In 1968 when Frank was thirteen and Tom, twelve, their uncle Brian, their father's younger brother by a year, was killed during the siege of Khe Sanh during the Vietnam War. The boys had been fonder of their uncle than of their own father. Frank, indeed, hated his father, Peter Morrissey. That same year another, even more traumatic tragedy occurred. Their mother, Jackie Morrissey, under the influence of a large dose of LSD, stepped off the balcony of their fifteenth-floor apartment on East Sixty-eighth Street.

Jackie Morrissey was thirty when she died. At sixteen, perky Jacqueline Hartstein had been president of the Bronx chapter of the fan club of a rockabilly star of the day. Peter, who was eighteen, was a gofer and rookie disk jockey at radio station WRST. On his second date with Jackie, he impregnated her. They were truly in love and as soon as she discovered she was pregnant they married. Frank was born seven months later. Both Peter and Jackie were among the earliest users of pot, LSD, and other hallucinogenic substances. They lived a hectic life in the popular music and record milieu, yet found time to march in civil rights and anti-Viet demonstrations and attend events like the mass gathering at Woodstock. Thomas was born the year after Frank, but their parents had little time for their children. The boys were left in the care of a random succession of housekeepers and baby-sitters. Peter became one of the most influential disk jockeys in the business and Jackie was soon appointed head of publicity for the hottest new independent record label. They lived wildly sybaritic and self-indulgent lives.

"My God," said Laura to Phyllis. "They sound like a rock-and-roll version of Scott and Zelda Fitzgerald."

The one stabilizing influence in Peter's and Jackie's lives was Peter's father, Michael. He understood his son's and daughter-in-law's problems more than might ordinarily have been expected. He tried constantly to get them to seek psychiatric and every conceivable form of other help for their drug dependency. He himself and his wife, Lois (nee Tyson), had both been alcoholics. Indeed he had met Lois at the first Alcoholics Anonymous meeting he had attended, shortly after having quit his job in the office of the city's planning commissioner. In a cafeteria on West Seventy-third Street, after their fourth joint AA meeting, Mike and Lois Tyson realized they were in love.

They went up to Mike's apartment, got drunk, went to bed, and conceived Peter. They resumed attending AA meetings and were doing quite well in beating their disease, when Brian was born in the second year of their marriage. They were sober the night he was conceived. Mike discovered that the best way to keep his mind off drinking was to bury himself in his work. He switched from being an alcoholic to a workaholic. He was also a fine architect and worked for several of the leading firms in the city. Lois, too, was successfully sustaining her sobriety, and was a good and loving mother.

And then came World War II. Right after Pearl Harbor, when Peter was five and Brian, four, Mike sat down with Lois one night after the boys had been put to bed.

"I've got to join up, sweetie," he said. "You think you can handle the kids?"

Lois came over and sat on his lap. She kissed him hard on the mouth, then softly and tenderly a half dozen times. Then, her eyes moist, her voice unsteady, she said, "I know Mike. I know you do. Sure, I'll handle the kids."

Mike went into the Navy and became an officer in the Seabees. Lois went to work at the USO Canteen in Times Square. She didn't mean to, but so many sailors and soldiers who came to the canteen reminded her of Mike, she couldn't refuse when they insisted she have just one drink with them. Each time she thought, what the hell, just one; just one can't hurt. AA had taught her better, but she missed Mike and just plain didn't have the strength of will. Too many times she wound up drunk, and in a seedy hotel room with a lonesome, desperate, horny boy in khaki or blue. A neighbor's daughter baby-sat for the kids.

When Mike came home from the war in September of 1945, he was a hero with a hopeless alcoholic for a wife. For the next nine years Lois was in and out of expensive sanitoriums until she died of cirrhosis of the liver in 1954.

"How awful, Phyll," said Laura, when Phyllis finished telling her the story of Mike and Lois Morrissey "It's no wonder Peter turned out like he did."

Phyllis nodded somberly.

"It's strange how differently siblings will react to terrible tragedies. Wild as Peter was, Brian was a good, solid young man, full of patriotic fervor."

She looked toward the children at the swing, and warned Marianne not to push young Phyllis too hard. Baby Frank, reclining in a stroller in the sunshine by her side, complained with a small cry. Phyllis saw that the comforter nipple had popped from his mouth. She replaced it, and he sucked contentedly and closed his eyes.

"The same kind of thing happened when Jackie killed herself." Phyllis continued her narrative. "Somehow, Tom, with his grandfather's help, came out of it fine. Went right through the university, worked hard, and turned into a first-rate architect himself."

"Where did you meet Tom?" asked Laura.

"I was secretary to a man named Horace Hazelton. He was president of an enormously successful real estate development corporation. They've built some of the most stunning skyscrapers in the city. Tom did his first major job for them."

Young Phyllis fell off the swing onto her knees and began wailing. Her mother jumped up from the lawn chair and ran to her. Laura followed. Between the two of them they quickly soothed the little girl. When they returned to their chairs, baby Frank was crying loudly because he had lost his comforter again. Phyllis found it and put it into his mouth.

"Where was I?" she asked.

"You were talking about how different two brothers can be . . ."

"Yes, of course. Tom handled it well. He somehow understood his mother's and father's problems. But Frank couldn't handle it at all. He hated his father bitterly. Tom thinks he believed his father was leading his mother into doing the drugs and living like they lived. Even though he was only five when it happened, in 1960, Tom says Frank even seemed to remember that their father almost went to jail. He was indicted for bribery. It seems the government discovered that record companies were paying disk jockeys large amounts of money and bribing them with all kinds of inducements to favor their records."

Laura nodded.

"They called it the payola scandal, but how could a kid of five know anything about it?"

Phyllis shrugged.

"Perhaps somebody mentioned it in his presence or told him about his father's part in it years later, when he was older."

"Is Peter Morrissey still alive?" asked Laura.

"Yes. Tom sees him once or twice a year. Frank still will have nothing to do with him. He's the manager of the station now, and he's married to a nineteen-year-old girl, the lead singer in a new all-girl rock band."

"Good lord, Frank is thirty!" exclaimed Laura. "How old is Peter?"

"He's only in his late forties, but he looks a mod sixty."

The nipple had popped from baby Frank's Cupid's bow mouth a third time. Phyllis automatically replaced it.

"At any rate, when Jackie killed herself, Frank ran off and somehow got himself a job on a merchant ship. He was only thirteen, I think, but big for his age. No one heard a word from him until, oh, I don't know, perhaps five years later, early in 1973. He'd been living in Ireland, in Cork, and he came back very, very Irish. He joined the police department about six months after he came back. I think he was twenty or twenty-one."

Laura knew a good deal about Frank Morrissey's "Irishness." Ever since he had moved into the apartment on the third floor of the Rivington Street building, right next door to the Hills, he had been courting Laura in a sort of old-fashioned manner. Frequently he asked her to have dinner with him, or attend a movie, but always quite shyly, hesitantly. Several times she had accepted his invitations and found him a charming and interesting man. She was surprised to learn he was only three years older than she.

He told her about leaving his ship in London one year and sailing across the Bristol Channel and St. George's Channel into Cork harbor and landing in Cork. He could not say why he headed for Cork. It simply seemed that he must go there. He liked it. He found a job as general handyman and bartender in a homey tavern owned by a hearty one-legged Irishman named McGonigal. McGonigal specialized in telling his patrons Irish folktales. Cork was near a small village called Shandon, and Frank took to going to church at St. Ann's there. St. Ann's had the sweetest-sounding bells he had ever heard and they sounded every hour on the hour.

On his days off Frank walked about the countryside. One day he came to Blarney just a few miles from Shandon, and went up into a ruined castle more than two centuries old.

"I'm sitting there, staring out at the lovely Irish countryside, than which there's none lovelier, Laurie, my girl," he told her over Irish coffee at P. J. Moriarty's restaurant on Third Avenue one night. "And—now you're going to say I'm daft—but I hear this squeaky little voice down at my feet. First I think it's a mouse I'm hearing. But I see—as Jesus is my witness—I swear, I see this little man."

Laura licked the cream of the Irish whiskey off her upper lip and smiled.

"How tall *was* he, Frank?"

"The best way I know how to describe 'im is as old William Allingham did in his poem, 'He's a span and a quarter in height.'"

He spread his short-fingered hand sideways before Laura, stretching thumb and small finger as far as they would go.

"What would that make 'im?" He grinned. "Some ten inches maybe, or perhaps twelve, if you've longer fingers. Anyway, about that, an' he says, 'Me name's Martin, lad. Oi'm 'ere t'inform ye it's time ye wuz goin home to that benighted land across the sea.' If I'd been drinking, I would have thought I was seeing and hearing things, but it was a Sunday morning, I'd just gone to church, and I hadn't had a drop."

He took more than a drop now of his Irish coffee, and licked the cream from his lips.

"Anyway, we had a nice chat, and we've been good friends ever since."

He lowered his head, studying the dark brown patches breaking through the thinning cream surface of his coffee.

"He told me once, Laurie, that I was going to marry a fair-haired lass with big blue eyes."

"Oh, he did, did he?" said Laura. "Have you met such a girl?"

He blushed and rubbed his cheek in embarrassment. He couldn't look at her. He said to the Irish coffee, "If I'm not mistaken, you yourself have golden hair and blue eyes."

"Oh, yes," teased Laura. "I suppose I do."

That was as far as Frank got. That night or any other night on the several occasions when she went out with him. Except one night in late March. She was in her study, making notes from a book on New York City during the Revolutionary War. There were some interesting chapters on George Washington's espionage system. It was early evening. The phone rang and Frank Morrissey said, "Laura, I'm glad you're home. Come on up. This celebrating alone doesn't work!"

"What are you talking about, Frank? I'm working. What are you celebrating?"

"It looks like we finally got the bastard," he said, a strong, exultant note in his voice. "Come on up!"

"Who? You got who?"

"Mejias! They handed down an indictment this afternoon. With Rico turning state's witness, and the coke and horse I got from his safe, I'm sure he'll be convicted. He should get at least seven years."

A month after the Operation Pressure Point action, Morrissey had arrested a dealer who admitted he was getting his supply from Mejias. He picked up his stuff at Mejias's Dreamland nightclub. Morrissey got a search warrant and in a wall safe in Mejias's office in back of the club they found ten kilos of cocaine and three of heroin. The dealer, Bruno Rico, agreed to testify against Mejias in the hopes of getting a lighter sentence himself.

Laura thought Frank Morrissey sounded a little drunk now. She had only been in his apartment once before, a week earlier, when he had had a small St. Patrick's Day celebration for some friends from the police department, his brother, Tom, and Phyllis, Leslie and Robey Hill, and Eddie Ferraro and herself. Now there was a sudden uncharacteristically roguish note in his voice, as he spoke again, since she had said nothing.

"Anyhow, you've been wanting to see my collection of Irish folktales and fairy books," he said.

She laughed. He had told her about his library of old Irish books and she had expressed an interest in seeing them. And his pleading was so earnest she could not resist.

"Well," she said lightly, "that's a nice switch on the old 'come up and see my etchings' routine. I'll be up in about a half hour."

She changed from a Jets sweatshirt and baggy slacks into a blouse and a pair of designer jeans, put on fresh makeup, and went to the third floor. Frank *was* a little drunk, and she had several glasses of Jameson Irish whiskey on the rocks with him. He did have some fascinating books, which he discussed with Laura as they sat side by side on the new sofa in his somewhat stark, masculine living room.

"This one's my favorite," he said, handing her an ancient-looking book from the small pile on the table beside him, *The Secret Commonwealth of Elves, Fauns and Fairies* by the Reverend Robert Kirk published originally in 1691. In *Fairy and Folk Tales of the Irish Peasantry*, edited by William Butler Yeats and published in 1889, he found the William Allingham poem he had mentioned to her at Moriarty's in describing his leprechaun, Martin.

"Charming," said Laura, and reached across him to pick up another of the books. This one was *The Coming of the Fairies* by Sir Arthur Conan Doyle.

"Is this the same Sir Arthur who wrote the Sherlock Holmes stories?" she asked.

"The one and the same," said Frank. "It's a true story, the full account of how two little girls in Yorkshire in England came upon a small group of fairies and actually photographed them. Here . . ."

He flipped open the book and showed Laura a rather indistinct photograph of a glen in which the tiny elflike figures near the gnarled trunk of a tree might indeed be fairies. While Laura was studying the photo Frank moved closer to her and tentatively eased his arm around her shoulder. He looked earnestly into her eyes.

"Laura," he said, his voice suddenly hoarse. "Do you believe a marriage between a highly educated girl and a stupid oaf who never finished high school could work?"

Laura was taken aback.

"Frank," she said quietly, "I have no plans to get married. But when I do, I doubt that educational qualifications will be my top consideration."

He took his arm from her shoulder, his face reddening, and went to the bar and poured himself another drink.

"Right," he said. "Right you are! To your health, Laura! And to your book!"

She drank with him.

37

In the month or so between Frank's sweet, oblique proposal and the time she received the phone call from Eva Konyi, Laura had had one of the most productive times yet on her book. The three families who had lived in the house on Rivington Street from the time of its settlement as New Amsterdam to this Easter Sunday, April 22 in 1984, had become clearer and clearer in her mind. And even as the characters evolved into flesh-and-blood human beings, who frequently peopled her dreams, the building on Rivington Street magically became the showpiece in the neighborhood's gentrification effort.

Inside the building every apartment had been remodeled, many walls knocked down, others newly added, all freshly plastered, painted, or papered. In the bathrooms new white enamel toilets, showers, and tubs sparkled. An efficient new boiler graced the cellar, where the termites had been evacuated and the entire area cleaned and fumigated.

The building's exterior had been sandblasted so that its sandstone and brick gave off a soft glow in the spring sunshine. Strikingly effective against the beige and warm maroon surface were the geometric lines of the gleaming ebony fire escapes, securely rebolted and freshly covered with multiple coats of expensive glossy paint. The wooden oblong frames of the windows matched the shining blackness of the fire escapes and not a single window was cracked, broken, or smeared with dirt or grime. Handsome black wrought-iron bannisters flanked the sandblasted front stoop, and the paneled double doors were freshly painted ebony.

But the most charming and attractive, if probably the most impractical, decorative touches were the glistening black flower boxes that rested on the sills of each window to the left of each fire escape. Laura had had a long, good-natured argument with Tom Morrissey and Eddie Ferraro over these flower boxes. Both Tom and Eddie insisted they were completely impractical, that there was no way to persuade, let alone force, tenants to keep them filled with flowers, or tend the flowers if supplied.

Laura cited the fact that the city was now sticking vinyl decals of potted plants, even shutters and Venetian blinds, onto the windows of abandoned buildings along the Cross Bronx Expressway to make them appear more pleasing to the eyes of passersby and, indeed, to the people in the neighborhood.

"Real flower boxes are certainly more attractive and practical than decals," argued Laura, "and how much can they cost?"

Eddie laughed.

"Some partner I got myself, Tom," he said. "Never worries about spending that extra dollar."

"Maybe she has something," said Tom, grinning.

They had filled the flower boxes with artfully made artificial red, pink, and white geraniums with rich green leaves. They looked most attractive and *The New York Times* ran a photograph of the building with its new face and a brief story emphasizing the flower-box touch.

Along with the reconstruction of the Rivington Street building, Laura was convinced that the neighborhood itself was gradually improving, that the gentrification program was working. The new black police commissioner, Benjamin Ward, had decreed that Operation Pressure Point would continue without letup right through the winter. More than two hundred uniformed police and forty undercover officers had been assigned on a regular basis to the Lower East Side area. The choppers patroled from the skies. The dogs sniffed out the few remaining galleries. Soon the usual lines of junkies, waiting to go into the abandoned buildings to buy their dope, had disappeared. The out-of-state cars, which used to come into the streets daily for their supplies, had ceased coming. Dealers abandoned the streets and went into the subways. Ward alerted the transit police, and their men drove the drug hustlers out of their new underground haunts.

Frank Morrissey was ecstatic. At the end of February he told Laura and Eddie Ferraro that the cops had made close to two thousand drug-related arrests since Operation Pressure Point began, and six hundred and seven of those were felonies. Robberies in the area dropped by almost fifty percent. More new stores, boutiques, art galleries, and restaurants were opening. Eddie's uncle Gino himself had opened a new Italian restaurant, half a block from the Rivington Street building. He placed a nephew, who was an accomplished gourmet chef, in charge.

On the Monday after Palm Sunday, Laura was attempting a first draft of an opening chapter for her story. She used the historical episode she had researched, wherein Petrus Stuyvesant ordered the impoverished young Dtuch boy to receive forty lashes for stealing a few tulip bulbs from his garden. In her story the boy was stealing the bulbs as an Easter present for a little Dutch girl he loved.

An idea struck her in midsentence. She threw on her light topcoat and went uptown to the area on the West Side in the twenties where the wholesale florists were located. She found a florist who specialized in tulips.

On Easter morning she came out of the building to go down to the corner newsstand for her *New York Times*. She walked across the street from the building and stared up at her newly remodeled, beautifully decorated house. She had had the artificial geraniums carefully removed from the flower boxes and set aside for future use. Real, live tulips—scarlet, gold, blue, yellow, white, brown—had been planted in their stead. It had been costly and the florist had had a dozen men work two days, but Laura grinned happily at the result. It was worth it!

Coming toward her from the Essex Street corner she heard happy whistling of what sounded like a Gaelic air. Frank Morrissey was returning from Easter Mass at the Most Holy Redeemer Church, where the pastor, Father John Kennington, was one of his best friends. He saw Laura standing on the sidewalk, gazing blissfully up at the building. He joined her and said, "You're a wonder woman, indeed, Laura. I don't know when or where I've seen a lovelier house."

And as they stood there admiring Laura's handiwork, Eddie Ferraro's car slid smoothly up before the building. He saw Laura and Frank across the street, looking up at his building. He could not see much of it from his position at the driver's seat of the car. He reached over and picked up the large lavender-foil-wrapped pot of purple and gold tulips in the front seat, and carefully backed out of the car, holding the plant in both hands. He started across to Laura and Frank. He turned and looked back and up at the building. His jaw dropped. He continued toward Laura and Frank. When he reached them, he handed the pot of tulips to Laura and laughed.

"Happy Easter, honey," he said. "Jesus Christ! Talk about coals to Newcastle!"

"Tulips to Rivington Street is better," said Laura, hugging the tulip pot happily to her breast.

Leslie and Robey Hill were having the Easter brunch this day, and they all went up to the Hills' apartment on the third floor, after Laura dropped off her tulip plant. Laura was exultant! Imagine Eddie bringing her tulips! He had never done that before. During the brunch, Frank went across into his own apartment and returned with a special gift for her. It was a tiny red leather shoe with a curled and pointed toe in a small glass case. He said it was a shoe Martin, his leprechaun, had made. He had long since informed her that all leprechauns were shoemakers.

"It'll bring you good luck and help you with your book," he said.

The copper bracelet with the tiny figure of the horse had created several visions in her dreams, not all of them beautiful or positive. One night, when she had worn the bracelet to bed, she had a nightmare about a black man being burned at the stake, while she sat on a horse on a knoll overlooking the burning site and the ghoulish, rejoicing crowd. Shocking visions or happy, romantic dreams, or hard historic research, she seemed to be getting to know her Dutch family, her Irish family, and her German-Jewish family better all the time. And tomorrow Eva Konyi would arrive from Washington, and she would experience a regression . . . and only the good Lord knew what she might learn!

SPECIAL NOTE TO THE READER

All the material Laura Van Gelder uncovered in her dreams and in her research, and what she learned during her regression, as well as many secrets never revealed to her, appeared in the stories of the Van Gelders, the Morrisseys, and the Kesslers in a prequel to this book. It is entitled "Remember This House."

ABOUT THE AUTHOR

JOSEPH CSIDA began his writing career at a very early age, trying out stories part time, while holding down a succession of full time jobs in the publishing, entertainment and music/record industries. In the late thirties he wrote short stories for *Black Mask*, the pulp home of Dashiell Hammett and other major suspense writers, and later continued to write short stories and novellettes for *Alfred Hitchcock Magazine*, as well as *Liberty* and *Country Gentlemen*. As president and chief writer for Crimewriters, Inc., he also wrote scores of true crime stories for the leading fact detective magazines.

He worked on *Billboard* magazine, a music trade journal for nineteen years and was eventually elected a vice president and appointed Editor in Chief. He left to become Assistant Director of Advertising and Public Relations for the Radio Corporation of America, and rose to become Director of Artists and Repertoire for the RCA Record Division. He was also Vice President in charge of Eastern Operations for Capital Records, President of Recording Industries Corporation, and President of the New York Chapter of the National Academy of Recording Arts and Sciences.

Csida finally formed his own talent management, music publishing, record and show production operations. In this period he was personal manager for such performers as Eddy Arnold, Bobby Darin, John Gary, and Jim Lowe. He was also executive producer of the syndicated Eddy Arnold television series, as well as producer of the John Gary television show.

In 1973 he turned to a full time writing career. He has written several novels: *Crime Is of the Essence*, *The Magic Ground* and *Unknown Shores;* as well as non-fiction books, *The Music/Record Career Handbook*, *Rape—How to Avoid It and What to Do About It If You Can't*, and *American Entertainment—A Unique History of Popular Show Business*, the latter two with his wife, June Bundy Csida.

Although he lived most of his life in New York City, he and Ms. Csida presently reside in Malibu, California, where they continue their writing activities.

Rusty's Story

By Carol Gino
Author of NURSE'S STORY

When Carol Gino first met Barbara "Rusty" Russell, the young woman was working as a nurse's aide in a nursing home. Immediately, Carol was impressed by Rusty's compassion and understanding of her often difficult elderly patients, and the two women quickly became friends.

As their friendship deepened, Carol began to uncover the layers of Rusty's life. At the age of fifteen, Rusty suffered a seizure at a football game and the incident propelled her into a medical nightmare. Rusty was institutionalized, overmedicated, and misdiagnosed as everything from a paranoid schizophrenic to a dangerous psychotic. Struggling to maintain a normal life, Rusty fought back against the medical system and appeared to have won by the time Carol met her. But, her nightmare was just beginning . . .

Rusty's Story

The harrowing true tale of the friendship between two women who join forces for the fight of their lifetime.

Available December 18 wherever Bantam Books are sold.